A Parallel Time & Place

Stand in the Gap Trilogy

Book 1

A Parallel Time & Place

A Story of a Modern Nation Running in Sync with a Biblical Land in an Alternate Reality

N. E. Kurz

Dogwood Publishing
Bolivar MO 65613

Published by Dogwood Publishing, Bolivar, MO 65613

Printed in the United States of America. First edition.

Library of Congress Control Number: 2024937538

Publisher's Cataloging-in-Publication data

Names: Sawyers-Kurz, Norma Eileen, author.
Title: A parallel time & place : a story of a modern nation running in sync with a Biblical land in an alternate reality / Norma Eileen Sawyers-Kurz.
Series: Stand in the Gap Trilogy
Description: Bolivar, MO: Dogwood Publishing, 2024.
Identifiers: LCCN: 2024937538 | ISBN: 978-1-6629597-9-0 (hardcover) | 979-8-9905216-1-2 (paperback) | 979-8-9905216-2-9 (Kindle)
Subjects: LCSH Time travel--Fiction. | Josiah, King of Judah--Fiction. | Biblical fiction. | Christian fiction. | Historical fiction. | BISAC FICTION / Christian / General | FICTION / Christian / Historical
Classification: LCC PS3619 .A99 P37 2024 | DDC 813.6--dc23

DEDICATION

THIS BOOK IS DEDICATED TO ALL

WHO SEARCH FOR TRUTH IN LIFE AND FIND IT

CONTENTS

A Parallel

Time & Place

Whatever is has already been,

and what will be has been before;

and God will call the past to account.

~ Ecclesiastes 3:15

1

EZEKIEL & YAFA

Jerusalem—598/597 BC

Boom …, boom …, boom …, the sound of the battering ram continuously and rhythmically beat its loud tune in the distance. But then, suddenly, the booming abruptly ended, and everything went silent. Soon after, a woman's high-pitched scream replaced the quiet, and all became still again. Yafa, in a deep sleep, heard the background sounds in her mind, turned over in her bed, and fell back into restless sleep.

She tossed and turned on the feathered mat as the wails of an infant invaded her mind. "Wahhh, wahhh, wahhh," the baby bawled, but then the infant's crying quickly ended.

The quiet was replaced by a blood-curdling repetition as a male voice yelled from afar, "Kill. Kill. KILL." The sleeping lady curled into a ball and pulled her covers over her head. The accumulating sounds, almost unbearable to hear, mixed into Yafa's dreaming mind until a montage of frightening and gruesome images awoke her.

Sitting upright in her bed, she cried out, "Ezekiel, help!" Her eyes wide with fright, Yafa glanced over at her husband Ezekiel beside her in their bed. Already awake, but with his eyes closed and his mouth silently moving, he fervently prayed. Yafa grabbed his arm. "Zeke!" Her voice trembled as she spoke. "I know the Jerusalem wall has been breached! I can hear the approaching warfare."

Ezekiel opened his eyes and quietly stared into Yafa's tear-filled orbs. Then he tenderly brushed away the teardrops from her cheeks. "Yes, it's finally happening, as we knew all along it would."

"That doesn't make it any easier." Yafa began to cry again. "What are we going to do now that the Babylonians have broken through the wall? Zeke, you don't even seem scared."

"Yes, this is a terrifying situation, Yafa, I admit, but I know God is with us whatever happens."

Yafa bit her lip to prevent herself from saying more. *I'm definitely not like Zeke,* she thought. *He always trusts in God whatever the circumstances.* A piercing scream nearby startled Yafa from her thoughts. She jumped from her bed immediately when loud banging was heard at their door. Her legs shook with fright as she desperately searched for a place to hide.

Ezekiel stood up, resolutely walked toward the door, and calmly asked, "Who is it, and what do you want?"

"It's Saphah, Rebecca, Hannah, and Anna," yelled a female voice. "Ezekiel, please let us in," Saphah pleaded. "Hannah is having sharp labor pains, and she needs Yafa's midwife assistance. Please, please allow us into the room!"

Ezekiel opened the door, the women rushed into the room, and Rebecca, who clutched a bag of clothes hanging on her shoulder, swung it around and slung it to the floor. Saphah and Anna followed suit.

"Ohhhh …, ohhhh …," moaned Hannah, agonizing in pain as she folded her arms over her extended belly. Bending over, she let out a scream.

Yafa quickly spanned the space between herself and Hannah. "Zeke, you and Anna need to go outside."

Ezekiel took the young lady's hand, and the two quickly walked out and shut the door behind them.

"Yafa, please hurry." Hannah, bent over in pain, moaned as sweat ran down her forehead.

"Yes." Yafa cleared her mind of fear for her safety as her midwife experience began to kick in. Grabbing the birthing stool, she helped the woman painfully settle her rump upon the seat equipped with a large hole.

With a loud groan of pain as she sat down, Hannah cried out, "Yafa, please hurry! It's coming! Now!"

"Hannah, with your next labor pain, give me a big push."

Saphah dabbed the sweat from the laboring mother's forehead, and Rebecca held her hand as they waited for the next pain. Almost immediately, Hannah groaned again. "Push …," Yafa encouraged. "Push …, you can do it. C'mon, push again." With all her strength, the expecting mother pushed once more, and with a gush, the little baby boy was born. As the other ladies both breathed a sigh of relief, Yafa continued her midwifery. She cut and tied the baby's umbilical cord, cleared his nose and mouth, and taking him up by his feet, she spanked him on the behind.

"Wahhh, wahhh, wahhh," the newborn cried as the ladies rejoiced at the arrival of new life. Saphah and Rebecca washed the baby, rubbed him with salt, and wrapped him in swaddling clothes from Yafa's midwife bag. In the meantime, Yafa attended to Hannah by discarding her afterbirth, washing her body, changing her clothes, and helping her to the bed.

"Now, I get the honor of presenting this sweet baby to his mother." Yafa picked up the precious infant in her arms and carried him to Hannah, now resting on the feathered mat.

"Oh, he's beautiful." Hannah caressed her little one.

Yafa called outside. "Ezekiel and Anna, you may come back in now." The two reentered the room. "Anna, you have a new baby brother! Would you and Zeke like to see him?"

"I sure would! Ezekiel, let's go see my new baby brother!"

Ezekiel and Anna hurried across the room to Hannah and the infant. "Hannah, congratulations on the baby boy."

"Thank you, Ezekiel." Hannah tenderly kissed the newborn. "My husband wants to call him Jesse."

"That's a great name for a boy," Ezekiel answered. "But where are Ebed, Shallum, and Huldah now."

"Ebed and Shallum are still at the palace, and Huldah is going to fetch them and bring them here."

"Good, but they need to hurry." Ezekiel motioned with his hand. "Quick. All of you. Come here."

As they gathered around Ezekiel, he continued in hushed tones. "You're all in extreme danger. Since I'll become a priest at age 30, Yafa and I'll be classified as elite and be spared. So, you all need to know you are family now, and you've been living with us. But Saphah …," he looked at her with a solemn gaze, "you'll be recognized as a foreigner by your eyes, hair, and skin. You won't pass as a Judahite. The cruel Babylonians will try to kill you because we're unable to claim you as family."

Ezekiel's words were so blunt, they caused Saphah to take a step back.

"You need to leave right now and escape to your own world." Ezekiel continued talking without a pause. "We can't talk about it anymore. I heard enemy troops coming closer, and they'll attempt to kill anyone mingled in with Jerusalem's soldiers. Everyone, say your goodbyes now, so perhaps Saphah can escape." But then he remembered. "She'll need water for her journey. Yafa, please get her a flask of water."

"Thank you." Saphah grabbed the flask and ran out the door. "Please pray for me, and I'll pray too!"

Oh dear, Saphah thought, *I can see the Babylonian soldiers approaching right now!* "My Lord and my God, please help me!" She prayed aloud as her heart began beating wildly. Then she spun around in her tracks as she heard the shriek of a woman's voice behind her. Aghast, she saw a Babylonian warrior pulling the blade of a sword from the female's stomach. Instantly, intestines and blood gushed from the victim's belly. Saphah felt like she was going to vomit.

Blahhhh …, Saphah expelled some of her previous meal. Blahhhh …, she vomited again and wiped her mouth with her hand. Sick with anxiety, she crouched in the shadows and saw a different soldier who tore an infant from the clutches of a woman. The mother screamed as the soldier slung the baby against a wall and then tossed the child aside as if it were trash.

Oh my God, how evil! How cruel to kill a precious little baby like that! Saphah stifled her own cries. *Have they seen me? Have they heard me? Will they be coming for me next?* Frozen in fear, Saphah couldn't move. Suddenly, remembering her own plight, she began to run as fast as she could.

"Kill them all," a rough voice bellowed and then laughed as a man of war heard a little child's fearful cry for help. Saphah dared to search for the child—only some fifty feet behind her.

"Help me, help me!" The young child yelled over and over. "Hel …!" The child's words were snuffed out by the blade of a sword.

Saphah screamed, "I can't take it! Lord, please help me escape!"

Saphah prayed as she continued to run. Almost out of breath, she barely jumped over a big rock in the street. Then she heard a person, who seemed to be in hot pursuit, breathing heavily behind her. Her heart fell. *Has an enemy soldier almost caught up with me?* She turned just in time to see the pursuing soldier trip over the rock and fall flat to the ground. "Praise God!" She sighed in relief. "Praise God!"

Saphah spied a side street and quickly took that route. *I'm getting close to the stairs to the Pool of Siloam. I think I know how to get there from here.* Dashing forward she soon reached the steps. Making it to the bottom of the flight, she stopped to catch her breath. Then, pulling up her skirt tail between her legs and tying it on her sash in front, she took a deep breath and dove headfirst into the Pool of Siloam. Swimming toward the Hezekiah Tunnel, she soon came to the spot where she could stand on her feet. *Alright, I must wade the water from here forward into the tunnel.*

Finally reaching the wall separating the Siloam Spring from the cave, Saphah jumped as she heard the voice of someone already standing there. She gasped as she recognized her prophet friend in the light of his candle. "Zephaniah, I'm so glad to see you!"

"As I am to see you." Prophet Zephaniah put an arm around her shoulder. "God sent me here to tell you that you must return to your own world now."

"But what will you do, Zephaniah? Can you travel with me to the future?"

"No, I can't." The prophet reminded Saphah of God's providence. "But as God's will is performed in your life, it'll also be performed in mine, so you must leave now."

"Alright." Saphah gave him a big hug.

"God be with you." Prophet Zephaniah returned the hug.

Saphah turned away and walked through the solid wall separating the Hezekiah Tunnel from the cave.

It is so dark in here.

"Yes, it is," noted a kind male voice. "Here, let me give you some light."

Saphah jumped in alarm at the sudden appearance of someone else in the cave. "You're a heavenly being, aren't you? I can tell by your glow." She continued to stare at the man. "But who are you?"

"I'm here to light your pathway," the man answered matter-of-factly. "So here, please take this candle."

Saphah reached over and took the lit candle in a holder from the celestial man. "Will you walk back with me all the way?"

Surely, I am with you always, to the very end of the age.[1] But, then he disappeared.

Saphah walked on, reflecting on what had just occurred. Then she remembered how and why she'd come to ancient Jerusalem in the first place. *I clearly remember being awakened early one morning from my sleep by a visiting angel. I was staring at a handsome man. I didn't know then that he was an angel.*

The man stood there like a statue, staring at me. I thought I was dreaming. I'm not sure what awakened me, but when I opened my eyes and saw him planted at the end of my bed, I froze with fear. He held his hand up as if to indicate he came in peace, and he didn't look as if he were there to harm me. I focused my eyes in the early morning light to view this muscular man with dark, wavy hair. His eyes were what drew me in …

2

Journey Into the Past

Saphah pulled the covers to her neck as she sat straight up in bed. She stared at the large, wide-set brown eyes of the man standing at the foot of her bed. *Who is this and why is he here?* Her heart raced.

He gazed back into the sleepy eyes of Saphah with deep compassion. "Don't be afraid. I've come to tell you something important. My name is Malek, meaning messenger, and I've been sent to you as a spokesman from the heavenly realm."

Saphah's eyes grew large as she continued to warily stare at the man at the end of her bed. "Are you an angelic being, or are you a dream?"

"I've been sent by God to guide you to a parallel time and place."

Saphah gasped. *What's happening?* Shielding her eyes, she dared to look upon the magnificent being who shone in brilliance as Malak was enveloped in a blinding light. Then her eyes blinked in amazement as the visage of Malak converted back into an ordinary human.

"Oh, you're really an angel!" Saphah covered her mouth in surprise.

Malak nodded. "Messenger angels usually appear to humans as persons, like they did when they spoke to Abraham[1] or to Samson's mother[2] in biblical accounts. That's why I first came to you as a man. But because you're afraid, I had to show you my true appearance as an angel. However, I'd like to keep speaking as a man, if that's okay?"

"I'd prefer you speak as a man, but I'm glad to know you're really an angel. But please tell me, what is a parallel time and place?"

"I can't tell you exactly." Malak spoke in a calm and gentle voice. "You'll need to personally experience it before you can understand it."

"But I don't know if I want to experience it if I don't know what it is." Saphah was still unsure about what was happening. "Can you at least tell me how I'll get to a parallel time and place?"

"I'm here to guide you to a portal where you can travel to a place which existed centuries ago in an ancient biblical land."

"Are we going to biblical Israel? Is that what you mean? Please, tell me how that can be possible?"

"*All things are possible with God,*"[3] came Malak's reply.

"But why are we going?"

"You've a mission to accomplish, and I'm an angel assigned to lead you in the first part of your journey." Malak smiled and nodded his head. "Now, please slip on your robe and slippers, and take my hand. We'll travel together to a place you've visited before. Don't be afraid when you suddenly find yourself standing in a cold river. We have to go there first for you to reach the gate to the portal."

Saphah reached for Malak's hand and felt her smaller hand disappear within his grasp. *I feel safe and secure grasping his hand.* She looked up into his compassionate eyes when her surroundings became a blur.

"Brrrrr …," Saphah shivered as the two of them landed hip-deep in frigid water. Her body quivered, her teeth chattered, and her folded arms shook as she glanced in all directions. "Malak, I do remember this place. We're standing in the stream where my cousins and I used to fish and swim as kids. Over there is the entrance to the cave where my cousin Ben explored by swimming underwater to get inside, but

I was too afraid to tag along into the cave. In this spot, there's only a few inches between the water and the low ceiling of the cave entrance."

"I knew you'd remember." Malak gave her a huge grin. "Are you ready to go into the cave now?"

"I guess." Saphah nodded her head with a huge frown on her face.

Observing Saphah's expression, Malak stifled another smile and then reassured her, "Saphah, it's alright. Just take a deep breath and hold it because we're going inside the cave."

Saphah had no chance to think or resist. She barely had time to inhale a large gulp of air and hold her breath. The angel grasped her hand, and they disappeared headfirst into the flowing water. In a flash of time, she and Malak popped up into the pool of water inside the cave, like two huge bobbers on her childhood fishing line. There was barely enough light to see the rock floor with a stream flowing beside it. "What's the source of light in here?" Saphah couldn't understand how they could see anything at all in the cave.

"Come on, we'll walk a little farther." Malak took her hand to guide her. "But close your eyes until we get there." Turning the corner he paused. "Open your eyes now, and look up. See the small sinkhole allowing a stream of light to shine in? Most caves have openings such as this scattered about. Some are large enough to provide access to the inside from various locations. They also allow air inside so that breathing is possible."

"That's so beautiful!" Saphah gazed at the pale sunlight casting its rays onto the floor of the dimly lit space. As they walked forward, the filtered sunlight washed over the pair from head to toe. "Isn't it remarkable? Even in the darkest places, there can be light."

"Yes." Malak shook his head in agreement. "That's because *Light shines in the darkness, and the darkness has not overcome it.*[4] Christ is the light of men from whom comes all spiritual illumination, and the darkness cannot prevent it from shining."

Glancing down, Saphah caught a glimpse of a shiny object on the cave floor. A few inches from her right foot lay an Indian arrowhead. Saphah quickly picked up the ancient artifact, stuck it in her pajama pocket, and the pair traveled on. Suddenly she felt something brush once, then twice, against her face. "What's that?" She flailed her hands to protect her head from the black creatures flying nearby.

"Don't be afraid, Saphah. It's just cave bats circling around. Look over in that little cove." Malak pointed to the left. "You'll see some hanging from the ceiling." He took a candle with its holder from his pocket, lit it, and then held it off to one side so she could see.

Although Saphah saw some of the creatures grasping the ceiling with their claws, her heart beat wildly as other bats blitzed at her head. As she ducked and swatted at more of the bats, Malak pulled her toward him. Hurrying away, the two spelunkers soon reached safety from the bombarding bats. "We'll reach the gate soon." Malak turned toward her with a smile. "You'll travel to the city of Jerusalem where you'll meet some people you've read about in your Bible."

"But why would God want me to visit the Holy Land in a past age?" Saphah wondered about the purpose of traveling to the past.

"You're a believer. Right?" Malak inquired.

"Yes, I've accepted Christ as my Lord and Savior." Saphah was very thankful for her salvation.

"One explanation from scripture for your salvation refers to the fact that your eyes are blessed *because they see, and your ears because they hear.*[5]

The ability to spiritually hear and see is given as a gift to believers rather than being the result of human cleverness. *The world cannot accept him, because it neither sees him nor knows him.*[6] Nonbelievers remain unable to spiritually see and hear until they believe. But the verse about seeing and hearing applies to you in another way."

"What do you mean?"

"You go by the name Saphah, rather than your actual name Tsaphah, don't you?" They continued walking farther into the cave. "Do you know what your real name means?"

"I go by Saphah because it's easier to say, but I really don't know what Tsaphah means."

Malak noted the chronology of the word. "In ancient Hebrew, it means watchman. Saphah, you're a watchman, or if you prefer a watchperson or watchwoman. Do you know what a watchperson does?"

"No, I don't. Please explain."

"Since a watchperson is someone equipped by God to see and hear, every believer has the potential to become one. But a watchperson doesn't just observe or hear. If danger is seen or heard, a watchman or woman must sound the alarm so people of their land can receive a message of approaching harm. It's as if God has not only trained their eyes to see and their ears to hear, but has also specially equipped them to give warning of coming danger."

"Well, I know that in the Old Testament, the Prophet Ezekiel became a spiritual watchman for Jerusalem." The two entered a large room in the cave. "Look, Malak!" Saphah admired various folded sheets of mineral hanging down from the ceiling in draped positions. "What are those?"

"Those are called curtains." Malak moved his candle around to bring into focus different aspects of the room. "Up there are icicle-shaped stalactites hanging from above, and below are inverted icicle-like stalagmites rising from the floor."

"The glow from your candle makes the room seem ethereal." Saphah stood motionless as she soaked up the beauty of the chamber, then she joined Malak to enter another narrow stretch of the cavern. "The Prophet Ezekiel was a spiritual watchman for Jerusalem, wasn't he?"

"Yes, he was." Malak stopped for a moment to talk directly to his protegy. "God called Ezekiel to be a watchman for his capital city and nation. But the Lord also wants you, Saphah, to be a watchperson for the people of your nation. When the Lord called Ezekiel, he said, *Son of man, I have made you a watchman for the people of Israel; so hear the word I speak and give them warning from me.*[7] Did you notice the Prophet Ezekiel was told not only to hear God's Word but also to give a message of warning to his countrymen?"

"Yes, I noticed Ezekiel was to both hear God's Word and to give a message of warning. But are you really telling me I've been called as a watchwoman for the people of America?" Saphah was surprised to hear God had called her for such a role. "Hearing what you've said makes me feel responsible to fulfill the mission. But it also seems incredible to me that God would call me, a mediocre person, to such a task! Me? A watchwoman for my country? That's too mind boggling to believe! I don't know how I can?"

"I have both a short and a long answer to your question." Malak stopped and pointed toward the cave wall. "Would you like to sit for a while on this natural outcropping while I tell you more?"

"I would." The two sat down and turned to face one another on the bench-like rock.

"Modern technology has made it easier to communicate with mankind everywhere on the globe." Malak began his two-part explanation. "Actually, it's less difficult in the present day for one individual to transmit information worldwide than it was in ancient times for a single person to share information to a city. So that's the short answer."

"Yes, that's very true. Now, please tell me the long answer."

"God told Ezekiel, *I looked for someone among them who would build up the wall and stand before me in the gap on behalf of the land so I would not have to destroy it, but I found no one.*[8] A city wall provided the best protection from foreign invasion in ancient times. Watchmen stood guard on the wall to warn of coming danger, and they blew shofars to sound the alarm when an enemy was nearby. But if a gap existed in a wall, the city would eventually be attacked. Here, the gap represented the danger facing ancient Jerusalem, the capital of a nation in spiritual decline. God planned to use an enemy nation, the Babylonians, to break through the gap in judgment. But God couldn't call anyone to successfully 'stand in the gap' to warn the people because the Judaens simply wouldn't listen to the warnings of danger."

Saphah grew solemn and became lost in thought for a few minutes. "Malak, I think I need to tell you something. It could be important. God may have already called me."

3

A City Set on a Hill

Malak was anxious to hear what Saphah had to say. "Alright, please tell me more."

"Recently, I personally asked the Lord if there was something I should know. Then I listened quietly to see if God would answer me."

"Did He answer you?"

"He did. I heard in my spirit four softly spoken words."

"Stand in the gap."

"The words, 'Stand in the gap,' seemed like a directive, but I didn't really know how to obey God's command. So, I researched trying to figure out what God wanted me to do. I also reasoned perhaps God wanted me to write as a method to 'Stand in the gap,' but I needed to learn more about what He wanted me to write. And I prayed about whether my book should be non-fiction or fiction. The Lord let me know it should be fiction, possibly written in an historical or a fantasy vein."

"Yes." Malak verified God's call on her life. "The Lord wants you to 'Stand in the gap' by writing and publishing a book. Possibly he might want several books, according to what transpires in the world."

"Well, Malak, I really didn't know what to do before, but since you've been sent to me as a messenger from the heavenly realm, I think I understand God's calling. But to tell you the truth, I don't feel capable of writing fiction. My experience is with writing non-fiction."

"We'll talk about your abilities later, Saphah. But for now, we must concentrate on you becoming a watchperson."

"Was there anyone in ancient times who stood in the gap to prevent destruction of the land?"

"There were prophets who spoke warnings from God to the people. But the rebellious men and women of that time wouldn't listen. God spoke about that to Ezekiel: Son of man, you are living among a rebellious people. *They have eyes to see but do not see and ears to hear but do not hear, for they are a rebellious people.*"[1]

"Did the Lord speak of that to other prophets too?"

"Yes, God's Word regarding the inability of the people to see and hear also came to both Jeremiah and Isaiah. The Prophet Jeremiah recorded God's warning: *Hear this, you foolish and senseless people, who have eyes but do not see, who have ears but do not hear. Should you not fear me? … These people have stubborn and rebellious hearts; they have turned aside and gone astray. …Should I not punish them for this?*[2] Other prophets also spoke truth to the people of their time, but these folk wouldn't listen."

"So, what did Isaiah say on the subject?"

"Isaiah referred to the hardening of people's hearts in his prophecy, and was quoted by Jesus. Saphah, do you want to look that up in this bible and read it to me?" Malak reached into his backpack and pulled out a Holy Bible

"Sure." Saphah took the bible and did a long search to find the right quote. "Here is what it says:

> *You will be ever hearing but never understanding; you will be ever seeing but never perceiving. For this people's heart has become calloused; they hardly hear with their ears, and they have closed their eyes. Otherwise,*

they might see with their eyes, hear with their ears, understand with their hearts and turn, and I would heal them.[3]

So, if I'm understanding this correctly, it wasn't because people were unwilling to stand in the gap that no one could successfully intercede for Judah. Instead, it was because most people were unresponsive to warnings of danger. Most of Judah's citizens were hardened to the point that they were beyond help. Am I right?"

"Sadly, that's correct. But Jesus pointed out that the people of your day can also have hardened hearts."

Saphah stopped for a moment and put her fingers to her temple in deep thought. "Please tell me, are present-day citizens of the U. S. also in danger of becoming hardened beyond help?"

"Yes, that's a very real possibility." Malak stopped walking and looked toward Saphah. "As God called the Israelites to be a light to the ancient nations, He has also called American Christians to be a light to the rest of humanity." As they continued through the cave Malek asked, "Do you remember John Winthrop from your own American History?"

Saphah thought a moment. "I think he was a Puritan in the early days of America."

"You're correct. Winthrop led the first massive wave of immigrants from England to America. In 1630, the Puritan wrote a message and shared his vision with the passengers of the ship Arabella, who would pioneer the new commonwealth. The man spoke of a unique nation being birthed into the world for the will and purposes of God. All other nations of the world would look to America as a nation to emulate: 'We must consider that we shall be as a city upon a hill. The eyes of all people are upon us.'"[4]

"The symbolism of a city upon a hill comes from the New Testament where Jesus noted that *a city set on a hill cannot be hid*,[5] if it is raised up by God as a light to the world. Of course, Israel was called by God to give light to the world when it entered into agreement with God and became a covenant nation. But just as Israel was directed by God to give light to the world, at the founding of America, Winthrop would likewise write about America: 'Thus stands the cause between God and us. We are entered into covenant with Him for this work.'"[6]

"Wait …," Saphah paused. "What exactly is a covenant nation?"

Malak smiled at her inquisitive nature. "Let's talk about it." He reached for a flask attached to his belt. "Are you getting thirsty? Here's some water." He offered Saphah a drink.

"Yes, I'm getting thirsty. I haven't had anything to drink since last night." Saphah reached for the flask, took several swigs, and handed back the container. "How much farther do we have to go?"

"We have quite a distance to travel, so what do you think about resting for a while as we talk?"

"That sounds like a good idea, but where will we sit?"

"I'm all prepared." The angel grabbed his backpack, pulled out two woven rugs, and spread them out on the ground. Saphah sat cross-legged on one of the soft mats, and Malak settled down on the other with his legs stretched out and his palms on the rug.

"Now, please go on with your explanation." Saphah rolled her shoulders and stretched her arms.

"Although Israel alone is recognized Biblically as a covenant nation, Winthrop's vision for America was based on God's covenant with

Israel. That covenant specified that as long as Israel kept the ways of God, the blessings of the Lord would fill their land. Likewise, the covenant rules that Winthrop prophesied for America concerned the good that would happen to the country if it followed God's ways: 'The Lord will be our God and delight to dwell among us, as His own people, and will command a blessing upon us in all our ways, so that we shall see much more of His wisdom, power, goodness, and truth. …We shall find that the God of Israel is among us when ten of us shall be able to resist a thousand of our enemies.'"[7]

Saphah thought for a bit. "To me, Winthrop's words are comparable to what God gave Moses to speak to Israel before they entered the promised land. What do you think?"

"Yes, I think they're comparable. And these similar prophecies by Winthrop were also given to the pioneers of the new Commonwealth before they entered the New World."

"Well, we all know that Winthrop's prophecies concerning America at its inception did come true. God lifted America as a light to the world and blessed it in all its ways until it became an exalted nation on earth."

"Yes, and God gave America great light for spreading the gospel, but you need to remember an important fact. To whom much is given, much is expected."

"True. But America isn't living up to expectations. At the present time, the moral condition of my nation is declining fast. In fact, the entire world seems to be spiraling out of control. It's really sad."

"It is sad. God's Word says: *Be very careful then, how you live—not as unwise but as wise, making the most of every opportunity, because the days are evil.*[8] And that's why Winthrop gave a prophetic warning of what would happen to the U. S. if it failed to follow God's ways:

'If we deal falsely with our God, if our hearts turn away so that we will not obey, but shall be seduced, and worship other gods and serve them, our pleasure and profits, so that we shall deal falsely with our God in this work we have undertaken, and so cause Him to withdraw His present help from us, we shall be made a story and a by-word through the world. We shall surely perish.'[9]

As you can see these words bore a strong resemblance to Israel's judgments if it departed from the Lord. Thus, when Israel failed in its role as a light to the nations, it was judged."

"Yes, Malak, I do see. Israel failed to be a light to the nations and was judged. So is any modern nation called by the Lord to be 'a city set on a hill' likewise in danger of judgment if it fails to fulfill its own role as a light to the world?"

"Saphah, it sure is. The result of that failure is God's judgment on any nation negligent of their spiritual role. Nevertheless, today God is again searching for those who'll stand in the gap to intercede for the present-day citizens of the U. S., through the work of *God our Savior, who wants all men to be saved and to come to a knowledge of the truth. For there is one God and one mediator between God and men, the man Christ Jesus, who gave himself as a ransom for all people.*[10] But the men and women of your nation desperately need to be warned while there's still time."

"Otherwise, are the people of my nation in danger of reaching the point of no return?"

"Well, the Lord doesn't want the people of any land to reach that point. He wants men and women worldwide to come back to him, to fight to restore the vision of God, and to continue to be a light to the citizens of the world. To do otherwise would be to fall from grace and to invite retribution from a just God who loves the people of the globe dearly, but can't allow sin and wickedness to prevail unabated."

"Enough for now." Malak pointed to a ledge in the cave where they could comfortably sit. "I've brought you refreshments, since you haven't eaten yet today. You need your energy for the journey ahead." Malak sat and motioned for Saphah to sit too. He pulled a big honey cake from his satchel along with a flask of water. "Here, Saphah. Nourish yourself."

Saphah thanked Malak and then whispered a quick prayer of thanks to God. She hungrily gobbled the cake and thirstily drank the water. Then, with her hunger and thirst assuaged, she settled back on the ledge and rested her head against the wall. As she rested, Malak's velvety baritone voice began to hum. She closed her eyes and reveled in the melodic tones.

"Hey! I know that hymn!" She wiped her mouth to smile.

"I know you do. You used to sing it at your church."

"How would you know that?" Saphah gave him a puzzled look.

"God knows everything about you, and the Lord has shared much about you with me, as your messenger, to help you."

"I'm so glad he knows me personally. The Bible tells me that he knows *when I sit and when I rise* ...[and] *is familiar with all my ways.*"[11] She took another drink and then looked with thanksgiving in her heart toward the kind angel. "I'm thankful God sent you to me, Malak. I loved hearing you hum. Would you like to sing the hymn with me?"

"I would love to sing with you, sweet Saphah." And so, in their rich voices, Malak and Saphah both sang. "'Softly and tenderly, Jesus is calling, Calling for you and for me. See on the portals He's waiting and watching, Watching for you and for me. Come home—come home. Ye who are weary, come home. Earnestly, tenderly, Jesus is calling—calling, O sinner, come home.'"[12]

"Oh, thank you so much for singing one of my favorites with me. May I tell you something else?"

"You're welcome, Saphah. Now, what else would you like to tell me?"

"Well, I'm older now, and I've enjoyed singing old-time hymns for most of my life, up until about ten years ago or so. That's when many churches transitioned into singing choruses instead of the old hymns. I like the up-to-date music too, but I'm glad to hear the old-fashioned words that characterize the hymns from my childhood."

"Well, I'm happy to tell you, Saphah, that all genres of music, from all ages of history, will be associated with the extremely joyous tone which will accompany mankind's first glimpse of Jesus." And with that, Malak broke out in song again. "'When we all get to heaven, what a day of rejoicing that will be! When we all see Jesus, we'll sing and shout the victory.'"[13]

"Oh, how I look forward to seeing Jesus, my Savior, face to face! And when the redeemed first see Him, I think there's a strong possibility we'll be worshipping our Lord by singing and shouting in victory!"

"I think 'In the sweet bye and bye, when we meet on that beautiful shore,'[14] Malak sang with a twinkle in his eye, "the redeemed are in for some pleasant worship experiences featuring all types of worship music."

"Malak, do I detect a sense of humor?" Saphah grinned. "Well then, 'Just over in the glory land, I'll join the happy angel band.'"[15] She burst out in tune.

Laughing, Malak asked, "Don't you suppose God created angels with a capacity for humor too? Besides, you should lighten up and laugh a little." As they walked into a vast room, Malak's tone turned serious, almost ominous, as he looked Saphah in the eyes. "Once you reach Jerusalem, you're going to experience both light-hearted and soul-wrenching times in the days ahead. You need to prepare yourself for that now."

"Malak, I will," Saphah solemnly promised.

4

THE APERTURE OF PROCESS

Malak and Saphah sat down in the spacious room which featured more stalactites and stalagmites, plus various shapes of mineral curtains adorning the walls. It also featured a large pool with water so clear objects could plainly be seen on the bottom.

"Saphah, do you want to see some interesting creatures who live and thrive in caves? Many of the critters are so rare they only exist in certain areas of the world."

"Yes, I do!"

Malak turned over a rock to expose some white snails. "These little pale creatures only exist in Southern Missouri caves, and over there, those completely white crayfish with long antennas and blind eyes, are most numerous in the cavern pools of the Southeastern U. S."

"Look, Malak, there's a little school of white fish swimming around in the pool."

"Yes, those are eyeless, unpigmented cavefish, and they use sonic clicks to communicate with others in their school."

"Fascinating."

"Indeed, God has created a fantastic array of life in the universe and made them suitable for their various environments." But then Malak asked, "You grew up on a farm, didn't you?"

"Yes, I did. A farm is the best place in which to grow up. But why do you ask?"

"Well, in your father and mother's farming operation, do you recall that your dad would temporarily leave some plots of land dormant so the soil could rest?"

"Of course, I remember that well. For example, my dad plowed the soil after corn harvest and left the field without sowing new seed so it could lie fallow. After the soil remained for a while in a dormant state, he plowed and tilled the ground again and planted seed for a new crop. I remember as a kid talking with my father about subjects like allowing the land to lie fallow, crop rotation, and so forth."

"Saphah, did you know that God's love is displayed through that illustration. A watchperson's experience is similar to a farmer's in tending the soil. He or she reminds people that their faith life has lain fallow too long. It's time for them to awaken from dormancy and arise to new life and spiritual growth. So, just as your earthly father wanted to revive the farm soil, your Heavenly Father wants to revive the souls of those in need of salvation through His Son Jesus Christ. He wants you to share the message that they aren't alone, because God is beside them, offering his love to them, and providing the way for them to return home."

Saphah thought about Malak's words for a few moments. "I think I understand my calling better now. But there's a big problem which might prevent fulfillment of my mission. I don't have ministerial training; I only have a Bachelor Degree in Biblical Studies."

"You only need to use whatever abilities or talents God has given you to sound the alarm that danger is near. You do recognize the ability God has given you, don't you?"

"Maybe. I've written three non-fiction books and independently published two of them. The other book was first published by a traditional publisher. Could writing be my ability?"

"Think about it. What if you became a writer because you were chosen to become a watchwoman in a late season of your life? Books you've already written have prepared you for writing and publishing books to warn people of approaching danger."

"I don't know." Saphah thought about it. "Jesus communicated with people using parables or stories. When I asked the Lord if He wanted me to write my book as a story, He let me know I should write in the Christian Historical Fiction or Fantasy vein. But I don't feel capable of writing fiction."

"Remember Esther in the Old Testament?"

"Yes, Esther was a capable woman who providentially became the queen of Assyria. God used her elevated position so she could intercede for her own people."

"But how do you suppose Esther felt when she was called? The ultimate coming of the Messiah was jeopardized by the evil Haman who wanted to destroy all the Jews living in the Assyrian Empire. When God called her to intervene, most likely Esther didn't feel capable of fulfilling her task. But her uncle Mordecai said: *If you remain silent at this time, relief and deliverance for the Jews will arise from another place, but you and your father's family will perish. And who knows but that you have come to your royal position for such a time as this?*"[1]

"It sounds like Esther felt inadequate, just as I do."

"That's right, but then she realized it wasn't about her. It was about Him, the One who called her to an important task to save the remnant of Jews living in Assyrian exile. Esther told Mordecai: *I will go to the king, even though it is against the law. And if I perish, I perish.*"[2]

Looking directly into Saphah's eyes, Malak said, "It wasn't about Esther, and it's not about you either. All you have to do is answer

God's call and follow His lead. It's your job to make people aware of coming danger by passing along God's message as recorded in the Word. Some who read will not understand, but others who read will comprehend. God's Word will not return to Him void. The results aren't under your control, but you'll be held responsible to clearly present the truth."

Considering Malak's words, Saphah inwardly prayed and then replied, "I'll go to the parallel time and place of which you spoke, but I'll leave the final results of what I write with God." The now silent pair rounded a bend deep into the cave. A brightly-colored undulating light appeared, but its features couldn't be distinguished at that distance. As they drew closer, Saphah saw a shimmering metal gate extending from floor to ceiling of the cave. Flashing light bathed the bars of the gate with radiant light.

"Malak, look! We've found the gate! See how beautifully it is lit up! How could there be a light like this in such a deep part of the cave?"

"It's heavenly light splendid in its radiance. Heaven has lent us this light for such a situation as this."

"Oh my," Saphah gasped as she jerked on the gate. "Look, it's locked! What're we going to do?"

"Only those who have a key can pass through the gate."

"Oh no, Malak. I don't have a key! We'll have to go back now." Large tears started to well in her eyes and slip down her cheeks. "I won't be able to fulfill my mission."

"Don't despair my friend." Malak gently comforted Saphah by placing one hand lightly on her shoulder. "I have some good news. Look! I have the key." The angel smiled as he held up the metal object in his other hand.

"You have the key. Oh, that's wonderful!" Saphah wiped her wet cheeks. "Now we can go through the gate. C'mon, Malak, let's go!"

Malak held up his hand. "Saphah, I'm sorry. But I can't go with you. I've led you safely to the gate, but now you must transition into the past alone. Then, using knowledge you gain there, you can travel back and forth as often as needed to do research and finish your book. While you're in the ancient land, nothing will change back in your world. No one will even know you've been gone."

"But aren't you going to Jerusalem with me? Oh please, come with me. I don't want to go alone." Worry lines creased her face and tears began to form in her eyes again.

"I can't, Saphah. I must stay on this side as your gatekeeper. But always know, you're never actually alone, for Jesus will be with you to assist in all He has called you to do. Remember what Jesus said: *All power is given unto me in heaven and in earth. … And, lo, I am with you always.*"[3]

"Yes, Lord Jesus, please stay with me always." Saphah gratefully smiled and wiped tears from her face with the back of her hand.

"Now, I need to explain supernatural time travel to you. First, the portal had to be in a geologically-stable region. This cave, with its stone walls of dense, stable matter has been positioned for thousands of years." The angel patted the wall with his hand. "This portal on the future side is your entryway into the Aperture of Process which lets you travel into the past."

"Uh-huh." Saphah listened to Malak as she walked to the gate. *This gate is magnificent*, she thought. *There must be symbolic meaning attached to it.*

"Second, when you're in the past, your presence won't tamper with events or the environment there. Your body will process into a supernatural form. No matter how long you're there, you won't age while you're gone. You can interact with your environment and other people, but after you leave the past, the environs and history of that time will remain unchanged."

I can't believe this is happening! Saphah pinched her arm to see if she were awake.

"You're listening, aren't you?"

"Yes, I am. It just seems unreal that I'm going to travel to an ancient land!"

Malak spoke in a serious tone of voice. "Well, you're going there, and you need to pay close attention. This is important!"

"I agree," Saphah realized that she needed to concentrate on what Malak was saying.

"Third, in regard to your time travels, once a time gate has been opened into the past, you may travel in either direction through the gates as long as they remain open. But once a time gate is closed, the link between the two timelines will be lost and can't be regained. Therefore, the gates must remain accessible, but continually guarded to protect them from intruders."

"Oh, that's why you can't travel with me. Now I understand why. It's important for you to stay and protect this gate."

"Fourth, and the most important thing you need to remember is that you're visiting the past to observe firsthand what happened to the people of a faraway land in a time long ago. You'll see for yourself their sin and disobedience foreshadow the immorality present in the world today. It's a place of parallel sins."

"Hmmm …," Saphah shook her head, "that's what you meant when you said I'm going to a parallel time and place, isn't it?"

"Definitely! Finally, you're going to cross barriers of time, geography, language, and culture that presently separate you from the ancient biblical land. Your time travels will both assist you in understanding the original meaning of biblical events and also help you to know the message God wants you to write for today's people."

"I want to get this straight. The primary goal of my time travels is to observe certain happenings in the times and locations where they occurred?"

Malak nodded.

"… and then to build a bridge between the ancient message of the Word of God and what's happening today. Right?"

"That's right." Malak smiled happily because Saphah was starting to understand.

Saphah rubbed her chin with her thumb and forefinger and stared down as she went through the process in her brain. "Alright, through my future writing, I'll share the significance of what happened back then with today's people. The citizens of my nation need to hear the same message as it applies to them today." She looked up at Malak. "I would like to know something though. Is the ancient message truly applicable to the people of the present?"

"Most assuredly, the God of yesterday is the same God as today and the people of today are similar to those of yesterday. Since people of your day share a common humanity with biblical persons, there is a universal aspect to problems faced and solutions received from God. The timeless nature of God's Word enables it to speak with power and relevance in every culture, period, and place. People can use the truths spoken in that time and apply them to similar-yet-different needs in the modern world. So, as God spoke to older generations, He still speaks to humanity today through the Word of God."

"I never thought of it that way, but what you've said makes sense."

"Well, you must be excited to continue your journey, so now I'll unlock the gate for your entry." Malak fitted the key into the lock. With a turning motion of the key and a click, the gate opened before the watchwoman. "If you're ready to transition into the past now, I want to wish you Godspeed and success in your mission."

"Thank you, Malak. Yes, I'm ready to go, and I truly appreciate everything you've done to help me. Would you mind if I take a few moments to say a short prayer before entering the gate?"

"Yes, please do."

Saphah placed her hands together and began to pray. "Heavenly Father, thank you for calling me to stand in the gap for my people, and I humbly accept your call. I pray you'll forgive me for all my sins and wipe my slate clean. Lord, please let your Word be to me, not as a silent written Word, but as a living Word empowered by the Holy Spirit as a light unto the hearts and souls of others. And, let it be to others, a Word not only heard with their ears or seen with their eyes, but also a Word imparted to their hearts as a living message unto their own souls. In the precious name of Jesus, I pray. Amen."

Finishing her prayer, Saphah opened her eyes and turned to the gate which seemed to beckon her forward. She glanced at Malak with a questioning look, and he gently nodded approval. Saphah arose from the floor and strode to the open gate. Her eyes sparkled as she observed the swirling rainbow around the perimeter of the portal. The center of the white aperture seemed to recede inward.

Cautiously, Saphah extended first one foot and then the other inside the pulsating mass. *This must be a little taste of heaven*, Saphah supposed, as she floated around inside the Aperture of Process. *I don't know what's happening, but I think this is one of the most pleasant things I've ever experienced.* Fluffy white clouds drifted around her body and the smell of fresh rain caressed her nose. *It's going to rain*, she thought, as a gentle rain shower began to fall around her. It reminded her of the old hymn, "There Shall Be Showers of Blessing."

She began to sing aloud, in her soft soprano voice, ""There shall be showers of blessing: This is the promise of love; There shall be seasons refreshing, Sent from the Savior above. Showers of blessing, Showers of blessing we need: Mercy drops round us are falling, but for the showers we plead."[4] Yes, dear Father in heaven," Saphah prayed. "Please send showers of blessing upon my nation. In Jesus' name I pray. Amen." There was a lull, and then all was still. Saphah's body gradually stopped swirling and her feet settled to the ground as she came to rest at a second gate.

"Hello, Saphah," said a pleasant, but muffled voice.

5

A Parallel Time & Place

The startled woman stood upright at the second locked gate. *Who spoke to me? That wasn't Malak's voice I heard.* "Hello, who's there?" Saphah spoke aloud. Suddenly there was a click and the gate swung open with a groaning sound. Saphah saw a young man waiting for her beyond the gate. She was taken aback by his piercing blue eyes that seemed to look straight through her.

"Welcome." The man brushed a hand through his blond, wavy hair. As he did, his image began to change. His chiseled features began to glow as his eyes turned into blinding beams of light and his white garment glistened with light.

Saphah gasped in amazement. But then, just as quickly, the angel's appearance became human-like once again, proving to her he was a heavenly personage. Saphah glanced down at her own garments, only to discover she was now fully garbed in a long cream robe with a brown sash tied on the side. A matching brown shawl covered her head, and sandals shod her feet. She felt a chain around her neck. *What's this?* She lifted the golden chain from her neck to find a tiny dangling key.

The nice-looking man interrupted Saphah's thoughts. "Welcome to a parallel time and place. I'm so glad you're here. My name is Nahal, which means 'provider of rest and refreshment.' You're now in the biblical past, and I'm your gatekeeper on this side within the cave. So, among other things, my mission is to refresh you with food, rest, and to equip you for your trip. As you already know, the gate here must remain unlocked so you can access it in your travels. While you're away I'll guard it from intruders. As long as the gate is unlocked, you can make your journeys back and forth to complete your mission."

"Thank you, Nahal, and I'm so pleased to meet you. Can you tell me about my journey ahead?"

"Of course, but you've been traveling several hours, so first I'd like to offer you a meal." Nahal glanced toward a little loaf of bread baking on a bed of coals.

"Oh, that would be great." Saphah's stomach growled as she took note of a low table with long cushions on two sides.

"Please make yourself comfortable on a pillow and rest while I get your food ready."

"All right. I'm feeling a little tired right now." Saphah's long walk had depleted her legs of strength. She lounged on the cushion and placed her head on a little soft pillow. *I'll just close my eyes for a few seconds.* But before she knew it, she fell sound asleep. Awakening shortly later with a start, Saphah quickly sat straight up on the cushion and glanced toward the angelic being who was busy cooking her food.

"Saphah, did you have a good rest? Your food is prepared now." Grasping a little loaf of bread baking on the coals with his bare fingers, Nahal quickly flipped the hot object into Saphah's bowl. "Ouch!" He fanned his hand in the air.

"Oh my! Did you burn yourself?"

"No," Nahal's mouth crinkled into a crooked grin. "I just wanted to check to see if you're awake."

"Well, I am now." Saphah snickered at Nahal's antics.

"I'm an angel, so I really can't get burned." Nahal laughed at the absurdity of the thought. "But I'd hoped to relieve your stress with a little joke."

"Actually, it worked. Malak pointed out that I seemed a bit nervous. But thanks to you two I'm becoming calm. I'm sure thankful God sent me two light-hearted angels!"

"Well, my friend, you've got to remember one thing. God's hand is upon you, so if you just trust in Him, you've nothing to fear. I'll be quiet now while you give thanks for your meal."

Saphah bowed her head, closed her eyes, and began to pray. "Father in heaven, thank You for sending Malak and Nahal to shore up the foundation of my faith and to help me realize that terror and fear have no part in my life. And thank You too for providing food for this meal. In Jesus name I pray. Amen."

Nahal offered Saphah fruit and cheese. "While you enjoy your meal, we can talk."

"Thank you for the wonderful food." Saphah dipped a piece of hot bread into a little cruse of olive oil. "I didn't realize I was so hungry and thirsty."

"You're welcome." Nahal filled Saphah's cup with a good vintage of wine. "Don't forget to try the raisin cakes too."

"Thank you, I will," Saphah took a bite of the sweet raisin treat and a sip of the smooth wine. "Your food is so yummy and just what I needed after walking all morning."

"I'm glad you're enjoying it. Now, please tell me about your transition through the Aperture of Process, and then I'll listen to any questions you may have."

"Well, my passage was a good experience. The best part, I think, was a gentle shower of rain falling around me at the end. It made me think of the old hymn, 'There Shall Be Showers of Blessing' and I sang it aloud as I twirled around in the Aperture of Process. Does the rain shower have any spiritual significance?"

"The inspiration for that hymn originates from a verse in Ezekiel, which occurs only once in the Word: *I will send down showers in season; there will be showers of blessing.*[1] While the verse specifically applies here to Israel, it states a divine principle which can rightly be appropriated by people in all eras that God 'will send down showers in season.' Thus, the first verse of the hymn sets forth that it is a promise of love that the Savior above will send seasons of refreshing upon people who long to return to the Lord."

"Yes, God deeply loves humanity. And, I know from experience that the greatest blessing in human life is a personal relationship with the Lord, which comes by the hearing of the Word and is obtained through the Lord Jesus Christ. The Word of God states: *As the rain and the snow come down from heaven, and do not return to it without watering the earth and making it bud and flourish …so is my word that goes out from my mouth: It will not return to me empty, but will accomplish what I desire and achieve the purpose for which I sent it.*"[2]

"Yes, all of mankind is blessed beyond measure by Jesus' death on the cross! Because of the message of salvation as shared in God's Word, people are made aware of what God has done to ensure their deliverance."

Saphah sighed with relief. "That's why I don't have to worry about the results from my book. God calls Christians to share the Word of the Gospel, while assuring us His Word will not return to Him void."

"That's right. When peoples' lives are bereft of meaning and they're searching in earnest for God, the Holy Spirit will send down showers of blessing because he loves mankind. Thus, the second verse of the hymn, 'There shall be showers of blessing, Precious reviving again, Over the hills and the valleys, Sound of abundance of rain,'[3] refers to the life-giving effects of revival. Just as rain revives a dry and thirsty land, the Lord causes spiritual revival whenever people become weary and faint."

"What about the third verse? Does it have special meaning, too?"

"It does. Verse three, 'There shall be showers of blessing: Send them upon us, O Lord! Grant to us now a refreshing, Come and now honor Thy word,'⁴ serves to remind people that, as a rule, the season of showers occurs when there's a great void in peoples' hearts."

"So, when souls are deeply longing and searching for God, that is a time when God will send showers of refreshing."

"True. And, the fourth verse helps men and women to recognize that they must have a personal relationship with God to be saved: 'There shall be showers of blessing: O that today they might fall, Now, as to God we're confessing, Now, as on Jesus we call.'⁵ To have a personal relationship with God, one must respond to his message by calling on him personally. But did you know the fifth verse is excluded from many hymnals?"

"I didn't know that. What does it say?"

"'There shall be showers of blessing, if we but trust and obey; There shall be seasons refreshing when we let Him have His way.'⁶ It mentions the need to obey God from the heart. The Lord has promised to bless us, but to receive his blessings, we must hearken to his voice and do his will. As the Word says: *If we confess our sins, he is faithful and will forgive us our sins and purify us from all unrighteousness.*⁷ So, the possibility of revival depends a lot on the actions of the people and the sincerity of their hearts. Spiritual revival only occurs when people humble themselves, confess their sins, and follow the path of obedience toward God."

Saphah took another bite of raisin cake and thought for a few seconds. "Nahal, could that mean that if men and women began to wholeheartedly return to God, the Lord might spread revival across an entire country or maybe even the whole world?"

"When people are sensitive to a need for personal revival in their own hearts and call upon the Lord to restore their souls, the effects can spread. Others will be drawn back to God. The hymn focuses on that kind of personal revival which can be contagious in the hearts of mankind. So yes, the hymn could apply to the whole earth. In Isaiah, the Word says: *This is what the high and exalted One says—he who lives forever, whose name is holy: I live in a high and holy place, but also with the one who is contrite and lowly in spirit, to revive the spirit of the lowly and to revive the heart of the contrite.*[8]

"So, God's forgiveness is available to all who are humble and sorry for their sins?"

"Yes, if the will and love of God had free course, showers of blessing would happen around the globe. The obstacle to revival worldwide is disobedience in the hearts of the people."

"Nahal, what about the outward appearance of the aperture? The swirling perimeter of the Aperture was bathed in rainbow colors, but the entrance itself was composed of a white powder-like mass receding inward. Is there symbolic significance to these things?"

"Yes. The rainbow symbolism belongs to God, who alone has the right to use the rainbow colors as a representation of an abstraction. Nevertheless, some have used the rainbow as a symbol of actions displeasing to God. The legalization of gay marriage took place in America in 2015, and in various other countries at different times. Two U.S. presidents have declared the observance of Gay Pride month and officials in other nations set aside special pride festivals to celebrate the LGBTQ life, with some U. S. states following suit."

"So, does the Bible say Homosexuality is wrong?"

"Yes, it proclaims the homosexual practice to be so sinful in God's eyes that those who continue to engage in the act deserve judgment: *If a man has sexual relations with a man as one does with a woman, both of them have done what is detestable.*[9] *…Because of this, God gave them over to shameful lusts. Even their women exchanged natural sexual relations for unnatural ones.*[10] *…Although they know God's righteous decree that those who do such things deserve death, they not only continue to do these very things but also approve of those who practice them.*"[11]

"Is that word continue important?"

"Yes, it is. The word *continue* refers to those who refuse to repent and abstain from doing 'these very things.' Only they are culpable in God's eyes. God is the one who created human beings to be male and female: *God created mankind in his own image, in the image of God he created them; male and female he created them.*"[12]

"Since God is our Creator, He has the right to rule over us. Is that true?"

"Yes, God is the One who has the right to specify that proper sexual conduct is only between a man and a woman. Any deviation from God's criteria is sin in our Creator's eyes. God's purposes are denied by any aberration from these commands, both on a personal or a governmental level. So, if any nation disobeys God by approving of practices going against God's righteous decrees, what do you think will happen? Do you think God will bless them?"

Saphah considered the fact that God is holy. "Oh my, I don't see how God can bless any country, state, or city for upholding immoral and unbiblical practices by passing laws in approval of the very things that God forbids."

"That's right, there are many countries around the globe where gross iniquity has been committed by those who pass laws that go against God's Holy Bible. People need to remember the actual symbolic purpose of God's rainbow. It is his promise that He will never judge the world again as he did in the days of Noah."

"So, does that mean the Lord will never judge the people of the earth again?"

"No, it doesn't mean there won't be judgments. The Word stresses that *He will judge the world in righteousness and the peoples with equity.*[13] And the Bible also says He will not only judge what has been done in the past, but will also judge what will be done in the future: *Whatever is has already been, and what will be has been before; and God will call the past to account.*[14] Thus, the Bible reveals that God is a judge who oversees the movement of the epochs of time and will one day call the entire past to account."

"True, and no one will escape his judgment: *God will bring to judgment both the righteous and the wicked, for there will be a time for every activity, a time to judge every deed.*[15] There will be a final accounting, as also pointed out in the New Testament: *The day of the Lord will come like a thief. The heavens will disappear with a roar, the elements will be destroyed by fire, and the earth and everything done in it will be laid bare.*[16] The Lord will judge the earth, but it will be judgment by fire and not by water."

"So, what's the meaning of the white powdery substance revolving inward in the Aperture of Process?"

"When you entered the revolving white mass in the Aperture, your body processed into a dimension capable of existing in the past. In a similar way, a baby created in the womb processes into a form capable of existing in the outside world after birth."

"So, the white powder is symbolic of baby powder used on infants?"

"Yes, it is. Yet there are those who've stolen the lives of unborn babies and destroyed them in the womb or even after live birth. But the Word of God says: *You created my inmost being; you knit me together in my mother's womb. …My frame was not hidden from you when I was made in the secret place …Your eyes saw my unformed body …I praise you because I am fearfully and wonderfully made.*[17] Thus, scripture informs us that God loves the little babies for it says we are 'fearfully and wonderfully made.' So, if nations of the world continue to allow the act of abortion, what do you think God will do? Do you think God will bless nations that pass unconscionable laws permitting the killing of unborn babies?"

"How sad. I can't comprehend how the Lord would bless any land for passing laws which condone the heinous act of abortion of tiny infants."

"That's right. The Lord can't bless countries that pass laws going against His law. And, those are only two examples of the forms of depravity in the world as it continues to depart from the ways of the Lord. Nahal, I'm curious about something else. …"

"Go ahead."

"Well, recently I read in Amos: *Surely the Sovereign Lord does nothing without revealing his plan to his servants.*[18] So, I asked God a question concerning the Covid 19 virus which began to occur in our world in December of 2019. I wanted to know what would happen next after the pandemic outbreak since it developed into a worldwide plague allowed by the Lord. The evil of mankind perhaps caused it, but God permitted it to occur. Then, I prayed and asked and silently waited to hear what God would say."

"So what did He say?"

6

WINNOW

Saphah said, "Although I'd asked the Lord to reveal to me what would happen after the worldwide Covid Pandemic, I didn't really expect a response."

"Well, did you get an answer?."

"To my surprise, I did. In my spirit, the Lord quietly stated one word."

"Winnow."

"God gave you the word, *winnow*?"

"Yes, that was all. He said no more, but immediately I sensed it was a word of great spiritual significance."

"So, what do you think the word, *winnow*, means?" Nahal wanted to learn about Saphah's understanding of the word.

"Winnow is an agricultural term about an aspect of harvesting grain. When my parents farmed, they raised various grain crops such as milo, sargo, corn, barley, or wheat. Harvests of large plantings of grains such as wheat required a machine called a combine which cuts, thrashes, and winnows the grain. But harvests of small plantings of crops such as milo were done manually. My father mechanically cut the stalks and hand-bound the sheaves. Later, Dad and I manually cut off seed clusters for added nutrition in our dairy feed mixture. I hated that job," Saphah confessed. "But I know manual winnowing is also required when processing small planting of crops like wheat for home use after the cutting and thrashing. To winnow wheat, the grain is slowly poured out in front of a fan to separate seed from chaff."

"Also, as you suspected, there's a spiritual meaning for 'winnow.'"

"I thought so. Please, tell me about it."

"Basically, here is the story of what happened in ancient Judah which should help you understand the implications for modern America. There came a time when the Lord knew Jerusalem and Judah had reached the point of no return. Their fall from grace had happened over the course of many years. Previously, a long line of kings, both good and evil, had reigned in the land of Israel, which was later divided into the northern and the southern kingdoms. The northern kingdom retained the name Israel and the southern became Judah. Apostate Israel fell first, and then after more years passed, Judah fell from grace too."

"Was this a consequence of their rejection of God?"

"Yes, it was. At that point, the Lord said to the Prophet Jeremiah: *Even if Moses and Samuel were to stand before me, my heart would not go out to this people. Send them away from my presence! Let them go!*[1] Here, God was likewise rejecting 'this people,' and he says not even a Moses or a Samuel figure could intercede for them. For God to dismiss the mediation of spiritual leaders such as a Moses or a Samuel, was to say judgment was unavoidable."

"So, what happened next?"

"Coming judgment was announced and described in terrifying terms. The Lord said to Jeremiah: *And if they ask you, 'Where shall we go?' tell them, 'This is what the Lord says: Those destined for death, to death, those for the sword, to the sword, those for starvation, to starvation, those for captivity, to captivity.*[2] Four kinds of adversity—death, sword, starvation, and captivity were explicitly mentioned."

"But what exactly occurred to bring about the adversity?"

"God attributed the effects of King Manasseh's reign as the reason for inevitable judgment: *I will make them abhorrent to all the kingdoms of the earth because of what Manasseh son of Hezekiah king of Judah did in Jerusalem.*[3] The judgment to come on Jerusalem and Judah derived from the overflowing wickedness of the reign of Manasseh and his son Amon, and from the continuing influence of their apostasy on a subsequent generation."

"But what did Manasseh do that was so bad?" Saphah felt certain that Manasseh had greatly led the people of Judah astray.

"Manasseh was extremely evil. He became king at twelve and reigned in Jerusalem for fifty-five years. Scripture provides a long list of his malicious deeds:

> *He rebuilt the high places …erected altars to Baal and made an Asherah pole. …He bowed down to all the starry hosts and worshiped them. …He sacrificed his own son in the fire, practiced divination, sought omens, and consulted mediums and spiritists. He did much evil in the eyes of the Lord, arousing his anger. …Moreover, Manasseh also shed much innocent blood, …besides the sin that he caused Judah to commit, so that they did evil in the eyes of the Lord.*[4]

But that is only a small fraction of all the wickedness he committed. One wicked deed, according to Jewish tradition, was the murder of the Prophet Isaiah by having him sawed in half."

"Oh my, what an evil man!"

"So, the Lord said to the people:

> *You have rejected me. …You keep on backsliding. So, I will reach out and destroy you; I am tired of holding back. I*

> *will winnow them with a winnowing fork at the city gates of*
> *the land. I will bring bereavement and destruction on my*
> *people, for they have not changed their ways.*[5]

God used the terrifying word *winnow* as a description of a future judgment which would fall upon Jerusalem and Judah for their rejection of the Lord."

"That's very frightening. Something similar is in the New Testament about end time judgment on the world. The Revelation of John shows judgments that will be poured out on the land as the seals of prophetic scrolls are broken.[6] The judgments are depicted as different horsemen riding on different colored horses—white (Christ), red (persecution), black (famine), and pale (death). John's prophecies in the Book of Revelation are intended to help people of my civilization understand that God's hand will move not only in judgment on the ungodly, but also in deliverance of those who have placed their faith in Him."

"It was a similar situation in the time of the Old Testament. Prophet Jeremiah's contemporaries in Judah were to see God's hand moving in judgment on the unrepentant, but also to observe his hand moving in deliverance of a believing remnant."

Saphah thought for a moment. "To tell you the truth, the current moral situation in America is quite disturbing. It's obvious to the observant eye that many people in my country are rapidly moving toward apostasy. In fact, it seems like the entire world has gone astray. Is my world ripe for winnowing too, like Judah?"

"Well, Scripture speaks of that when it notes that all humanity, *like sheep, have gone astray: each* [individual] *has turned to his own way.*"[7]

"But, as scripture also points out, it doesn't have to remain that way. Although all sheep have initially wandered from their Shepherd, any who choose to do so can return to Jesus Christ. Jesus died for the sins of all mankind: *He himself bore our sins in his body on the cross, so that we might die to sins and live for righteousness; by his wounds you* [believers] *have been healed. For you were like sheep going astray, but now you have returned to the Shepherd and Overseer of your souls.*[8] The Lord Jesus Christ is like a shepherd who searches for his lost sheep and calls them to return to him. Because of His death on the cross and His love for mankind, those who return to the 'overseer of our souls' can receive everlasting salvation from sin."

Nahal noted that the spiritual meaning of the word *winnow* was further clarified in the Old Testament. "Here, the prophet Jeremiah spoke about God winnowing a different country, Babylon, on a separate occasion: *I will send foreigners to Babylon to winnow her and to devastate her land; they will oppose her on every side in the day of her disaster.*"[9]

"Like when farmers such as my dad used the process of winnowing the grain to separate the grain from the chaff." Saphah recalled again the agricultural method used by farmers to winnow grain.

"Exactly. The winnowing of grains in ancient times was an entirely manual process. Farmers tossed the cut grain, such as wheat or barley, high into the air so wind currents could separate the grain from the chaff. So, just as the heavy, good grain fell to the threshing floor, and the unwanted, useless chaff was blown away, God metaphorically blew away Babylon like chaff. Babylon's foreign enemies were God's winnowing fork opposing Babylon on every side until the country was destroyed."

"Oh, my! Are the countries of the world in such a late stage of apostacy that judgment will soon come down upon us?"

"The nations of the world will reach a point where they're beyond help." Nahal was being honest and frank with Saphah. "And that time may be closer than some people think. The entire world is presently under the shadow of judgment. But in the meantime, God has given a window of opportunity to the unsaved of the globe to return to Him for salvation. God's mercy and grace are free, as the last verse and chorus of an old hymn, 'At Calvary,' proclaims in song."

"I love that old hymn. Could we sing it? I know the words."

Nahal began to sing in his beautiful tenor voice, and Saphah joined in with harmony as they sang: "'Oh, the love that drew salvation's plan! Oh, the grace that brought it down to man! Oh, the mighty gulf that God did span, At Calvary! Mercy there was great, and grace was free; Pardon there was multiplied to me; There my burden found liberty, At Calvary!'"[10]

"I loved singing that with you, and I see what you mean. If people simply remembered that Christ's gifts of salvation, mercy, and grace are completely free at Calvary, God wouldn't have to winnow."

"How true!"

"Now I understand why you and Malak both told me the time is short and that I need to warn people quickly."

"Yes, that's why you need to leave here for Jerusalem soon. But first, I want to tell you about your travel gear."

"Yes, I'd really like to hear about the travel supplies for the trip to Jerusalem." Saphah stood up to stretch her legs.

"First of all, I'll give you a writing case equipped with straps." Nahal pointed toward the object. "You can wear it on your back. Inside are a scroll, pen, and ink, along with a few additional supplies. Since you'll need to make lots of notes about your observations in Jerusalem, I've also included some candles to aid your nighttime writing. Some loose silver is hidden in a secret pouch, and a map is enclosed to prevent you from getting lost. Your writing case should remain locked when you're not using it. You've already found a tiny key on a chain around your neck to lock the case. Also, here's a flask of water for your trip, which you can hang by a strap on your shoulder. Please use your little key now to open your case and get the map."

Saphah removed the chain and key to open the case. "It looks like the map is here on top." She handed Nahal a small piece of cured animal skin with a detailed map drawn on it.

"Alright, let's take a look. Here's where you are right now." Nahal pointed toward an X on the map marking where they stood. "From here, you're going to continue quite a distance, so you need to know some things you'll encounter. About midway through at the second X, you'll arrive at a spacious room with an underground lake. You'll notice some tiny, strange animals swimming in the lake or crawling on the surrounding rocks. There are cave pseudoscorpions, crabs, crayfish, beetles, and other small creatures, all acclimated to cave life. The white pseudoscorpions, for instance, have the appearance of real scorpions, but their tails produce venom less harmful to humans. Nevertheless, I suggest you keep walking by the pool and don't linger too long."

"Alright."

"In addition, there's a sinkhole in the ceiling not far from the lake. Bats fly in and out of the cave from that sinkhole on foraging missions. There are also large bat-hunting cave snakes in that area. The snakes work in tandem to snag small bats on the fly by hanging from outcroppings on cave walls. They make a kind of fence by dangling down in pairs or trios across the area where bats are grabbed in midair. Remember, they're after the bats, not you. So, just leave them alone, and they won't bother you."

"That reminds me of the black snakes that lived in the barn lofts of our area when I was a kid. The snakes killed mice, so I knew to leave any I encountered alone. It was still frightening to see them when I played with my cousins or friends in the lofts. Nahal, thanks for telling me about the cave snakes."

"You're welcome. Now, let's take another look at the map." Nahal pointed to an X. "From here you'll walk through the cave until you reach a walled-off area at the Spring of Gihon, right here." He traced the map with his finger to the spot. "You may hear the gushing sound of the spring which periodically releases spurts of water."

"Did you say the Gihon Spring is walled off at that point? If so, how do I get to the spring?"

"Just keep walking forward." Nahal was being patient with Saphah.

"What do you mean?"

"Remember? Malak said the Aperture of Process would transform your material body into a different state. Although you look the same as before, your body has changed, so you can do things you couldn't do before. You've been through the Aperture. Right?"

"Right, but I still don't understand how I'll get through the wall."

"The best answer is that your body processed into a more substantial form in the Aperture of Process, so now you can just walk through the wall to get to the spring."

"Wait a minute. It's a solid wall, not a cloud or fog I can just walk through." Saphah shook her head in wonder.

"Let me explain it another way. Back in your own world, you could walk through a fog bank because your body was more solid than the water vapor or mist. Since you've gone through the Aperture of Process, your body has changed into an even more solid form than a stone wall. Therefore, the walled-off area of the cave will now seem like tissue paper as you walk through it. Does that explanation make any sense to you, Saphah?"

"Like everything else that has happened so far, it seems very strange. But I think I do understand what you're saying."

"Good." Nahal pointed at the map again. "Here, the Spring of Gihon flows into an area of the cavern outside the city wall, south of the temple in Jerusalem. King Hezekiah, the great-grandfather of King Josiah, knew the water supply here was vulnerable to attack by adversaries. Because it exists outside the walls of the city, he sought to secure it from enemy forces. Hezekiah built a tunnel 1,750 feet in length and cut through solid rock from the Gihon Spring to the Pool of Siloam, located inside Jerusalem."

"Will I be able to walk through the length of the tunnel?"

"Yes, you should be able to walk most of the tunnel without any issue. At times, where the ceiling is low, you'll need to walk hunched over or maybe even crawl, and that'll slow you down some. The tunnel height is very irregular and varies from about four to twelve feet high and averages two feet wide. The water depth in the tunnel is never higher that twenty-seven inches, and in most places, it's only between ankle and knee deep. You'll need to follow the marked route to enter into the city of Jerusalem at the pool of Siloam."

"How long will it take me to get there?"

"You should be able to make it to Jerusalem in a few hours after you leave here. The rest of the map pertains to the city of Jerusalem and the surrounding area, so you'll need to study it more when you get there."

"Alright, I will."

"Saphah, just think, the first place you're going to visit is Jerusalem during the reign of King Josiah. Manasseh was Josiah's grandfather and Amon his father. Amon came to the throne when he was twenty-two, and he was king for two years. *He did evil in the eyes of the Lord, as his father Manasseh had done.*[11] But Josiah's reign began when he was eight years old, and he was destined to rule for thirty-one years. Unlike his father and grandfather, *He did what was right in the eyes of the Lord.*[12] My friend, right now as you're entering Judah, Josiah is almost twenty-one-years-old and the lingering effects of the evil reigns of Manasseh and Amon are still evident."

"Does the bible say anything special about Josiah coming to the throne?"

"Definitely, scripture says that God sent a prophet from Judah to Bethel in the northern kingdom of Israel to prophecy about King Josiah before he was born, and this is what the Lord told him to say: *A son named Josiah will be born to the house of David.*[13] The same prophet also foretold the future king's role as a reformer who would rid the land *of the priests of the high places who make offerings.*[14] And this would happen as far north as Bethel."

"So, King Josiah was born to be a reformer, and he reigns in Judah now as I'm about to enter Judah?"

"Yes, he does."

"Will I meet King Josiah?" Saphah shook her head in amazement.

"Yes. Later in his rule, King Josiah brought about reforms resulting in revival which lasted his entire reign. You'll be able to see the reforms. he made to bring about change in his land."

"Oh, that's wonderful. Maybe reforms can also be applied to some situations in my present-day world. Nahal, do you think God, in His mercy, might hold off on bringing calamity on my world, at least for a time, like he did during the reign of Josiah?"

"Saphah, God's forbearance is actually up to the citizens of the world. In Deuteronomy the Lord spoke to ancient Israel, and he is still speaking to the people of your modern world, about his offer of life and death:

> *See, I set before you today life and prosperity, death and destruction. For I command you today to love the Lord your God, to walk in obedience to him, and to keep his commands, decrees and laws; then you will live and increase, and the Lord your God will bless you in the land …But if your heart turns away and you are not obedient, …I declare to you this day that you will certainly be destroyed.*[15]

God offers life and death to men and women today just as he did to the ancient Israelites, but it's up to each individual to accept His offer of salvation." Nahal went on to explain: "It's really not a difficult choice, for God said:

> *Now what I am commanding you today is not too difficult for you or beyond your reach. It is not up in heaven, so that you have to ask, 'Who will ascend into heaven to get it and proclaim it to us so we may obey it?' Nor is it beyond the sea, so that you have to ask, 'Who will cross the sea and proclaim it to us so we may obey it?' No, the word is very near to you; it is in your mouth and in your heart so you may obey it.*[16]

All that human beings are required to do is to obey God by sincerely turning to Him by faith for salvation. Then all they need to do is follow up by obeying his moral precepts as set forth in His Holy Word: *If you fully obey the Lord your God and carefully follow all his commands, …All these blessings will come upon you and accompany you if you obey the Lord your God."*[17]

"True." Saphah nodded her head in agreement. "It isn't difficult to accept God's free offer of pardon for sin. It seems to me that through his Word God has gone above and beyond to present his plan for salvation to the world. Yet people still refuse to believe."

"Sadly, they do. But the Word of God says that in the last days scoffers will come who will ask:

> *Where is this 'coming' he promised? Ever since our ancestors died, every thing goes on as it has since the beginning of creation. …But do not forget this one thing, dear friends: With the Lord a day is like a thousand years, and a thousand years are like a day. The Lord is not slow in keeping his promise, as some understand slowness. Instead, he is patient with you, not wanting anyone to perish, but everyone to come to repentance.*[18]

That last sentence reveals the fact the Lord is a long-suffering God."

"And that's because he desires everyone to be saved and none to perish!"

"Yes, the Lord would like for all to come to him before it's too late, and He is using this time to draw humanity to Himself. We don't know the day or the hour, but we do know the day of God's final judgment is going to happen, because the Word says *that day will bring about the destruction of the heavens by fire, and the elements will melt in the heat. But in keeping with his promise we are looking forward to a new heaven and a new earth, where righteousness dwells.*"[19]

"And since the Lord is waiting for all who'll come to repentance, the sooner believers share the Word and invite others to the Savior, the sooner that day will dawn. Isaiah prophesied about it in the Old Testament: *See, I will create new heavens and a new earth. The former things will not be remembered, nor will they come to mind.*[20] And, John confirmed it in the New Testament:

Then I saw a new heaven and a new earth, for the first heaven and the first earth had passed away, …And I heard a loud voice from the throne saying, 'Look! God's dwelling place is now among the people, and he will dwell with them. They will be his people, and God himself will be with them and be their God. He will wipe every tear from their eyes. There will be no more death or mourning or crying or pain, for the old order of things has passed away.'"[21]

"Isn't that wonderful! Glory to God in the Highest." Angel Nahal raised his hands in praise to God. "The 'former things' and the 'old order of things,' referring to the suffering, pain, and sorrow of the present age in your world, will no longer exist in the new heavens and new earth. So, get your things ready now, because you need to reach Jerusalem while it's still light."

"Okay. This is so exciting!" Saphah picked up her bag and checked to ensure it was secure before placing in on her shoulders. Adjusting her water flask she asked, "May I say a short prayer before I leave?" Saphah retrieved the Bible from her writing case again.

"Of course, go ahead with your prayer." Nahal nodded his head in agreement.

"I'm going to adapt some scripture to myself and my world in this prayer." Saphah kneeled, placed her hands together, and voiced her prayer:

Heavenly Father, I lift up my eyes to the mountains—where does my help come from? My help comes from the Lord, the Maker of heaven He will not let [my] foot slip—he who watches over [me] will not slumber; indeed, he who watches over [civilization] will not sleep. … The Lord will watch over [our] coming and going both now and forever more.[22] *You guide [us] with your counsel, and afterward you will take [us] into glory. [Our] flesh and [our] hearts may fail, but God is the strength of [our] hearts and [our] portion forever.*[23]

Thank you, Lord, for being the sustainer of those who place their faith and trust in you. In Jesus' precious name I pray. Amen."

Nahal handed Saphah a newly lit candle with holder. "Goodbye Saphah. I look forward to seeing you again as you travel back this way. If you have any questions at that time, I'll try my best to answer them."

"Goodbye, my friend," Saphah waved as she left him. She carried her candleholder before her with one hand and protected the flickering flame of the candle with the palm of her other as she traveled alone farther and farther into the dark cave.

7

THE WALL

Although Saphah continued to walk on into the depths of the cave after leaving Nahal, she still felt terrified about walking all alone into the dark bowels of the earth. Nahal had sparked her fears when he'd told her earlier of a spacious cavern room with strange creatures. But when she finally reached the spot, she wondered why she'd been so afraid.

The underground lake was so clear, so serene. As she gazed into the soothing waters, her spirit calmed. It was so tranquil there she sat down on a rock beside the lake to rest and enjoy the unusual critters flitting about in the water. Deciding to relieve her aching feet by soaking them, Saphah pulled up her skirt tail to her knees. Stretching her arms over her head, she laid her body down on the rock as her feet dangled in the water.

Saphah awakened from sleep shortly later and absentmindedly reached down to scratch her legs. "What's that?" Dozens of tiny, white pseudoscorpions were crawling up both legs. Yanking her feet from the water, she jumped to her feet with a scream. "Lord Jesus, please help me!" In near panic, she brushed off the strange creatures briskly with her hands. Then she inspected her itching legs. *Oh, thank goodness. These itching places aren't overly red or swollen.* Quickly moving away from the edge of the lakeshore, she lowered her skirt and put on her sandals.

Entering a new area of the cave, she traveled quickly for several minutes before noticing there was a branch in the cave off to her left. *That must be where bats fly in and out at dawn and dusk. Nahal said snakes hang down from ledges near the ceiling to grab them, but I don't see any snakes.* "Whew!" She sighed in relief. "It must not be dawn or dusk yet."

Passing the fork in the cave, Saphah strolled on. Now here she stood, realizing God's protection anew. She'd encountered the scorpions and escapted unscathed. The frightful snakes she'd imagined hanging from the ceiling of the cave weren't even there.

Saphah suddenly felt ashamed when she remembered the story from the New Testament of the seventy disciples Jesus sent out. They had reported back to the Lord that even the demons submitted to them in his name. Then Jesus said, *I saw Satan fall like lightning from heaven. I have given you authority to trample on snakes and scorpions and to overcome all the power of the enemy; nothing will harm you.*[1]

Oh my, Saphah thought, *when Jesus sends his followers into danger, He promised that no ultimate harm will befall them. Even death cannot harm them, for they will live again. He is sovereign over any danger. The Lord Jesus is with me*, so *I have nothing to fear or dread when I call on His name.*

Now unafraid, Saphah continued her journey. From that point on, the pathway meandered in a winding direction. *Oh, this cave is so dreary! It must go on forever!* Once her candle burned low and flickered, so she replaced it with another candle from her writing case.

To help pass the time Saphah began to sing "God Will Take Care of You," a favorite old hymn:

> Be not dismayed whatever betide, God will take care of you;
> Beneath His wings of love abide, God will take care of
> you—God will take care of you, through every day, Over
> all the way; He will take care of you, God will take care of
> you—No matter what may be the test, God will take care
> of you; Lean, weary one, upon His Breast, God will take
> care of you—God will take care of you, through every day,
> Over all the way; He will take care of you, God will take
> care of you.[2]

After walking and singing her way through the rest of the cave, she reached the spot Nahal told her about. She stood directly in front of the wall built to block access to the Hezekiah tunnel. She looked left, right, above, and below, but nowhere was there any way forward. The cave wall in front of her declared in strong terms—no entry.

Saphah stood stupefied in front of the solid wall for several minutes contemplating what she should do next. "There's no way around it. No way through it, under or over it. What should I do? Lord, please help me!"

A quiet, but firm voice replied, "Go forward."

Saphah's eyebrows raised in surprise. *Oh my goodness,* she thought, *the Lord really wants me to walk through this wall.* "Yes, Lord," she answered with a smile on her face as she finally took action. Placing her candle holder on the cave floor, she took her skirt tails and tucked them into her sash in front. Closing her eyes and taking a deep breath, she picked up the candle holder and decisively stepped forward through the wall as if it didn't exist. Clearing the solidly constructed wall, she stared down in wonder at her candle. *Wow! The candle flame didn't even go out as I passed through the wall, and it was like walking through tissue paper!* She smiled again at the thought.

When Saphah heard a remote but distinct gushing sound, she took off her sandals and held her candle in the direction of the sound. As she did, she saw a cascading flow of water rushing into the channel where she stood. It engulfed her feet and legs in frigid water up to her knees. *This must be from the Spring of Gihon, for it is clear and cold, like the flow from a spring. Now, if I just keep wading the tunnel according to Nahal's map, I should reach the Pool of Siloam shortly. I must be in the right place.*

As Saphah waded on, she reflected on a passage in Exodus about the escape of the Israelites from Egyptian bondage. Moses, their leader, told the people that God would provide for their escape. When the time came for them to cross the Red Sea through the parted waters, Moses kept crying out to God for help. The Lord finally said to Moses: *Why are you crying out to me? Tell the Israelites to move on.*[3]

I've been crying out for help just like Moses, Saphah thought, *even though Nahal told me I could get through the wall to the Hezekiah Tunnel by 'walking forward until you get there.' The Lord showed His power to Moses by parting the Red Sea so the Israelites could 'move on.' Likewise, He reminded me of His supernatural ability by processing my body so I could 'go forward.'*

Saphah looked up to heaven. "Heavenly Father," she fervently prayed aloud. "Thank you for reminding me that the ability to walk through the wall depended on your power and not on anything I could do on my own. And, in the future, Lord, when I come to a wall, physical or spiritual, please help me to remember I don't have to stress about it. I just need to trust in you and 'go forward.' Whatever you've called me to do, and whatever I face because of it, I can accomplish it because I'm not doing it on my own, but by the power of the One who can do all things. Thanks too, for changing my attitude from disbelief and fear to faith and trust in the divine intervention you've performed on my behalf. In Jesus' name I pray. Amen."

Well, according to the map, Saphah thought. *I'm now in the Hezekiah Tunnel on the east side of Jerusalem outside the wall. This should be inside a slope which leads down into the Kidron Valley. I probably have no more than around 1,700 feet left to walk in the tunnel until I reach the Pool of Siloam, so I should be able to arrive at my destination soon.*

Setting off again at a fast clip, Saphah quickly covered territory. Unaware of the changing height of the ceiling, she often struck her head on the rock surface above until knots and bruises appeared on her forehead. Then she reached a spot where she had to crawl on her hands and knees, which slowed her progress. Her skirt tails escaped from her sash and became dirty from the wet silt under her knees.

Saphah stopped when she heard a faint sound from ahead. Placing one hand on the cave wall and standing stock still, she listened. *Do I hear people talking?* She strained her ears to hear. *Yes, that is human voices I'm hearing nearby.*

With her fingers lightly touching the surface of the cave wall, Saphah felt a strange texture. Holding up her candle with one hand so she could see, she rubbed her fingers carefully over the spot. *Is that an inscription on the wall?* Slightly moving the angle of her candle, she reexamined what seemed to be words cut into the rock on one side of the tunnel. *I must be looking at a Hebrew inscription.* Suddenly, she gasped out loud. "Oh my, I can read these words!" The writing was interspersed with dots but lacked inscription at others. She read the Hebrew words to herself by translating them into English in her mind:

> …the tunnel …and this is the story of the tunnel while …the axes were against each other and while three cubits were left to [no inscription] …the voice of a man …called to his counterpart [no inscription], there was [unknown word] in the rock on the right …and on the day of the tunnel [no inscription], the stonecutters struck each man towards his counterpart, ax against ax and flowed water from the source to the pool for 1,200 cubits. And [no inscription] cubits was the height over the heads of the stonecutters …[4]

Saphah thought about what she'd read: *Perhaps the inscription records the construction techniques for the tunnel. It seems that work on the tunnel began at each end simultaneously and advanced until the workers met in the middle. But I'm amazed I could even read the inscription!* The watchwoman suddenly realized that God had given her knowledge of a foreign language. *It's simply incredible what God can do!* Saphah perked up her ears again. She heard a youthful male voice speaking in Hebrew.

"Has anyone here seen a pilgrim to Jerusalem?"

After a pause, she heard a different person, who sounded like an older man, reply, "No, I haven't seen a traveler, and I've been here for a bit with my servants filling our water jugs for the evening."

Saphah wondered, *Is the young guy asking about me? But how could he even know I'm here?*

8

THE CITY OF GOD

Walking faster, Saphah rounded a bend in the tunnel and then glimpsed some people immediately ahead standing on the far side of the Pool of Siloam. In just a few strides she came to the pool and walked directly from the tunnel into its deeper waters. She noticed that natural walls extended above the pool on two sides. "Hello, here I am," she spoke up in her new language. "I'm a pilgrim to Jerusalem."

A tall lad, with curly brown hair and light blue eyes, abruptly stopped climbing the stone steps from the Pool of Siloam. He turned around and stared curiously at Saphah. Taking a water jug from atop his head, he set the large container down on the steps and ran back down to the pool. "You, over there in the water, if you're a pilgrim, why're you standing in the Pool of Siloam?" He shouted the words.

His loud question took Saphah by surprise and made her think he was angry. *Why Is the young man disturbed about my presence in the water?* she wondered. *Does he think I'm a foreign spy sneaking around in the Hezekiah Tunnel and the Pool of Siloam?*

"Why are you inquiring, young man?" Saphah was disturbed at his query. "And, how did you know I'd be here?"

"My master's wife instructed me to fetch a pilgrim at the Pool of Siloam, so I just followed her instructions." The teen boy's tone mellowed. "Please forgive me, I didn't mean to be rude. You just startled me, that's all."

"It's alright. I'm a little confused too." Saphah crossed the pool to the stone steps that led out of the water and to the City of Jerusalem.

"Here, please grab my hand." The young man offered assistance, leaning over and extending one hand toward Saphah.

"Thank you so much." Saphah grasped his hand and slowly ascended from the water. She realized that ancient peoples were often formal in greetings, so she asked, "Who do I have the pleasure of meeting?"

"My name is Ebed, and I'm a mesharet to Shallum. He is the husband of the Prophetess Huldah and the Keeper of the Wardrobe for King Josiah.[1] My sister Rebecca is a mesharetet to Huldah, who supervises and teaches at the Jerusalem School. My sister and I are two of her students."

"How nice that you and your sister can both work and attend school." Saphah stepped out of the water and loosened her skirt tails from her sash. "That arrangement must keep the two of you very busy."

"Yes, it does." Ebed skillfully balanced the heavy water jar atop his head again, and the pair began walking up the steps toward the landing to the Fountain Gate Square. "My sister and I are Rechabites. We're descendants of an Israelite sect named for Rechab, the father of Jehonadab, an ally of King Jehu of Israel. King Jehu was used by God over 200 years ago to rid the land of worshippers of Baal, a Canaanite fertility deity."[2]

"Please tell me more."

"Our ancestors, the Kenites, accompanied the Israelites when they first entered the Holy Land and lived among them.[3] The main branch of the Kenites adopted settled ways of life and dwelt in cities. Our branch became nomadic because we were forbidden by a forefather named Jehonadab to live in cities or to engage in farming since it is associated with the Canaanites. We are followers of Yahweh, the God of Israel, and our people are noted for their faithfulness to Him.

Therefore, we remain separate from activities that might detract from our fervent faith, such as drinking wine, as Jehonadab commanded us to do."[4]

"What happened to cause you and your sister to become servants to Shallum and Huldah?"

"Well, our Rechabite clan needed a literate person to replace our scribe, who is elderly and ready to retire. So, my parents arranged with Shallum and Huldah for me to be a servant to Shallum in exchange for my education at the Jerusalem School. Huldah suggested to my parents that my sister Rebecca, whom I call Becca, become her servant so she could be educated to become a teacher for the Rechabite children of our clan."

"Shallum and Huldah must be very special people. I'm truly looking forward to meeting both of them. Can you tell me a little about them before we meet?"

"You're right. They're wonderful people. My master holds a position of prominence in the royal court as Keeper of the Wardrobe, so he's in charge of King Josiah's clothes and robes for all occasions. I accompany him each evening to assist in tasks regarding Josiah's wardrobe, like doing measurements for creation of new clothes or doing alterations to older clothing he has almost outgrown. I've often had the opportunity to listen to conversations of Shallum and King Josiah and even joined in at times in talking to Josiah, whom I call Jo in private by his permission. He calls me Eb, which is alright with me. Anyway, King Josiah has become a follower of Yahweh and has been talking about his intent to begin religious reforms in our land."

"Really," Saphah said with a knowing grin. "It's wonderful you've had the opportunity to befriend King Josiah and to speak to him about spiritual matters. Does he know that your people, the Rechabites, are noted for their fidelity to God and adherence to His laws?"

"Yes, I've told him. He also knows that his great-grandfather Hezekiah was a godly man. But he knows too that his grandfather Manasseh and his father Amon were both extremely evil."

"Please tell me about Huldah. I would really like to know more about her."

"Huldah is a prophetess and the leader of our school, where she teaches. She is highly respected in Judah and admired by all the good people of our land. After supervising and teaching at the school all day, she sits near a city gate in the vicinity of the temple as a ministering prophetess to women and girls. At dusk, she returns to her quarters, which are part of the school complex. That's also where my sister Rebecca lives."

"She really sounds like an outstanding person."

"She is. But just remember Huldah can often be plain-spoken and blunt when she talks. But don't worry. She has a heart of gold and a spirit of love even though she puts on a firm face."

"I'll keep that fact in mind. Ebed, look, we've finally reached the top step, and I'm sure glad. My legs feel like rubber, and my feet ache. I've been walking all day to get to Jerusalem and I've climbed all these steps. Could we rest a minute?"

"Sure, we've reached the landing to the Fountain Gate Square and the King's Garden is South of here." Ebed turned and pointed toward the two main features of the area. "Soon you'll meet Shallum for yourself as he greets pilgrims to Jerusalem, and you can rest some more when we get there."

The first thing Saphah noticed when she stepped on the landing was the city's beauty. The sun was low on the horizon, and the hues of the sunset bathed everything she saw in awe-inspiring beauty. "God's sacred presence in Jerusalem is palpable," she whispered in wonder. She lifted her head as a fragrant breeze brushed her cheeks and gently blew her hair from her face. A wind chime in the distance tinkled a succession of pleasing musical tones. "It's sublime in this place."

"So, you've noticed it too?"

"Yes, as God's Word proclaims: *The heavens declare the glory of God; the skies proclaim the work of his hands. Day after day they pour forth speech; night after night they reveal knowledge.*[5] It's true that the heavens above reveal that God is real."

"That's a psalm of King David! King Josiah has access to David and Solomon's scrolls through the High Priest Hilkiah, so I've read from them, and I recognize that verse. But how do you know about King David's writings?"

"I'm also a follower of the Lord God. So, in my country, we too have access to the Psalms of David and the Proverbs of Solomon."

"Really. Where are you from? Please tell me more about your nation."

"I'm from a land far away. No one here knows much about it, except for some of your prophets in a veiled sort of way. My country is called America, and it's very much like your country, Judah. Many people in my land have slipped into alienation from God. He has become distant to some people in their thinking, their hearts, and their behavior as never before. For older believers like myself, it's a time of great sadness because our world has fallen so far away from God and changed so quickly. Many of us don't even recognize it anymore."

"Do you think that has something to do with why you're here?"

"I do. I think the Lord sent me here to learn about the reforms of your good King Josiah. He'll be God's instrument of revival and reform for the people in your land. After all, God named him before he was born and destined him to inherit the throne so he could carry out God's plans to give your people more time to repent."[6]

"Well, I'm glad you're here."

"Thank you, Ebed." The two continued to quietly soak up the beauty of a sunset in the City of God.

9

SHALLUM & HULDAH

Ebed and Saphah were mesmerized by the beauty of the sunset in the city of God. The stately palms, the buildings, and all features of the Fountain Gate Square glowed in the light as the two stood transfixed admiring the ambiance of the place.

As the sun sank lower in the sky, Saphah frowned as she noticed a look of alarm on Ebed's face. "What's wrong, Ebed?"

"If I'm going to introduce you to Shallum, we must hurry now. We need to get there before Shallum closes for the day outside the gate. C'mon, Saphah, we can make it." The two walked hastily toward the Fountain Gate entrance to Jerusalem. "There he is." Ebed waved toward a 30-ish aged man gathering up his things outside the gate and shouted, "Shallum, I've found the pilgrim to Jerusalem you wanted to greet. Huldah sent me to get her at the Pool of Siloam."

"That's good," Shallum answered with a smile. "I'd almost given up on you. Who do we have here?"

"Shallum, I want to introduce you to a pilgrim from a faraway land. God sent her to observe the events in Judah for the benefit of her own people." He chanted his words as he pointed with both hands toward her: "Shallum, I present to you Saphah—Watchwoman from America." Then Ebed intoned as he motioned with both hands toward the man: "Saphah, may I introduce you to Shallum—Keeper of the Wardrobe."

Saphah was shocked. "Wow, Ebed, how did you know that I'm a watchwoman?" Her eyes widened as she raised her eyebrows and looked toward him.

"I think Huldah plans to explain that to you later," Ebed answered.

"Watchwoman Saphah from America," Shallum spoke grandly, "I'm so pleased to meet you, a pilgrim to our land. Welcome to Jerusalem, the capital of Judah. How was your journey here?"

Saphah kept in mind that ancient greetings in foreign lands were often formal. So, thinking fast, she likewise addressed the man by his title and spoke in grand terms, "Shallum, Keeper of the Wardrobe, I'm very pleased to finally meet you. My travels went well, and I'm looking forward to my stay here in Jerusalem."

"Well, in my other official role as Greeter at the Jerusalem Wall," Shallum replied in lofty tones, "it would be my pleasure to offer you a refreshing drink of water now. Please take a seat." He motioned toward a bench attached to the outside of the Jerusalem wall. "And, please accept this small jar of water to quench your thirst after your long journey."

"Thank you for your hospitality." Saphah forgot to use flowery speech. She threw herself down on the bench in exhaustion, took the water, and heartily drank from the jar. She hadn't realized how exhausted and thirsty she was. "Shallum, may I ask you a question?"

"Please ask any questions you wish." Shallum smiled graciously. "I'm here to assist you in whatever way I can. No need to be formal now."

Thank goodness! Saphah smiled in relief. "Why are there so many benches attached to the wall here?"

"The gate areas in Judean cities are hubs of activity. Visitors, such as yourself, merchants, messengers, judges and others visit gate areas and conduct business here. So that's why benches line this entire area where people meet for their various purposes. At this late hour, the area is deserted, except for us, so there isn't anyone else sitting here."

"I have another question? How did you and Ebed know I could be found at the Pool of Siloam?"

"I'm sorry I can't directly answer that question. You'll have to ask my wife Huldah when you meet her. She's the one who said you could be found at the Siloam Pool. She also said to extend you an invitation to be our houseguest and to sit at our table while you're here."

"Oh, thank you. I would be honored to accept your invitation, but I've no method to pay you." Saphah paused as a thought came to her. "… except to offer my services to your family as a servant in some capacity."

"We'll be home soon, so you can ask Huldah about arrangements while we all enjoy supper together. Ebed and I join Huldah and Rebecca at home for our evening meal. Then Ebed and I return to the palace to complete my duties as Keeper of the Wardrobe and Ebed assists me."

"So, if I may ask, Ebed, what are your responsibilities each night at the Palace?" Saphah asked as the three strolled on.

"First of all, my role as Shallum's assistant is to set out King Josiah's clothing on a special stand for the next day's wardrobe changes. After that, each evening, we create new clothes or make alterations. Then, when our work is done for the day we enjoy a little free time, often shared with King Josiah. Sometimes we just talk or tell riddles. Other times we play games or read from the scrolls of King David or King Solomon. The king usually has snacks brought in. After that, we go to bed in our separate quarters. As for me, after I get to my room, I say my evening prayers and then collapse into bed and fall fast asleep."

"Yes, it's a good arrangement for all of us," Shallum added. "Of course, on the Sabbath, we're off work, so we attend worship and spend family time together on that day. Huldah and Rebecca are also off the day before Sabbath, so they make all the preparations. Scripture says that God worked six days and then he rested,[1] and that's what he wants us to do as well."

"We're almost home, and I can already smell something delicious cooking." Ebed inhaled a big whiff of air through his nostrils, stopped in his tracks, sniffed again, and exclaimed with a whoop, "Alright! It is quail cooked with wild mushrooms! Father and mother must have visited today."

"How wonderful. Do your parents get to visit often?"

"They buy supplies in Jerusalem every few weeks, and when they can, they stop by after they shop. Whenever they visit, they try to do so by late afternoon, so Becca and I can both see them after school. They usually bring us some provisions from the camp. And I can tell from that wonderful aroma that today it's quail they've raised and wild mushrooms they've gathered."

"Oh, Ebed, I caused you to miss seeing your parents. I'm sorry." Saphah was concerned about the fact.

"Don't be sorry. We're planning to visit my parents on my sixteenth birthday, and that's only a week away. Anyway, I'm just glad you're joining us for supper so you'll get to taste some of the wonderful quail my sister has prepared. Don't tell her I told you, or she'll get the big-head, but I have to admit she's a pretty good cook."

"I'm really looking forward to the quail dish, too. I grew up on a farm, and my father hunted wild quail on our land each year during hunting season. I haven't had quail since I was a child, so this is going to be a special treat for me too." Saphah glanced around the area. "Is this the New Quarter? The houses are larger and look newer."

"Yes, you're right. This is the New Quarter or what some refer to as the Second Quarter. As you noticed, the New Quarter houses are roomier than some you saw near the Fountain Gate Square. They're large enough to house a family plus a few animals in some cases. Living accommodations for our home, which is built of dressed stone, are situated on three sides surrounding the courtyard area. Some Jerusalem houses in poorer areas do not have courts." Shallum pointed across the street. "And here we are!"

"Oh, yeah, we're home! Now let's go inside. Ladies first." Ebed motioned toward the opening to the courtyard. "Welcome to our home, which is part of the Jerusalem School complex."

As Saphah stepped through the door into the courtyard, she was surprised to see several young palms waving in the breeze and various groupings of small bushes and plants. Admiring the greenery, she moved her head in unison with the gently waving palms that lined the courtyard. Then she walked across the smooth, flat rocks fitted close together paving the courtyard floor. "You grow legumes and greens, too?" She inspected some plants in larger containers.

"Yes, the courtyard also serves as our garden." Shallum proudly pointed toward several clay planters holding young herbs, onions, and garlic. The lower floors inside our residence are constructed of fl at rocks, but many of the more common homes in Jerusalem have dirt floors."

"Don't they get dusty or muddy?" Saphah questioned.

"The dirt floors are swept clean, but rugs or mats for a covering keep the dust down." Shallum guided Saphah toward a sitting area in the courtyard where she noted the long slabs of stone sitting on small rectangular rocks at each end and forming benches in between the plantings.

"We like to sit out here on these stone benches to relax." Ebed plopped down on one of the sturdy benches. "Becca wove this beautiful fabric canopy to shade the area where we can sit on summer days. Sometimes, she grinds flour out here in the shade, and she also loves the stone cooking area with storage for cooking utensils and a large oven for baking. It's nice for her to be able to cook in our out-door area during the hot summers."

Shallum pointed toward a different area. "Over in that corner sits a deep basin of clean rainwater used for ritual cleansing and for washing hair."

"The court entrance to your home is both beautiful and practical. I just love it."

"Well, it ought to be beautiful." Ebed gave a huge sigh. "You wouldn't believe how many trips to the Pool of Siloam or the cisterns I make each day to fetch water for all this greenery."

Shallum crooked his arms, placed a fist on each side of his hips, tilted his head, and stared at Ebed with a frown.

Seeing Shallum's reprimanding look, Ebed blushed and quickly added, "Of course, I'm very thankful God placed my sister and me with Shallum and Huldah. They've provided us such a wonderful home."

A slightly gruff voice spoke up. "You should be, young man!" The matron of the Jerusalem School, who looked to be mid-thirty, entered the courtyard from the doorway of the washroom. "Where have you been all this time?" The woman with flaming red hair glared at him. "Your sister has been cooking for you ever since she came home from school."

"Oh, Huldah." Ebed looked perplexed. "What can I say? You know I've been searching for the pilgrim to Jerusalem as you instructed me." He shrugged his shoulders.

"Oh, sure." The tired-looking woman answered as she turned toward Saphah. "And who is this fine lady?"

Undisturbed by his wife's grumpiness, Shallum immediately stepped forward toward Saphah to begin casual introductions. "Saphah, this is my wife Huldah. Huldah, this is our new houseguest, Saphah."

"Saphah, I was expecting you." Huldah's demeanor changed as she turned toward their guest. "I'm very pleased to meet a watchwoman from another nation. You're the first female I've ever met who's a watchperson for her country. But, as I've learned from personal experience, God doesn't play favorites."

"No, he doesn't. I'm happy to meet you too, Huldah. I never thought I'd have the pleasure of meeting a woman who is both a prophetess and an educator. But I'm curious. How did you know I would be at the Pool of Siloam and that I'm a watchwoman?"

Shallum interrupted the conversation. "My wife can explain that to you at supper time. Right now, we still need to introduce you to Rebecca and finish the tour of our home."

"Okay, I'm really looking forward to meeting Rebecca."

"Saphah, right this way." Shallum led the way toward the first doorway to the left. "The door we're entering is the living area. As you can see the room has two areas. Our meal preparation center on the left includes a place for a fire on a stone base, along with a small oven. The lounging and dining area on your right includes a fireplace, a built-in bench, and a low dining table on an area mat, along with cushions for relaxing and eating."

"Hello, Becca." Ebed suddenly spoke up as a slender young girl with sun-bleached hair and brown eyes entered from another room.

"How's my little sister?" He playfully pulled on a loose strand of her hair.

"Ouch!" Rebecca gave him a pained look with a hint of a grin. "Quit it!" She tugged at a hunk of his curly hair. "I was great, Ebed, until you got here," the pretty young lady said with a laugh. "Father and Mother were here when I got home from school. They both looked well, and I was so happy to see them. Mother is expecting again! So, if all goes alright, in a few months, we'll have a new little brother or sister."

"Oh, wow! We're getting a new little kid to spoil. That's wonderful! Did you tell them I was on an errand for Shallum and Huldah?"

"Yes, they were sorry they missed you, but they're expecting us on your birthday next week. They brought an assortment of goodies for us." A playful grin played across Rebecca's lips. "I'll bet you can't guess what we're having for supper."

"Let me guess," Ebed closed his eyes in mock contemplation. Opening them wide again in feigned surprise, he pretended to guess. "Oh, I think it's quail and wild mushrooms, one of my favorites."

As if surprised, Rebecca asked, "How in the world did you know?"

"Alright, you two, quit picking on each other. That's enough," Huldah scolded. "We have a new houseguest who'll be staying with us an unforeseeable time. Shallum would like to introduce Rebecca to her."

"Oh, I've been hoping to have someone else around besides Ebed." Rebecca stuck out her tongue at her brother as she gave Saphah a wink.

Without a word, Shallum raised his hand toward Rebecca and gave her a stern gaze. "Enough." Then he turned back toward their guest again. "Saphah, I'm glad to introduce you to Rebecca, the youngest member of our family. And Rebecca, I'm greatly pleased to introduce you to Saphah, who'll be a guest in our home."

"I'm so happy to meet you, Rebecca." Saphah smiled at the young girl. "I've heard a lot about you."

"I'm sure glad to meet you too." Ebed's fourteen-year-old sister shook Saphah's hand. "Huldah said you were coming, but I didn't know what to expect when she said you're from a land I've never heard of before."

"We'll talk about it at supper, Rebecca. Go ahead and set out the food now, because we'll soon be back after we show Saphah the rooms." Huldah led the way toward her room.

"Saphah, the next room we're going to visit is my private quarters and office. Since the house is built in a u-shape, we can just walk from one room to the next by going through the doors in each room. Since our house is one of the residences for school personnel, it contains features which are uncommon in most regular housing in Jerusalem. For example, the bedrooms in houses in the school complex have beds which provide comfortable accommodations for the staff. As they all walked into the room, Huldah held out her hand toward her bed. "I'm so thankful for my built-in bed with a cushioned mat and I'll tell you why. I supervise boys such as Ebed at the Jerusalem School, a place of strict study during the day."

"Do girls attend the school too?"

"Yes, two girls also attend the school, Rebecca and her friend Tamara. They're from the Rechabite clan, a group which allows both males and females to attend. As the matriarch of the Jerusalem School, I'm authorized to allow the girls to receive tutelage in my office there. Although Rebecca lives with us, Tamara lives with another family while attending school. Additionally, after each school day is over, I minister to females of all ages near a city gate, so I'm very exhausted each night and a little cross sometimes too, I admit."

"So, you're responsible for the spiritual education of both male and some female students?"

"Yes, the Torah is the law on which our faith is founded, the first five books of scripture which include Genesis, Exodus, Leviticus, Numbers, and Deuteronomy. Some of the Torah, especially from Deuteronomy and Leviticus, was lost during the reign of King Manassah. But I have the capability to teach the Law to students because I memorized parts of the Torah during my own education."

"Huldah, how do you do all that?" Saphah admired Huldah's diligent efforts to educate youngsters and minister to women in Jerusalem.

"Well, God has blessed me tremendously, but I do have my limits." Huldah solemnly shook her head. "That's one reason I'm glad you're here."

Saphah raised her eyebrows as she gave Huldah a curious look. "What do you mean?"

"Well, I hear that you've arrived here to learn about reform efforts in Judah," Hulda explained her understanding of the situation. "But while you're here perhaps you can help me out at the same time?"

"I'd be happy to help. But what could a pilgrim like me do to assist you?"

"Oh, you could be of great assistance to me. Since you speak Hebrew, you could fill in for me occasionally as a teacher when I'm away or sick. And you could also assist with my ministry to women and girls at the gate."

Saphah was speechless. *Huldah wants me to be a teacher in her place when she's absent? I don't even know for sure if I can write Hebrew. What should I say? Lord, please help me to know what to do.* Then in her spirit she heard a quiet voice.

"Remember Philippians 4:13?"

Yes Lord, I remember. Saphah contemplated what God had said: *I can do all this through Him who gives me strength.*[2] She said a silent inward prayer: *Lord, thank you for reminding me that I can do all things through Christ.* "Huldah, I will fill in for you whenever needed at the school and at a city gate to the best of my God-given ability."

"Thank you, Saphah. That'll be wonderful. Now, here at the end of my bed is a storage box for my clothing and underneath is a long drawer for shoe storage. You'll have the same in your room."

Saphah noted two lamps, one on a bedside table and one on the desk. There was a stool by the desk, and school supplies and scrolls were stored on side shelves underneath the desk. She hoped there would be a desk in her room, too.

"As you can see," Huldah pointed toward the mostly blank surface of a plastered wall in her room, "I've begun a mural. But I've been far too busy to get it completed."

"The next bedroom is Rebecca's, which is mostly like mine in furnishings, except that instead of a desk, she has a small loom on a table on one side of the room. Her sewing area has a table to hold supplies and a lamp to give light. Although she has a good start on her mural, it is uncompleted like mine. The small windows here and throughout our home have shutters that open from inside."

"Saphah, you've seen our two bedrooms in the u-area at the far end of the house. Now, we're ready to view the large guest bedroom where you'll be staying." Huldah lowered her voice. "The guest room is the most spacious room in the house, and each of the two built-in beds has a clothes and shoe storage box at the end. A small library of religious scrolls is stored on shelves on one side and a desk and stool sit on the opposite. You'll have lamps for light." Huldah stopped midstream and gave them a serious look. "When we go into the room, please speak quietly. We have another house guest who is probably asleep now on one of the beds."

"Oh, we have another house guest." Ebed felt both surprised and left out. "Why didn't I know we have another visitor?"

"When I saw you earlier, I didn't know," Huldah explained. "I brought the lady home with me from my ministry at the city gate. The young woman has been abused by her husband, her parents are deceased, and she doesn't have anywhere else to go. Her name is Hannah, and she's also a relative, so I certainly wanted to help her out. She had no place to rest her head last night, so she probably didn't get much sleep, if any. She's resting now."

"I'll try to be as quiet as I can," whispered Saphah.

"As will Ebed and I," Shallum quietly added.

"Before we go in, Saphah, I want to ask you a question. Do you have anything to go in your storage box?"

"No," Saphah shook her head. "All I have is my writing case."

"Don't you even have one change of clothes with you?"

"No, I don't."

"Well, we're going to have to do something about that, don't you agree, Shallum?" She shot him a suggestive look.

"Yes, indeed." Shallum nodded his agreement. "Please tell Rebecca later to take Saphah to buy fabric for new clothes tomorrow."

"Alright," said Huldah. "Rebecca will need to measure Saphah to find out how much material is needed for two changes of clothes. Ebed can assist Rebecca tomorrow morning when he stops here on his way to school." Huldah looked toward the woman and instructed, "Saphah, please come closer so I can see what I'm doing. Come a little closer." She impatiently pulled on the skirt tail of her frock. "I want to take a closer look at your robe."

Curious, Saphah stepped closer to the lady of the house.

Huldah reached down and lifted the tail of Saphah's robe. "Oh, my! Your frock is made of the finest linen I've ever seen. It can serve as your garment for worship and as your ceremonial clothing when you meet the king. All we'll need to do is sew a more elaborate sash and a matching headdress, plus a fine shawl with fringe on each end. All of these articles will need to be hand embroidered. Tassels will also need to be added on the bottom edge of the robe. Does your nation have a symbol or a creed we can use for the embroidery work?"

"Yes, the Bald Eagle is our symbol and our creed is 'In God We Trust.' I could do a drawing for you of our symbol and creed if you wish. I also know how to sew and embroider, so I could even do the sewing and the embroidery work if you like."

"Yes, that'll work fine." Huldah was pleased that Saphah knew how to sew and embroider. "Shallum knows the Worker of Embroidery at the palace. He can borrow those supplies and send them by Ebed tomorrow morning. You'll still need the other two additional changes of clothes since you'll be participating at times in teaching and ministering activities."

"Oh, how wonderful." Saphah took a step back away from Huldah.

"Wait a second," Huldah tugged at Saphah's skirt to pull her back. "My lady, don't step away yet. I want to know something." Huldah's voice raised a pitch. "Why is the knee area of the skirt tail of your beautiful robe so dirty?" She raised her head with a scowl on her face. "What did you do anyway? Did you cross a river and then crawl in the mud after you reached the other side?" Her tone was cross.

"Well …," Saphah hung her head in shame, not knowing what to say.

"And, what's wrong with your forehead?" Hulda noticed the bumps and bruises on Saphah's forehead for the first time. "Has someone been hitting you on the head?" Her voice softened as she gently touched Saphah's forehead.

Saphah reached up to touch her forehead with her fingertips. *Oh dear. I have knots all over my brow from hitting my head on the ceiling in the Hezekiah Tunnel.* "I …, " Saphah trailed off. "I …," She glanced at Ebed, who stood behind Huldah. He shrugged his shoulders and raised his eyebrows but didn't say anything. Then she remembered what Ebed had told her earlier about Huldah's bluntness. Saphah relaxed a bit and took a deep breath. "I'm very sorry I got my skirt tail dirty. And I promise you that no one has been hitting me."

"It's all right," Huldah finally answered, now with more compassion in her voice. "I was afraid someone had been beating you."

"Supper is ready." Rebecca announced as she walked into the room.

"Whew!" Saphah breathed a sigh of relief. "I'm so glad Rebecca showed up and rescued me from this awkward situation."

"Who's that!" Rebecca jumped in surprise seeing someone stir in one of the beds.

"I'm sorry I didn't get a chance to tell you we have another visitor." Huldah turned to the young lady who was now sitting up in the bed. "Saphah, Shallum, Ebed and Rebecca, this is Hannah, a new guest in our home and a relative of mine. And Hannah, I'm pleased to introduce you to Saphah, another guest of ours. This is Shallum, my husband; Ebed, Shallum's mesharet; and Rebecca, my mesharetet." She pointed to each one respectively. "Ebed and Rebecca are like a son and a daughter to us."

Saphah couldn't believe her eyes. *Is this beautiful young lady really Huldah's relative? But how could that be?* "I'm pleased to meet you, Hannah." Saphah tried to hide her genuine surprise. "I guess we'll be guest roommates in this fine home."

"Speaking not only for myself, but also for Ebed and Rebecca, we're likewise pleased to meet you," Shallum graciously said in his welcoming voice. "Would you like to join all of us for our evening meal?"

Staring at the floor in shyness, the tall, ebony girl slowly arose from the bed and stood. "I'm happy to meet all of you too. And thank you for inviting me to supper, because I sure could use a good meal."

10

THE TWO PROPHETS

Rebecca stood quietly and perked up her ears. "Listen! Is someone knocking outside?" Everyone stood still and remained quiet.

"I wonder if that is who I think it is?" Huldah spoke aloud to no one in particular.

"Well, I don't know who's outside, but I do know I'm starving." Ebed moaned and gave Huldah a wistful look. "Could we just go eat now?"

Shallum answered for his wife. "Yes, it's definitely time to go eat. Rebecca, please go see who's at the door, and the rest of us will begin cleaning up for supper in the wash room."

"Hooray." Ebed rubbed his hands together. "I thought we were never going to get to eat." He started to head for the dining area, but Huldah stopped him. "Don't forget to wash up."

"Alright." The hungry teen rushed over to a basin, poured water from a large jar, then quickly splashed the liquid all over his face and onto both his arms. Grabbing a hand towel, he dried his face and hands and threw the towel on the table. "Quail and mushrooms, here I come." He lunged toward the door.

Huldah grabbed the neck of his robe and pulled him back with a stern command. "Come back here young man and hang that towel on your peg."

"Alright. Alright." Ebed quickly hung the towel and headed to the door, but stopped as his sister blocked the way. "Becca, who's that?" Ebed whispered as he saw a man standing directly across the court.

"I don't know," Rebecca said softly. "Huldah, come here please."

The curious matron stared across the courtyard toward a middle-aged gentleman of medium height and dark skin. He turned toward her from across the court and greeted her with a pleasant smile. "Zephaniah, hello," Huldah spoke up. "I'm so pleased a great man like you is here for a visit at our humble home." She walked across the courtyard to the finely-dressed man and began a low-toned but animated conversation with him. Finally looking back toward the group of five in the doorway to the washroom, she beckoned to her husband. "Shallum, would you and the others please join us?"

"It would be our pleasure to greet such a fine guest." Turning to Ebed, he quietly but firmly stated: "Please wait while the ladies finsh washing up, and then join us properly as we walk toward our main living area. We have a new guest who will most likely join us for supper. Ebed and Rebecca, I want you to show our guests how polite and respectful you can be. Do you understand?"

"Yes, Shallum," both teens answered in unison.

"You'd better." Shallum shot them a warning look while hanging up his towel. "We don't need any more shenanigans out of you two. He started toward the door of the courtyard and the others followed. Midway across the court from the main living area, Shallum momentarily stopped to talk to the women guests. "Ladies, do you see the ladder that reaches to the doorway to the second story?" He pointed toward the area on the opposite end of the court. "You'll need to use that ladder to reach the loft area. Rebecca, later when you get a chance, please show our guests the two upper rooms at the end of the courtyard and the two open roof areas—one on each side of the court."

"Okay, Shallum. I'm sure they'd like to see our main library and our spinning, weaving, and sewing room too. They'll also want to look at the two open roof areas on each side—one for sleeping cool in hot summer weather and the other for laying out clothes or produce to dry."

"Rebecca, thank you." Shallum nodded with a big smile. "Alright, group, now let's go meet our other guest and then eat supper."

~

Prophetess Huldah introduced everyone to Prophet Zephaniah. Then the two entered the dining room first, and the rest of the group brought up the rear.

"Your table looks beautiful." Saphah admired a fringe-ended linen runner decorating the middle of the long table. "Who made this handsome table runner with its hand-embroidered pomegranates in a bowl?"

"Rebecca did both the weaving and the embroidering, and I think she did a fine job." Huldah elaborated on her work with pride. "And, if you look over in the cooking area, you'll also see some pottery that Ebed hand-painted, with great attention to detail, I might add."

Saphah and Hannah walked over to examine Ebed's beautifully done jars portraying various wild and domesticated animals. "Rebecca and Ebed are definitely artistic." Saphah examined one of Ebed's painted jars. "They both do such fine work."

"Yes, they do." Hannah examined a jar featuring a lion. "I already know how to weave cloth, but I sure wish I could learn to paint and embroider."

"If you wish, Rebecca and I can teach you." Ebed volunteered for both his sister and himself. "What do you think, Becca?"

"Sure." Rebecca was all in favor. "Hannah, I just want to tell you that I'm glad you're going to live with us. I'll be happy to teach you to embroider."

"Would you really?" Hannah was both surprised and pleased.

"Of course, I'd love to." Rebecca gave her a big smile.

"You bet." Ebed wanted to assure Hannah of their willingness to teach her. "Our current art project is the bedroom murals we're painting. Huldah is planning to finish the one in her room, Becca is working on hers, and I'm planning to do the guest room. Hannah, would you like to help me draw a mural that you and I can paint in that room?"

"Yes, I sure would!" Hannah was joyful about the prospect of learning how to draw and paint. "Thank you."

"Hannah, would you also like to assist me with a small drawing project?" Saphah looked toward her with a questioning look. "I need to do a drawing of my nation's symbol and another of our creed for a new sash, headdress, and shawl for my wardrobe. If you and I worked together, you could learn how to draw embroidery patterns for your own projects."

"Oh, I would love to do that too!" The excitement was evident on Hannah's beaming face.

Turning toward Huldah, Saphah pointed out, "I don't have papyrus or parchment for the embroidery patterns, but I do have some silver to purchase supplies."

"Don't even think of using your silver." Huldah wanted her to save the money for emergencies. "Tomorrow, when you all go shopping, you can pick out what you need. I'll give Rebecca money to buy it."

"Oh, thank you. I appreciate so much everything you and Shallum are doing for Hannah and me."

Hannah chimed in. "Yes, thank you for helping us!"

"Give thanks to God, for He is the one who supplies all our needs." Huldah reminded Hannah of God's providence.

"Yes, scripture says that *God will meet all* [our] *needs, according to the riches of his glory in Christ Jesus*,[1] who is the Messiah to you," added Saphah.

"I agree. Thanks be to Messiah." Hannah voiced her appreciation for God's mercy.

"See, Zephaniah?" Huldah nodded her head. "I told you that Hannah would fit right in here at our home."

"Well, it looks like you're right," Zephaniah said in his magnificent low bass voice.

That's amazing! Prophet Zephaniah looks a little like the American actor James Earl Jones, especially when he smiles. He sounds like him too with his bass voice. Saphah forced her eyes to look away from the prophet. She was afraid of embarrassing herself if he caught her staring.

"I want to express my profound appreciation to all of you for the hospitality you've shown my niece Hannah." Zephaniah continued on in his wonderful voice. "Her husband has a history of mistreating her, especially in regard to her religious values and her faith in God Most High. The man has tried to force her to follow all the false gods he worships instead of worshipping the One True God, but Hannah has refused to do so. There's a lot more I could tell you about his abuse, but I'll let Hannah tell you herself when she feels ready."

"Yes." Shallum agreed that Hannah should be allowed to share or not share more about her situation. "Now, before another moment goes by, let's all get acquainted over this fine meal Rebecca has prepared." He turned to the dark-skinned man. "Zephaniah, honored prophet in our land, please sit here on this cushion at the low table, and Hannah, virtuous houseguest, please join your uncle beside him. Saphah, American Watchwoman and favored guest, please sit on the second side. Huldah, esteemed prophetess and my dear wife, please sit beside me on the third side. And Ebed and Rebecca, valued members of our family and household helpers, please take your positions on the remaining side. And now that we're all seated and ready, Prophetess Huldah, would you please say a prayer over the food Rebecca has prepared?"

The prophetess closed her eyes and began to pray. "Lord, thank You for hearing our prayers, for providing sustenance for our bodies, and for providing us with a place to lay our heads. Thank You also for bringing Hannah under our care and Saphah into our home. Please lead and guide both women in all their endeavors for the benefit of others and for the glory of God. Lord, please guide our family to be good hosts to our special guests according to Your providence and planning. Thank You too for laying Your hand on Your servant, the Prophet Zephaniah, who is one of Your faithful spokespersons to the people. Now, Lord, please bless this food to our bodies. Amen." Huldah glanced toward Ebed with a smile. "Ebed, I think it's finally time to eat, don't you?"

"I sure do!" Ebed gave Huldah a grateful glance. "Lord, thank You for giving me a wonderful sister who knows how to cook such great food. Let's eat!"

"After supper, Zephaniah has some prophecy he wants to share. And, later, he and I each have additional short messages for Saphah and Hannah to hear," said Huldah. "But in the meantime, we just need to enjoy the quail and mushrooms, the hot bread, and the fresh fruit the

Lord has provided. Rebecca and I will serve you now." The two arose from the table and began to serve the food.

Saphah inhaled the wonderful savor of the quail and mushroom dish. *That smells so good!* Her mouth watered in anticipation. She glanced at Hannah whose eyes were glued on the quail Rebecca would serve. *She's famished too,* thought Saphah.

"Alright, Eb." Rebecca smiled at her brother. "Since this is the early birthday supper I've prepared just for you, I'm going to serve you first. And because you were nice to me for once, I'm going to give you two servings of quail and mushrooms—unless you object to that."

"Oh, I don't object." Ebed answered quickly but then rolled his eyes upward as he paused to think and then added, "That is, unless one of the others wants two servings."

"Does anyone want two servings?" Rebecca questioned the group. Waiting for a reply but not hearing one, she ladled up two hot quail breasts, smothered with mushroom gravy, into Ebed's bowl. "I'm due a payback," she whispered in his ear. Ebed rolled his eyes and feigned a moan, but then quickly grabbed a roll from Huldah, who followed up Rebecca with a basket of hot bread in one hand and a bowl of fresh fruit in the other.

"Watch your manners, young man," Huldah whispered in Ebed's ear. "You forgot to thank Rebecca."

"Oh, I guess I did." Ebed sighed in regret. "Becca, thank you so much. I admit I'm glad you're my sister."

"You're welcome. I guess I'll keep you as my brother." Rebecca flashed him a big smile.

Hannah was thankful. "What a delicious meal. The food was so good!"

"It sure was," Zephaniah sat back in satisfaction. "The food was superb!"

"What a wonderful ending to a great day," Saphah added, "with yummy food and congenial company."

11

THE DAY OF THE LORD

The ladies cleared the table of dishes and food after supper. Then they lounged around the table, enjoying the fellowship of conversation after their meal. "Saphah," Huldah said, "remember what you told me earlier about your writing case?"

"… that I need to always keep my writing case with me because I might need to take notes at any time."

"Well, then, why don't you get your writing supplies out and ready so you can take notes when Zephaniah or others speak?"

"Sure." Saphah quickly set up her writing paraphernalia on the table. "Huldah, thanks for reminding me. I'm all set."

Shallum turned toward Zephaniah. "Sir, are you ready to begin?"

"Yes, thank you. I'll speak first to Hannah, my niece, and then second to Saphah, the American Watchwoman. In honor of my niece, I'll read a Psalm, written by the second ruler of Israel, King David." He took out a sheet of papyrus from a pocket in his robe.

Saphah quickly moved over to her scroll, dipped her pen into a little jar of ink, and poised it above her scroll. *Lord,* she silently prayed, *please help me to quickly and efficiently translate what I hear so I can write it down in English shorthand. In Jesus' name, I pray. Amen.* She was thankful now for taking that shorthand course in high school.

Prophet Zephaniah turned toward Hannah and began reading a Psalm to her. "King David said of God:

> *You are my Lord; apart from you, I have no good thing. I say of the holy people who are in the land, they are the noble ones in whom is all my delight. [But]* *those who run after other gods will suffer more and more. I will not pour out libations of blood to such gods or take up their names on my lips. Lord, you alone are my portion and my cup; you make my lot secure. ...I keep my eyes set always on the Lord. With him at my right hand, I will not be shaken.*[1]

Then, the prophet turned toward Shallum. "My friend, would you please interpret for my niece?"

"I would be delighted." Shallum turned toward Hannah. "Young lady, as King David said, please keep your eyes always on the Lord because 'with Him at your right hand, you will not be shaken.'"

"Thank you, Uncle Zephaniah and Shallum. Yahweh alone is 'my portion and my cup. He makes my lot secure,' now and forevermore."

"Now, Zephaniah, are you ready to deliver a prophecy from God to the American watchwoman Saphah?" Shallum asked.

"Yes, I'm ready," Zephaniah replied. "although I have prophecies of my own directed toward ancient Judah and Saphah's modern world, tonight I'll use Isaiah's prophecy which is related to your civilization."

Saphah took up her pen and held her breath in anticipation.

Zephaniah began, "Here is the quote from the Prophet Isaiah:

> *See, the day of the Lord is coming—a cruel day, with wrath and fierce anger—to make the land desolate and destroy the sinners within it. The stars of heaven and their constellations will not show their light. The sun will be darkened and the moon will not give its light. I will punish the world for its evil and the wicked for their sins.*[2]

Now, Shallum, would you please interpret for Saphah?"

Shallum turned to Saphah with a downcast countenance. "American Watchwoman, the Prophet Isaiah is talking here about the day of the Lord—a day of terror and a day of imminent destruction—which will fall upon all creation as a judgment for mankind's sin. In this future day, God 'will punish the world for its evil and the wicked for their sins.'"

"Cosmic darkness is also associated with the day of the Lord in the Book of Joel." Zephaniah began reading from his copy:

> *I will show wonders in the heavens and on the earth, blood and fire and*
> *billows of smoke. The sun will be turned to darkness and the moon*
> *to blood before the coming of the great and dreadful day of the Lord.*
> *And everyone who calls on the name of the Lord will be saved."*[3]

"How wonderful! Praise God!" Saphah raised her hands high in praise. "In other words, anyone who sincerely calls on the name of the Lord will be saved. And no one will be turned away."

"Yes, praise God!" Huldah raised her voice in joyful exclamation. "Our God is so good!" The others all raised their hands and voices in praise and thankfulness.

As Saphah continued writing what Prophet Zephaniah and Shallum had shared, a thought came to her. *I remember Jesus also said something very similar in the New Testament. In part of it, I think he was quoting Isaiah. I'll consult my bible later and include it in my writing.*

> *Those will be days of distress unequaled from the beginning, when God*
> *created the world, until now—and never to be equaled again. If the*
> *Lord had not cut short those days, no one would survive. But for the*
> *sake of the elect, whom he has chosen, he has shortened them. …But*

> *in those days, following that distress, 'the sun will be darkened, and the*
> *moon will not give its light;' the stars will fall from the sky, and the*
> *heavenly bodies will be shaken. At that time, people will see the Son of*
> *Man coming in clouds with great power and glory. And he will send*
> *his angels and gather his elect from the four winds, from the ends of*
> *the earth to the ends of the heavens.*[4]

Saphah finished her writing and her thoughts returned to Huldah as she heard her speaking.

The prophetess spoke directly to her, "Watchwoman Saphah, the writings of Prophets Isaiah and Joel remind us of what will happen in your world at the end of the great tribulation. The two outcomes of the coming day of the Lord will be blessing for all who've called upon the Lord, but judgment for all the unfaithful who've turned away from Him. Two aspects of God's character—compassionate love and holy justice comprise a mixture of hope and judgment, which should not be a surprise. Basic to the nature of the covenant between God and mankind is both 'blessing for obedience'[5] and 'cursing for disobedience.'[6] Saphah, you must let your people know that the end of the world is impending, and for those who rebel, there will be disaster, but for those who repent, there will be joy."

"Yes," Saphah said with determination in her voice. "I must give the people in my land warning that their final destiny draws near. Coming judgment is certain, *but about that day or hour no one knows, not even the angels in heaven, nor the Son, but only the Father.* [Therefore], *be on guard! Be alert!* [For we] *do not know when that time will come.*[7] It's greatly imperative that the masses examine their spiritual condition before it's too late."

"Exactly," Huldah conveyed the seriousness of scripture. "You must let them know that even during times of tribulation, they can seek the Lord. Sections of scripture like Deuteronomy became lost in our time. But earlier, my father memorized parts of scripture that later vanished. I memorized those verses too and this is one of the verses:

Thou shalt find him, if thou seek him with all thy heart and with all thy soul. When thou art in tribulation, and all these things are come upon thee, even in the latter days, if thou turn to the Lord thy God, and shall be obedient unto his voice; (For the Lord thy God is a merciful God;) he will not forsake thee, neither destroy thee.[8]

Those who sincerely search for the true God will find Him."

"What beautiful and wonderful words." Saphah was profoundly moved by Huldah's quote. "Praise God that he has provided a way for all human beings to have a chance to repent of their sins, return to the Lord, and partake of the joy, hope and deliverance provided by our Savior!"

12

THE TWO MESSAGES

Everyone at the table remained silent as they reflected on the warnings from Isaiah and Joel of future judgment on Saphah's world. The watchwoman's eyes stared without seeing at the bowl of fruit on the table in front of her. She was thinking long and hard about the sobering words. But then she remembered that Huldah had also said that the two prophets had some personal messages to share about the events of the day. Unable to hide her curiosity any longer, Saphah finally blurted out: "Huldah, do you and Zephaniah want to share the other messages now?"

"Of course." Zephaniah was ready to speak. "At the start of Huldah's afternoon ministry to women at the gate, I received a message from God and shared it with her: 'Huldah, you'll have two houseguests tonight. One will be a black woman, a native of Judah, who'll arrive at the gate where you minister today, and you'll invite her to your home. But the other houseguest will be a white woman who's a watchwoman for her country, America. You'll tell Ebed he can find her at the Pool of Siloam.'"

"Oh, now I see!" Saphah exclaimed, "Huldah, that's how you knew I was a watchperson and that I could be found at the Pool of Siloam. Earlier, Zephaniah told you!"

"Now," Huldah added, "here's the message from God for Zephaniah, which I heard in my spirit after he gave me his message at the city gate: 'Zephaniah, you'll speak tonight at my home to the two women you told me about. First, you'll speak a word of encouragement to the black woman, Hannah, your niece. Then you'll prophecy about the day of the Lord to the white woman, Saphah. In her role as a watchwoman for her country, she carries a shofar.'"

Jaws dropping, Hannah and Saphah looked toward each other in wide-mouthed amazement. "Oh!" Hannah voiced her surprise. "Zephaniah, that's why you knew to come to Shallum and Huldah's house tonight. You already knew that Saphah and I would be here."

"Yes, but Huldah, I don't carry a shofar." Saphah raised her shoulders and eyebrows in exasperation.

"And how could I be your relative?" Hannah frowned in her curiosity. "I'm black, but you and Shallum are white." She shook her head in doubt.

"One at a time, ladies," Huldah said to the skeptical ladies. "Saphah, look in your writing case."

Saphah searched all around inside her writing case. "I don't see any kind of musical instrument in here."

"What's this?" Huldah pointed to a rectangular-shaped box on one side of the case.

Saphah placed her fingers on a flap on the box and felt a small outcropping of wood. She pressed up on the section of wood to release the flap, and then rolled the flap upward like a roll-top desk. *Oh, this must be the secret compartment Nahal told me about.* Saphah looked inside. "Well, there are two sacks in here, a smaller and a larger one."

Intrigued, she opened the smaller, which contained a small quantity of silver and quickly closed it again. *Alright,* she thought, *that must be the stash of money Nahal mentioned.* Returning the silver to its spot, she opened the larger. "Well, look at that!" She was surprised to find a ram's horn in the sack. "I guess I do carry a shofar!"

"Huldah, what you said about Saphah is correct, but I don't see how your reference to me as a relative can be true. Although I'm related to Zephaniah, how can it be that I'm also kin to you and Shallum?" She shook her head in confusion. "You don't have the same skin color I have, so how can we be relatives?"

"I know it's baffling, Hannah, but actually, you're not only related to Prophet Zephaniah, Shallum, and me, but you're also related to King Josiah." Huldah began her case. "That's because each of us is a descendant of Judah's last good ruler, King Hezekiah. Josiah is the great-grandson of King Hezekiah, and the rest of us are descendants from different branches of the same family tree. Zephaniah, would you like to tell Hannah a little about your ancestry from Hezekiah?"

"My dear niece, Hannah." The Prophet Zephaniah's kind, dark eyes looked into hers. "My family line involves a Cushite, an Ethiopian—hence my dark skin. My brother was your father—thus both his and your dark skin. But we are also descendants of Hezekiah. At the beginning of my prophecies, my family line reads that I am the son of Cushi, the *son of Gedaliah, the son of Amariah,* [and] t*he son of Hezekiah, during the reign of Josiah son of Amon king of Judah.*[1] All the people Huldah mentioned can state a similar yet different ancestry back to Hezekiah, and Huldah's branch can be traced back much farther since she's a direct descendant of Rahab, the daring woman who hid the Israelite spies, who were on a secret scouting mission, just before the battle of Jericho."

"Oh," Hannah shook her head in understanding. "It makes better sense now. Thank you for explaining."

"It was my pleasure." Zephaniah put his arm around his niece and kissed her on the cheek.

"I hate to leave good company, but now Ebed and I need to get back to the palace." Shallum remembered that he and Ebed had more work to do on King Josiah's wardrobe. "Zephaniah, would you like to walk along with us? I hear that your place is not far from here and on the way."

"Thank you." Zephaniah was pleased he could walk back to his home with them. "It's not safe to walk alone in Jerusalem in the evening."

Rebecca turned to Shallum. "I hate to interrupt, but could I tell you something before you leave?"

"Go ahead." Shallum nodded toward Rebecca.

"My parents said Eb could invite anyone he and I wish to his dinner next week. So, you're all invited to come one week from today to my parent's camp where the celebration will be held. Father and Mother stopped by the palace earlier to invite King Josiah."

"Yes!" Ebed was overjoyed to hear about Josiah attending. "Please come to my birthday celebration, everyone. I can't wait. Even King Josiah is coming!"

"I would love to come." Zephaniah accepted the invitation, as did the others, but Huldah remained silent.

Shallum turned to his wife to discretely ask, "Huldah, if it's a school day, will you be able to attend?"

"I wish I could." Huldah sighed with sadness. "Maybe next year, if Saphah is still here at that time she can fill in for me at school after she receives her training. I may not be able to be there in person this year, but I'll certainly be there in spirit. "I'm sorry, Ebed." She side-hugged the young man.

"Oh, it's all right, Huldah." Ebed tried to console her. "I understand, but we'll miss you a lot."

"We sure will." Shallum and the rest all agreed.

Saphah had an idea. "Huldah, I want to ask you a question. Why couldn't I train with you at the Jerusalem School before the celebration so you can go this year?"

"Well, we have a lot going on." Huldah paused to think. "Let's see. Tomorrow you and the girls are going shopping for sewing supplies and so forth. The next day you'll begin working on your projects. After that, the following two days, we ladies will need to do our preparations for the Sabbath and then attend worship the next day. So, how would the first day of next week work?"

"Okay, that would be great, and I'm really looking forward to learning your routine." Saphah was thrilled she could help. "But could Hannah come along with us too? The reason I ask is because she and I need to do our embroidery work, and we could get some embroidering done along with observing your teaching procedures. That way she could sub for you at times too. What do you think?"

"I think that is an excellent idea!" Huldah was excited she could go to Ebed's birthday celebration after all. "So, let's plan on both of you coming, that is if Hannah would like to come. Hannah, would you like to tag along and learn my routine too?"

"Yes, that would be great." Hannah glanced first at Huldah and then at Saphah with a big smile. "I can't wait."

"Alright, thank you for permitting us both to visit your classes. But I do have another question. Regarding the Sabbath, would it be appropriate for me to have my own private service here in your home? I could worship God, read scripture, sing hymns, and praise the Lord for what he has done. What do you think, Huldah?"

"Yes," Huldah approved of Saphah's request. "That would be an excellent way to accommodate your worship needs in a setting where you feel comfortable. But if you ever want to join us in our worship setting that would be good too."

"Thank you so much! We're worshipping the same God, but you're looking forward in anticipation to the saving work of the Messiah, and I'm looking backward to the Messiah's finished work on Calvary. Thank God that He has provided a way for all of us to be his people!"

"Yes, praise God from whom all blessings flow." Huldah looked upward in thankfulness.

"Amen, praise be to Yahweh." Zephaniah then turned to a different subject. "I've been to see King Josiah today. I'm one of his advisors for the spiritual reforms he plans to initiate. However, since he wants to do everything in a way pleasing to God, he'd like to meet with close friends, relatives, and trusted palace personnel to discuss the matter. Likewise, he wishes to talk to the Rechabite clan about reforms that occurred two hundred years ago to hear their ideas. Ebed's birthday celebration, with members of the clan in attendance, would be a perfect opportunity for everyone to have a discussion after the festivities. King Josiah told me the names of certain people from the palace he trusts, and I'm supposed to give them invitations so they can attend."

"That sounds like an excellent idea." Huldah approved of the plans. "Zephaniah, can you think of anyone else that Ebed and Rebecca should invite?"

"I don't know if Jeremiah is in Jerusalem right now, but if he is, you might want to invite him too. He's another young lad I mentor in spiritual matters, and he's around Ebed and Josiah's age. It would be nice if they could all become acquainted. As a trustworthy relative, he might be able to add input regarding possible reforms. He's studying for the priesthood right now, but who knows what God may have in store for his life."

Ebed was pleased with the idea and gave approval to invite Jeremiah.

"Alright." Shallum formalized the plans. "I'll inquire about Jeremiah at the city gate while I'm there tomorrow and send Ebed to invite him if he's in town."

Rebecca looked up at her brother. "Eb, I would like to invite my friend, Tamara. Would that be alright?"

"Of course." Ebed patted her shoulder with one hand. "Becca, why did you even ask? You know that would be fine with me."

"Alright, it all sounds good, and I'm looking forward to going." Prophet Zephaniah turned toward Rebecca. "Young lady, I want to thank you for the marvelous supper, and thank all of you again for your splendid hospitality. My niece, Hannah." He smiled at her. "I'm so pleased Shallum and Huldah have so graciously taken you in. Please remember, I'm always here for you too." He stepped closer to Saphah and shook her hand. "Dear, I'm very happy I got to meet you and look forward to seeing you and the others next week. Prophetess Huldah, I'm delighted we were able to finally meet at the gate where you minister. I hope we can get together there again soon."

"I hope so too." Huldah was happy to become acquainted with another prophet. "We definitely need to take time out from our busy schedules to discuss the spiritual condition of both the men and the women in Judah."

"We must leave now, because it's nearing dusk." Shallum gave Huldah a farewell kiss and waved toward the three ladies. "Farewell." He and the other two men walked out the door.

"I'm so tired," Hannah sighed and then suppressed a yawn, covering her mouth with her fist.

"Me too." Saphah stretched her arms and legs before getting up.

"Huldah, may we help with the dishes?"

"No, it's been a long day for you both, so you're excused now," said Huldah. "Rebecca will get some clean clothes for you, Saphah. Hannah, is there anything you need?"

"No, I'm fine. Thank you so much for everything." Hannah gratefully expressed her appreciation.

"Yes." Saphah wanted to show her gratefulness too. "Thank you both."

"Come with me, ladies." Rebecca escorted the two. "We'll stop by Huldah's room to get some night clothes for Saphah."

"Ladies, good night and sweet dreams," said Huldah.

"Good night, Huldah." Saphah and Hannah said their goodnights in turn.

Quickly but carefully rummaging through Huldah's storage trunk in her room, Rebecca soon found a night wrap and a suitable change of clothes for Saphah. "Please let me know if you need anything else."

"Thank you and good night." Saphah took up the clothes.

"Yes, good night, Rebecca." Hannah and Saphah departed for the guest bedroom. "I'm so glad this day is almost over." Hannah sat down on her mat and stretched her arms above her head.

"Me too." Saphah yawned in her sleepiness. "Why don't we get ready for bed now. We're both so tired, and we can talk tomorrow.."

"Let's do." Hannah immediately began putting on her nightclothes and climbing into her bed. "Good night, Saphah."

"I don't blame you. Good night, Hannah." Saphah began changing clothes too, but then she remembered something else she needed to do. Although weary, the American woman had promised herself to look up the scriptures she'd written down earlier in summary form. She made the necessary corrections on her scroll by the light of a lamp on the desk, but then she decided to research in her Bible to find out the dates of the reigns of Hezekiah, Manasseh, Amon, and Josiah.

Hmmm …, Saphah thought. *It says here that the period after the godly King Hezekiah's reign in* 716 – 687 BC *was marked by religious decay and spiritual rebellion. At that time, true worship was perverted by the evil reigns of his son Manasseh in* 687 – 642 BC *and his grandson King Amon in* 642 – 640 BC. *But here it says that early in the reign of Hezekiah's great-grandson Josiah in* 640 – 609 BC, *Zephaniah began to warn his people of the impending judgment of God, caused by the reigns of Josiah's grandfather and father. But it also says he gave warnings of judgment on my world too which would occur before the end. Oh, I must read that!*

However, now I need to compare the accounts of Josiah's reign in 2 *Chronicles and* 2 *Kings.* Saphah discovered that 2 Chronicles recorded in detail the execution of the purging of the two lands, but the 2 Kings portrayal of reforms didn't begin until the time of the restoration of the temple in Jerusalem. *Evidently, the accounts began in different time frames, but both agree that major restoration of the temple started when Josiah was* 26. *So, the spying out of the land and the early reforms evidently began before that time.*

Saphah considered what she needed to do: *Going forward, I'll compare the two accounts about King Josiah, …but not tonight.* She yawned widely. Struggling to keep her eyes open, Saphah stopped reading and crawled into her bed. Whispering a short but thankful prayer, she drifted off into a sound sleep.

~

A shrill scream awakened Saphah with shivers up her back. Her frightened eyes saw the outline of Hannah's thin form, in the dim light from the window, sitting up on the edge of her bed. The girl placed her face in the palms of her hands and began to sob mournfully, moving her body rhythmically from side to side. "Hannah, what's wrong." Saphah rushed to the side of her friend's bed to comfort her. As Saphah gently stroked Hannah's shoulder, the girl cried.

"Oh, Saphah," Hannah sobbed, "I had the most terrifying nightmare. In my dream, I was pregnant and suffering birth pains of delivery. I gave birth to a beautiful baby girl and held her in my arms. But then, suddenly, my husband Jude roughly stole my newborn away and ran off with my screaming infant in his own arms. Then I awoke." The young woman began crying even more bitterly.

"What would cause such a horrifying dream?" Saphah gently asked.

Hannah's weeping began anew. "I think I may be pregnant because I haven't had my monthly flow for over four months."

Saphah lightly rubbed Hannah's shoulder. "You don't know for sure you're pregnant yet. For now, just be happy you're staying with a wonderful family that cares about your welfare. You'll be safe here with us, but more importantly, you'll be safe because God is with you. Do you remember what you said after Zephaniah read that Psalm?"

"Yes, I do, and thanks for reminding me. I said that Yahweh alone is my portion and my cup; He makes my lot secure, now and forevermore." Hannah stood up and gave her new friend a hug.

Facing Hannah, Saphah placed her hands on the young woman's thin shoulders, turned her so the moonlight from the window bathed her face, and looked intently into her teary, brown eyes. Her heart went out to her as she said, "Hannah, I think you can depend on this entire household, and Zephaniah too, for support if you're with child. You should also share with Huldah that you might be expecting. She is the female head of household and needs to be aware of your pregnancy ahead of time. You might want to wait until tomorrow night to tell her because everyone will be busy in the morning."

"You're right. But do you think she'll have a bad reaction to the news?" Her eyes revealed sudden fear. "A new baby will mean there's another mouth to feed and clothe in this household."

"Well, she might be initially shocked, but from what Ebed has told me, that reaction won't last long." Saphah reassured Hannah she had nothing to fear. "And, if you really are pregnant, I think everyone will be supportive of you. In fact, I think Ebed and Rebecca will probably be thrilled, so don't worry your tender young head about any of us."

"Thank you so much, Saphah." Hannah yawned as her body began to relax from the anxiety she'd been experiencing.

"You're welcome," Saphah said with tenderness. "Now, let's both get some more sleep because we have a big day ahead of us tomorrow." She returned to her warm bed and settled into the covers.

13

THE SHOPPING TRIP

To Saphah it seemed like she'd just gone to sleep when she abruptly heard Rebecca's voice. "Wake up ladies. Huldah has breakfast ready. She wants us to come over in our nightclothes because she must leave soon. Wake up. Wake up." She repeated her refrain several times.

"Alright." Saphah stretched and yawned after being awakened. "Good morning, Rebecca and Hannah." She sat upright on the side of her bed, rubbed her eyes, and slipped on her sandals.

"C'mon, Hannah," Rebecca said, "It's time to get up."

"Yes," Hannah replied in a sleepy fog, sitting up in her bed but then immediately flopping back down again with a giggle. Still laughing at her own antics, Hannah arose and joined the other two women, tip-toeing in her bare feet. They all walked into the washroom to tidy up and then across the courtyard to join Huldah.

"What's for breakfast?" Rebecca inquired as they walked into the room.

"Boiled eggs and breakfast cakes with honey. Rebecca, I was very pleased this morning to discover that wild honey and goose eggs were among the supplies your parents brought in from their camp when they were here yesterday."

"Sounds yummy!" Hannah didn't waste any time in settling down on one of the cushions. "I'm really hungry this morning."

"Well, get started eating because I must leave soon, and I've several things to tell you first."

"I still need to take Saphah's measurements." Rebecca picked up the measuring tape and set it down where she was sitting. "Then Ebed can estimate how much fabric I need for the creation of her new garments and the accessories for her other robe."

"Alright, when Ebed gets here, he can sit down and eat while you measure Saphah." Huldah was trying to work things out so they wouldn't waste any time. "Meanwhile, everyone, help yourself to the food. Saphah, would you please say the prayer?"

"Of course." Saphah sat down on a cushion on one side of the table and served herself a breakfast cake and egg. "This is a supplication to God called 'The Lord's Prayer.' At the beginning of the day, I like to pray it along with the rest of my morning prayer:

> *Our Father which art in heaven, hallowed be thy name. Thy kingdom come. Thy will be done on earth, as it is in heaven. Give us this day our daily bread. And forgive us our debts, as we forgive our debtors. And lead us not into temptation, but deliver us from evil. For thine is the kingdom and the power, and the glory, forever.*[1]

And Heavenly Father, please guide us in everything we do today. Please watch over our coming and our going, please protect us from all evil, and please bring us safely home again. Lord, thank You for the wonderful breakfast You've provided and Huldah has prepared. Please bless it to our bodies, I pray. In Jesus' name. Amen."

"Good morning, everyone," Ebed's cheery voice called out. "Is breakfast ready?"

"Good morning, Ebed. How's Shallum this morning?"

"Oh, he's fine. He's already on his way to greet pilgrims to Jerusalem at a city gate."

"I'm glad to hear that. Please tell him hello for me when you see him later."

"Will do, Huldah."

"Alright, I've cooked extra cakes, so please take all you want."

"Great!" Ebed sat down, bowed his head, and silently said a short prayer of thanks. "I'm so hungry." He grabbed his bowl and filled it to the brim with breakfast cakes. He plunged a rolled cake into his container of honey and bit off a big hunk. "Mmm, Mmm, good." He profusely relished the cakes. "Becca, have you taken Saphah's measurements yet?" Taking up a boiled egg with his fingers, he dipped it into a bowl of salt and took a hearty bite.

Rebecca saw that Saphah's food was finished, so she stuffed the last bite of her breakfast cake into her mouth. "I'll do it right now. Come on, Saphah." She began to take measurements for the new clothing with her flax measuring line. "Eb, I'm writing her measurements on a scrap piece of papyrus."

"Alright. When you get finished, I'll write down the amounts of material you need on the other side of the papyrus. I've also brought along drawings and patterns for each garment. Since Saphah is a representative for her country, she needs an attractive wardrobe to wear for engagements. So, I've chosen two nice patterns from the palace selection for Judah's queens. Also, I've brought embroidery supplies. Here you go." Ebed handed a small wooden box filled with patterns, drawings, and embroidery supplies to her. "If you need anything else, just let me know, and I'll get it for you."

"Ebed and Rebecca, thank you so much." Saphah looked through the box and removed the drawings for her new garments to show the others. "Ebed, you have such good taste. I really love the patterns you chose for my new robes."

"You're welcome, Saphah." Ebed shoved the last bite into his mouth. "Oh, Huldah, by the way, Zephaniah gave me a bag of money for Hannah's shopping, and Shallum also gave me a bag for Saphah and Becca's purchases at the market." He got up to leave and left the two little bags of loose silver on the table.

"Good, I'm about ready to walk over to school with you, but I just need to tell the ladies a few things before we go."

"Alright, I'll wait outside." Ebed stepped out into the courtyard.

Huldah addressed the girls. "I've made a list of everything with the amount to spend on each purchase. Rebecca, you'll need to weigh out money for each item and place it in individual bags. You should also weigh Hannah's money from Zephaniah and Saphah's money from her writing case for future emergencies. Remember, you may have to haggle with merchants to buy items at an affordable price. If a merchant won't reduce the price, you must look for a merchant who will."

"Hannah, here's the money Zephaniah left for you." Huldah handed a little bag of silver to her.

Hannah looked in her bag. "There's a note in here from my uncle Zephaniah instructing me to use a portion for a nice birthday gift for Ebed, but to use remaining money for whatever I desire."

"Rebecca, here's Saphah's money from Shallum. Now weigh out her silver. She doesn't know the value of our money yet, so you'll need to help her with purchases. The bag also has money for the two of you to each purchase a birthday gift for Ebed. Rebecca, we'll have something easy for supper tonight. I've already put lentils on to cook over a low fire. All you'll need to do is add seasonings and a little olive oil when you return, and you'll have the soup all prepared. We also have the goat cheese and dried apricots your parents left us."

"That'll be great, because we might be really tired after all our shopping." She gave the other girls a wink and a grin. "Thank you, Huldah."

"Alright, Rebecca, Hannah, and Saphah." Huldah looked from lady to lady as she spoke. "I want you three to stay together while you do your shopping today. It's not safe for a woman to be out alone in Jerusalem. Be careful, and God willing, we'll see you back here late this afternoon."

"We will." They all shook their heads in promise.

"Goodbye, ladies." Huldah and Ebed left the courtyard.

"Bye, Hannah, Saphah, and Becca." Ebed turned with a big smile on his face and waved.

The trio stood at the open doorway and waved goodbye. "Becca, you're fortunate to have a brother who's both handsome and polite." Hannah's eyes were still on Ebed as he walked away.

"Thank you, Hannah, and I agree he's a wonderful brother, but don't ever tell him I said so, or I'll never hear the end of it. Now, let's make our plans for the day. Huldah has graciously allowed me to stay home from school to get shopping done, so let's do our chores so we can go."

"Good idea, let's get this show on the road." Hannah was enthused to go on a shopping trip. "Okay, girls, what chore should we do first?"

"Does this sound like a good plan?" Rebecca listed the chores in order. "First, let's go to the washroom to clean up and get dressed. Second, let's make the rounds of the bedrooms and tidy up. Then, let's go to the outdoor cooking area, and I'll put on a pot of water to heat so we can wash the breakfast dishes when we get back."

"Yep, that sounds like a plan." Hannah was ready to get started.

Rebecca pointed out the cleansing agents, lotions, toiletries, perfumes, and other washroom essentials. "Hannah, tell us about your parents as we wash and get dressed."

Hannah began her story with a sigh. "Well, I'd been married to my husband Jude for a short time when Father and Mother decided to travel to Ethiopia to visit relatives and do some business. As they neared Jerusalem on their way back home, they were waylaid by robbers who stole all their money and valuables, killed them both, and left their bodies beside the road. They were found by someone who recognized them, and that's how I found out what happened. I was devastated because of the loss of my beloved parents and because my marriage to Jude wasn't working out well. Without my parents, I had nowhere to turn for help or support."

Rebecca regretted her question. "Hannah, I'm sorry I asked…"

"No, that's fine. Actually, I need to talk about it." Hannah sighed again. "I hardly even knew my husband, who called me 'woman' or 'wife' in his surly way, instead of by my actual name. I was subject to his every whim without a way to achieve my own wishes or desires. If I did the least little thing wrong in his eyes, he flew into a rage and hit me with the force of his fists with hate in his eyes. I had to get away from him to protect my own sanity, yet I had nowhere to go until Huldah took me in."

"Oh, Hannah, that's terrible, and I'm so sorry you've had to endure his mistreatment." Rebecca's eyes began to glaze, but she pursed her lips tightly together to get her emotions under control. "I'm so glad Huldah could take you in."

"Thank goodness she did! To top it off, Jude wanted me to worship the false gods Molech and Baal in addition to Yahweh, which I wouldn't do. He even threatened to sacrifice our first child to a false god if I got pregnant." Hannah began to cry and gave Saphah a knowing glance.

"Oh, my dear friend," Saphah tried to suppress her own tears while stroking the young lady's back. "God won't let that happen. He'll help you." She was striving to appease the girl into a peaceful state of mind.

"Yes, if you reconcile with Jude and become pregnant by him, the Lord will help you," Rebecca consoled. "Let's pray for Hannah."

"Yes, please pray for me," Hannah sobbed pitifully, "…and my baby."

Rebecca gave her a startled look.

"I know I'm pregnant because after I had a terrible nightmare last night, I felt my child move in my loins. Then I was unable to fall back asleep quickly. That's why I had a hard time waking up this morning."

"I'll pray for you and your little one." Crying out to God, Saphah prayed: "Heavenly Father, we lift up our voices to you, our Lord and our God, in solemn petition for our friend Hannah and her unborn child. She puts her faith and trust in you. We know from the Psalms that *the salvation of the righteous comes from the Lord; he is their stronghold in time of trouble. …He delivers them from the wicked and saves them, because they take refuge in him.*[2] Lord, our friend Hannah has taken refuge in You. So, we give thanks for Your compassion and Your protection. Amen."

"Thank you so much for praying for me and my child. *God is* [my] *refuge and strength, a very present help in trouble..*"[3]

"You're welcome."

"Oh, I think it's wonderful you're expecting a baby!" Rebecca was pleased there would be a new baby in the household. "Are you going to tell the others about your pregnancy tonight?"

"Well, I was already planning to tell Huldah privately, but now I think I'll announce to everyone tonight at supper that I'm expecting!"

"I think you should." Saphah knew it would be best for Hannah to tell them. "Now, let's finish our chores, so Rebecca can weigh the money and then we can go shopping. I'm really looking forward to touring the marketplace and seeing some of the sights in Jerusalem. Please help me to remember to bring my writing case."

"Go get it right now." Rebecca laughed. "Because otherwise, if you're like me, you'll probably forget."

"You're right, I need to get in the habit of putting it on first thing after I get dressed each morning." Finally completing their morning routine and weighing out the money, the trio left the school complex and headed toward the marketplace. "I'd like to know something. What are you two planning to buy Ebed for his birthday?"

"I'm thinking about buying Eb a bow and arrow set, that is, if I can afford it," Rebecca shared. "He talks all the time about his trips to the target range with King Josiah, where they take turns shooting arrows with the king's bow. I think he'd love to have his own bow and quiver of arrows."

"Becca, does your brother ever get to go hunting with his father?" Hannah wanted to know more about Ebed.

"So far, he hasn't done any hunting with Father, but I know he'd love to, if I can just get him a bow and arrows."

"In that case, do you think he'd like a knife for hunting trips?"

"I think Eb would really like to have a knife! He could also carry it in a scabbard for self-protection as he goes about the city. He has to run errands by himself almost every day, and I fear for his safety."

"Oh, my, Eb really needs a knife and scabbard set, so I hope I can afford to get him a set for his birthday. We don't want anything bad to happen to him in Jerusalem doing his chores and errands."

"No, we don't," agreed Saphah. "That reminds me. Perhaps we should stop and pray again before we reach the marketplace. There's a stone bench over in the shade. Let's go sit down and pray. Rebecca, would you please make our praises and requests known to God?"

"I would be pleased to. Dear Jehovah, I come to You today in thanksgiving and praise, grateful for all You've done for us. Lord, thank You that my friend Hannah and my mother Miriam are both expecting new life, precious babies that You love so much. Please watch over the rest of our family members today, and please take care of Saphah, Hannah, her unborn child, and me, as we do our shopping. Lord, please help us make wise decisions in purchasing our sewing supplies and our gifts for Eb. And Lord, please guide our feet every step of the way in everything we do today. To You be the glory and honor, we pray. Amen."

As the three reached the market, Saphah paused to take in their surroundings. "What a remarkable place! This group of shops is like a fair or bazaar with all the various stalls and people of all sorts swarming around everywhere."

"I enjoy coming here just to observe all the adults as they mill about and the little children as they play," Rebecca explained. "You never know what types of people you might encounter when you come here."

"Yes, I noticed some Judahites are dressed in what seems to be regular clothing," Saphah said, "but others are dressed in deep shades of purple, red, and blue. Some of their flashy garments, with heavy embroidery, look very expensive. In fact, their clothing seems strangely different from what we're wearing. Why is that?"

"I think I can answer your question by quoting prophecy." Hannah began telling them more about her Uncle Zephaniah who had shared some of his prophetic writing with her. "Although my uncle memorizes the words of prophecy God reveals to him, he also records all the prophecies on scrolls, just like the other prophets. Some of the prophets even dictate to scribes who accurately write down every word."

"It's wonderful the prophets of your age record the words God has given them by the Holy Spirit." Saphah was glad to hear firsthand about the way God spoke through the prophets. "Scripture attests to the inspiration of its words: *For prophecy never had its origin in the human will, but prophets, though human, spoke from God as they were carried along by the Holy Spirit.*[4] God was the source of the content, so what the human authors actively said came from God as 'they were carried along by the Holy Spirit.' Hannah, did you know that Zephaniah's prophecies are in my bible?"

"No, I didn't. Please tell me more."

"The prophecy written on scrolls by the prophets in ancient times later became a part of scripture compiled into the Bible in modern times. But the fact that the prophetic scrolls weren't compiled into a book yet in your era doesn't mean they weren't God's Word. They are the Word of God in ancient times and the Word of God in modern times. They are God's eternal Word and can be quoted as such in any age, because *the word of the Lord endures forever.*[5] Now, please continue with what you were telling us about Zephaniah's prophecy."

"Alright. Uncle has even spoken on the subject of apparel regarding God's warning of coming judgment against Judah for worshipping Molech and other false gods. Here is a section of Zeph's prophecy, which is the Word of God directed toward the people of Judah:

> *I will stretch out my hand against Judah and against all who live in Jerusalem. I will destroy every remnant of Baal worship in this place, and the very names of the idolatrous priests—those who bow down on the roofs to worship the starry host, those who bow down and swear by the Lord and who also swear by Molech, those who turn back from following the Lord and neither seek the Lord nor inquire of him. ... [And] I will punish the officials and the king's sons and all those clad in foreign clothes.*[6]

Hannah continued her explanation. "The people clad in foreign clothes are Judahites who worship false gods. In Judah, wearing the clothes of the Canaanites, Babylonians, Assyrians or other foreigners who worship false gods shows conformity to their ways of life and religion. In other words, they're trying to become like those who worship the many fake gods. In fact, my husband Jude dresses like them. He tried to force me to dress that way too by buying an assortment of foreign frocks for me, but I refused to wear them."

"Good for you!" Rebecca piped up. "I'm so glad you got away from that wicked man."

"Me too. Who're those pitiful folk sitting in a row on the side of the street over there?" Saphah inquired.

"They're beggars," Rebecca said. "They're sitting there for a variety of reasons. Some are blind, others are sick or crippled, but still others are mentally deficient or incapable for other reasons. Most of these people depend on the compassion of strangers to move about or get food and water. Ebed brings them water to drink from the cisterns or the Pool of Siloam as often as he can, and Shallum gives them money when he comes here. The beggars always display deep gratitude for anything done for them. I feel so sorry for these sick and desperate people."

"As do I. Before my parents died, mother would bake bread for them when she could, and father and I would deliver the nourishing loaves. I miss my parents so much." The bereaved girl let out a huge sigh of longing for her mother and father. "They were such good and compassionate people."

Rebecca tenderly gave Hannah a loving hug. The trio walked on with Saphah in the middle and a girl on each side holding one of her hands.

"Alright ladies. Let's stay on the lookout for the stalls and shops where fabrics, weapons, and art supplies are sold. If we shop and make our purchases first, then we can take in the other sights of the marketplace at our leisure." Saphah was hoping to do some sightseeing.

"Saphah, have you decided what you're going to buy Ebed for his birthday?"

"Well, Rebecca, does he have the art supplies for doing the mural in the guestroom?"

"No, I don't think he does, so he needs supplies for sketching an outline on the wall and for painting in the various colored areas. Hannah, since Eb invited you to help him with the project, do you know what he's thinking about painting for the mural? That would really help Saphah in buying colors."

"Oh my." Hannah stopped for a minute and scratched her head as she searched for an answer. Her eyes suddenly lit up. "He hasn't told me, but I know what we could paint. What about mountains, a waterfall, and wild animals as a scene for a mural?"

"I think Ebed would like to do a mountain scene because that would make a very nice mural. I'm glad you came up with that possibility, because now I have an idea of some color pigments to purchase. Also, maybe we can get papyrus at the art shop, both for our embroidery patterns and for a small sketch of the mountain scene. That way, you and Ebed can refer to the sketch while you work on the mural." Saphah noticed some important-looking men sitting over at tables taking money. "Who are those well-dressed men?"

"Oh, those are tax collectors and money changers. We definitely want to stay away from the money changers because they often cheat people when making change by using false weights on their scales. That's why we used our own scale when we weighed our money at home. It has honest weights. I also brought along my flax measuring line to measure the fabric we want to buy. That way we can be sure it's an honest measurement of cloth. Sadly, many of the people shopping here are too poor to have their own scales or measuring lines at home."

"Is that a millinery shop over there?" Saphah exclaimed in surprise. "Because if it is, we could look at the various types of headdresses, turbans, and other headgear to give us an idea of the type I might need."

"Step right over, ladies," called a foreign-looking madame from the street. "Come pick out your millinery right here." The hawker called out loudly again.

"Should we go over and take a look at the headgear?"

"Go ahead. But, Saphah, just remember we're only looking, because I'm sure her already-sewn products are very expensive."

"C'mon, Saphah." Hannah grabbed her hand and half-dragged her over to the woman's stall. "let's see what kind of headwear would look best with an embroidered eagle, the symbol of your country, America."

The ladies walked toward the woman selling head-gear. "Hello, madame." Saphah examined several types of headwear.

The lady was eager to push her wares. "What can I sell you today?" She draped a flashy red shawl around Saphah's neck.

"Let us look around for a few minutes first. Then we'll ask you for help."

"Yes, go ahead." The lady retrieved her shawl.

Saphah quickly glanced over the offering of headgear and considered which type might be best to highlight the embroidery. "What do you ladies think?"

"Well, I like the round or square types of headwear best. You could wear a linen shawl under them or wear them alone," Hannah explained.

"You know, I was thinking the same thing. In America, we call them pillboxes because they look like the little containers we use to hold medicine pills. We could embroider the eagle on the bottom front part before we sewed either the round or square top part onto it, so that type of headwear would work great. What color do you think would highlight the symbol best?"

Rebecca noted her choice of color. "I think the royal blue one is nice, because you said your national colors are red, white, and blue. Your sash could be made of the same material since it will be embroidered with your motto, 'In God We Trust.'"

"Could we see both the square and the round cap type in royal blue?" Saphah asked the Madame.

"Of course," The lady in charge placed two of the cap types on the counter in front of her. "These caps are lined in fine linen and would look quite nice on you. Would you like to try one on?"

"Yes." Saphah examined the interior of a square pillbox to see how it had been constructed. "How does it look on me?" She tilted her head toward the girls.

"It looks very nice," Hannah observed, "but try on the round one too."

"Alright." Saphah removed the square one and placed the other toward the back of her head like the American First Lady Jacqueline Kennedy wore her pillbox hats in the 1960s.

"I think the round one looks just beautiful on you." Hannah admired the way the cap brought out the blue in Saphah's eyes.

"Me too, that's definitely the headgear for you. We'll keep this one in mind," Rebecca politely informed the owner.

"Well, it may be gone when you get back." The hawker tried to pressure them to make the purchase. "You better buy it now while you're here."

"Thank you," said Rebecca, "but we need to shop around a bit more before we make a decision."

The three ladies walked on and browsed the stalls as they looked for articles they needed to buy. Saphah was surprised at the variety of products for sale at the various stalls located in the area. "Look ladies, over there a woman is weaving baskets out of flax; beside her is a man making pottery at his wheel; across from them is a jewelry maker working with gold, silver, and fine jewels; and near him is a tanner working leather. But now, I'm smelling something delicious, so we must be getting near the food businesses."

"Yes, we are." Hannah was wanting to use some of her extra money from Zephaniah to buy a treat. "They're making hot mixed nuts over there. See the lady pouring out a fresh batch of the hot walnuts, almonds, and pistachios right now? Should I buy some for us to share?"

"Oh, that sounds good." Rebecca was pleased Hannah wanted to purchase some hot nuts. "And I brought along a flask of water from home that we can share."

"Yes, the nuts smell so wonderful my mouth is watering," Saphah agreed.

"Alright, that settles it," Hannah briskly walked to the stand and bought both a medium and a small bag of the mixed treat. "Why don't we go sit down on the ground under that tree."

"I've never had these before, and they're yummy." Rebecca was enjoying the taste of the sweet and spicy nuts. "Here, Hannah and Saphah." She offered them a drink of water from her flask.

"The weaponry stall is right over there." Hannah pointed toward it, took a big drink from the flask, and then offered it to Saphah. "Let's go to that stall next. Then we could price both the bow and the knife sets."

Saphah took a drink of water and handed the flax back to Rebecca. "That's a good idea. I'm looking forward to seeing what types of weapons they sell."

"Okay, let's go." Hannah attached the smaller sack of mixed nuts to her sash.

"We're ready." Saphah and Rebecca arose, and the three walked over to the shop. After much haggling with the attendant over prices, the three walked out of the weaponry store in triumph. Rebecca sported a quiver of arrows strapped on her back and a bow on her shoulder, and Hannah proudly wore a knife in a scabbard around her waist.

"Well, that went well." Hannah smiled at Rebecca and congratulated her for making a good buy on her gift. "At first, when you gave the man your money, I thought he was going to cheat you. When he said there wasn't enough silver in your bag for the bow and arrow set, I was worried."

"I've seen merchants like that before, and I wasn't about to let him get by with his conniving tricks." Rebecca was resolute in her dealings with people trying to cheat others. "That's why I told him to get an honest scale. When I told him the head of our household works for King Josiah and frowns on anyone who doesn't abide by the law …"

"The merchant certainly changed his tune." Saphah laughed as she cut in on Rebecca, "He even gave you a good buy on the knife and scabbard set Hannah wanted."

"Yes, he did!" Rebecca laughed heartily. "Now, we need to find the sewing supply area."

"I see looms and yarns ahead, so the sewing supplies shouldn't be far away," Hannah observed.

"Oh, I see the fabric stalls right over there." Saphah spied several tables with beautiful rolls of cloth ready for sale. It looked like other tables were filled with baskets of sewing accessories such as needles, thread, and embroidery supplies.

"Rebecca and Hannah, please help me to choose the right material for my robes and accessories."

They shopped from table to table looking for affordable nice linen cloth. "What do you think about the fabric on this table?" Hannah asked.

"I love the feel of this linen." Rebecca ran her hand over the smooth material. "Saphah, come over here and feel of this cloth."

"Yes, that's very nice, and I like the muted shades of the material on this table too." She was happy they found something they all liked. Continuing to shop, the ladies found everything they needed to make Saphah's new garments, including her headwear and changes of undergarments. Relying on Rebecca's expertise in bargaining with shop owners, they purchased all their sewing supplies at affordable prices. Saphah stashed the sewing supplies in her writing case, and the three headed on toward the art supply area nearby.

"Alright, what kind of art supplies am I looking for?" Saphah didn't know what types of art supplies, such as paints or brushes, were available in Judah.

"Well, we need papyrus and sharpened charcoal sticks or hard earth color sticks in yellow, red, or brown for the preliminary sketches of the mural and the embroidery patterns." Rebecca tried to recall everything they needed. "We'll also need color pigments for mixing the different shades of paints, plus assorted camel and calf hair art brushes for painting the mural."

After tying the sack of art supplies to her sash, Saphah decided to let Hannah and Rebecca shop for the papyrus. "Ladies, I'm getting tired, so I'm going to rest over on that bench in the shade. You girls can go find the papyrus. Just get a few small sheets for the embroidery patterns, and a couple of larger ones for the drawings for the mural."

Reaching a bench some distance away, Saphah plopped down with a huge sigh of relief. After being on her feet for two days in a row, her feet hurt. She smiled at the two young ladies who were completing their purchases. She was thankful for her new friends. As she rested in the shade, she closed her eyes for a few minutes. A noise caused her to open her eyes again, and she turned in concern to check the whereabouts of Hannah and Rebecca. Searching for the girls, Saphah noticed a man dressed in foreign garments off to the side staring at Hannah.

Who is that man, and why is he staring at my young friend?

14

THE ENCOUNTER

Saphah was startled to see a stranger in flashy clothes moving toward Hannah. *Oh my*, she thought. Her skin prickled as she came to a frightening conclusion. *That must be Hannah's husband! He doesn't look happy with that frown on his face. I must warn her!* Saphah arose from the bench where she was sitting and took fast strides toward Hannah and Rebecca.

Approaching Hannah from behind, the arrogant young man knocked off her turban and grabbed a fistful of her hair. Violently jerking her around to face him, he poked his angry face into hers. "Wife, what are you doing here? You're coming home with me right now!" He made his demand through clenched teeth.

Hannah trembled in fright as tears welled in her eyes. Defiant and more confident, she stared him in the eyes, and firmly declared, "No, I'm not going with you!"

Rebecca tightly grasped one of Hannah's arms to pull her away from the disgruntled man, but he still held her by the hair.

"Jude, quit pulling my hair," Hannah screamed out in pain. "You're hurting me."

Saphah noticed firewood in the next stall, so she quickly grabbed a stick of the wood. In stealth mode, she approached Jude from behind, but he didn't notice her in his fit of rage at his wife. In one fell swoop, Saphah brandished her weapon like a baseball bat and whacked the bully with full force squarely on his back.

Losing his grip, Jude fell to the ground with an irreverent oath.

"Run, girls!" Saphah exclaimed, throwing down her stick of firewood and running in the opposite direction from Hannah and Rebecca. Terrified, she kept running, only pausing for a second to see if Jude was in pursuit. She watched him doubled over in pain on the ground.

Jude rose from the ground, still cursing in anger and rubbing his sore back in pain. Then he spied Saphah and shouted furiously at her. "Hey you, woman, stop right now! You're going to be sorry when I get my hands on you!"

With her heart pounding a hole in her chest, Saphah turned a corner out of Jude's sight. She spied a group of people entering a building. She mingled with the crowd and shuffled along with them into a large room where strange music began to play. Sparsely-clothed women wearing foreign headdresses and bangles on their wrists and ankles began a vulgar dance on a platform. Men clad in bright Canaanite garb also danced in a vile and immoral manner on a different dais.

"What is this place? Who are the dancing men and women on the stages?" Saphah grilled a woman standing nearby.

"This is a Temple of Baal, the god of fertility and agriculture. It is a shrine where we worship him with our ritual acts of fertility which symbolize the union of heaven and earth that brings about blessings of rain and crops."

Saphah was repelled by the smell of her breath heavy with alcohol. The woman pointed toward an ugly statue of the false god Baal perched on a little stand in a concave area at one end of the room.

"The people dancing are temple prostitutes." The woman's voice slurred in her inebriated state. She left Saphah to join the drunken crowd swaying and chanting the name of their god to the beat of the music.

"Baal, Baal, Baal," came their repeated cry.

Suddenly, the chanting stopped, and the women dressed in sheer and scant garments descended from their platform. Dancing in a sultry manner, they reached out toward others in the throng. Likewise, the men prostitutes descended from their stage, dancing with vile bodily movements and initiating contact with the crowd.

Oh my, I remember what God's Word says about temple prostitutes, Saphah thought. *No Israelite man or woman is to become a shrine prostitute.*[1] [For by doing so, they] *prostitute themselves to other gods and worship them.*[2] *This is a wicked place and I've got to find a way to get out of here!* Saphah's legs began to shake, and her mouth became dry as she frantically searched the room for an escape route. *On my goodness, I think I might be trapped! What am I going to do?* Worming her way through the crowd, she saw a man and a woman prostitute walking toward her hand-in-hand. *Why are they walking toward me?* She was relieved when the man's eyes turned toward a door she hadn't spotted. *Maybe that's my way out. I didn't notice that door until now.* As she headed toward the doorway, a loud, male voice called out:

"Stop, woman!"

Saphah momentarily paused, looked back, and saw two men, dressed in priestly vests of foreign origin, following her. Instead of obeying the man's command, Saphah ran through the door. *Oh, no! Shaking with fear, her worst thoughts were confirmed. I'm only in a hallway. There are open doors everywhere. The couple must have gone through another doorway farther down. Hopefully, there's an exit at the end of the rooms.* Saphah sped down the hallway and passed the room where the half-naked couple engaged in frenzied copulation.

Saphah glanced sideways as she passed the room. *Ugh!* Saphah turned her head and put her hand to her mouth at the lewd sight. *Ugh! Did I just see an example of the ritual acts of fertility? Is that what the drunken woman meant?*

Near panic, Saphah frantically ran toward the last doorway, only to discover it was an opening to another cubicle, not an exit. Rattling the locked door across the hall, she discovered it wasn't an exit either. *There's nowhere else to go. There's only a blank wall.* Her entire body began to shake violently without control. Her knees weakened as if she were going to faint. Saphah didn't know what to do. She turned around and saw the two priests bearing down on her. One harshly shouted, "Stay right there, woman!"

"Lord, please help me," Saphah prayed in desperation. The gentle voice in her spirit instructed:

"Go forward."

"Oh Lord, I forgot you've given me a special power." Without more ado, but with great confidence, Saphah walked through the wall. On the other side, Saphah fell to her knees, lowered her head, and prayed a brief prayer of thanks. "Heavenly Father, thank you for helping me. I've been so afraid. Amen." Then the voice softly whispered:

"Why are you afraid?"

"I'm sorry, Lord, please forgive me and please help me in the future to trust you as I should," She felt guilty that she hadn't remembered the portion of the Psalm she'd quoted in her earlier prayer for Hannah: *The salvation of the righteous comes from the Lord, … He delivers them from the wicked and saves them, because they take refuge in him.*[3] Suddenly her spirit heard the softly spoken words:

"Surely, I am with you always.[4]*"*

"Stay with me always, Lord," Saphah earnestly whispered. But then she heard:

"To the end of the age.[5]*"*

"Lord, I love and thank you from the bottom of my heart." Saphah was deeply touched by the words of her Savior.

Calm once again, Saphah arose from the ground, looked around, and continued on her way. *Now, where am I, and where should I go? Shallum must be at one of the gates*, she reasoned. *So if I just keep walking, I'll eventually reach the Jerusalem Wall. I can keep following it until I find him greeting pilgrims at a gate.* Feeling confident she was doing the right thing, Saphah kept walking in a straight line at a fast gait, knowing she would eventually reach the wall.

"Saphah, stop," a deep, male voice called out. "Wait right there."

~

Have the false priests found me after all? Saphah wondered with a tinge of renewed fright. *But wait a minute. The priests don't know my name.* Stopping short in her tracks, Saphah heard the approaching steps of the person behind her.

15

THE WORD WAS GOD

Saphah heard the kind voice of the man now standing in front of her. "My dear friend, please raise your head and look at me."

Slowly, the weary Saphah raised her head and then smiled in sudden recognition of a face she knew. She was overjoyed. "Zephaniah, you don't know how happy I am to see you! You're a Godsend!"

"Saphah, my dear, why were you running just now?" Zephaniah asked in concern. "What has happened? Are you alright?"

"Yes, I'm alright."

"Good, but has someone been chasing you as you walk all alone in Jerusalem? Why aren't Hannah and Rebecca with you?" He stayed with his line of questioning as he placed one arm over her shoulder. "There …, there …," he said in a soothing voice as he looked at her quizzically. "Please tell me what happened."

"Hannah, Rebecca, and I've been through a dreadful ordeal." Saphah related the details of events leading up to that moment. "Now, I don't know where I am; I don't know the whereabouts of Hannah and Rebecca; and I don't know the location of Shallum, Huldah, or Ebed. But praise God, I've found you!" Saphah sighed with relief.

"Yes, I'm so glad we've crossed paths, and you're alright. But, do you think Hannah and Rebecca successfully escaped from Jude too?"

"Yes, I do, because the last time I saw Jude, he was shouting and swearing in hot pursuit of me."

"Thank Yahweh, the three of you have gotten away from Hannah's evil husband."

"Yes, thank God. Zephaniah, would you mind if I get the Jerusalem map from my writing case so you can show me our location." Saphah rummaged in her case. "I just need to get my bearings."

"Of course." Zephaniah waited as Saphah retrieved her map. The prophet pointed to the spot where they stood and traced with his finger toward an imposing building located quite some distance away. "King Josiah's palace is right there." He ended his trace with a tap of his finger on the drawing. "The school complex is even farther away, so what do you think about going to the palace first?"

"Zephaniah, I agree. Since the king's palace is closest, and Shallum might be there for a break or a meal, it might be best to go there first. Of course, we can keep a lookout for Hannah and Rebecca as we walk. I'm very concerned for their safety."

"Yes, if Shallum isn't at the palace, surely someone will know the gate he's working today." Zephaniah turned toward Saphah and extended his arm. "Dear, please take my hand now, because we don't want to get separated. I think you've probably escaped from Hannah's husband and the two false priests, but we might run into them again. So, let's play it safe."

"Thank you, Zephaniah." Saphah gratefully grasped his outreached hand.

"Saphah, when we reach the palace, I'll inquire about Shallum first, but then I'll ask permission for an audience with King Josiah. I know the king personally, so I'd like to inform him of the events of today. He needs to know the terrible way my niece Hannah was mistreated by Jude. But he also needs to learn of the Baal Temple where the false god is worshipped through vile and immoral acts."

"Are you telling me King Josiah is uninformed about the temples to other gods, the high places, and the other locations of false worship in your land?"

"Unfortunately, King Josiah is unfamiliar with much of the evil in our kingdom. He came to the throne when eight years old, so up to this time the young king has been sheltered from knowledge of what's occurring. Yet the chronicles of our sacred history tell us that even the temple itself became defiled by the disrespectful acts of various kings."

"Zephaniah, wait a minute. I think I remember reading something along those lines. Are you going to tell me about King Ahaz? If so, I'm going to get out my Bible to find the scripture so I can directly quote it later."

"Alright." Zephaniah paused while Saphah retrieved her bible and then continued: "King Ahaz was one of our apostate rulers, who did egregious things that were not right *in the eyes of the Lord,*[1] and *became even more unfaithful to the Lord.*"[2]

"I found it, and here is some of what it says about Ahaz:

> [He] *gathered together the furnishings from the temple of God and cut them in pieces. He shut the doors of the Lord's temple and set up altars at every street corner in Jerusalem. In every town in Judah, he built high places to burn sacrifices to other gods and aroused the anger of the Lord.*[3] *Ahaz and others turned their faces away from the Lord's dwelling place and turned their backs on him. They also shut the doors of the portico and put out the lamps. They did not burn incense or present any burnt offerings at the sanctuary to the God of Israel.*[4]

Sadly, during the time of Ahaz, there was grave neglect of worship of God in favor of worship of foreign gods."

"Then King Ahaz was succeeded by his son Hezekiah," Zephaniah added.

"Well, thank goodness for that!" Saphah was more familiar with the reign of the good King Hezekiah. "Zephaniah, could you wait a bit while I locate information about Hezekiah in my bible." She hurriedly skimmed over a longer section of material about the next king. "Alright, I'm ready now."

"As I was saying," Zephaniah smiled at Saphah and began again. "After the reign of evil King Ahaz, his son Hezekiah became king."

"Alright, briefly here is some of what scripture says about Hezekiah. He did what was right in the eyes of the Lord. In the first year of rule he opened the doors of the temple of the Lord. Then *he brought in the priests and the Levites, assembled them in the square on the east side and said: 'Listen to me, Levites! Consecrate yourselves now and consecrate the temple of the Lord, the God of your ancestors. Remove all defilement from the sanctuary. Our parents were unfaithful.'*"[5]

"But after Hezekiah's death, what do you think happened next?"

"Hmm …," Saphah's eyebrows contorted into a questioning look. "Did things take a turn for the worse again?" She let out a sigh and consulted her bible. "Oh my, I see material on that subject here where it notes that following Hezekiah's rule, Manasseh his son and Amon his grandson both had evil reigns and influenced their people to do wrong."

Saphah flipped some more pages. "And here it says that Judah returned *to the sins of their ancestors, who refused to listen to my words. They have followed other gods to serve them. … You, Judah, have as many gods as you have towns; and the altars you have set up to burn incense to that shameful god Baal are as many as the streets of Jerusalem.*"[6]

"Yes, I'm afraid that's true," Zephaniah acknowledged. "So, Judah was sealing its own fate by continually returning 'to the sins of their ancestors.' Thus, the Lord said, *'I will bring on them a disaster they cannot escape.'*"[7] Remember, Saphah, you saw for yourself that at least one of the temples 'to that shameful god Baal' are located inside Jerusalem. So, I think it is high time that King Josiah is made more aware of the apostate condition of our nation, don't you?"

"Yes, I do," Saphah solemnly agreed.

"He needs to know that many of Jerusalem's citizens worship one or more of the false gods of foreign countries, alongside Yahweh, who is the actual One True God. But, even worse, some of our people have completely abandoned worship of God Almighty. They prefer to exclusively worship foreign gods instead."

"Zephaniah, I understand what you mean." Saphah could see the similarity between Judah and America. "Many of the citizens of my own country believe that multiple religions are equally true or valid. But New Testament Scripture strongly refutes that belief: *For there is one God and one mediator between God and mankind, the man Christ Jesus, who gave himself as a ransom for all people.*[8] In addition, Jesus said: *I am the way and the truth and the life. No one comes to the Father except through me.*"[9]

"I see what you mean." Zephaniah understood what Saphah was telling him. "Jesus Christ is the only way to God, and the godly people of my age look forward toward his saving grace and those of your generation look backward in faith toward his atonement."

"Yes, Christians share Scripture's objective truth that salvation *is by the name of Jesus Christ of Nazareth,* [who was] *crucified but whom God raised from the dead,*[10] and that *salvation is found in no one else for there is no other name under heaven given to mankind by which we must be saved.*[11] *We also proclaim what all the prophets testify about him that everyone who believes in him receives forgiveness of sins through his name.*"[12]

"Saphah, I want to learn more about your Bible." Prophet Zephaniah was quite intrigued by this time.

"You want to learn more about God's Word, the Holy Bible. Well, I'd be honored to tell you more."

"Yes, please do."

"Well, the Bible is a compilation of 66 different books. They were written over the course of time by various authors, beginning with Moses and ending with John. These writers were called by God and inspired by the Holy Spirit to write for mankind the message of the Good News of Salvation through Jesus Christ. Through Jesus, God the Father did for humanity what we couldn't do for ourselves: He provided a way for us to gain a right relationship with him. This wonderful news was given to us through God's Word, the Holy Bible. Zephaniah, did you know your book is included in the Bible?"

"Really! I knew God wanted me to record on a scroll the prophetic words he gave me, but I didn't know those words would become a part of what you call the Holy Bible."

"Well, my Bible is a translation written in English, the predominant language of America, so would you like to see it?" Saphah asked. "In my world the Bible has been translated into almost every language from the biblical languages of Hebrew, Aramaic, and Greek."

"Definitely! I would love to see your Bible."

"Alright." Saphah handed her Bible to the Prophet. "This is God's Word in its completed form, the Holy Bible."

"Oh my." The prophet gently rubbed his hand over the leather cover and opened the book to the first page. "I've never seen anything like this before." He felt the smoothness of the pages and carefully turned a few. Zephaniah glanced at Saphah with his mouth open in amazement. "Saphah, my dear friend, would you please show me where my writing is located in this book?"

"By all means." Saphah turned pages to the place where most of the prophetic writings are located. "Zephaniah, here is your book as it appears in English in my Bible."

"Thank you so much for letting me see the placement of my book in God's Word. Now, would you please tell me more about Messiah?"

"Zephaniah, I would be delighted to tell you more about the Lord Jesus Christ. In fact, since you're familiar with Isaiah's writings, I'll refer to some of the prophecies God gave him about Messiah. Now, as I quote from Isaiah, listen and then tell me if you remember the following words: I*n love a throne will be established; in faithfulness a man will sit on it—one from the house of David—one who in judging seeks justice and speeds the cause of righteousness.*"[13]

"Yes, I do remember those words. I'd also noticed that more than once in Isaiah's prophetic writing God spoke of a descendant of David ruling over Israel and Judah in the future."

"The following verse is a promise of the Messiah," said Saphah. "We know that because the Lord has given us a sign to confirm that the word of Isaiah is a true promise of God by saying: *Therefore, the Lord himself will give you a sign: The virgin will conceive and give birth to a son, and will call him Immanuel* [God is with us].[14] Also, Jesus the Messiah is in view, in the following verses:

> *The people walking in darkness have seen a great light; ... For to us a child is born, to us a son is given, and the government will be on his shoulders. And he will be called Wonderful Counselor, Mighty God, Everlasting Father, Prince of Peace. Of the greatness of his government*

and peace there will be no end. He will reign on David's throne and over his kingdom, establishing and upholding it with justice and righteousness from that time on and forever. The zeal of the Lord Almighty will accomplish this.[15]

The great light to come would accompany the birth of a child, so a person reading the scripture would recall Isaiah's recent promise of God with us, Immanuel. So, Zephaniah, does all of this make more sense to you now?"

"Yes, it does. In the past when I thought about Isaiah's prophecies and even my own, I was confused. The message from God sounded almost too good to be true. I knew that the Wonderful Counselor was to be a descendant of Adam, yet he was also to be Mighty God and Everlasting Father. In addition, I also knew that Isaiah was clearly bringing good news, yet it was a mystery to me, and to others of my generation, how it would all come about and when it would happen. So, if I may ask, when in the future did it occur?"

"Well, the period before Christ's birth is called BC (before Christ), but the time after Christ's death and resurrection is called AD (after death). So, to give you reference points, in your ancient world you're living in the sixth century BC or before Christ, but in my modern world (when I'm there) I'm living in the twenty-first century AD or after Christ's death."

"Oh, I see. Please tell me more!"

"Alright, in the Book of Matthew," Saphah said as she turned to the book in her Bible, "the inspired author presents a genealogy of Jesus by beginning with its most important theological elements: *This is the genealogy of Jesus the Messiah, the son of David, the son of Abraham* …[16] and then he numbers the generations from Abraham to Jesus in verses 2-16 since he assumes first-century readers will understand his purpose, demonstrating Jesus is the Savior for all people everywhere."

"That's amazing! Jesus is the Savior for all people!"

"Yes, He is. Then after that there's more about Prophet Isaiah," Saphah continued. "In Matthew, the author tells of the conception and birth of Jesus, by referring to Isaiah 7 and setting forth that Jesus' birth is a fulfillment of prophecy: *The virgin will conceive and give birth to a son, and they will call him Immanuel, which means, 'God with us.'*[17] That verse is a powerful demonstration that Jesus is a fulfillment of God's prophetic actions and possesses a rightful place in God's promises to Abraham, and that he does, indeed, stand in the direct line of God's redemption."

"Hallelujah! It's so wonderful to hear what you're saying. How great it is to know that God came to be with all of us to offer salvation to people everywhere and in all times. So, as the people of my ancient time look forward in faith toward his saving activity, the people of your modern time look backward in faith toward it too. Praise God, praise God, praise God!" Zephaniah looked upward, raised his hands, and shook them rhythmically back and forth with each word of praise that came from his lips.

"Yes, glory to God in the highest!" Saphah exclaimed as she turned to the book of Luke in her Bible. "Listen to what an angel said to Mary the mother of Jesus: *Do not be afraid, Mary; you have found favor with God. You will conceive and give birth to a son, and you are to call him Jesus. He will be great and will be called the Son of the Most High. The Lord God will give him the throne of his father David and he will reign over Jacob's descendants forever; his kingdom will never end.* Then Mary asked the angel a question: *How will this be, … since I am a virgin?* So, the angel said to her: *The Holy Spirit will come on you, and the power of the Most High will overshadow you. So the holy one to be born will be called the Son of God.*[18]

Gabriel's announcement to Mary is significant, because Jesus will be the Messiah who will fulfill God's promise to King David that his family, of which Jesus would be a descendant, would be established forever."

"That's right!" Zephaniah knew about God's promise to King David that his family would be established forever more.

"And God announced to David that he was going to build a house for him: *Your house and your kingdom will endure forever before me, your throne will be established forever.*[19] In other words, David will have sons who will rule over Israel. But there will be one very special Son, Jesus Christ, through whom all the promises God made in scripture pertaining to the kingdom of God will be fulfilled. God's promises are fulfilled in his first coming and will be consummated in his return to earth at the end of time."

"Remarkable! That means that in Jesus all of David's hopes, and all of mankind's hopes as well, are fulfilled!"

"Yes, the New Testament centers on the identity of Jesus and how his presence manifests God the Father," Saphah said as she turned the pages of her Bible to the book of John. "Here we see that there are three great truths about Jesus, as we read that: *In the beginning was the Word, and the Word was with God, and the Word was God.*[20] Here, John draws the reader's attention to three important truths about Jesus."

"What does he mean when he says, 'In the beginning was the Word?'" Prophet Zephaniah asked.

"When he says, 'In the beginning was the Word,' he is pointing out the eternal nature of Jesus and his words echo those of Genesis, where Moses writes: *In the beginning God ….*"[21]

"Well then, what about the phrase, 'The Word was with God.' What does that mean?"

"By saying, 'the Word was with God,' he is pointing out that Christ was distinct from the Father and yet in union with him, which is the foundation of the doctrine of the Trinity, the belief that there is one God who exists in three distinct persons—Father, Son, and Spirit."

Zephaniah smiled broadly, "Saphah, I think I already know the answer to the last part."

"Yes, I bet you do." Saphah smiled back at the prophet. "When he states, 'the Word was God,' he is saying that Jesus is God in bodily form and he is completely God."

"Yes!" Prophet Zephaniah jumped up and down. "Yes! Jesus Christ is truly God!" Zephaniah clapped his hands and shouted with joy.

"Just think how the disciples must have felt when they first realized that Jesus Christ was truly God," Saphah rolled her eyes and shook her head. "I'm sure they were overjoyed too. They got to see him face to face, but someday you and I and all God's children will get to see him too! In the meantime we have the Holy Spirit to help and guide us. And we have access to the Father through prayer in Jesus' name."

"Wonderful! Don't stop. Tell me more."

"At one point, when Jesus was talking to one of his disciples, Philip, he said that anyone who has seen me has seen the Father. ...*The words I say to you I do not speak on my own authority. Rather it is the Father, living in me, who is doing his work.*[22] Jesus was reminding his disciple that only the Father could do the works that Jesus has done. Then Jesus explained that *whoever believes in me will do the works I have been doing and they will do even greater things than these.*[23] The word *greater* denotes the idea of greater in depth! So, what could be greater than raising the dead? The answer is clear: Preaching the gospel of eternal life that Jesus gives to those who believe!"

"Yes," said Prophet Zephaniah. "All the prophets foretold the good news of Jesus Christ which is to be proclaimed until he returns."

"That's right." Saphah turned again to the book of Luke, "Jesus even quoted Isaiah's message about the Messiah from a synagogue scroll: *The Spirit of the Lord is on me, because he has anointed me to proclaim good news to the poor. He has sent me to proclaim freedom for the prisoners and recovery of sight for the blind, to set the oppressed free, to proclaim the year of the Lord's favor.*[24] The Gospel Age is the time when salvation will be proclaimed throughout the earth."

"Yes, it is. But please remember, Saphah, the period of the gospel will soon come to an end for your world," Zephaniah explained with sadness in his voice. "Do you remember what I told you about the return of the Lord?"

"I do." Saphah turned in her Bible to the book of Zephaniah. "Yes, here's the part where you began talking about the Lord's return: *The great day of the Lord is near—near and coming quickly.*[25] In the dramatic, but lyrical passage which follows, the Lord inspired you to describe the destruction that will sweep the earth on that day: *That day will be a day of wrath, a day of distress and anguish, a day of trouble and ruin, a day of darkness and gloom, a day of clouds and blackness. ... I will bring distress on the people ... because they have sinned against the Lord. ... The whole earth will be consumed.*"[26]

"But did you see what God inspired me to say after His warning of future calamity because of sin?" Zephaniah asked.

"I sure did. He inspired you to warn about God's chastisement for sin which can be applied to peoples of all times and places:

> *Gather together, gather yourselves together, you shameful nation*[s], *before the decree takes effect and that day passes like windblown chaff, ... before the day of the Lord's wrath comes upon you. Seek the Lord, all*

you humble of the land, you who do what he commands. Seek righteousness, seek humility; perhaps you will be sheltered on the day of the Lord's anger."[27]

"People definitely need to remember that last part about seeking the Lord," Zephaniah pointed out. "Even when destruction looks imminent because of growing apostasy, there is still time to be sheltered from the storm if only people will humble themselves and repent."

"Zephaniah, you're a prophet in your ancient land, so you've been called to warn people of all periods and nations they need to repent. But I'm just a citizen of my modern world without a title, so what should someone like me do to let the people of my time know to repent?" Saphah was uncertain.

"Well, God called me to be a prophet," Zephaniah began. But then a trace of irritation entered his voice. "But, Saphah, have you already forgotten that the Lord called you to be a watchwoman?"

"No, I haven't forgotten," Saphah was defensive. "But I don't know how to tell people to repent. Who am I to tell them?"

"It's simple! Just as God called prophets of my ancient land, such as myself, to give warning of coming danger, the Lord also called contemporary watchpersons of your modern world, such as you, to give warning. The people of your land who haven't accepted God as Savior need to realize their need of him before the coming day of the Lord. As you write your books you are to quote from God's Word, the Holy Bible, to warn others of coming calamity. Remember, you aren't telling folks they need to repent of their sins, but God is the one, through the Holy Spirit, who is actually speaking to them through the scripture you quote."

"Oh, I understand now," Saphah answered. "The results from my writing will be from God doing his work, not from my own doings."

"That's right." Zephaniah nodded his head. "Now, don't forget what I said!"

"I won't." Saphah gave her solemn promise.

16

BE ON THE LOOKOUT FOR ADVERSITY

Saphah said, "Zephaniah, that reminds me, I need to tell you something significant. A short time before I came here to your ancient land, God spoke to me after prayer in a still small voice:

"Be on the lookout for adversity."

"I didn't know exactly what God was referring to," Saphah said. "So, I inquired of the Lord: 'Is something going to happen to me or my family? Or is something going to happen to my country or the world? Lord, what do you mean? What kind of adversity am I to look for?'"

"So, what do you think the Lord actually meant by telling you to 'Be on the lookout for adversity?'"

"I didn't know what to think in the beginning, but after I thought about it longer, I realized the Lord had spoken to me as a person responsible to be on the lookout for danger facing either the world in general or America in particular."

"In other words, God was speaking to you as a watchperson."

"Yes, I think so." Saphah became somber. "In regard to being on the lookout for adversity, I realized there could be three types my nation might face—from external, internal, or natural sources. So, I began looking for external dangers because I remembered what God had said earlier about what would happen after the Covid Pandemic. Here's what the Lord told me:

'Earlier the Lord gave me a word, *winnow,* an agricultural term for the processing of grain, used metaphorically in the Bible when God speaks of using a nation's foreign enemies to chastise them through war."

"So, did that help you to know you needed to begin your lookout for adversity starting with dangers facing America externally?"

"Yes, I had a sudden epiphany that I should read and listen to world news. And, that's when I noticed that autocratic leaders of two nations, Russia and China, were displaying war mongering tendencies. Then, in January, 2022, I found out China was building up militarily in Cuba and the Caribbean, and preparing to invade Taiwan in the future. In addition, I learned Russia was building up a force of over 100,000 troops to invade Ukraine. I also found out Russia has the capability to use cyber warfare on Ukraine, and experts think Russia might retaliate with cyberattacks against the U. S. too, if our leadership forcefully works against them through sanctions or other actions."

"How did all of this affect you?"

"The idea of America being faced with war was mind-boggling. I knew if cyber warfare occurred and the U. S. power grids went down, the ensuing chaos could be enough to win a war against us. Then I read that William Cohen, former U.S. Defense secretary, had said:

> 'The possibility of a terrorist attack on the nation's power grid—an assault that would cause coast-to-coast chaos—is a very real one. …It is possible and whether it is likely to happen soon remains to be seen. …It wouldn't even be necessary for terrorists to wreak havoc by way of an EMP attack in which a burst of electromagnetic radiation wipes out most of the nation's power. You can do it through cyberattacks …[that] are able to shut down our power grid.'[1]

He predicted that 'a major outage would cause large-scale economic damage and civil unrest throughout a country. …In a war situation, this could be enough to bring about defeat.'[2] A situation like that might even cause the U. S. to decline into a third world country."

"What was your reaction to what you were learning from your research?"

"I was shocked!" Saphah shook her head in dismay. "Since the Lord had informed me to 'Be on the lookout for adversity,' I wondered if war might be on the horizon for America. After that, the thought of eminent warfare somewhere in the world was always in the back of my mind. But I vacillated between thinking a war like that would be confined to Ukraine or Taiwan and harboring thoughts that if such a conflict occurred in one of those countries it might spread to Europe or even the United States."

Zephaniah frowned and shook his head too. "Saphah, I don't know anything about cyber warfare or its results except for what you just told me, but what you said definitely sounds like some kind of ominous warfare that could be used against your country!"

"I agree. It was ominous that Russia and China were revving up for war and even posing a future threat to America. But then, when the 2022 China Winter Olympics began, I learned Russia and China had formed an agreement of noninterference:

> 'China and Russia on the opening day of Winter Olympics declared a no limits partnership, backing each other over standoffs on Ukraine and Taiwan with promise to collaborate more against the west. … Beijing supported Russia's demand that Ukraine should not be admitted into NATO, as the Kremlin amassed 100,000 troops near its neighbor, while Moscow opposed any form of independence for Taiwan, as global powers jostle over their spheres of influence.'[3]

This was an agreement that if either country started a war, the other nation wouldn't interfere. Then in February, 2022, Russia began an unjustified war against Ukraine. So far, Russia and China's agreement has held up. China has refused to condemn the incursion as provided in their partnership agreement of noninterference."

"It is very dangerous for two autocratic nations to form partnership."

"It sure is! But that's not all," Saphah added. "Then, in March, 2022, I learned:

> 'There's lots of chatter suggesting that if China is going to move on Taiwan now would be the opportune time. … The Russian conflict plays into this because, of course, it's a big distraction for the United States. In October, 2022, President Biden pledged to defend Taiwan if China attacked. … [But], the conflict in Ukraine limits the resources the U. S. can dedicate to protecting Taiwan from China. If Russia and China are each fighting back-to-back in their own regions, that's going to overstretch American resources, give them inroads in their own regions, and I think heightens the risk of a conflict over something like Taiwan.'[4]

I also think there's a strong possibility China might want to attack us while our current president is in office."

"Oh my, I see what you mean."

"But guess what?" Saphah turned to Zephaniah with her eyebrows raised high in consternation.

"What?" The prophet asked in surprise.

"There's even more." Saphah shook her head at the thought. "First of all, in November, 2022, the news media reported that Chinese

President XI Jinping had told his military to 'devote all its energy to and carry out all its work for combat readiness.'[5] The article also informed: 'China has the world's second highest military spending after the U. S. and is trying to extend its reach by developing ballistic missiles, submarines and other technology. Xi has refused to renounce the use of force to unite Taiwan with the mainland. He is sending a message to the United States and Taiwan,'[6] Willy Lam, a senior fellow at Washington-based Jamestown Foundation noted."

"China definitely seems bent on conquest of Taiwan." Prophet Zephaniah could see the clear implications of the situation.

"Yes, and listen to this. In December, 2022, Russia's defense ministry said that 'Russia and China completed naval drills in the East China Sea, after a week of joint exercises like …practicing how to capture an enemy submarine with depth charges and firing artillery at a warship. … Once the leader in the global Communist hierarchy, Russia after the 1991 collapse of the Soviet Union is now a junior partner to a resurgent China which already leads in some 21st century technologies.'"[7]

"Those two seem to be in cahoots for sure."

"Yes, but now China is the main Communist leader, not Russia. General Mike Minihan, a four-star Air Force General thinks the same thing and he predicted in a memo 'that the U. S. will be at war with China by 2025 and advised his commanders to prepare.' Minihan believes 'war with China is imminent in the next two years due to the upcoming 2024 elections in the U. S. and Taiwan, which he claimed will distract Washington and Taipei and enable China to make a move on the Island.'"[8] A U. S. Congressman, Mike McCaul, agreed that 'The odds of conflict with China over Taiwan are very high,'[9] as did several additional persons of influence. But William Burns, CIA Director reported 'that Chinese President Xi Jinping has ordered his military to be ready for action no later than 2027.'"[10]

"I just hope the action doesn't involve your country." said Zephaniah.

"Me too."

"I hate to have to tell you this, but from everything you've said has happened, and if nothing changes to alter the situation, I'm afraid your country may be in for conflict with China." Zephaniah threw his arm over Saphah's shoulder and gave her a side hug.

"That's scary!" Saphah clasped her hands together at her chest and rhythmically shook her head in fear. "But I also need to tell you something else. A suspected high-altitude Chinese spy balloon was first seen above Montana, one of our 50 states, on February 1, 2023. 'China claimed that the airship is a civilian research craft that was blown off course by prevailing winds, and that it regrets the incident.'[11] However, listen to the following:

> 'The Pentagon said that it acted immediately to protect against the collection of sensitive information from the balloon. But geopolitical experts said there is little reason to believe those efforts were successful, as the balloon almost certainly transferred surveillance data over to China as it flew over several military bases. Brandon Weichert, author of *Winning Space*, said he 'believes China successfully gathered U. S. military and technological information through its spy balloon.'[12]

Furthermore, Gordon Chang, a senior fellow at Gatestone Institute, said 'it is all but confirmed China's mission was successful.'[13] The Pentagon waited to destroy the balloon until it had traversed the entire country and was hovering over the Atlantic Ocean."

"Saphah, did the balloon travel over your state?"

"It sure did! I live in Missouri, a state in the heartland of America, and the China spy balloon traveled over our air force base. Here is what Eric Schmitt, a Missouri senator, observed as the Chinese balloon was getting close to Whiteman Air force Base, where the B-2 strategic stealth bombers are stationed. Schmitt tweeted that the Chinese 'spy balloon' is 'right now' heading for Whiteman Base, 'home of the stealth bombers,' which is 'absolutely unbelievable.'[14] Whiteman, a key military air base where the U. S. 8th Air Force's 509th Bomber Wing is located, is the sole unit equipped with B-2 Spirit strategic bombers. I'm telling you, Zephaniah, it broke my heart that American leadership allowed the China Spy Balloon to transgress the airspace of this base, and other air force bases across America."

"Why did your government allow this to happen?"

"It is beyond my comprehension." Saphah abjectly shook her head. "About all I can say is it was a dereliction of duty that the balloon wasn't shot down over the Pacific Ocean before reaching the U. S."

"Do you think the purpose of the Chinese was mainly to use the balloon to spy?"

"Maybe their intent was to spy or perhaps it was to check out how our leadership would react. But possibly it was meant to be a dry run."

"What kind of dry run could it be."

"Here is what retired Air Force Major David Stuckenberg, a leading expert of electromagnetic pulse (EMP) devices, who previously led the Defense Department's EMP Task Force, said, 'It was most likely a type of dry run meant to send a strategic message to the USA. We must not take this for granted.'"[15]

"What kind of message is he talking about?"

Major Stuckenberg reported: "China's recent balloon flyover of the United States is clearly a provocative and aggressive act. … The high-altitude Chinese surveillance balloon that is traveling across the U. S. could be a dry run to deliver a nuclear device that would wipe out America's power grid."[16]

"It definitely looks like your country might be facing a threat from China to take down America's power source."

"Yes, it does. But we face additional dangers if China or Russia takes aggressive actions against the U. S. Others might join the fracas, such as North Korea or various Middle East nations. In fact, in February 2023, 'North Korea fired a Hwasong-15 intercontinental ballistic (ICBM) in a sudden launching drill.'[17] And, on another front, 'In the aftermath of [America's] troubled withdrawal from Afghanistan, new concerns over terror groups rebuilding have mounted within U. S. intelligence communities. … [Florida] Representative Mike Waltz expressed his concern about the simmering powder-keg in the Middle East.'[18] Additionally, a new report is out that 'Iranian Uranium enrichment [is] dangerously close to nuclear bomb capability.'"[19]

"Well, it certainly looks like there is no lack of evil authoritarian leaders who might want to invoke war against your country."

"You're right. God's command to me to be on the lookout for adversity certainly fits my calling as a watchwoman looking for signs of danger to my country and world. External threats of adversity from world leaders are abundant. But, as I said before, internal threats of adversity are numerous too."

"Saphah, please inform me about what's happening in your country internally."

"I'd be glad to, because right now, my modern world is spiraling out of control. What is good is called evil, and what is evil is called good. But scripture proclaims: *Woe to those who call evil good and good evil, who put darkness for light and light for darkness.*[20] Yet, calling 'evil good and good evil' seems to summarize the moral condition of many people in my land and even of some who claim to belong to the church. An increasing number of people are failing to follow God's transcendent moral precepts."

"What do you think is causing this?"

"Presently, there's an internal spiritual battle going on in our land for the very heart and soul of our nation. It is dominated by a faction whose minds are blinded. The bible says that *the god of this age* [Satan] *has blinded the minds of unbelievers, so that they cannot see the light of the gospel that displays the glory of Christ, who is the image of God.*[21] Here the Word of God says that the devil, the god of this age, is the unseen power behind all unbelief and ungodliness. His followers have in effect made him their god. Hence, the insanity of the notions of this group makes it difficult to characterize their movement. Yet the Bible speaks of this very condition in the New Testament. I'll need to go over the first chapter of Romans to explain what's currently happening, but I'll try to be as brief and I can."

"Of course, please continue."

Saphah grabbed her bible and began to read:

> *The wrath of God is being revealed from heaven against all the godlessness and wickedness of people who suppress the truth by their wickedness, since what may be known about God is plain to them, because God has made it plain to them. For since the creation of the world God's invisible qualities—his eternal power and divine nature—have been clearly seen, being understood from what has been made, so that people are without excuse.*[22]

"Who wrote that?" Zephaniah asked. "What the author said is very true. No one, in any age, has an excuse for not honoring God, because the entire creation reveals him. Our Creator has every right to be angered by the behavior of His creatures. That is essentially what wrath really is: Divine anger! When unrighteous people are hostile to the truth of God and 'suppress the truth by their wickedness,' it greatly upsets our Creator. People don't realize that it is a serious thing for them to deviate from God's holy standards, but it is even more serious for them to seek to hold back God's truth."

"We have the Apostle Paul to thank for writing much of the New Testament, including Romans," said Saphah. "And I agree with you about what Paul said. The tendency he spoke of is on display in the day and age in which I live. Many people reject God's holiness in their own experience because they can scarcely allow themselves to face God's truth. Therefore, they seek to suppress the truth in their own consciousness and in the consciousness of others. Hence, they call 'evil good and good evil.'"

"I don't know who these individuals are." Zephaniah frowned at what he was about to say. "But if they're deniers of God and his law, they're without excuse. God's eternal power and divine nature are clearly displayed by the beauty and wonder of nature. If they claim ignorance, it is both willful ignorance and suppression of the truth."

"That's right." Saphah noted. "Even the simplest of persons is able to consider creation in such a way as to draw the conclusion that it was made by Someone who displays eternal power and whose essence is of a higher order than anything in the universe."

Zephaniah said. "Well, the gospel your bible presents is itself a divine revelation. Of course, it's not a revelation deducible from the natural world. But if deniers were willing to recognize the manifestation of God which creation gives them, they'd be in a position to search out the will of God from His Word, which is readily available at this time in your world. However, as long as they suppress the true witness of nature, they're unable to make progress in the area of discovering God's will for themselves. Instead of searching out truth from the Bible, those who turn away from God deny his existence. They do not want to acknowledge accountability for unrighteous behavior."

"So true! Here is the way Paul explained it:

> *For although they knew God, they neither glorified Him as God, nor gave thanks to him, but their thinking became futile and their foolish hearts were darkened. Although they claimed to be wise, they became fools and exchanged the glory of the immortal God for images made to look like a mortal human being and birds and animals and reptiles.*[23]

Something similar to this darkening process has repeated itself in my modern world. As the universe is studied more and the evidence for the Creator mounts, still some in the scientific community claim that there is no basis for belief in divine creation by a supreme being. Therefore, even in my advanced world, such people, although 'they claimed to be wise,' in reality 'they became fools.'"

"When people fail to glorify God and to thank Him for what He has done, they practice idolatry in their own hearts toward themselves," Zephaniah rightly pointed out.

"Yes, I hadn't thought about it that way, but that's true. In Paul's day, this folly to which the image of God was degraded happened when men created idols made in the likeness of mortal man, of birds, of animals, and of reptiles:

> *Therefore, God gave them over in the sinful desires of their hearts to sexual impurity for the degrading of their bodies with one another. They exchanged the truth about God for a lie, and worshipped and served created things rather than the Creator—who is forever praised.*

> *Amen. Because of this, God gave them over to shameful lusts. Even their women exchanged natural sexual relations for unnatural ones. … [and] men committed shameful acts with other men and received in themselves the due penalty for their error.*[24]

This idolatry led to an awful consequence: God gave them over to their own iniquity."

"Yes, in wrongly directed worship toward created things, rather than toward the Creator, the creature becomes the focus of everything, the idol."

"But that wasn't all God did: *Furthermore, just as they did not think it worthwhile to retain the knowledge of God, so God gave them over to a depraved mind, so that they do what ought not to be done.*[25] Once again, 'God gave them over' to something. Since they did not retain the knowledge of God, He gave them over to a 'depraved mind.' Gay sin cannot be comfortably engaged in when the human mind is thinking about God. A person's common sense makes clear that male and female are suited for sexual union, but deviant sexual activity requires ignoring the very structure of nature and creation."

"Yes," Zephaniah noted, "God 'gave them over' to a 'depraved mind,' because they refused to retain the knowledge of Him in their hearts and minds."

"Yes, they themselves were the cause of God giving them over. If, instead, they would just hold God in their minds, plus accept and honor Him in their hearts, they'd be able to overcome temptation: *God is faithful, who will not suffer you to be tempted above that ye are able; but will with the temptation also make a way to escape, that ye may be able to bear it.*[26] If they would only allow Him, the Lord of the Universe would help them because He is faithful."

"Yes, God loves fallen mankind, so He is faithful in all temptations!"

"He sure is! But the actual purpose of this discourse is to reach the next section of Romans 1 where it shows that the refusal to keep God before the mind is not limited to this type of sinner. Human beings in general are prone to do away with the idea of God. Some go to great lengths to deny, distort, or explain away His existence because the thought of accountability is painful. But when they banish God from their mind, God simply allows them to possess the natural result: a depraved and defected mentality. They possess a mind that lacks acuity, so they do what 'ought not to be done,' as noted in the following long list:

> *They have become people filled with every kind of wickedness, evil, greed, and depravity. They are full of envy, murder, deceit, and malice. They are gossips, slanderers, God-haters, insolent, arrogant and boastful; they invent ways of doing evil; they disobey parents; they have no understanding, no fidelity, no love, no mercy.*[27]

This description of mankind's moral state certainly lays out the broadness of God's displeasure with sin."

"That's right. The writer wasn't describing unique cases of depravity, but the universal condition of mankind."

"Yes, and later, the author will note that 'there is no one righteous, not even one.'[28] The entirety of unsaved humanity is under judgment for sin unless they repent and turn to their Maker for salvation. The very nature of the unrepentant loudly proclaims why 'the wrath of God is revealed from heaven against all the godlessness and wickedness of people who suppress the truth by their wickedness,' as I read in the beginning."

"So, is the terrible state of affairs you talked about becoming worse in America?" Zephaniah wondered if Saphah's nation America was becoming apostate just like his own nation Judah.

"Yes, the normalization of LGBT behavior has become apparent. For instance, recently, in some libraries in mainly larger American cities, drag queens have been allowed to do readings for children in their facilities, but readings by authors of Christian books for kids are disallowed. Here is what happened to Christian book author Kirk Cameron: 'I wanted to have a book reading at a public library, and over 50 Woke libraries denied my book. At the same time, they're hosting drag-queen story hours. … Those same institutions, …[also] allow reading events for LGBT friendly books.'"[29]

"When libraries disallow Christian material from being read to children at their facilities, they are 'suppressing the truth' by their actions." Zephaniah let out a sigh of sadness for the little ones. "But, I also think it is pure wickedness for some of them to be promoting drag-queen story hours for, of all people, innocent children."

"I agree. It is enough to make any parent or grandparent enraged! But there are other evil things occurring against little kids in my land."

"I almost dread to hear it." Zephaniah sighed again. "What are they doing?"

"Anti-religious bigotry is starting to rear its ugly head in some places. Here's an example:

> 'A …lawmaker in Nebraska is being accused of anti-religious bigotry … after she proposed to ban children from attending church youth groups or vacation bible schools. [The] State Senator says her amendment, which would ban children under 19 years of age from attending a religious indoctrination camp [i.e. church youth groups or vacation bible schools] is intended to kill the underlying bill, LB 371, a measure put forward to ban minors from attending drag performances. It is a tongue-in-cheek response to those who have said children should not be exposed to explicit sexual

content at drag shows. [The Senator] said that this is an amendment that I will use to make a point. This amendment obviously won't pass. … It's a device to make a point'[30]

"Prophet Zephaniah, isn't that astounding?"

"It's beyond astounding!" Zephaniah pressed the palm of his hand against his forehead. "This woman's 'tongue-in-cheek' remark reveals her anti-Christian bias. In addition, she is promoting 'evil as good' and 'good as evil.' To me this is an example of the waywardness of these people."

"Yes, it is, but here is another example of their insanity. The headline reads: 'The FBI has found a gateway to declare Christians as criminals: Federal whistleblower.'[31] Evidently, the corrupt FBI wants to blame riots in our country and so forth on Christians by declaring them as criminals."

"Who is the FBI, anyway, to call these Christians criminals?" Zephaniah was perplexed.

"They're the Federal Bureau of Investigation, an arm of our federal government, and what they are planning to do is an infringement of religious freedom. A federal whistleblower and former FBI agent noted:

> 'An internal document from the bureau's Richmond field office allegedly vowed to spy on radical traditionalist Catholics [those who worship using the Latin Mass] and their ideology. …[But some Catholic young people attend] traditional [Catholic] school where [they] actually learn Latin in fifth and sixth grade and all the way through high school, [so] it doesn't seem reasonable. … [But the FBI thinks] they have found a gateway in what they consider fringe Catholicism in order to move into Christians in general and

declare them to be the actual criminals in this country or the potential terrorists.'"[32]

"But why is the FBI so intent on targeting Catholic Christians?"

"The document is opposed to more than traditional Catholicism:

> 'The document … was written by someone who believes abortion rights must be upheld and the LGBTQ agenda has to be pushed down the American people's throats. …It is the state of the FBI at this point that they are so desperate to find White Supremacists that they're going to look at the Catholic Church. …[The whistleblower] stated the very simple statement that if they're going to go after radical traditional Catholics, then radical traditional Baptists are next and radical evangelicalism and anyone else that espouses essentially what [they consider] radical, which is just [the entire traditional] Christian faith.'[33]

Isn't it amazing that this wicked movement has even infiltrated the FBI, a federal department in my nation."

"I think this goes to show that evil people are in control of your country, and they're attacking the foundations of your freedoms, including religious rights. That is very dangerous!"

"Zephaniah, it certainly is, but what is so sad is that the movement has even slipped into some of our school systems in larger cities, where they're indoctrinating our little children in their evil ideology. It's everywhere. It affects many large corporations, most news media, part of politics, some entertainment, segments of government, elite universities, the military, the medical field, and even some churches and religious organization. You name it and this evil movement has probably slipped its tentacles into some part of it. It has caused an increase in lawlessness, corruption, civil unrest, division, crime, and all forms of unrighteousness as listed in Romans 1:29. In addition, in many major metropolitan areas people are stealing, looting, rioting, and burning without any punishment."

"Saphah, I see what you mean! Your nation is suffering from the effects of a wicked internal attack. It is the work of the evil one and the blinded who follow him."

"Therefore, I'm wondering what the implications might be of this worsening adversity. All these forms of adversity—external, internal, and also natural adversity—such as earthquakes, hurricanes, drought, and so forth, are getting worse and worse in my land and evidently in your time and place too. For instance, in my modern world an extremely bad earthquake recently occurred. An AFP news headline on February 13, 2023 read: 'Turkey-Syria Quake Deaths to top 50,000 …The United Nations [Relief Chief] has warned that at least 870,000 people urgently need hot meals across Turkey and Syria. Up to 5.3 million people may have been made homeless in Syria alone.'[34] Zephaniah, why do you think internal, external, and natural sources of adversity are becoming more rampant?"

"Well, do you remember your first two scriptural quotes when you began talking about the internal spiritual battle going on in your land?"

"Yes, first of all I quoted what scripture says about 'the god of this age [Satan].' He has 'blinded the minds of unbelievers, so they cannot see the light of the gospel that displays the glory of God.' Hence, their unbelief, ungodliness, and distorted thinking verge on insanity. Then, I quoted the part that says 'the wrath of God is being revealed from heaven against all the godlessness and wickedness of people who suppress the truth by their wickedness.'"

"Does that give you any idea of how you should interpret all the lunacy and mayhem going on in your world?" Zephaniah asked.

Saphah thought about it for a few minutes. "Come to think about it, it does. Those who are blinded because they do not acknowledge God are the godless and wicked ones who suppress the truth by their evil doings. Therefore, 'the wrath of God is being revealed from heaven' more and more frequently because our Creator God is angry at these rebellious people."

"Then, do you remember quoting the long list of the unseemly things ungodly people do?"

"When human beings do not see fit to retain God in their knowledge, their character and behavior reflect an abundance of all kinds of 'unrighteousness, immorality, greed, and malice,' along with all the other listed evil deeds."

"So, what does all that cause?" Zephaniah asked.

"It causes a display of God's anger in all generations toward the behavior of mankind. Therefore, I need to share with people soon about how they can be delivered from God's anger. Is that right, Zephaniah?"

"You're right. As said before, all men are subject to God's anger as a result of their sinful behavior."

"True. But He is *the Lamb of God, who takes away the sin of the world!*[35] If we return to Him and receive Him as Savior, we not only receive God's approval but also gain access to Him from whom we were formerly estranged. This gives us great inner strength, for we are righteous by faith in Him and not by good works. And *since we have now been justified by his blood, how much more shall we be saved from God's wrath through Him! For if, while we were God's enemies, we were reconciled to him through the death of his Son, how much more, having been reconciled, shall we be saved through his life!*[42] This causes us to *joy in God through our Lord Jesus Christ, by whom we have received the atonement.*"[37]

"What a wonderful truth."

"Yes. But I'm very concerned about the times in which I live, so I'd like to learn more about the implications of everything we talked about."

"Good idea." Zephaniah replied. "So, let's talk about the adversity and apostasy happening in both your land and mine so we can compare. I think you'll see that our ancient and modern worlds aren't that different. Then we can talk about the implications of it all."

"Zephaniah and Saphah, wait up," shouted a young male voice. "I need to talk to you."

"Ebed, where are you going?" Zephaniah asked.

"King Josiah sent a runner to the Jerusalem School to let Huldah and me know that Hannah was accosted by Jude. I'm running to the palace to find out more." Ebed panted as he stood bent over with his hands on his knees. "He also said Rebecca and Hannah are safe at the palace, but they're worried about you, Saphah. I'm sure glad I've run into both of you here."

"That's where we're going too," said Saphah. "Are you sure the girls are alright?"

"Yes, they're alright." Ebed said, "But the runner said Jude really roughed up Hannah. Frankly, I'm really angry, because she's such a nice girl who loves the Lord, and she's just so beautiful with her wavy hair and tawny skin. But that husband of hers is a scoundrel!"

"When we get to the palace, I'm planning to ask for an audience with the king to tell him about these events." Zephaniah briefed Ebed. "Although Hannah can't get a divorce from Jude on her own, King Josiah could grant her one. Ebed, do you want to see the king too?"

"I sure do. I want to do everything I can to help Hannah. And, if she does get a divorce, Zephaniah, I'd like to ask for her hand in marriage. That is, if Hannah will have me."

Saphah glanced at Zephaniah who was smiling in wide-eyed surprise at Ebed. "Young man, you certainly have my permission to marry my niece. But you'll also need to talk to Shallum, Huldah, and your own parents. Let's talk to King Josiah first to find out if he'll grant Hannah a divorce. Then you can consider marriage."

"Yes, you're right." Ebed nodded in agreement. "It's just I realized Hannah was a special woman from the beginning."

"Ebed." Saphah gave the young man a big smile. "I do know this. When you and Huldah left for school this morning, Hannah told Rebecca she was lucky to have a brother who is both handsome and polite. So, I think she already likes you, but just keep that to yourself."

"Really, she cares for me too!" Ebed joyfully smiled and ran one hand through his curly hair. "Thanks for telling me."

"Yes, Ebed, I think Hannah cares for you. But I'm really worn out now, so why don't you go on ahead of us to let the ladies know I'm alright? Then, Zephaniah and I can rest here on one of the stone benches and finish an important conversation."

"Oh, I'd be glad to. I'm anxious to check on Becca and Hannah. But, especially, Hannah." He winked at Saphah and ran off to the palace.

"Look at him run." Saphah smiled as she observed Ebed kick up both heels to one side and click them together, but then kick them up and click them together again as he ran. "I think we're seeing a case of budding love in the air."

Zephaniah chuckled and nodded in agreement.

17

BEGINNING OF BIRTH PAINS

Zephaniah was ready to resume the conversation. Now, let's get back to our conversation about the similarities of the moral decline in ancient Judah and modern America. But where should we sit to talk?"

"See that bench over there under a tree?" Saphah pointed toward an open bench. "Let's go over there and sit in the shade."

"Sounds good." Zephaniah sighed as he sat down on the bench and crossed one leg over the other. "To tell you the truth, I'm tired myself. Should I begin or would you like to start?"

"I'd like to start with a question," said Saphah. "How did it happen that a Baal temple is located right here in Jerusalem in the 6th century BC? In the past I'd noticed in scripture that some people of Judah possessed little idols which they worshiped in addition to Yahweh. Also, I'd read high places existed where they venerated false gods. But I'd never realized the extent of the apostacy in this land, that is, not until I observed some of it here firsthand for myself."

"Saphah, to answer your question about the apostasy in Israel, Judah, and Jerusalem, I'll probably need to briefly explain some history of our land so you can understand what occurred."

"Yes, please tell me the details of what happened to cause the decline in Judah and Israel. Because, as you can see, my modern world is headed toward a similar fall from grace."

"Alright, but you need to know that our nation's deterioration actually began long ago. It originated with Moses and his message to the people of Israel as they entered the promised land after their sojourn in Egypt. Through Moses, God reminded the Israelites: *You have now become the people of the Lord your God."*[1]

Saphah interrupted "I need to break in with another question. Even though it's true the Israelites became the people of God on that day, isn't it true that Christians are God's people too? The New Testament says that Christians are children of God because salvation is by faith, not by law/works:

> *So also Abraham believed God, and it was credited to him as righteousness. Understand, then, that those who have faith are children of Abraham. Scripture foresaw that God would justify the Gentiles by faith, and announced the gospel in advance to Abraham: All nations will be blessed through you. …So in Christ Jesus you are all children of God through faith, …If you belong to Christ, then you are Abraham's seed, and heirs according to the promise.*[2]

William Hendrickson, author of *More Than Conquerors*, summarized that fact beautifully, and noted the scriptures he used as well, when he said:

> 'Scripture emphasizes the fact that the church in both dispensations is one. It is one chosen people in Christ. It is one tent; one vineyard; one family—Abraham is the father of all believers whether they are circumcised or not—one olive tree; one elect race, royal priesthood, holy nation, people for God's own possession; one beautiful bride; and in its consummation one new Jerusalem whose gates bear the names of the twelve tribes and whose foundations are inscribed with the names of the twelve apostles.'[3]

I think Hendrickson gave a convincing summary that all believers are one chosen people, don't you?"

"Yes, he did. Likewise, it seems to me that the Bible teaches that all believers are children of God. This leads to the conclusion that God promised all his children *blessings*[4] for obedience to him; however, he warned of *chastisement*[5] for disobedience. But these judgments on nations such as from *war*,[6] from *plague*,[7] and from *dispersion*[8] had just one goal—to turn the straying nation from disobedience. I think it would be proper for us to keep that fact in mind as we continue to talk about both my nation and your nation's descent into apostasy."

"As do I," Saphah agreed. "As the Bible tells us, the Lord *does not willingly bring affliction or grief to anyone.*[9] Rather, the Lord is pleased when people turn from their evil ways. That is why God says: *Turn from* [your] *ways and live. …Repent! …Then sin will not be your downfall. Rid yourselves of all the offenses you have committed, and get a new heart and a new spirit. …For I take no pleasure in the death of anyone. …Repent and live!*"[10]

"Correct, God doesn't want to bring adversity upon people. But unfortunately, ancient Israel and Judah tipped the faithfulness to God scale to the disobedience rather than the obedience side, and chastisement followed. Psalm 106 is a history of Israel's descent into apostasy. It tells us that in Israel's history, the blessings and judgments followed a pattern. First, the psalmist recalls the Red Sea experience, when the Israelites in their panic didn't believe God and wanted to turn back. But God miraculously led them through the sea and drowned the Egyptian army. In response they believed God and praised Him, but then they quickly forgot what He had done."[11]

"Isn't that sad." Saphah looked downcast. "People in my modern era, including myself, act the same way at times. I continually need to ask God to forgive me and help me do better."

"I'm always praying for God's forgiveness and help too," Zephaniah confessed his own need for forgiveness. "Then, Psalm 106 informs us the attitude of the Israelites went from bad to worse as they went into the wilderness. They tested God and questioned the leadership of Moses. They also had Aaron create a golden calf for worship. Thus, God said that he would destroy them, had not Moses stood before him in the gap to turn away His wrath. They yoked themselves to Baal and other lifeless gods so that the Lord's anger was aroused. Then a plague broke out, but Phinehas intervened and the plague was checked. But when they got to the promised land, even though God had promised them the land, they lacked the faith to enter in."[12]

"Again, that just goes to show that although God rescued his people over and over after such episodes, they always forgot what He had done." Saphah lamented that imperfect mankind in every generation continually forgets what the Lord has done for them.

"We're all guilty of that sometimes. Psalm 106 says that when the people entered the promised land, they became like the other nations. Saphah, please read that part from your bible."

"Yes, here is what it says:

> *They mingled with the nations and adopted their customs. They worshiped their idols, which became a snare to them. They sacrificed their sons and their daughters to false gods. They shed innocent blood, the blood of their sons and daughters, whom they sacrificed to the idols of Canaan, and the land was desecrated by their blood. They defiled themselves by what they did; by their deeds they prostituted themselves.*[13]

And in response to their sin, God allowed Israel to be overpowered time after time:

> *Therefore the Lord was angry with his people and abhorred his inheritance. He gave them into the hands of the nations, and their foes ruled over them. Their enemies oppressed them, and subjected them to their power. Many times he delivered them, but they were bent on rebellion and they wasted away in their sin. Yet he took note of their distress when he heard their cry; for their sake he remembered his*

covenant and out of his great love he relented. He caused all who kept them captive to show them mercy.[14]

So, during this early period when Israel's leaders were judges, there existed a constantly revolving change in the nation's loyalty."

"Yes, they'd serve God for a time, but then backslide and face hostilities again. Each time the Lord would raise up a deliverer, but then the cycle would repeat again."

"Throughout my own nation's history until recently, we've generally been a God-fearing nation. In fact, up until what we call 9/11, the date in 2001 when our country was first attacked on our own soil, God always delivered us from evil. But now, moral conditions in my land have deteriorated. Many people seem to have forgotten God. Sorry for the diversion, Zephaniah."

"I'm glad you spoke up. We need to frequently compare our two lands." Zephaniah continued his discourse. "When the days of the judges ended, God gave kings such as Saul and David and Solomon as national leaders of Israel. Nevertheless, the same cycle continued, with good kings who followed the Lord and bad kings who led the people astray. Later, when the nation split into the Northern Kingdom (Israel) and the Southern Kingdom (Judah), the pattern continued. After the split, Israel was afflicted with one wicked ruler after another, with no respite. Therefore, the Northern Kingdom was eventually destroyed by Assyria, the people were exiled, and other surrounding peoples were brought in to inhabit the land."

"My country is already split in their thinking," Saphah noted. "The citizens of rural and middle America generally see things one way, and the citizens on both coasts and near the Great Lakes in many big cities usually see things another. Do you think there's a possibility my own nation might split?"

"I don't know." Zephaniah was uncertain. "I really need more information. After I finish telling you about Israel and Judah's descent into apostasy, I'm looking forward to hearing more about America's apparent decline."

"Alright," Saphah answered. "Now go on with what you were telling me about Judah."

Zephaniah related more historical facts. "In Judah, however, some kings followed the Lord and brought reform. As mentioned earlier, Hezekiah was a good king who moved Judah back toward God. He abolished idolatry and pointed people to temple services."

"What was the next king like?"

"Judah's golden days ended when Manasseh, Hezekiah's son, became king. All Hezekiah's reforms were undone by his son as the nation reverted to its Canaanite roots. The Judahites worshipped Baal, sacrificed their children to Molech, and built idolatrous places for their worship. What does your bible say, Saphah?"

"It says Manasseh's dark reign *led Judah and the people of Jerusalem astray, so that they did more evil than the nations the Lord had destroyed before the Israelites. The Lord spoke to Manasseh and his people, but they paid no attention.*[15] I can definitely see that both your country and mine have the problem of good and bad leaders. In our nation one president will bring about good, but then another president will come into office and undo all the good the previous president had done."

"After Manasseh died, *Amon his son succeeded him as king.*[16] He did *evil in the eyes of the Lord, as his father Manasseh had done. Amon worshiped and offered sacrifices to all the idols Manasseh had made.*[17] But then, …" Zephaniah's tone changed as he cheerfully spoke up, "a son was born to Amon who became our present king. King Josiah told me he began to seek the Lord in his teens and he wants to obey the Lord. It is my hope that God will use him to bring about reform in this land. So that's where Judah is at this point. Now, let's get back to our conversation about the problems facing America."

"The U. S. is declining fast," Saphah continued her report on her nation's downfall. "The changes in my country over the course of my lifetime are amazing. Just a short time ago, a Christian who publicly supported the right to life, backed laws protecting God's view of marriage, and spoke freely of Christ's love for fallen humanity was universally recognized as an upstanding person. But things have changed. In today's world there are people who try to destroy an outspoken man or woman such as this. God-fearing people are often vilified and harassed for being loyal to God's values."

"Do you think the present circumstances in your country and world are similar to happenings in Jerusalem and Judah in my own time?" asked Zephaniah.

"Yes, I do!" Saphah emphasized. "In America we are struggling through a downward stage right now, with all that entails, just as Judah did under leaders such as Manasseh and Amon. But then good King Josiah arrived on the scene in your land just in the nick of time."

"I agree. If Josiah hadn't arrived when he did, I think Judah would already be in big trouble." Zephaniah declared.

"In America we elect a new president every four years," Saphah pointed out. "Yet we're in fast moral decline under present leadership, and it's obvious our nation needs a 'Josiah figure' soon. We need a strong and upright leader who'll guide our country back toward God like Hezekiah and Josiah. But it is up to our citizens to vote for moral leaders who uphold the Christian values that've made the U. S. great. If they do otherwise, they'll be allowing evil to prevail in our land."

Zephaniah reminded Saphah of a very important fact: "Perhaps modern Christians need to pray that God will provide a 'Josiah personage' to lead the citizens of your land back to God. But now, please just go ahead and tell me about the history of your nation up to the present."

"I will. Fervent prayers are needed in America today. Our country was founded on Christian principles because the signers of the Declaration of Independence mainly had Christian affiliations, but from different denominations. In the past our country remained great because of our adherence to our Christian heritage."

"What was the Declaration of Independence and what are denominations?" Zephaniah asked.

"The Declaration was a statement of independence from the nation of Great Britain, who considered our own nation to be their colony." Saphah explained. "But the people of my land wanted freedom from the oppressive and unjust rule of Britain. We wanted to be in control of our own destiny. Christian denominations existed because our people wanted religious freedom, the opportunity to worship as we pleased. Although the majority of our citizens were Christians, they differed in outlook and worship practices, and this led to the many denominations. These various Christian churches spread across our nation, and God blessed our land."

"So, God was with America when your country was founded, just as He was with Israel in the beginning. Is that true?"

"Yes, like the Israelites, Americans gained control of the land God gave them because the Lord approved of their venture and blessed them. Therefore, both the Israelites and the Americans obtained freedom from tyranny, and the two nations grew strong as they worshipped and obeyed the Lord."

"How long did that last?"

"America's fall was subtle but insidious, with a gradual but cumulative effect, like a cancer silently eating away until it spells doom to its host. Our downfall began slowly, but picked up steam until now our country is full of corruption, lawlessness, immorality and sin. In addition, many people in our land are estranged from God. But, from what you've told me, Zephaniah, Israel started worshipping other gods and sacrificing their own children early in its history. They left out God, so He left them too, and the nation was split in two. Then, over the course of time Assyria captured Israel and now Babylonia wants to attack Judah."

"It's true that Israel and Judah's apostasy started quickly in history, but it looks like both Judah and America ended up in a similar situation over the course of time. Why do you think this happened to the United States?"

"Modern America didn't learn from the past mistakes of God's ancient people," noted Saphah. "So, I'm concerned that as God left your country, He might leave my nation too. We seem to be at a tipping point with perhaps a little over half the population following God, at least nominally, but the other half lacking faith in Him. So, the percentages aren't good. And, if our downward spiral continues and non-Christians become the majority, I greatly fear for our nation. And there's more that makes me think that" Saphah noted. "We call ourselves a Christian nation, but we're not following God's will. Like Judah, we're sacrificing our children but killing them before they're born. Many are worshipping other gods, and for some that means they're serving 'created things rather than the Creator.' Thus, America has replaced internal peace and harmony with violence, lawlessness, and destruction from within. But now we're also in danger of adversity from without. So everything is a great big mess!

Unless we can turn our country around, I'm afaid that someday God will allow us to be overthrown by our enemies." Saphah's tone was desperate.

"I understand your distress," said Zephaniah. "What you're saying about American history could also be a description of Judah's escapades over the course of time."

"I agree. Earlier when you told me about Judah, your recollections were like a mirror reflecting an image of the downfall in my own world. Our globe is spiraling downward faster and faster, but there's still time to share the gospel before the end. Right?"

"Right. The Lord has not returned again because He is waiting for men and women to come to repentance."

"Yes, He is graciously waiting. When Jesus' disciples asked him the signs and the time of His coming, Jesus answered:

> *Watch out that no one deceives you. For many will come in my name, claiming, 'I am the Messiah' and will deceive many. You will hear of wars and rumors of wars, but see to it that you are not alarmed. Such things must happen, but the end is still to come. Nation will rise against nation, and kingdom against kingdom. There will be famines and earthquakes in various places. All these are the beginning of birth pains. Then you will be handed over to be persecuted and put to death, and you will be hated by all nations because of me. …Because of the increase of wickedness, the love of most will grow cold. But the one who stands firm to the end will be saved. And this gospel of the kingdom will be preached in the whole world as a testimony to all nations, and then the end will come.*[18]

America is now suffering from the 'beginning of birth pains.' God loves humanity, but soon there'll come a time when the world is too far gone and 'then the end will come.'"

"So, you realize that if the moral condition of your world continues to decline and if most of the people refuse to return to the Lord, that will usher in the end of the age?"

"Yes! I've read about all these things in the New Testamen. At that time, Satan will be loosed to deceive the nations and to manipulate them into waging a war against believers. In Revelation, the final book of God's Word, John the apostle writes:

> *I saw an angel coming down out of heaven, having the key to the Abyss and holding in his hand a great chain. He seized the dragon, that ancient serpent, who is the devil, or Satan, and bound him for a thousand years. He threw him into the Abyss, and locked and sealed it over him, to keep him from deceiving the nations anymore until the thousand years were ended. After that, he must be set free for a short time.*[19]

This portion of scripture describes 'the thousand years' which is a long but undetermined period of time."

"When does the thousand years occur?"

"The figurative thousand years (millennium) describes the present reign of Christ in heaven over his realm as described in Matthew 28:

> *Then Jesus came to them and said, 'All authority in heaven and on earth has been given to me. Therefore, go and make disciples of all nations, baptizing them in the name of the Father and of the Son and of the Holy Spirit, and teaching them to obey everything I have commanded you. And surely I am with you always, to the very end of the age.'*[20]

Zephaniah, would you like to hear more about the millennium?"

"Yes, I would."

"There are three basic approaches to the millennium. My bible has a commentary with a summary of the main outlooks which are: Amillennialism, Premillennialism, and Postmillennialism. But the traditional outlook, Amillennialism, is the outlook I think is most biblical. It takes the bible at face value and can be understood by any believer. Here is a summary of that outlook as delineated in the bible commentary:

> 'The millennium describes the present reign of Christ in heaven over his realm (Mt 28:18-20), along with the souls of deceased believers, and in the hearts and lives of living believers on earth. The present form of God's kingdom will be followed by Christ's return, the general resurrection, the final judgment and Christ's continuing reign over the perfect kingdom on the new earth in the eternal state.'[21]

Thus, Christ now reigns from heaven over his realm, 'along with the souls of deceased believers and in the hearts and lives of living believers on earth.' Christ must reign over the course of history and in the lives of his people who are spiritually born again. This reign will continue throughout the present age."

"So, what will happen after that?"

"The New Testament says: *When the thousand years are over, Satan will be released from his prison and will go out to deceive the nations in the four corners of the earth—Gog and Magog—to gather them for battle.*[22] Here, 'Gog and Magog' symbolize the nations of the world as they band together for a final assault on God and his people. At the end of this age and before Christ's return, Satan will be released to deceive the nations and manipulate them into waging war against believers."[23]

"Are there other New Testament passages describing the end time events in this way?"

"Yes, there are similar passages. They speak of a falling away: *At that time many will turn away from the faith and will hate and betray each other.*[24] They also say *that day will not come until the rebellion occurs and the man of lawlessness is revealed.*[25]

> *For the secret power of lawlessness is already at work; but the one who now holds it back will continue to do so till he is taken out of the way. …The coming of the lawless one will be in accordance with how Satan works. He will use all sorts of displays of power through signs and wonders that serve the lie, and all the ways that wickedness deceives those who are perishing. They perish because they refused to love the truth and so be saved. For this reason, God sends them a powerful delusion so that they will believe the lie and so that all will be condemned who have not believed the truth but have delighted in wickedness.*[26]

This means that Satan is still bound in my modern world and has been stripped of authority until the time when 'many will turn away from the faith.'"

"So right now the influence of the devil is limited?"

"Yes, regardless of the evil that permeates the present era in my world, the influence of the devil is restrained. All those who turn to God for salvation can experience triumph through submitting to the reign of Christ. And they pass on that triumph to other people by spreading Christ's rule and will continue to do so until the end. But then at the last hour, Satan will make one final attempt to crush the church, the people of God. In that dark moment, Christ will return to earth. The present form of God's kingdom will be followed by the general resurrection, the final judgment, and Christ's continuing reign over His kingdom in the new heavens and earth where we will live with Him forever."

"So Christ is reigning now and will use His church to spread His reign through the earth until His return?"

"Yes, the story of spiritual warfare in history will climax as Satan is loosed to deceive the nations. But Jesus says: *Look! I am coming soon! My reward is with me, and I will give to each person according to what they have done.*[28] This viewpoint presents a clear and simple picture of Christ's reign and return. I don't think it's my place to critique the outlooks of others. Zephaniah, do you understand my position?"

"I certainly do. Saphah, God has called you to warn others, not to engage in end time philosophies." Prophet Zephaniah stood up and put his arm around Saphah's shoulder after she arose. "Let's go, my dear. I'm sure Hannah and Rebecca will be greatly pleased to see you."

"Yes, let's go. I can hardly wait to see them again!"

$$18$$

THE AUDIENCE

"Look Saphah, we've reached King Josiah's palace."

"What a lovely building!" Saphah stopped to stare at the magnificent tall white columns decorating the front.

"Zephaniah and Saphah, I'm over here." Ebed motioned to them from a side entrance. "I was about to come looking for you because Hannah and Rebecca were starting to get worried again."

"Sorry it took us so long." Zephaniah apologized.

"Oh, that's alright. Shallum isn't back yet either."

"Good afternoon, Benjamin." Ebed addressed a palace guard by name as he walked toward them. "Do you know if Shallum is still greeting pilgrims at a city gate?"

"I'm not sure." The young guard furrowed his brow in uncertainty. "He usually arrives back here by mid-afternoon to eat, so he's probably on his way now. He's greeting pilgrims at the Fish Gate today."

Zephaniah entered the conversation. "Thank you for giving us that information. We're going with Ebed to see Rebecca and Hannah in Shallum's quarters. Also, I'd like to put in a request for an audience with King Josiah for Ebed and myself. Hannah, my niece, has been in an altercation with her husband, Jude, today. The row also involved Rebecca and Saphah. So, I'd like to report to King Josiah the details of what happened. Ebed also has information he'd like to share."

"Alright," said Benjamin. "But first, would you please introduce me to your friend."

"Of course, I'd be glad to." Ebed turned toward the man to speak. "Benjamin, Royal Guard of the Palace, I'm very pleased to introduce you to Saphah, Watchwoman from America, who is a pilgrim to our land."

"I'm very pleased to meet you, Guard Benjamin." Saphah curtsied toward him.

"I'm happy to meet you too, American Watchwoman Saphah." The guard gave her a bow in return. "Would you also like to request an audience with King Josiah?" he politely asked.

"Thank you for asking, but I think I'll wait to see if the king requests to see me. The Prophet Zephaniah has important information to share with the king, so I'll stay with the ladies in Shallum's living quarters while the men visit King Josiah."

"Alright," Benjamin gave her another bow. "Now come right this way, and I'll take you to Shallum's living area."

"Oh, the palace is magnificent." Saphah tagged along with Zephaniah and Ebed behind Benjamin as they walked down a hall with marble floors. As the group walked toward the staff quarters, she stroked the cedar walls with her hand and admired the alabaster ceiling with her eyes.

Benjamin stopped at an engraved door and spoke to the three in hushed tones. "Before we enter Shallum's quarters, I want to inform you that when the ladies arrived at the palace, they were greatly distressed. Rebecca told me they'd escaped from a physical confrontation with Hannah's husband so they needed to see Shallum. But when I told them he wasn't available, they requested to wait for his arrival back at his quarters. They were greatly worried about you, Saphah, so I'm sure they'll be pleased to reunite."

"Praise God." Saphah looked upward in thanks. "I'm so grateful that the girls are safe here in the palace!"

"Yes, praise Yahweh." Zephaniah expressed his thankfulness. "You lovely ladies have experienced a most distressing and unsettling event. Benjamin, would it be possible for them to receive a nourishing meal and a refreshing drink here in the quarters while they wait for our return from the audience?"

"Yes, Zephaniah. I'll certainly order some food delivered from the palace kitchen. Now, while you're all visiting, I'll request an audience for you and Ebed with the king."

"Thank you, Benjamin."

"Yes, thank you, Ben." Ebed was walking back and forth impatiently. "I'm ready to talk to the king right now!"

"I'm glad I can assist you." Benjamin glanced at Ebed with a smile.

"Now, are all of you ready to enter the quarters?"

"Yes," said Saphah, "I don't think I can wait another moment to see them."

Benjamin knocked on the door, entered the room, and announced: "Hannah and Rebecca, you have three visitors, Zephaniah, Saphah, and Ebed. Do you want me to let them in?"

"Saphah!" Hannah called out her friend's name. "I'm so glad to know she is alright!"

"Thank you, Lord, thank you!" Rebecca chimed in as she gave Hannah a big hug. "Yes, hurry, please let them in!"

Glimpsing Saphah's smiling face, Rebecca and Hannah's rushed to reunited with her for a group hug. "Saphah, you've no idea how worried I've been about you." Tears streamed down Hannah's face. "Jude is such a brute I was fearful he might harm you."

"Me too." Rebecca smiled through her tears. "I'm very glad to see you're safe. Thank you so much for helping Hannah!"

"Yes, thank you!" Hannah planted a kiss on Saphah's cheek.

"Hannah, are you still feeling alright?" Ebed quietly asked as he slipped his arm around the beautiful girl's waist.

"Yes, Eb, I'm alright." Hannah smiled as she turned her head toward him and shyly stared up into his blue eyes. "Thank you for your concern for me and the baby."

"Oh, I'm so glad to see you're both alright." Saphah expressed her thankfulness. "Ladies, I feel like a weight has been lifted off my shoulders. God is so good!"

"Yes, he is." Zephaniah embraced first Hannah and then Rebecca. "Ladies, who wants to say the prayer of thanks for what God has done?"

"I do." Hannah immediately began her prayer. "Yahweh, thank you for intervening in our lives today and for saving us from evil. Thank you too for the good people you've placed in my life, for I recognize your hand upon them. We love you Lord and thank you again for everything you've done. Amen."

"Thank you, my niece," said Zephaniah with tears in his eyes.

They all heard a knock at the door, and then Benjamin entered and announced, "Men, I'm pleased to inform you that King Josiah accepts your request for a personal audience and invites you to join him now. And ladies, you'll soon receive your delivery of food and drink. I hope you enjoy your meal which consists of leftovers from King Josiah's repast. After you finish eating, you're also invited to join the king, and I'll return to get you later. All right, men, your King is expecting you. Please follow me."

"Thank you so much, Benjamin," Saphah said as the men walked out the door.

"Yes, that's wonderful," Rebecca joined in. "I've always wanted to eat a meal here at the palace. Ebed talks about how good the food is all the time. And then we're also going to meet King Josiah."

Hannah's mouth opened wide in amazement. "Oh my, we're actually going to get an audience with King Josiah. I never thought I'd get to meet him personally!"

"We're going to meet the king!" Rebecca skipped around in the room and then grabbed Hannah's hand. "We're going to meet the king. We're going to meet the king." The two girls skipped around and gleefully repeated the refrain.

Saphah laughed as she watched Rebecca and Hannah's antics. "Shhhh! Be quiet!" Saphah whispered and then perked up her ears. "Someone is tapping on the door!"

Hannah opened the door to discover two men, one pushing a serving cart of delicious smelling food and the other balancing a jar on his head.

"Kitchen delivery." One man announced their presence before entering the room with his cart.

"You're just in time," the other man proclaimed, setting down his jar with a thud. "If you'd been much later, the leftovers from King Josiah's meal would have gone to the dogs."

"Whew," Rebecca laughed, "I'm glad we got here when we did."

"Me too," Hannah giggled. "After all that running, I'm really hungry."

"Thank you for bringing us the meal." Saphah turned toward the kitchen staff with a smile. "We really appreciate it."

"It was our pleasure. I'm Aaron, and I'll be your server." The older man removed a folding table from a closet, placed a fine linen cloth upon it, and positioned three stools around the table. "Please be seated." The three ladies took their seats. Opening double cart doors, he brought out and arranged a service for three on the table. Then, he placed covered food trays and lifted the lids while describing each one.

"Your first dish is braised lamb with broad beans and artichokes; your second is spinach salad with radishes, new onions, and peppers, along with yogurt dressing. Next, you have plates of hot bread and butter. Finally, your dessert is fig and walnut cakes with a sweet crème sauce."

"I'm Luke, and I'll serve your drinks." The younger man placed cups for their drinks on the table and poured fresh pomegranate juice into each. "Could we get you anything else?"

Hannah smiled sweetly at the servers. "No, we don't need anything. But thank you both for the wonderful meal and drink."

"Thank you," Saphah and Rebecca each said in turn.

Aaron and Luke bowed and then left the room.

"What a great meal." Hannah sniffed the aroma of the delicacies spread before them. "Lord, thank you for this wonderful food and bless it to our bodies I pray. Amen."

"Let's help ourselves to the food before it gets cold." Rebecca began filling her plate.

Hannah cut off a slice of the braised Lamb. "Saphah, what happened after you struck Jude with that stick of wood? We were worried sick about you and sent up many prayers for your safety."

"You'll never believe what happened to me." Saphah related her frantic ordeal at the Temple of Baal and ended with a description of her fright. "I've never been so scared in my life as I was trying to escape from those false priests. My entire body was shaking and my knees were knocking together. I was afraid the priests in that evil place would detain me and never turn me loose."

"After I got out of that detestable place, I didn't know where I was, but Zephaniah found me, praise God. So here I am no worse for the scare, but I'm thankful you both escaped too. Please tell me what happened to you after we so abruptly parted."

"Becca grabbed my hand and we ran as fast as we could toward the palace," Hannah related. "We didn't even stop for a second to look back. My heart was pounding out of my chest and I couldn't quit crying."

"Yes, we knew the king's palace was the closest safe place to go, and Shallum might be here too," Rebecca explained. "But as we neared the palace, at one point we had to stop to remove our sacks from our sashes because they were starting to get loose. We didn't want to lose any of our purchases, so we carried them by hand the rest of the way."

"Benjamin saw us running toward the palace and realized something was wrong. So, he sent a runner to escort us the rest of the way," added Hannah. "When we finally got to the palace, Ben listened to our story about what happened and relayed the information to King Josiah. The king then sent the runner on to the school to inform Huldah and Eb. After that, Ben took us to Shallum's room where we prayed and tried to rest while we waited."

"When Eb got here, we were overjoyed to learn you were safe with Zephaniah," Rebecca said. "But we couldn't really relax because we needed to see for ourselves you were okay."

"Someone is knocking again." Saphah arose from her stool and walked toward the door. "Who is it?"

"It's Benjamin. I've come to take you for your audience with King Josiah."

"Oh, that's wonderful, Ben. But could you give us just a few minutes to tidy up?"

"Of course, I'll wait outside. Just let me know when you're ready."

"Alright, we'll hurry. We don't want to keep King Josiah waiting."

The ladies scurried around as they combed their hair and smoothed their skirts. "Becca," Hannah asked, "would you please help me with my turban? I'm so nervous I don't know if I can get it on straight."

"Sure." Rebecca wrapped the turban around Hannah's head and tucked it in. "There, you look nice."

"Alright, are we ready?" Saphah asked.

"I think so." Hannah adjusted her sash.

"Yes," Rebecca answered. "Let's get this audience started."

"Benjamin, we're ready." Saphah smoothed some loose tendrils of hair back from her face.

"Right this way." Benjamin motioned as he led them through more wide halls into the presence of King Josiah.

Saphah saw Zephaniah and Ebed standing before the king, and Shallum was present too. Ebed even glanced over at Hannah with a smile on his face and she smiled back. But Saphah's heart jumped and then sank with a thud when she suddenly saw Jude enter the room from another hall. *What is he doing here?* She tried not to look at him. She noticed handsome King Josiah was sitting tall on his throne and staring straight at Jude as he entered the room.

The three ladies were brought forward toward the king. Each lady bowed and then curtsied before him as they were presented. Then, Zephaniah introduced his niece to the king.

Hannah responded nicely to King Josiah. "I'm so pleased to meet you."

"As I am to meet you, Hannah." King Josiah kindly spoke to Hannah and nodded his chin.

Then Ebed introduced his sister.

"I'm very happy to finally get to meet you." Rebecca smiled graciously at the king.

"Yes, I'm glad to meet you too, Rebecca. I've already heard a lot about you." The king pleasantly smiled back at her.

Finally, Shallum introduced Saphah, who responded: "I'm highly honored to meet you, King Josiah. I never thought I'd get to meet a Judean king."

"I'm greatly honored to meet you too, American Watchwoman. Welcome to Judah."

Then finally, a guard stated Jude's name and motioned him to stand before King Josiah.

"Do you have anything to say?" King Josiah asked sternly?

"No, Your Majessssty." Jude rudely prolonged the king's title as he glared at the ruler's face.

"I've heard disturbing things about you." King Josiah's tone was stern. "Is it true that you mistreated your wife today at the market?"

"No, she deserved what she got. She needs to come home and fulfill her duties." Jude turned toward Hannah and stared a hole through her. "I demand you send her home with me right now. She is my wife."

"No!" King Josiah answered firmly. "Hannah wants a divorce from you. Is that correct Hannah?"

"Yes, that's correct." Hannah, unnerved by Jude's gaze, turned away from him and looked at the king.

"Well, she can't have a divorce. By Jewish law women can't divorce their husbands in this land."

"No, they can't," King Josiah agreed.

"Well, wife, come here right now." Jude angrily spoke to Hannah. "We're going home!"

"Ebed stepped over to grasp Hannah's hand. "Don't go," he whispered.

"Who're you? Get your hands off my wife, you bastard." Jude yelled and then rushed toward Ebed.

"Grab Jude," King Josiah commanded a guard. "Now listen to me." The king angrily addressed Jude. "It is correct that women cannot divorce their husbands, but it is also true that kings in Judah can grant women divorces from husbands. I have the power and authority to grant Hannah a divorce from you. You have disrespected her in word and deed, and there are several witnesses to your actions. I hereby grant her a divorce decree from you this day. Do not ever come near her again, for if you disobey you'll be banished from Jerusalem forever. Take him from my presence."

"It's alright." Ebed spoke with assurance to Hannah. "He's gone."

"Oh, thank God." Hannah breathed a sigh of relief and wiped tears from her eyes. "Thank you, King Josiah!"

"You're welcome, Hannah," King Josiah's voice was compassionate. "Ebed wants to talk to you privately. Please go with him to the hall where you can talk."

Hannah looked up at Ebed, who nodded his head and took her hand. "Come with me. I want to ask you an important question."

Ebed and Hannah walked hand in hand out of the room. "Hannah," Ebed said as he took both of her hands and they faced one another. "I've loved you from the moment I first laid eyes on you. You are the most beautiful woman I've ever seen, inside and out. I humbly ask for your hand in marriage, because I don't think I can ever be happy without you. Will you marry me?" Ebed placed his hands at the sides of Hannah's waist as he tenderly waited for her answer.

Hannah stared into his eyes for several moments before placing her hands on his shoulders and then slipping them around his neck. "Oh, Eb, I've loved you from the beginning too. You are the sweetest man I've ever met. Yes, I want to marry you," she answered his proposal joyfully. "I'd be greatly honored to become your wife."

"Oh Hannah, I love you." Ebed's voice was passionate.

"I love you too." Hannah answered softly with a smile.

Ebed bent down and gently kissed Hannah's lips, and then the two embraced. "Let's go tell the others," Hannah said, her face lit with joy. The two walked together arm in arm back into the room.

"We've an announcement," Ebed spoke up. "Hannah and I want to tell you that we're betrothed. I've already gotten permission from Zephaniah for Hannah's hand, and Shallum has given his blessing for me to marry her. Zephaniah and Shallum will travel with me to my parent's home to ask their blessing this evening. I'm sure they'll be pleased and happy to help me set a date."

With that, the entire audience, along with the king and the guards, burst into applause. "Congratulations Ebed and Hannah." King Josiah bestowed his sincere blessings on the couple. "I'm so happy for you both." Everyone added their own congratulations. The king dismissed the group, they departed from the audience, and then they all left the area to meet up again in Shallum's quarters.

"I'm so glad we've been able to meet here again before we part," said Shallum. "Now, Zephaniah, Ebed, and I need to get on our way to the Rechabite camp so we can arrive there before dark. We'll stay all night and start back in the morning at first light."

"Alright men, let's grab some water and get going so we can reach the camp before nightfall." Zephaniah instructed. "Goodbye, everyone."

"I hate to leave good company, but we must be on our way." Ebed stole a quick kiss and then embraced Hannah in a lingering hug. "Bye, honey, I'll see you in the morning."

"Bye, Eb," Hannah watched as Ebed walked out the door from Shallum's quarters with the others. "Bye Zephaniah and Shallum. See you in the morning."

"God bless you Ebed, Zephaniah, and Shallum. See you in the morning," Saphah said as they departed.

"Yes, see you all later." Rebecca joined in as the men parted from the ladies and each group traveled their own way.

"This has been a tumultuous day for all of us." Saphah sighed in her relief it was all over. "But I'm so glad it has ended on such a happy note." The ladies began walking toward the school complex. "Let's hurry home because I know Huldah must be worrying about us right now."

"Yes, we need to let her know we're all safe, and I want to tell her about my betrothal to Ebed. Let's hurry!" Without saying another word, they broke into a faster walk, as they hurried toward the school housing area. Arriving home, the ladies rushed into the dining area. The table was set, and they could smell supper cooking, but Huldah wasn't there. They headed toward Huldah's bedroom and found her fitfully sleeping on her bed.

"Shallum!" Huldah cried out in her sleep. "Where are you? Shallum!"

"Hush, Huldah." Rebecca soothed as she gently placed her hand on Huldah's arm. "Hush, dear lady, everything is alright."

Huldah opened her eyes as she awoke with a start. "Oh, Rebecca, I had a terrible nightmare. I was tired so I came in here to rest, but then I must have fallen asleep. I dreamed that Jerusalem was under siege, but the enemy had broken through the wall. I found Ebed at the palace, but when I searched for Shallum there, I couldn't find him anywhere." Huldah turned her head to look toward Saphah. "Do you think this dream was a warning from God?

"I don't know for sure, but I think it may be a warning not only for your world but also for mine," said Saphah. "Zephaniah and I talked and we agree that your ancient land and my modern civilization seem to be parallel worlds. At the present time in your civilization, you seem to be in a period of temporary reprieve before a great future calamity. Circumstances seem to be similar in my civilization, except that we don't know whether God will allow a temporary respite for my land too. Zephaniah and I had a long talk about it, and he thinks I need to give warning to my people of coming danger."

"Oh my," Huldah agreed. "Zephaniah is a wise man who is in touch with God. If he is thinking this way, I think we should both take heed."

"Yes, Huldah, I think you're right."

"Well, supper is ready," Huldah informed the ladies. "I'm certainly glad we planned ahead for this meal."

"Oh, Huldah, would it be alright with you if I skip supper?" Saphah wasn't hungry after her stressful day. "If you don't mind, I'd just like to get a good night's rest."

"Of course, go ahead. Good night, Saphah. See you in the morning."

"Yes, good night," Hannah and Rebecca echoed.

"Good night, everyone." Saphah turned and walked toward the guest bedroom. Quickly reaching the room, she got into her nightclothes and sat down exhausted upon the side of her bed. *I need to read God's Word and say my prayer,* she thought, *but I'm almost too tired.* Saphah sat there several seconds contemplating what she should do. Despite the fact she felt exhausted, she finally recognized her need to get in touch with God. Reaching for her backpack, she grabbed her bible, it fell open to Isaiah 42, and she began reading aloud:

> *Hear you deaf, look you blind and see! …You have seen many things, but you pay no attention; your ears are open, but you do not listen. It pleased the Lord for the sake of his righteousness to make his law great and glorious. But this is a people plundered and looted, all of them trapped in pits or hidden away in prisons. They have become plunder with no one to rescue them.*[1]

Oh, Saphah thought, *Isaiah is talking here about the people of this ancient land being plundered and looted by first the Assyrians and then the Babylnians.* She continued reading:

> *Who handed Jacob over to become loot, and Israel to the plunderers? Was it not the Lord, against whom we have sinned? For they would not follow his ways; they did not obey his law. So, he poured out on them his burning anger, the violence of war.*[2]

Saphah's heart dropped as she contemplated what she was reading: Here Isaiah writes about Assyria and Babylon conquering Israel and Judah because God was chastising his people. But the commentary in this bible says that when God poured out his anger, "Israel had a foretaste of the day of the Lord.[3] Then she read: *It* [war] *enveloped them in flames, yet they did not understand; It consumed them, but they did not take it to heart.*"[4]

Saphah thoughts turned to her own people: *Many in my country have rejected the truth of God's Word, so society is becoming less moral and our world is in desperate need of Jesus. Because ofsin God allowed Assyria and Babylon to conquer the Holy Land and to take over Jerusalem. This happened because the*

Lord was upset with his people, but He knew what was needed to turn them back to Him. God responds to sin with consequences, but He responds to repentance in love. So, as He disciplined Israel and Judah, He will discipline America too. But God still loves us. Even the plight we are in now is designed to help and instruct us, not to harm us. But will the lesson be learned?

Saphah considered in her mind: *The heading for this section of Isaiah is called 'Israel Blind and Deaf,' but today in my land it could be called 'America Blind and Deaf.' And scripture on this topic is true for today too,* Saphah realized. *'You have seen many things, but have paid no attention; your ears are open, but you hear nothing.' For ancient Israel and Judah it was 'a foretaste of the day of the Lord,' but for current America it is a forthcoming reality and danger of the 'day of the Lord.'*

"Oh Lord, please help the people of my nation," Saphah earnestly prayed. "You are our only hope. Please open the eyes and the ears of those who cannot see or hear, please give us time for reform and repentance, and please use me however you see fit. I pray these things in Jesus' name. Amen."

19

FELLOWSHIP OF HIS SUFFERINGS

Oh, she is sleeping so peacefully, Saphah thought, *I mustn't awaken her.* Golden beams of sunlight cast their rays upon Hannah's form as she slumbered upon her bed. Saphah sat up, threw her legs to the side of her bed, and silently said her morning prayer, beginning with a recital of the Lord's prayer and followed by a personal word of her own:

> *Father in heaven, thank you for your love shown to your people in all ages. Please guide and take care of the people in my own land today: my family; my friends; my acquaintances; plus, all the good citizens of my world. Dear Lord, please do likewise for my new friends in this ancient place, and especially for those in Jerusalem and Judah who face adversities like those of my own nation. I praise and thank you for all you have done, for all you are doing, and for all you will do in the future. I pray these things in Jesus' name. Amen.*

A change of clothes was set out for Saphah on her storage case. *Huldah must have set these out last night before we ladies arrived home,* she thought. *She is such a hard-working lady and carries out all her tasks with diligence and efficiency.* Saphah took up her clothes, quietly left the room, and headed toward the wash room. After cleaning up and dressing for the day, she washed her dirty clothes and hung them on one of the lines strung high across one side of the room. *Huldah has already washed her clothes,* she noticed, *and neatly hung them here to dry. I'm glad she is already up so she and I can talk a bit.* Crossing the court and entering the kitchen area, Saphah was surprised to see Huldah already sitting there on a cushion sipping from a mug.

"Good morning, Saphah." Huldah sounded rested and chipper. "Did you have a good rest?"

"Yes, but what about you, did you get a good night's sleep?"

"Actually, I did. Rebecca and Hannah kindly offered to do the dishes for me, and I gladly accepted their offer, because I really needed to rest and calm down after all the stress from yesterday. They did tell me about Ebed and Hannah's marriage plans, and, by the way, they hope to marry soon. So, I went off to bed extremely relieved about Hannah's circumstances and so happy for the two. Saphah, would you like a mug of hot herbal tea?"

"Yes, I'm feeling a little hollow this morning after skipping dinner last night."

"Here, Saphah, take a seat on this cushion." Huldah motioned for her to sit down and quickly got up to retrieve a pot of tea and pour some for her friend. "Do you have any suggestions for breakfast?"

"Thank you, Huldah." Saphah took a sip of the tasty hot beverage. "Well, I noticed earlier you still have a big container of dried apricots, so I was wondering if we could make fried apricot pies this morning. I haven't had them since I was a little girl. My father's family had relatives in the western United States, and apricots were one of the fruits grown on their ranch. Most summers, some of our family members from middle America would travel to visit those relatives. When they'd return home, they'd invariably bring back a supply of the delicious dried apricots."

"I've never heard of fried apricot pies before. Please tell me how to make them."

"I remember watching grandmother make the pies. She'd mix flour, shortening or butter, and water for the crust and roll it out thin. Then she'd cut circles out of the pie crust." Saphah used her hands to show Huldah the size of the circles. "She'd simmer pitted dried apricots, sugar, and water together for the filling, but you and I could use honey as a substitute for sugar. After that, she'd heat a deep layer of shortening or oil in a pan to fry the pies. To form them, she'd spoon some of the apricot mixture on one side of each circle, fold the other half over the apricots, and pinch the edges together. When the oil was very hot, she'd place several pies into the hot liquid, brown on one side, and then turn over and brown the other."

"Fried apricot pies sound delicious, and I do think we have all the ingredients. Ebed and Rebecca's parents sent us some goat butter. Would that work to make the crust?" Huldah was looking forward to making the pies.

"Definitely," Saphah said happily. "Butter makes wonderful pie crust, and we could fry the pies in olive oil. You have that too, don't you."

"Yes," Huldah was getting enthused. "Let's make apricot pies! What do you want me to do?"

"I'll make the crust and you can make the filling. Then we can work together to form the pies and fry them. Let's get all the pans and ingredients together first."

"Sounds good," said Huldah. "We can make the pies and talk while we work."

Huldah built a fire under the outdoor grill and Saphah searched around inside for the ingredients and suitable utensils to make the pies. "While you were gone, I found everything except the olive oil for frying the pies. Where is the oil Huldah?"

"It's in that jar over there." Huldah pointed to the largest jar in the room located on the floor in a corner. "Let me get the oil, because it must be dipped or poured out of the jar, and it's not an easy task."

"Thank you."

"You're welcome." Huldah began dipping out oil and pouring it into a pan. "Hannah and Rebecca told me about what happened yesterday. Saphah, thank you so much for helping the girls escape from Jude."

"Oh, you're welcome. I'm just glad I was there to help."

"Me too." Huldah quit dipping the oil and looked at her. "They also told me about your escape from the despicable temple of the false god Baal. I've heard rumors that such temples exist in Jerusalem, but I didn't know for sure if it was true."

"Well, being there was the scariest thing I've ever experienced," Saphah said. "But praise God I escaped from that terrible place!"

"Can you scc now why women, or men for that matter, shouldn't walk alone in Jerusalem?" Huldah gave Saphah a questioning look.

"Yes, I can, but believe it or not, it's like that in the big cities in my country too. It's not safe to go there alone anymore."

"Really." Huldah was surprised. "Was it safe in the past?"

"Yes, it was safe to go about anywhere up until recently. But there's a lot of rioting, looting, killing, and lawlessness in big cities now. Yesterday, after I escaped from the false temple, Zephaniah and I had a talk about conditions in modern America. Things are getting bad. He reminded me again that I need to warn the American people soon that our nation is in danger."

"Do you want to give me more details about what's happening?"

"Well, before I left, an autocratic dictator of a country called Russia had invaded a sovereign country Ukraine without any provocation from the people of that land. Thousands and thousands of people have been killed or injured there."

Saphah mixed flour, butter, a dash of salt, and cold water for crust for the apricot pies. Forming the mixture into a ball, she paused and asked, "Huldah, do you think this'll make enough crust for around 14 or so small pies?"

"I think that'll be enough."

With both hands resting on the ball of dough in the bowl, Saphah elaborated. "The evil leader has done this type of thing before against other countries and is guilty of atrocities such as chemical warfare and sabotage against innocent civilians. He is guilty of crimes against humanity, and no one has been able to stop him."

"Why not?" Huldah wondered.

Saphah spread a thin layer of flour on the counter, patted out the pie dough on it, and began cutting out circles of dough. "World leaders don't know how to stop him, because they're afraid he'll retaliate with some type of chemical, nuclear, cyber, or other form of warfare on any country that tries. Instead, the United States and other nations have endeavored to help the attacked country Ukraine by sending war supplies and providing technical support. Nuclear warfare is very dangerous and especially capable of triggering a third world war scenario."

"Oh my, your world has already had two world wars, but what is nuclear warfare anyway?" Huldah raised her eyebrows high and stared in exasperation at Saphah.

"Yes, we've already had two horrendous world wars." Saphah stopped working with the pies to explain. "One of my grandfathers fought in the first world war, my father and two of my uncles were engaged in the second world war, and I was a baby during that second event. Now it looks like conditions are ripe for a possible third world war."

"Oh my, It's difficult for me to imagine wars that affect the whole world."

"Believe me, Huldah, there's a strong possibility a world war could happen again. But right now we need to fry these pies. Alright, the circles are ready. if you want to put apricot filling on one side of each circle, I'll fold over the dough and pinch the sides together. Is the oil hot yet?"

"Let me check." Huldah picked up a little piece of leftover pie dough and dropped it into the hot oil. "Please tell me about nuclear war."

"I think the oil is hot enough to fry some pies." Saphah noticed the piece of dough was sputtering in the oil. Then she carefully dropped three pies she'd just made into the hot liquid before answering Huldah's question. "Nuclear warfare is fought using nuclear bombs, a weapon that destroys infrastructure and kills people within a radius of many miles, leaves other people maimed for life, and inflicts huge damage on structures and the environment. In addition, it leaves nuclear fallout that is harmful to any living organism within a certain radius. If such a war continued, it could eventually involve the entire world and destroy it. What are we to do?"

"Evil must be contained, one way or another. It doesn't matter whether it's caused by the evil leader of a country, or a mean man who abuses his wife. Look at Jude. King Josiah knew Jude must be constrained, so he granted Hannah a divorce. The cruel man might harm or kill Hannah or the child she carries, so Jude must stay away from her. It is a similar situation with your nation and mine. Both are becoming more and more evil, and many people have turned away from God."

"Please tell me, Huldah, what should the national leaders of our nations do?"

"From what Zephaniah told me, God has sent the young leader King Josiah to Judah, and he's evidently planning to start reforms here."

Saphah turned over the first batch of pies to brown on the other side. "But what can be done in America?"

"You and other Christians need to fervently pray that God will raise up a strong leader like King Josiah to help stop the evil."

Saphah was vehement. "Well, I agree! We desperately need assistance from God to prevent our society from going down the drain. Those in my world who refuse to live in righteousness and to serve God are causing all this lawlessness and havoc. They are the ones trying to redefine things that go against God's standards and normalize those forms of unrighteousness by getting rid of God and his laws. But right and wrong can't be redefined: Evil cannot be defined as good; good cannot be defined as evil. When people try to redefine things in this way, that removes God from the picture. It's frightening!"

"It is, Saphah. They can't normalize evil like that without getting rid of God. And, when God is removed and evil and sin increase out of control, that's when your world will reach the point of no return. It's the work of Satan and those who follow him." Huldah let out a deep sigh and shook her head in consternation.

"Yes, scripture says the *one who does what is sinful is of the devil, because the devil has been sinning from the beginning.*[1] *Everyone who sins breaks the law; in fact, sin is lawlessness.*[2] The bible goes on to add that *He* [Satan] *was a murderer from the beginning, not holding to the truth, for there is no truth in him.*[3] So, 'the devil has been sinning from the beginning,' from the time he first rebelled against God, before the fall of Adam and Eve. He is the instigator of human sin, and those who continue to sin belong to him and are his children. The Word says he is *in the world*,[4] and *the whole world* [of unbelievers] *is under the control of the evil one.*"[5] Huldah, I need to take up these pies. Please hand me a tray."

"Here's a large flat pan that'll hold them all."

"Thank you." Saphah took up the first savory batch, and placed more pies to fry in the hot oil. "Huldah, I think it's the consensus that things need to change in both my land and yours. Hopefully, things will get better as King Josiah begins reforms here. And we can pray that the Lord will send a leader or leaders to help my nation too."

"Yes, a time of reform is needed for your modern world because wickedness must be halted there one way or another or your land will go into end time tribulation."

"Agreed. Huldah, I need to talk to you about that period immediately preceding Jesus' return and the persecution the bible says will occur at that time. Also, a second subject I'd like to discuss with you has caused me much consternation and angst, but I don't think there'll be time to talk about it today. Rebecca and Hannah will be getting up soon, and the men will be returning right away too, so we'll need to discuss it later."

"Go ahead with your first concern, and perhaps we can talk about your second subject during breaks and lunchtime when you visit Jerusalem School to learn my routine."

"That sounds good." Saphah was pleased that she would get to learn Huldah's routine at the school. "Well, here's my concern. In the book of Matthew, Jesus talked about a time of birth pains, and Zephaniah and I agree that seems to be what my modern world is experiencing now. But the Lord said that's when believers will be persecuted:

> [And] *be put to death, and you will be hated by all nations because of me. At that time many will turn away from the faith and will betray and hate each other, and many false prophets will appear and deceive many people. Because of the increase of wickedness, the love of most will grow cold, but the one who stands firm to the end will be saved. The gospel will be preached as a testimony to all nations; then the end will come.[6]*

Therefore, this gospel of the kingdom will be preached in the whole world as a testimony to all nations. And, that's when the end will come. But thats where my next question arises. There are two main viewpoints about End Time persecution and the two are complete opposites."

"Please explain."

Some people say there'll be a rapture at that time, and Christians will be removed before the suffering and persecution occur. They use a verse from Revelation as their proof: *Since you have kept my command to endure patiently, I will also keep you from the hour of trial that is going to come on the whole world to test the inhabitants of the earth.*[7] But the Greek for this phrase can mean two different things. The phrase, 'keep you from,' can mean either 'keep you from undergoing,' or 'keep you through,' the hour of trial or testing that precedes the consummation of the kingdom.[8]

"What else does the Word of God say on this subject?" asked Huldah.

"Here are some examples of what the bible says. Jesus said, *I am coming soon. Hold on to what you have, so that no one will take your crown. The one who is victorious I will make a pillar in the temple of my God.*[9] James writes about patience in suffering: *Be patient then, brothers and sisters, until the Lord's coming.*[10] Since believers will be suffering unjustly at the hands of the wicked, they are to look forward patiently to the Lord's return. James goes on to say: *Be patient and stand firm, because the Lord's coming is near. …The Judge is standing at the door.*[11] The statement, 'The Judge is standing at the door,' is a reference to Christ's second coming and to the judgment associated with it."

"So, what lies behind the New Testament's insistance on patience in suffering?"

"It arises from the fact that the 'last days' began with the incarnation, and we've been living in the 'last days' ever since. However, evil in the world is getting worse and worse, so the next big event in redemptive history is Christ's second coming. Scripture doesn't say when it'll take place, but believers are advised to watch for it. In the light of that, James expected the imminent return of Jesus,[12] but he also gave an Old Testament *example of patience in the face of suffering ... the prophets who spoke in the name of the Lord. As you know we count as blessed those who have persevered.*"[13]

"Saphah, we simply don't know what suffering we may have to endure in our lives. And, that includes you as well as myself, because both of us live in evil times."

"Yes, we do. Anyway, I consider myself fortunate to personally know two prophets, you and Zephaniah."

"Thank you, Saphah. I consider myself fortunate to know you as well." Huldah took up a fried apricot pie. "Should we share one to make sure it tastes all right?"

"Definitely, we need to be sure it's good," Saphah giggled.

Huldah split a pie, handed half of it to Saphah and then took a big bite out of her half. "Oh, that tastes wonderful!" She savored the tangy flavor of the honeyed apricots and crust on her tongue.

"So, you think the pie is alright?" Saphah smiled and took a huge bite herself. "Hmmm, if I do say so myself, that's good! Thank you, Huldah for helping me make them. Now, back to our conversation. As I mentioned earlier, although some Christians think God will 'keep us from undergoing' the hour of trial, others, including myself, interpret Revelation 3:10 as saying that God will 'keep us through' the hour of testing and suffering that precedes the consummation of the kingdom. And other portions of scripture attest as well to this interpretation."

"Would you please tell me about some of those scriptures?"

"Certainly. For example, in Revelation, John speaks of 'A beast coming out of the sea,'[14] and:

> *It was given power to wage war against God's holy people and to conquer them. And it was given authority over every tribe, people, language, and nation. All inhabitants of the earth will worship the beast—all whose names have not been written in the Lamb's book of life, the Lamb who was slain from the creation of the world. Whoever has ears, let them hear. If anyone is to go into captivity, into captivity they will go. If anyone is to be killed with the sword, with the sword they will be killed. This calls for patient endurance and faithfulness on the part of God's people.*[15]

John's beast has the combined characteristics of Daniel's four beasts from the Book of Daniel in the Old Testament, where beasts are normally used metaphorically to depict enemies of God and His people."

"Did Daniel say anything else about the End Times in scripture?

"Yes, he did. For one thing, he talked about an archangel, Michael, the great prince who protects your people, who'll arise. There'll be a time of distress such as hasn't happened from the beginning of nations until then. But at that time everyone whose name is found written in the book will be delivered: *Multitudes who sleep in the dust of the earth will awake: some to everlasting life, others to shame and everlasting contempt. Those who are wise will shine like the brightness of the heavens, and those who lead many to righteousness like the stars forever and ever. But you, Daniel, roll up and seal the words of the scroll until the time of the end. Many will go here and there to increase knowledge.*[16]

In my modern world, we live in a time when knowledge has increased dramatically, so I think Daniel is speaking of my era."

"Yes, from what you've told me, I do too. So, is something similar in the New Testament?"

"Mark talks about the elect, the chosen people of God when he says that those will be days of distress unequaled from the beginning, when God created the world, until now, and never to be equaled again and if the Lord had not cut short those days, no one would survive.

> *But for the sake of the elect, whom he has chosen, he has shortened them. ....At that time men will see the Son of Man coming in clouds with great power and glory. And he will send his angels and gather his elect from the four winds, from the ends of the earth to the ends of the heavens.*[17]

And in the Old Testament, scripture says that he *will bring them out from the nations and gather them from the countries.*"[18]

"But, does the Bible say anything about those who'll be slain during the tribulation?" Huldah asked.

"Here is a reference to the slain in Revelation:

> *When he opened the fifth seal, I saw under the altar the souls of those who had been slain because of the word of God and the testimony they had maintained. They called out in a loud voice, 'How long, Sovereign Lord, holy and true, until you judge the inhabitants of the earth and avenge our blood?' Then each of them was given a white robe, and they were told to wait a little longer, until the full number of their fellow servants, their brothers and sisters, were killed just as they had been.*[19]

Scripture also says *there will be terrible times in the last days. …In fact, everyone who wants to live a godly life in Christ Jesus will be persecuted, while evildoers and impostors will go from bad to worse, deceiving and being deceived.*[20] All those who live godly lives will be persecuted. And, if there is no respite, and if circumstances get worse and worse, the Lord will return at that time to rescue his remaining people. Then the remnant, those who know the Lord, will be saved. So, Huldah, what do you think? Do you think Christians will remain on earth during the End Times?"

"From what you've told me, there seems to be overwhelming evidence that God will 'keep [Christians] through' the hour of testing that precedes the consummation of the kingdom, rather than 'keeping them from undergoing' it."

"Huldah, I agree. Now, I want to ask you something else. My world is enduring the period Jesus called 'the beginning of birth pains,' so the signs of the end, which have been evident throughout the entire course of this age, are now becoming more apparent. The despair of humanity and the groaning of creation are telling us that God must soon intervene to undo the consequences of human sin. And, that's why Jesus described this evil time in history as resembling a woman's birth pains. Birth pains become more frequent and grow in intensity as the moment of birth draws near."

"Things in your modern world are really getting bad, aren't they?"

Saphah took up the last of the fried pies. Then Huldah poured two cups of freshly brewed tea, and they each sat back down on a cushion. "Yes, it's horrendous. In the U. S., lawlessness and evil are starting to hold sway. Enemies are within our borders and enemies are without, and discord and hate are readily apparent everywhere. Thus, mankind in my world is steadily descending the ladder of moral corruptness and getting closer and closer to the bottom rung with every step."

"Yet, those who presently lack the eyes of faith are unable to discern what is happening around them and will be caught unaware even though the signs of the Lord's coming are apparent to others. Thus, *while* [these] *people are saying 'peace and safety' destruction will come on them suddenly, as labor pains on a pregnant woman, and they will not escape.*"[21]

"Saphah, you know what you need to do, don't you?"

"Yes, I do. Christians must be bold to share the gospel even if only a few will comprehend. Of course, those who don't understand will undoubtedly spew hatred and vitriol toward those who try to warn them. Therefore, we Christians may be badly persecuted for sharing our faith at that time. Huldah, please tell me what Christians should do to persevere in the face of the coming persecution and suffering."

"For one thing, your people need to remember that the signs of the end are a guarantee that Jesus Christ is coming again soon to end the age."

"True, so true!" Saphah nodded her head in agreement. "And, since Christ suffered for us, surely we can suffer for others too in the hope they'll turn to Him for Salvation. Jesus said that those who are persecuted are blessed, *for theirs is the kingdom of heaven. Blessed are you when people insult you, persecute you and say all kinds of evil against you because of me. Rejoice and be glad, because great is your reward in heaven, for in the same way they persecuted the prophets who were before you.*"[22]

"Yes, Isaiah is one of the leading examples of an Old Testament prophet being persecuted, and there are many others."

"Yes, and Paul is an example from the New Testament of a persecuted prophet. Yet Paul wrote from prison to the Philippians telling them to persevere under persecution because suffering is a gift: *For it has been granted to you on behalf of Christ not only to believe in him, but also to suffer for him, since you are going through the same struggle you saw I had.*[23] Additionally, Paul knew his justification, sanctification, and glorification all came from Christ by faith: *That I may know him, and the power of his resurrection, and the fellowship of his sufferings, being made conformable unto his death.*[24] Hence, persecution is all about the fellowship of sharing Christ's sufferings for the sake of others."

"Yes, it is, and even to the point of death for the cause of Christ," Huldah pointed out. "Do you know if your bible provides guidance especially for persecution?"

"Definitely," Saphah answered. "In fact, the main purpose of the Book of Revelation written by John is to comfort the church in its struggle against the forces of evil. It is chock-full of assistance for persecuted and suffering saints. We realize, of course, that the real author is not John but God Himself:

> *The revelation from Jesus Christ which God gave him to show his servants what must soon take place. He made it known by sending his angel to his servant John, who testifies to everything he saw—that is, the word of God and the testimony of Jesus Christ. Blessed is the one who reads aloud the words of this prophecy, and blessed are those who hear it and take to heart what is written in it, for the time is near.*[25]

And, one of the main takeaways is that 'blessed are those who hear it and take to heart what is written in it.'"

"So, the Book of Revelation was actually written for all people living in the period after Christ's ascension?"

"Well," Saphah pointed out, "the starting point for Revelation owes it origin to contemporary conditions in John's time and for believers living in that age. It is the Lord's answer to prayers of the severely persecuted Christians scattered about the cities of Asia Minor at that time. The conditions that prevailed in the last decade of the first century AD provided the immediate context for this prophecy. But the writing was for both those who first read it, and for all believers throughout this dispensation. The entire church is in mind and the counsel and consolations of the words were meant for Christian believers of all centuries thereafter."

"So, what is the focus of the Book of Revelation?" Huldah wanted to better understand what Revelation taught.

"The theme is the victory of Christ and His church over Satan (the dragon) and his helpers. This apocalypse is designed to show us that the things which happen are not what they appear to be. For instance, in the case of the two witnesses, who may symbolize believers who testify in the final period before Christ returns,[26] the beast that comes up out of the abyss appears to be victorious because:

> *He will attack them, and overpower and kill them, [and] their bodies will lie in the public square of the great city—which is figuratively called Sodom and Egypt—where also their Lord was crucified. For three and a half days some from every people, tribe, language and nation will gaze on their bodies and refuse them burial. The inhabitants of the earth will gloat over them and will celebrate by sending each other gifts, because these two prophets had tormented those who live on the earth.[27]*

But the gloating and celebrating are premature, because actually it is the believers who triumph."

"Are there other examples of happenings that are not what they *appear* to be."

"Yes, throughout Revelation there are instances of believers who *appear* to have prayers that are not heard,[28] but the judgments sent upon the earth are God's answer to those prayers.[29] There are other times when believers *appear* to be defeated, yet in reality they reign![30] Still other times there are evildoers such as the dragon, the beast, the false prophet, and Babylon, *who appear* to be conquerors, but they are actually defeated.[31] In short, the theme of Revelation is stated supremely in these words: *They will wage war against the Lamb, but the Lamb will triumph over them because he is Lord of lords and King of kings—and with him will be his called, chosen and faithful followers."*[32]

"So, Christ is pictured throughout Revelation as victorious. Is that right?"

"Yes, it is. He conquers death, hades, the dragon, the beast, the false prophet, and the worshipers of the beast. He is victorious, and as a result, so are believers, even if we seem to be defeated. Believers need to always keep that fact in mind, because as God's people are faithful to their calling and bear testimony concerning the truth, tribulation will aways follow. And, the church is in the world, so it will also suffer along with the world. Christians will not escape the horrors of such things as war, famine, and plagues. It is the church in tribulation. But it is made clear that all these trials are controlled by the One who is sitting upon the throne."

"Will some believers be released from tribulation?"

"Revelation 7 points out that a great multitude in white robes will be freed. They're composed of individuals:

> *Who have come out of the great tribulation; they have washed their robes and made them white in the blood of the lamb. Therefore …He who sits on the throne will shelter them with his presence. Never again will they hunger, never again will they thirst. The sun will not beat down on them, nor any scorching heat. For the Lamb at the center of the throne will be their shepherd; he will lead them to springs of living water. And God will wipe away every tear from their eyes.*[33]

The Lord is watching over them and shepherding them for eternity."

"What does all of that mean?"

"The point is that believers will come out of their trials. They'll get beyond the suffering. These saints whom John beholds in a vision, have 'washed their robes and made them white in the blood of the Lamb.' In other words, they've placed their trust in the saving blood of the Lamb, Jesus Christ, and by means of His blood they've been made white. Therefore, they're before the throne of God in heaven, that is, in His immediate presence. And, the One who sits on the throne will 'lead them to springs of living water,' which symbolize eternal life and salvation. And, finally, the most blessed part of all, 'God will wipe away every tear from their eyes.' Nothing but heavenly bliss, perfect fellowship, and abundant life remains!"

"How beautiful! Praise God."

"Yes, praise God for his tender mercies!"

~

Rebecca and Hannah walked in the door. "Good morning girls," Huldah greeted them. "Saphah and I made apricot pies."

"Yes, good morning, Rebecca and Hannah." Saphah pointed with her arm toward the location of the pies. "Would one of you please bring the platter over to the table?"

"Oh, they smell so good." Rebecca picked up the tray. "Thank you."

"Yes, thanks for making these apricot pies. I've never had them before," said Hannah. The girls each grabbed a pie and sat down on the cushions by Huldah and Saphah.

"Anybody home," came a voice from outside. "I've got a surprise."

"Oh, that sounds like Ebed." Hannah jumped up from her cushion and headed for the door. "Good morning, Ebed. What is your surprise?"

Ebed held up a big flopping bird by both feet to show Hannah. "Good morning, Hannah. Look what father and mother sent. I hope you like baked goose."

"Oh, roast goose sounds good." Hannah smiled appreciatively at Ebed. "It's been a long time since I've had delicious poultry!"

"Huldah, when do you want me to dress the goose for cooking?" Ebed asked.

"Just put it in the birdcage for now, Ebed. The ladies and I are going to be very busy today doing preparations for the sabbath and starting the sewing projects," said Huldah. "You'll need to wait until the day after Sabbath to get the goose ready. You can come early that morning to prepare the goose before breakfast. Then, you can leave a little early from school that afternoon to build a fire in the outdoor oven for Rebecca and Hannah to bake the goose."

"Alright." Ebed stuffed the big goose back into a sack and tied it with a cord so he and Hannah could take it to the birdcage.

Huldah stood waiting at the door. "Alright now, you two come back in so we can have breakfast. But where are Shallum and Zephaniah?"

"Zephaniah needed to get back home, and Shallum wanted to talk to King Josiah, so they're skipping breakfast this morning. But they both said to tell all of you hello for them."

"Oh, alright. Now go wash your hands in the pan of water over there and then help yourself to the fried apricot pies Saphah and I made."

"Apricot pie, that's what I'm smelling. Well, I've never heard of pie before, but it sure smells good!" Ebed turned toward Hannah, gave her a kiss on the cheek, and then headed over to wash his hands.

"Eb, how were father and mother and the kids?" Rebecca asked.

"Becca, they're all fine. Mom and dad were surprised and pleased to hear of my betrothal to Hannah and happy to know they'll soon be grandparents. Mom suggested that under the circumstances, we should be wedded soon and the supper should take place at their home along with the birthday celebration. Since the birthday event was already planned, it would be simple to turn it into a prelude to the wedding activities." Ebed turned toward Hannah, and sweetly asked, "Does all of that sound alright with you, Hannah? Mother and father wanted me to be sure to ask if you approved of these plans."

"Oh, yes, I approve. It sounds like your mother and father are very nice people, and I'm very pleased I'm going to become a part of your family." Hannah was genuinely happy that Ebed's parents were so kindly welcoming her into the clan. "I just wish my parents could meet you, Ebed."

"Me too." Ebed shook his head sadly. The young man said a short prayer and they all began eating the apricot pies. "Oh my, is this fried pie ever tasty! I'm sure glad you've come to visit our land." He shot a big smile over toward Saphah and gave her a wink.

"Well, I'm glad to be here too."

20

LEARNING THE ROPES

Saphah had enjoyed being in Jerusalem for the Sabbath. On the previous day, the family had made all preparations for the day of worship and rest by cleaning the house, preparing the food, and doing the personal cleansing procedures. Thus, everything had been made perfect for a time of complete devotion to God and relaxation on that day. But Saphah had also prepared for her own private devotions in a corner of the guest bedroom.

Then, on the Sabbath, when the rest of the family went to temple for sacrifices, the American woman remained behind to worship her triune God—Father, Son, and Holy Spirit—in her corner space of the guest bedroom. Everything was tranquil and Saphah was at peace as she worshipped Him during her private devotions. After reading from the Bible, she asked for God's guidance. "Dear Heavenly Father, thank you so much for all of your blessings" Saphah prayed, "Please help me tomorrow to gain insights from Huldah as we talk on the important subject of America's children. Lord, please give me guidance on this vital subject I pray. In Jesus' name. Amen."

~

"Ladies, wake up!" Rebecca urged. "You need to quickly get ready because this is your day to learn the ropes at school. Hannah and Saphah, don't forget to sack up your embroidery stuff so you can both work on completing your embroidery work today. Then we'll have plenty of time to finish the other sewing projects before the celebrations on Wednesday."

"Oh my!" Hannah jumped from bed and then rushed around the room frantically searching for her clothes and project materials.

"It's alright, Hannah. Your embroidery stuff is over here by mine," Saphah informed her.

"Oh, good. I'm scared I won't be able to get everything ready before my wedding. I'm just afraid something will go wrong." Hannah's voice broke as she talked.

"Be at peace, Hannah. …Be at peace. …Everything will be alright." Saphah tried to calm the young girl by stroking her hair away from her face.

"Yes, Hannah." Rebecca kissed her friend on the cheek and hugged her. "We'll all work together to get everything done."

"Now, take a deep breath through your nostrils, Hannah." Saphah was instructing her on a method to calm down.

"Alright." Hannah inhaled a big breath of air through her nose.

Saphah added, "Now, let it out slowly through your mouth. Okay, do it again, over and over several times." Saphah waited for Hannah to finish. "Is it helping?"

Hannah inhaled and exhaled slowly over and over. Finally, she stopped and gave them a relieved smile. "That does help!"

"Now, let's get our morning chores done so we can head to school. We don't want to be late," Rebecca reminded them.

~

"We're here." Rebecca led Hannah and Saphah toward the outdoor entrance to Mrs. Huldah's office at the Jerusalem School. When they reached the door, Rebecca raised her index finger and touched it to her lips as a warning to the others to be quiet. "We must always talk in low voices here at the school." She wanted to be sure her new friends were aware of the strict expectations for quietness.

"Alright," Hannah whispered back and Saphah shook her head in agreement. Quietly, they slipped into the room. Mrs. Huldah was gathering some supplies from a wall of shelves located on the far side of the room, and a tall girl with long brown hair was sitting on a stool behind a desk. The teacher, holding her basket of supplies for the day, turned to greet the new arrivals.

"Good morning, ladies," Mrs. Huldah softly said. "Thank you for being here on time."

"Good morning, Mrs. Huldah." They all smiled and quietly returned her greeting. "Rebecca, would you please introduce Tamara to our visitors?"

"Good morning, Tamara," Rebecca greeted the intelligent looking girl sitting on her stool with her back held straight in perfect posture.

"Good morning, Rebecca," Tamara's big brown eyes widened and a huge smile spread across her face as she turned to speak to the two visitors. "Hello, ladies," she said in her pleasant contralto voice.

I can already tell I'm going to like her, Saphah thought.

Rebecca looked first at Tamara, and then toward Saphah. "Tamara, this is my new friend Saphah from America, a country far, far away. She's here today to learn how to fill in or substitute for Mrs. Huldah when she's away from school."

"Hello Saphah." Tamara arose from her stool, shook her head to adjust her long hair, and then stepped toward Saphah to give her a welcoming hug.

"Tamara, hello," Saphah said and returned the hug.

"Now, Tamara, I want to introduce you to Hannah, who'll soon be my new sister-in-law," Rebecca said proudly.

"Oh, my goodness, you're betrothed to Ebed! Congratulations!" The young girl happily hugged Hannah.

"Thank you, Tamara." Hannah smiled at her and returned the hug. "Ebed has told me about you. He and I would like to invite you to his birthday celebration and our wedding supper. The two events will both be held on the same day."

"Thank you. I'll be looking forward to it." Tamara answered. "Just tell me the day and the time and I'll be there."

"Alright girls, quiet down now," said Mrs. Huldah. "Other students will be arriving soon, so if you need to talk you must use quiet voices. Tamara and Rebecca, please take your seats, and here is a list of your assignments." She handed them a small piece of papyrus on which she'd written her notes. "You know what to do in regard to your recitations and school work. Now, Saphah and Hannah, I'm about ready for you to go with me. But first, Saphah, please note that the school supplies are all located here in my office. Alright, right this way." The two ladies followed Mrs. Huldah into a hall. "The first room to your left is Mr. Caleb's room. He is the teacher of the younger students."

"Good morning, Mrs. Huldah. I see you have visitors today." Mr. Caleb gave them a welcoming smile as he stepped into the hall.

"Yes," Mrs. Huldah said. "This is Saphah, an American lady, who is here to learn about subbing for me when I need to be away. I'm so pleased she has agreed to help me."

"Oh, that's good." Mr. Caleb looked toward Saphah. "I'm glad to hear you'll be filling in for Mrs Huldah. She really needs someone to take her place when she's away. If you ever have a question or need help with a discipline problem, just let me know. I'll be glad to help."

"Thank you," said Saphah. "I'm happy I can be here to help out Mrs. Huldah. And, when I come back to fill in for her, I'll probably need to take you up on your offer."

"And, this is Hannah," Huldah introduced her to Mr. Caleb, "who is betrothed to Ebed."

"Hannah, congratulations." Mr. Caleb's eyes brightened. "I think you're betrothed to a very fine young man."

"Thank you, I think so too. I'm quite happy to be marrying Ebed."

"The next room on the left is our dining area and the room on the right is my schoolroom where I teach older students." Mrs. Huldah motioned toward each area. "The door at the end of the hall leads into the foyer where a cloakroom is located on one side and storage compartments for student supplies are on the other. But the door at the end of the building is the main entrance." She unlocked and opened the door and glanced toward the rising sun. "Oh my, the location of the sun tells me it's time to head back to the classroom. The students will soon be here." The teacher led the way and the ladies followed her into the classroom. "Hannah, did you bring your embroidery work?"

"Yes." Hannah held up her hoop for Huldah to see.

"Good." Mrs. Huldah said, "Hannah, why don't you sit on one of the stools over there and begin embroidering while I show Saphah around the room?"

"That'll be great." Hannah sat down, took up her threaded needle, and started embroidering. "I'm really hoping I can get this done today so I can finish my sewing projects tomorrow."

Mrs. Huldah and Saphah slowly walked around the classroom as the students quietly entered and took their assigned seats. "My friend, here is the desk where I usually sit to observe the class when they're doing schoolwork, but the stand over there is where I do recitations and give interpretations of quoted material. We are short on paper for student use, so we use vocal methods for much of our learning here. In vocal learning, instructors speak a short oral lesson and the schoolchildren recite it back using harmonized voices and speaking in unison to help them retain it in memory."

"So, what material will I use for recitations when you're away?" Saphah was beginning to wonder if she'd made a mistake in saying she'd fill in for Mrs. Huldah.

"When you're subbing, you'll find scrolls or other written materials you need for recitations on this desk, along with plans for the day. You'll also find a roster and attendance scroll on which to check off absentees. Items for discipline wlll also be here in a drawer, such as a leather shoe strap, a wooden switch, and a paddle. If a student is recalcitrant, please feel free to handle punishment according to your discretion. Discipline is vital when teaching young people, and especially so when you're teaching four grade levels. So, I'll warn my students that anyone giving you problems will answer to me when I return. Just keep a list of any students who give you trouble."

"Alright, I will. What discipline problems might I encounter?"

"Problems that could happen might pertain to inattentive students or those who won't recite back lessons as required. You may correct them by using this leather shoe strap which is a less severe form of corporal punishment. However, if a student remains incorrigible you are permitted to use either the switch or the paddle. Young men in this age group have been known to test a new teacher to see if they'll maintain control. I really don't think you'll run into difficulties, but in case you do, I just want you to be prepared. Also, remember Mr. Caleb is next door and he'll be glad to assist if you have a disobedient student."

"Alright, I'll remember."

After all the students arrived and all the stools were occupied except for a missing student, Mrs. Huldah addressed her pupils: "Good morning students. I'm pleased to tell you that you have two visitors today who're houseguests at our home. Everyone, this is Saphah, who'll be your substitute teacher when I'm away and Hannah, who is betrothed to Ebed. Now, students, please welcome Saphah and Hannah." The students vigorously clapped for the two ladies. "Now, everyone please stand up." They all arose and Huldah addressed one young man: "Joel would you like to begin our day with prayer?"

"Yes." The young man with black hair and brown eyes began the opening prayer. "Heavenly Father, we are thankful for the blessings you bestow upon us each day. Please forgive us our sins, provide for our needs, and help us to be upholders of your law and upright citizens of our land. Please help and guide Mrs. Huldah as she teaches us. Thank you that she now has Saphah to sub whenever she is sick or away. We're glad she is our guest today and that Ebed's betrothed, Hannah, is our guest too. Please lead and guide us in all we do today. Amen."

Saphah tried to do as much embroidery work as she could while observing Mrs. Huldah as she gave oral lessons and the students as they recited material back. All pupils were obedient except for a new student who began the day by refusing to recite. Mrs. Huldah warned the little guy several times to begin reciting, but each time he refused.

So, she began slowly walking around the room as she continued the oral lessons. "Now everyone, please recite after me," she said again as she drew near the boy. He stubbornly refused again, but then was startled to feel the sharp flick of a leather shoe strap striking his arm.

"Ouch!" he yelled loudly.

"Recite," Mrs. Huldah repeated in an authoritative voice. But the youngster shook his head no, so the schoolmarm flicked him again, this time on his forearm. "Recite," she commanded again.

"Alright! Alright!" Then the youngster quickly began to recite the lesson after Huldah.

That's a painful way to learn to be obedient, Saphah thought to herself as she observed red welts on the boy's arm, *but it's an effective way to teach pupils a lesson.* She remembered a time in early childhood when she attended a rural one-room school and her teacher used a switch on a disobedient new student.

The teacher grabbed the child by the arm, took her outside, cut a little switch from a tree, and switched the girl on her bare legs. When the two came back in, the other students could see the red marks left by the switch. So, it was a lesson for both the new girl and the other students who might be considering misbehavior. Of course, since one teacher was instructing eight grades, nary a parent said a word. They knew teachers must maintain order and obedience so all the students can learn.

Midmorning soon arrived with time for a break, and that's when the young people asked to have a spelling contest. But Saphah was surprised when one of the students piped up, "Mrs. Huldah, since our new substitute is here, and she can give us the words to spell, would you be a contestant alongside us?"

At this, the other students began chanting, "Mrs. Huldah, Mrs. Huldah, Mrs. Huldah."

"Oh, my goodness, you want me to be in your spelling contest?"

"You heard them." Saphah smiled at Mrs. Huldah. "They're drafting you."

"I don't know." The instructor tried to get out of participating. "Why don't you spell instead of me, Hannah?"

"Oh, go on up, Mrs. Huldah." Hannah waved her hand forward and smiled as she urged the teacher to go up front with other contestants. "I really need to get my embroidery work done today."

Mrs. Huldah continued to stand there.

"Mrs. Huldah, Mrs. Huldah, Mrs. Huldah," the boys happily chanted again.

"Oh, alright." The teacher handed Saphah the spelling list and slowly walked to the front. Then all contestants stated their names one by one, and Saphah began giving them spelling words.

Although the students all did well, by the end of break contestants were down to two—Amos and Mrs. Huldah. Although Saphah kept giving them new words to spell, neither one misspelled a word." Finally, Saphah asked in frustration, "I think breaktime is over, so what do you two want to do?"

"Let's call it a tie," Amos said laughing.

"Whew, I agree." Mrs. Huldah was getting tired of spelling words. "Let's shake hands." The two shook hands and the class erupted in cheers.

"That was fun," Saphah said. "Maybe we can do it again when I sub for Mrs. Huldah later on." The rest of the morning went well and the sub apprentice was able to glean lots of vital details for subbing at the Jerusalem School.

"Alright Saphah, it's about time for lunch. When we get to the dining hall, we can start our discussion. But if you don't mind telling me now, what are we going to talk about?" asked Mrs. Huldah.

Saphah whispered as softly as she could, "Remember how I told you earlier that many in my world have turned away from God? They possess debased minds and think they know everything without knowing God. Some people of this sort in big American cities are pushing others every way they can with their insanity. They're doing crazy things that make no sense and even trying to indoctrinate and sexualize our smallest citizens, the little children."

"Who're these people?" Mrs. Huldah was so dismayed to hear what Saphah had said, she forgot to speak quietly. As a result, several inquisitive students looked up from their work at the two women.

Saphah waited a few seconds until the students returned to their work to quietly speak again. "They're 'educators' in mainly large cities who're out to destroy the innocence of our kids by indoctrinating them in theories such as CRT, inclusion, equity, transgenderism and associated issues. But I think the last issue, transgenderism, is the most troublesome and has caused me the most angst."

"Oh, my! Why are the 'educators' trying to sexualize little children? And, how did this state of affairs become acceptable in America?" Mrs. Huldah frowned as she whispered.

"We'll need to wait to begin our conversation until we get to lunch, don't you think?" Saphah asked. "Is there a spot away from the other students where we can discuss this privately?"

"Yes, of course. Grab your lunch, and I'll tell the youngsters." Mrs. Huldah reached for her own sack lunch and turned toward the boys. "Students, you're going to have different seating arrangements in the dining hall today. Instead of sitting spread out in groups, you're going to sit all together on the far side. We have two guests, Saphah and Hannah, along with Rebecca, Tamara, and myself. We ladies are planning to sit separate from you to talk privately. Don't forget your lunches and jars for your drinks, and now we'll mosey down to the dining hall. Please be quiet so we won't disturb Mr. Caleb's class."

Rebecca and Tamara walked into the room. "Hello, ladies. Please join us as we go to the dining area," Huldah instructed.

"Hannah, how is your embroidery work coming along today?" Saphah softly whispered as they walked along.

"It's coming along fine. Do you want to see what I've done?" Hannah held out her embroidery hoop so Saphah could see her work.

"Wow! You're embroidering like an old pro. Great Job!" Saphah whispered and then held out her own hoop for Hannah to see.

"Oh, that looks just wonderful!" Hannah ran her fingers across the smooth embroidery work on the fabric in Saphah's hoop as they continued walking.

The male students filed into the dining area first, stood in line to get milk, juice, or bakery items from farm maidens selling their products, and sat on the far benches. Then Mrs. Huldah and Saphah, plus the three girls, also stood in line for their drinks and sat on two other benches away from the young men. "Rebecca, Tamara, and Hannah, I hope you enjoy your lunches. While we eat, Saphah and I are going to have a private talk about some things happening in her world, so please excuse us for dining apart from you."

"Oh, that's fine," Rebecca said. "We've some things to talk about too, like Eb's birthday celebration and the wedding supper."

"And, who knows what else." Tamara laughed and winked at Hannah, who smiled and blushed as she opened her lunch sack.

"Alright," Saphah said. "Enjoy your lunches." The two ladies sat down as far from the others as they could and opened their lunches which consisted of flat bread, goat cheese, almonds, and raisins.

"Finger food," Saphah said. "This is a perfect lunch for us to eat today while we talk. Thank you."

"You're welcome. That's what I thought, too. Now, let's both say our prayer, and then you can tell me more. How long have you known of the situation with the 'educators' at big city schools indoctrinating children?"

"Well, ordinary people began to realize something was going on around the time we had the Covid Pandemic which began late 2019. Since the plague was worldwide and many people were dying, the citizens of most nations, including the children, were partially quarantined for long periods of time."

"You had a worldwide illness?" Mrs. Huldah was greatly intrigued by the idea. "How could an illness spread to every country in your world?"

"Do you remember the scripture I quoted you earlier written by an Old Testament prophet named Daniel?"

"Yes, I do."

"Do you also remember the last sentence of the quote?"

"Actually, I do. It was about people going here and there to increase knowledge."

"Well, that's what it's like in my advanced society. Knowledge has increased to the point where we've learned to build self-motorized carriages in which we can travel at amazing speeds. And, we've also invented forms of communication that are almost instantaneous. That's why we can have worldwide wars and pandemics. In fact, there was a pandemic around 1918 to 1920 which killed an estimated 20 to 50 million victims worldwide. The movement of soldiers and civilians during World War 1 contributed to the rapid spread of that pandemic around the globe."

"So, what actually occurred during the Covid Pandemic that caused your citizens to know something nefarious was affecting education?"

"During the pandemic many American kids had to do their school work at home by virtual learning to prevent them from catching covid. That's when parents in large cities began to realize something fishy was going on in some of the educational systems."

"Please explain to me about virtual learning. What is it?"

"You've asked me a tough question which is impossible for me to adequately answer. Again, remember what Prophet Daniel said about knowledge increasing in the end times. Well, our knowledge has increased in my time and place to the point that we're able to have machines on which all kinds of information can be disseminated. These machines are called computers and even children can use them to gain knowledge and do schoolwork. It's very, very complicated so I can't really explain it to you. You'll have to take my word for it that such machines exist."

"Oh, I believe you, but it is all very amazing to me. I'm going to have to take a moment or two to let that all sink in." Mrs. Huldah sat in contemplation for several minutes. "So, did the parents of the children doing virtual learning look at the homework of their kids on the machines, computers I think you called them, and discover something unethical the big city teachers were doing?"

"You're very intuitive. Yes, while the children were doing virtual learning assignments at home, some parents discovered the students were being taught false theories about things like race relations, white privilege, and systemic racism. Kids were even being indoctrinated to believe in a new founding date for America which they said was 1619. Also, the 'educators' were promoting activism by teaching students Critical Race Theory, which is often masked as Diversity, Equity, and Inclusion. These people were even infusing the brains of the little ones with climate fatalism, a deceiving theory frightening to undeveloped minds. And, that's just part of the list of crazy things they've been indoctrinating children to believe."

"I don't know anything about these theories, but from what you're telling me, it sounds like these people are trying to completely change your educational system."

"True! These moms and dads were shocked to suddenly realize that American education had taken such a radical turn. Occurring right before their very eyes was proof that a slow-rolling but effective takeover of our educational system was happening. But some of the most disturbing things the 'indoctrinators' were teaching the kids were false and aberrant sexual theories."

"Oh, my goodness, Saphah. That is almost unbelievable!" Mrs. Huldah was astonished that such a thing was happening.

"Unbelievable!" Saphah shook her head up and down in agreement. "It's like watching a terrible stage play where everything about the country I love is being destroyed, including the innocence of little children. Here is a saying of Jesus about little kids from the Word of

God: Let the little children come to me, and do not hinder them, for the kingdom of heaven belongs to such as these.[1] Yet, in America, some 'educators' hinder 'the little children,' by instilling false outlooks into the minds of youngsters."

"What are some of the false outlooks?"

"Among other things, little ones are taught to abhor their bodies and the genders they possess. The fake 'educators' in mostly big city schools indoctrinate youngsters to think they can change genders by removing or adding parts or by using hormone therapy to change the bodies that God created *male and female*.[2] Even physicians, who take an oath to a code of ethics to heal and not to harm, are denying the oath by mutilating the bodies of kids too young to know enough to reject the wrong and choose the right,[3] as scripture phrases the aspect of a child's ability to discern right from wrong."

"Why in the world are they doing this?" Mrs. Huldah could hardly believe her ears.

"It seems that good and evil have become so subjective in their minds that they've turned everything upside down. They don't believe in the objective truth of God's Word, so they promote evil as good and good as evil."

"In that case, these people are subjects of the evil one," said Mrs. Huldah. "He is their father."

"In the New Testament," Saphah noted. "Jesus said that the devil *is a liar and the father of lies*,[4] so those who belong to [their] *father, the devil, …want to carry out* [their] f*ather's desires*.[5] Truth is foreign to Satan and those who are his. On the other hand, *whoever belongs to God hears what God says*.[6] They believe the objective truth of God's Word and obey it. The Holy Spirit guides them into all truth, teaches them all things, tells them of things to come and much more. But the only way for people to receive the gift of the Holy Spirit is for them to repent of their sins and to accept the Lord Jesus as their personal savior."

"The problem of those who follow Satan is basically spiritual," Mrs. Huldah pointed out. "So, that indicates what is happening in your modern world is a spiritual battle. That is why those who follow the 'father of lies' are rejecting God and His truth in a willful manner. How long has this evil trend been going on?"

"Actually, it began years ago. Our big city educational systems are the product of a secular left hell bent on tearing down the foundations our country was built upon. But this plot happened so gradually and quietly that most Americans were basically unaware of it until the last few years. Misguided people, including some metropolitan school teachers, are seeking to dismantle the core values that created America and to replace them with a secular and godless society. It's a coordinated attack on all areas of American culture such as familial, social, political, religious, and educational."

"I can certainly see why you're so concerned. Please go on."

"As you can imagine, every area of life in my land is affected by the threat of this ideology, but today we'll only have time to discuss the educational aspect. This anti-American and anti-Christian outlook was taught first in higher educational facilities, or perhaps I should call them indoctrination universities, where students were taught all the false theories of the secular left. It was the campus craziness that first made us aware that a problem existed."

"So that's when you first became aware something was awry, but what had led up to all this resistance against your Judean/Christian culture?"

"It is a belief in Marxism, a theory assumed by elitists to explain the inequalities of society, but it leads to communism."

"What is communism?"

"I'll be glad to tell you the shocking truth about this theory because, 'to date, more than 100 million people have been killed by communist regimes around the world in their desire for this utopian fantasy.'"[7]

"Oh my goodness, go on!"

"Some American students are being led astray because 'educators' are ignoring to tell them the truth about the fantasy of 'communism [which] emerged in the 19th century as a political, societal and economic ideology. Karl Marx, in his Communist Manifesto, set the goals and measures necessary to achieve communism including the abolition of private property, abolition of rights of inheritance, the establishment of a classless society, and the centralization of power in the hands of the state. It also specifically called for the destruction of all aspects of the old system through violence and revolution.'"[8]

"So, what is the first example of this occurring?"

"The first attempt happened 'in Russia in 1917, as Vladimir Lenin's initial promise of peace, land and bread quickly devolved into terror, collectivization, famine and civil war leading to deaths of almost 7 million people …[and again] under Josef Stalin who killed upward of 20 million Soviets.'[9] Although the Soviet Union fell in 1991, communism still exists elsewhere."

"Please tell me more about the other instances of the brutality of communism."

"Sadly, 'today one-fifth of humanity still lives under its brutal rule. North Korea threatens nuclear war from a sprawling, 21st-century gulag; Cuba continues to jail, torture and murder dissidents who dare to dream of democracy; Vietnam arrests citizens for simply posting messages critical of the party; and China commits genocide in mass re-education camps, separates families, forcibly sterilizes minority women, uses forced and child labor, and harvests organs of political prisoners.'"[10]

"That's terrible! If students in America aren't taught the truth about communism, they'll fail to understand the danger the system presents to their nation."

"That's so true. And, they need to know that those attempting takeover of their country are using a sinister method. Instead of just aiming for a form of state supremacy like in China, Cuba, Laos, North Korea, and Vietnam, they're shooting for a cultural Marxism, a gradual transformation of our culture into one based on ungodly secular values rather than Christian morality. The Marxists are trying to destroy American culture as we know it and replace it with godless communist ideology. They're seeking to dismantle all the core values that made America so great."

"So, all of this is not just happening?" Mrs. Huldah asked.

"You're right. The things they're doing are not random occurrences but part of a carefully scripted and orchestrated plan to take down the United States of America as we know it."

"What are some of the other things they're doing?"

"The list of their activities is long and includes: delegitimizing our Judea-Christian past to make way for a secular society; using diversity to divide and destroy our people; stifling and shaming those who uphold a Christian worldview; using propaganda to sell their Marxist theory as a noble cause; changing school curricula to lead children to sexual confusion and warped identity by teaching transgenderism; shaming and vilifying those who disagree with them; striving to destroy freedom of speech; and other efforts too numerous to mention."

"Oh, I see what they're doing." Mrs. Huldah was distraught about the situation. "They're trying to erase God from any and all aspects of life in your country and thus destroy your nation."

"Yes!" Saphah shook her head in dismay, "And, some of those who've attended the indoctrination universities have graduated as teachers, so now they're busy 'educating,' or to put it more bluntly, indoctrinating K-12 students in big city schools in their false ideology. They're targeting young people whose minds are not fully formed yet so they're easily indoctrinated. Here is an example from computer social media that an 'educator' posted, but it contains foul language. Huldah, do you still want to hear it?"

"Yes, I definitely do."

"Alright, here goes. A Maryland teacher who described herself on social media as 'proud as f*ck to be liberal' called for an urgent fight against capitalism. The teacher wondered aloud, 'Does anyone else feel like we can skip math, skip the science, like we'll do that next year.' She also posted about providing 'Marxist literature' to kids and said, 'f*ck capitalism!' She shared in one post that she was 'tired after a long day of indoctrinating students.' In a video, she said, 'revolutions involve violence,' and a voice in the background music said, 'Ain't nothing wrong with that.'"[11]

"The language of the teacher is evil, and she is advocating for anarchy. But what this woman should be teaching is regular classwork like the math and science she mentioned, not chaos and carnage and revolutions."

"It sure seems that way. But listen to the following by an elementary music teacher who posted about confusing children about gender.

A teacher described a talk she had with a co-worker, where students allegedly asked the 'other teacher' whether the music teacher was male or female. The co-worker noted the students said that they 'just can't figure it out. It's just so hard. I can't figure it out.' The music teacher then laughed after she described the students remarks and said, 'I was just like, that's the goal. That's the goal.' Social media users 'didn't hesitate to criticize the music teacher for bragging about intentionally confusing the children about her gender.'"[12]

"How horrible to treat little children like that!" Mrs. Huldah was disgusted. "Saphah, please explain the word *transgender* to me."

"'Transgender refers to 'a person whose sex assigned at birth (i.e. usually based on external genitalia), does not align with their gender identity (i.e., one's psychological sense of their gender). Some people who are transgender experience gender dysphoria, psychological pain that results from incongruence between one's sex assigned at birth and one's gender identity. Transgender people may pursue … gender affirmation, including social (e.g., changing name and pronouns), legal (e.g., changing gender markers on government documents), medical (e.g., pubertal suppression or gender-affirming hormones), and/or surgical affirmation (e.g., vaginoplasty, facial surgery, breast augmentation, masculine chest reconstruction, etc.)'"[13]

"What you're describing sounds like some kind of mental incapacity," Huldah observed.

"Actually, it *is* a mental derangement. However, many people 'don't understand that it is a mental disorder some people go through [psychologically] in their head.'"[14]

"But an individual can't change whether they're male or female. That is God's prerogative, for *God created mankind in his own image, in the image of God he created them; male and female he created them,*"[15] Huldah asserted. "Yet school staff and medical people in your country are talking little children into allowing physicians to change their bodies by surgery or medication. How can such procedures be considered safe and proper?" Mrs. Huldah questioned the safety and propriety of the mutilation of a young person's body.

"No, a person cannot change whether they're male or female," Saphah said. "It is scientific fact that males have a pair of chromosomes X and Y in each somatic cell of their body which cannot be changed and women have a pair of chromosomes X and X in each somatic cell. Therefore, a man can never be a woman and a woman can never be a man. Gender reassignment surgery is unable to transmute an X chromosome into a Y chromosome or vice-versa. The surgery does not affect gender at the cellular level. Those who profess to be a gender other than what they are classified by objective science are suffering from the insane delusion of the mental illness called gender dysphoria."

"So, I was correct in stating that a man can never be a woman and a woman can never be a man."

"That is right," Saphah confirmed. "And procedures to attempt to change bodies of children aren't safe or proper. The Association of American Physicians and Surgeons, a national organization of physicians in all specialties, 'warned there are inherently unknown long-term risks to gender-affirming care for minors. Consequences of removing normal, healthy organs are generally irreversible. ... Gender-affirming in minors is medically and ethically contradicted because of a lack of informed consent and the consequences of removing normal, healthy organs are irreversible.'"[16]

"To go back to the big city teachers," Mrs. Huldah observed, "it seems evident that some of them don't even try to hide their activities, but are proud of what they do to confuse kids about their genders and to promote revolution against their nation."

"That's right. They're not worried about getting into trouble because America's big city K-12 school teachers are backed by their big city teachers' unions. 'The teachers' union monopoly wants to force kids to attend their residentially assigned, government-run institutions that they staff. It's about maintaining power. It's about maintaining a monopoly on the minds of other people's kids.'"[17]

"So is that why some of these teachers are so open about what they're doing."

"Yes, a 'new report shows that teacher union contracts with some of the United States' largest cities have aimed to indoctrinate students in leftist ideas through curricula. The defense of Freedom Institute [DFI] released a report …It shows that teacher union contracts with some of the United States' largest cities have aimed to indoctrinate students in leftist ideas through curricula. …The example …in the report is the deal between the Minneapolis Public Schools [MPS] and the Federation of Teachers [MFT]. …The deal, … included a section—titled Protections for Educators of Color—contractually obligating MPS to hire and fire teachers based on race. The DFI asserted that the terms were clear violations of the U.S Constitution's Equal Protection Clause.'"[18]

"The parents in your nation need to know about this."

"Yes, the report shows 'there's a reason why parents throughout the United States keep encountering Critical Race Theory and so-called anti-racist equity curricula, policies, and teaching methods in K-12 classrooms: union contracts often require it. If your child attends school in a unionized school district, you need to understand what is in the collective bargaining agreement with the union because it plays a significant role in what's taught in the classroom'"[19]

"We definitely need to continue our talk about American education." Mrs. Huldah stressed the importance of the subject. "But it's time to head back to the classroom now. What do you think about going with me today after school to the gate where I minister to women and girls? We'll probably get a chance to talk more there."

"Sounds good. Let's resume our talk after school at the gate."

21

THE HULDAH GATE

Mrs. Huldah turned to Saphah as they walked toward the Huldah Gate. "I'm so glad you're going with me to the gate where I minister to women and girls."

"Thanks for inviting me. Please tell me more about what you do there, Huldah, if I may call you that again."

"Of course, after school hours there's no need to precede my name with the formal designation, 'Mrs. Huldah.' Anyway, at the gate the ladies and girls honor me by referring to me as prophetess."

"They do well to designate you as prophetess. I'm in awe of your talents and achievements in Jerusalem. Please fill me in on what you do at the gate, Prophetess Huldah."

"Thank you, Saphah. I'm greatly concerned about the needs of the females, both women and girls, who come to my gate. As you've probably noticed, many women, such as Hannah, aren't respected by their husbands as they should be, so I try to help them however I can. Females in Jerusalem aren't usually allowed to even attend school, and that is one of the reasons I accepted Rebecca and Tamara as students, so they can become teachers for their Rechabite clan. The Rechabites are fine people, and their men generally honor women in a godly manner."

"Well, that is one reason I'm glad Hannah and Ebed are betrothed. She certainly deserves a good man like him."

"Yes, she does. And, Ebed is gaining a wonderful wife and a baby to boot. But there are so many females in Jerusalem who're not that fortunate, and God has called me to minister to them. I try to assist them with the problems they face as females in a male oriented society and with their spiritual needs so they're more mindful of obeying God's commands and aware of His great love and care for them."

"Oh, Prophetess Huldah, that's wonderful."

"The glory goes to God for allowing me this privilege, Saphah."

"Yes, and the glory goes to God for calling me, an ordinary woman, for such a time as this in my modern world. I pray for his guidance every day, because I cannot do this on my own."

"None of us can, my dear, for we're all dependent upon Him in every way for all he has called us to do. After all, it is His work."

"Yes, it is!"

"We're almost there. You're going to see what they refer to as the 'Huldah Gate,' where females congregate to exchange ideas."

"Oh, great. I can't wait." Saphah perked up her ears. "What's that wailing sound?"

"I don't know," Huldah thought the wailing was coming from near her gate. She broke into a brisk walk and Saphah followed suit.

A woman's voice wailed again and then screamed, "Don't take my baby."

"Let's hurry, Saphah."

"Alright." Saphah huffed and puffed as she tried to keep up with her friend.

"Prophetess Huldah, Prophetess Huldah," a pregnant woman yelled as she ran toward them.

"What's wrong, my lady? Tell me what's wrong?" Huldah inquired of Mary, her assistant at the gate.

"A couple have experienced a terrible tragedy. Their little baby was found dead in her crib!" Mary sobbed and buried her face in the palms of her hands.

"Where are they?"

"Over there." Mary pointed toward one side of the Huldah Gate.

The two women looked toward the gate and saw the young mother clutching her dead baby to her chest and a young man crying beside her. Huldah let out a huge sigh, her mouth turned down, and big tears spilled from her eyes. "Oh, Saphah, it's our niece Eve, her husband Jonathan, and their little baby girl, Abigail." Overwhelmed by the tragic loss of her great-niece, Huldah was so overcome with grief she couldn't hold back her tears.

"Come on dear, let's sit down for a moment." Saphah took the prophetess by the hand and led her to a stone bench. "You need to take a moment for yourself before we walk on. Here, put your head on my shoulder and let it all out." She wrapped her arms around the woman as she cried on her shoulder.

"Saphah, please pray for us," the prophetess sobbed.

"Yes, I'll pray for all of you." Saphah's tone was consoling. "Heavenly Father, thank you for your love and care for your people in all times. I come to you today in prayer for Eve and Jonathan who've lost their precious baby Abigail, and for their Aunt Huldah and Uncle Shallum who've also lost their great niece. Lord, please help Eve and Jonathan at this time of emotional loss, and please help Huldah and Shallum as they deal with their own grief too. Lord Jesus, please strengthen me as well so I can assist these special people and perhaps lighten their load. In the precious name of Jesus, I pray. Amen."

"Thank you, my friend." Huldah and Saphah arose.

"Are you sure you're ready to go on now?" Saphah gently asked. Huldah composed herself and sadly moved her head up and down. "Well then, later after you give your condolences to Eve and Jonathan, will you introduce me to Eve and tell her that I've also lost a young daughter and understand her loss."

"Yes, I will." Huldah braced herself for what lay ahead. She wiped her eyes, blew her nose on a hanky, and gave Saphah a brave smile. "Let's go now."

The two walked hand in hand again toward Eve, who continued to clutch her dead little baby to her chest, and Jonathan, who bowed his head in grief beside her. Huldah walked toward the grieving parents. "Oh, Eve and Jonathan, I'm so sorry for your loss." She offered each one consoling words and kissed them both. "I want to introduce you to my new friend, Saphah, who understands how you feel because she also lost a child, her young daughter."

"Hello, Eve and Jonathan, I'm glad to meet you both and so sorry to hear about the tragic loss of your baby girl, Abigail. Could I hold your baby?" After a brief pause, Eve tenderly handed her baby to Saphah.

Saphah admired the tiny baby girl from the top of her curly head to the tips of her bare toes. "She's beautiful."

"Yes, she's beautiful." For the first time Eve began to cry. "She is my baby girl. What will I do without her?"

Saphap handed the little one back to Eve. "Right now, I know you feel as if you can't go on. But please remember what I'm going to tell you: God is with you. It'll take a long period of time, but gradually you'll begin to recover. You'll be able to go on. There's a beautiful psalm which helped me in my grief after the loss of my own child: *Weeping may stay for the night, but rejoicing comes in the morning.*[1] Although the dark night of your grief will probably last for a long time, the dawning of your recovery will remain for eternity for God will eventually turn your sadness into joy."

"But how can I have joy when there's so much grief in my heart?"

"Eve, right now your grief is fresh and painful, so it's overwhelming. But God is at your side and will help you in your journey to recovery. And yes, there's a kind of joy that can coexist with grief. You can be grieving and yet have joy, hope, and peace in your heart. That was the route of my own recuperation. You may discover a different route to reach your destination, but with God's help you'll gain your recovery too. Thus, the same Psalmist could later say: *You turned my wailing into dancing; you removed my sackcloth and clothed me with joy, that my heart may sing your praises and not be silent. Lord my God, I will praise you forever.*"[2]

"Oh, Saphah, thank you for reminding me that with God's help I can survive this grief." Eve kissed her new friend on the cheek.

An older woman approached Eve and gently asked. "My daughter, are you ready now for me to prepare your little one for burial?"

"Yes, I don't think I can do it. Mother, please take care of Abigail for me," Eve said in tears. "I remember the day Aunt Huldah read to the ladies here at the gate about our past King David losing a baby son. As recorded in the scroll from which she read, King David said of his son: Can I bring him back again? I will go to him, but he will not return to me. So, along with King David I can say of my daughter,

'Can I bring her back again? I will go to her, but she will not return to me.'"[3]

"Yes, sweet daughter." Eve's mother hugged and kissed both of them. Then, ever so gently she took her granddaughter Abigail into her own arms. She Looked toward the couple again with tears in her eyes. "As Saphah reminded you, never forget that God is with you. But also remember that we are with you too."

"Thank you, mother. I love you." Eve and Jonathan clung together in tears as they watched their precious Abigail being carried away.

"Huldah," a man's voice cried from a distance. "Huldah."

"Shallum, thank God you're here."

"I came as fast as I could after I heard what'd happened." Shallum took Huldah in his arms, and they sobbed together. Then they went to the grieving couple and Shallum gave condolences. "Jonathan and Eve, we're so sorry for your loss." Shallum and Huldah hugged them each in turn. "Please let us know if there's anything we can do to help."

"Yes," Huldah agreed. "Jonathan, are you and Eve going home with relatives?"

Jonathan motioned his head toward a large group of waiting relatives. "Yes, we are."

"Alright, but why don't you two come over to our home later, have supper with us, and stay all night?"

"I agree," Shallum said. "King Josiah has given me time off, so Ebed and I'll be there for you Jonathan, and the ladies will be there for you Eve."

Jonathan put his arm around Eve's shoulder and looked at her. "What would you like to do, dear?"

"Let's do what they suggested. Let's go to your parent's place first, and then we can go to Uncle Shallum and Aunt Huldah's home for supper and sleepover there, that is, if that's alright with you. It'll be quieter there."

"Of course." Jonathan tenderly hugged Eve. "Let's go sweetheart." He took her hand and the sad couple headed slowly toward their waiting relatives.

"Huldah, I'm going to help you out this afternoon here at the gate." Shallum put his arm around Huldah and kissed her cheek. "King Josiah told me to take off as much time as needed because of the upcoming events of Abigail's burial and the birthday and wedding events."

"Oh, Shallum, that was so nice of the king. Sweetheart, thank you so much for coming." Huldah was grateful for Shallum's thoughtfulness.

"You're welcome, dear." Shallum gave her a hug. "Why don't I announce to the group waiting at the gate that you'll be away because of the tragedy that's occurred and that Mary and I'll fill in for you today."

"Thank you, Shallum, I love you."

"I love you too." Shallum kissed Huldah on the cheek and departed for the gate.

"Saphah," Huldah said, "Let's go to the court area where we can sit privately. But first, I'm going to get us a snack and drink from the vendor here. Would walnuts and apple juice be all right?" Huldah retrieved her flask which was tied to her sash.

"Yes, I feel depleated of energy. Thank you." Saphah handed her own flask to Huldah.

The two walked with their refreshments toward an empty stone bench beside a stone table where they could set their snacks and drinks. "Saphah, I'm so sorry to hear you lost a daughter."

"Thank you. My young daughter was killed in a tragic accident all those years ago."

"So, it was a long time ago. But how are you doing now?"

"I'm doing alright. It's still difficult and more so on anniversaries. But I'm doing well now, because God has healed me. In fact, recently a friend, who is going through difficulties of her own, commented that she could tell I'd been healed. I praise and thank God for healing my heart. I also thank Him for all my remaining relatives, and especially for my son and family and my second husband to whom I'm happily married. All members of my family are dear to me."

"Praise God for all His blessings."

"Huldah, will you please tell me more about Eve and Jonathan?"

"Yes, I'll be glad to. Jonathan was one of my best pupils in school, so Shallum and I were pleased he became betrothed to our niece Eve. Jonathan is supervising cook in the palace kitchen, so he resides at the palace. But Eve started staying with his parents here in Jerusalem after they got married. Please don't say anything about this to anyone, but Eve told me that she and Jonathan's mother don't really get along well. Therefore, the other women in the family ignore Eve most of the time as well. Eve gets lonely living with her in-laws, but at least Jonathan is with her on the Sabbath and for other religious events. And, she did have her little baby Abigail to keep her company, that is until the baby died."

"Oh, I'm sorry and sad to hear that. Under these circumstances, Eve is going to feel so isolated and alone after her child's death. Where do her parents live?"

"Her parents live on one of King Josiah's farms outside of Jerusalem where her father is a supervisor, so it's difficult for Eve to go there to see them. She loves Jonathan and doesn't want to leave him, so she's stuck staying with his parents. Eve visited my gate with Abigail almost every day so she could talk to me and others she met at the gate. Since she lost her dear little girl, she'll feel so alone now if she has to continue to live with her in-laws. It just breaks my heart."

"That is heart-breaking. I'm so glad Jonathan and Eve are coming to our house tonight for supper and to stay for the night."

"Yes, me too." Huldah sighed. "Let's say a prayer for them." Huldah and Saphah each bowed their heads and said a silent prayer for Eve and Jonathan's situation.

"Saphah, are you ready now to get back to the discussion we were having at the school?"

"Yes, but are you sure you're up to it, Huldah? Maybe we should postpone it until later."

"No, I don't think we should put it off. We need to discuss it because the education of children is an important topic in all ages. From what you've already told me, it sounds like some youngsters in America are subject to indoctrination by their teachers. But the question is, what can be done about it?"

"Yes, according to Betsy DeVos, a former education secretary under a previous president in the U.S., 'The system has failed our kids.'[4] However, she thinks there is a way to fix K-12 education in America. But it requires bold policymaking that interrupts the status quo by 'taking education-related decisions away from the federal government and returning them to the states, local school districts, and families. Her goal? For children to no longer be hostages of an education system built to protect itself and failed so many children.'"[5]

"I think she's right about the system failing some American children in large cities."

"Yes, Betsy's kind of thinking is a beacon of hope for millions of American parents in big cities who realize their 'education system is controlled by adults who are using our children as hostages to their cause, be it more regulations on teachers, shutting down competition from charter schools, or the promotion of woke ideology.'"[6] The lady notes that the answer is education freedom which means giving families 'choices of how to use education dollars—resources already being spent—funding kids, not systems or buildings. It means giving teachers freedom to innovate and grow in their profession. It means re-empowering the parents behind the podiums at school board meetings.'"[7]

"Have any states in your land made progress in education freedom?"

"Seeds have been planted in capitols of some states with expanded or new school choice programs. For example, 'Gov. Ron Desantis recently signed groundbreaking reforms to Florida's education system, … expanding school choice to every student in the state.'[8] And, Iowa's Gov. Kim Reynolds 'inked her signature on a law that will allow any Iowa family to use taxpayer funds to pay for private school tuition. …Reynolds touted the law's benefits for families, saying Iowa will be funding students instead of a system.'[9] In addition, 'lawmakers in North Carolina are poised to push ahead with school choice legislation and other education reforms …[using a new] veto-proof supermajority in the house.'"[10]

"That sounds like a good start."

"Yes, it's happening because 'school choice has gained tremendous momentum in recent years. Thirty-one states have at least one program that provides public financial help to enable children to attend private schools."[11] And, it may be a good time for more charter schools, either secular or religious. Recently, John O'Connor, Attorney General of Oklahoma,

> 'ruled the state's laws prohibiting religious charter schools are unconstitutional. The prohibitions, he found, run afoul of the Supreme Court's recent decision in Carson V. Makin, which held that Maine's exclusion of religious schools from a tuition-assistance program for students living in rural school districts violated the Constitution's free exercise clause.'"[12]

"Do other states have charter school laws?"

"Yes, 'forty-five states have charter school laws. All, like Oklahoma [in the past] have required charter schools to be secular and most, like Oklahoma [in the past] also prohibit them from being operated by or affiliated with religious institutions.'[13] But, the constitutionality of these restrictions is at issue."

"Well, it sounds like those other forty-five states should follow Oklahoma's lead."

"I agree. And the implications of Oklahoma's decision to permit religious charter schools are great, 'especially if …the Supreme Court eventually agrees with O'Connor's legal conclusions. …Opening the door to religious charter schools will result in the creation of new religious schools, adding valuable pluralism to the American educational landscape.'"[14]

"That sounds hopeful. Are there additional choices for adding pluralism?"

"Yes, there are several, and I'll tell you briefly about them, but then I'll elaborate on two additional choices which seem especially valid for education in my modern world. Concisely, here are some of the options:

> Home school where the student is educated independently by their parents or guardians; Distance education in which the student is educated by and conforms to the requirements of an online school; Hybrid home school or flex school where the student splits their time between home school and a traditional school environment; Home school cooperatives where there is a cooperative of families who home school their children; Web 2.0 which is a way to simulate a homeschool cooperative online.[15]

And there're numerous other similar types."

"What're the other two choices you were going to tell me about?"

"One choice I'm impressed with is the classical education movement which stresses a return to traditional and historic liberal arts education. It 'focuses human formation and learning on the liberal arts (including the natural sciences) as well as classical literature, the fine arts, and the history of civilization, and emphasis on classical skills such as memorization, recitation, imitation, and grammar.'"[16]

"Please tell me more."

"For example, Florida Governor Ron DeSantis says a movement by Hillsdale College to be 'a model for education nationwide …as part of a larger movement to restore classical education—a liberal-arts curriculum designed to cultivate wisdom and teach children to pursue the ancient ideals of truth, beauty, and goodness.'[17] And, Angel Adams Parham and Anika Prather, …wrote in the Washington post noting:

'As black educators, we endorse classical studies [because] rooted in the fullness of this history, classical education invites us and our students to learn from this rich crossroads and to enter into a millennia-long conversation what it means to be human, the essence of freedom, how to live well and what constitutes a good society.'"[18]

"So, some of the classical schools are already well established?"

"Yes, there are several well established types, such as:

> Around 300 classical Christian schools [that] are members of the Association of Classical Christian Schools. There are also hundreds of public charter classical schools including networks such as the Barney Charter School Initiative and Great Hearts Academies. Nyansa Classical Community also provides after-school programs. Almost 200 classical Catholic schools are part of the Institute for Catholic Liberal Education. The U.S. has many homeschooling communities, with over 1000 communities that are part of Classical Conversations, and over 100 that are part of the Scholé Communities Network.[19]

Additionally, the movement has inspired several graduate programs."

"Well, the classical school movement does sounds like a good choice for educating America's children. But now, please tell me about the other school choice you mentioned."

"Yes, another viable choice for educating our precious children is the re-emergence of the one-room-school like the one I attended up to fourth grade. Or, as it's called today in modern parlance, the micro-school."

"So, did a lot of one-room-schools exist in your nation at that time?"

"Yes, in fact, the one-room schoolhouse was once a signature of the American education landscape:

> [While only] 190,000 such schools [existed] in 1919, today, roughly 400 remain. [Although] many would characterize it as a relic of the past or a remnant of rural America, the one-room schoolhouse may instead be a vision for the future of education. The kind of teaching and learning that takes place in such an environment is much needed in today's world and a modern-day version of the one-room schoolhouse can serve as a model for renewal of education."[20]

"What was it like going to a one-room-school?"

"It was a lot like the Jerusalem School. In the one room-school I attended, students of all ages from grades one to eight learned in a single classroom with a single teacher. But, here in Jerusalem School students from all grades learn in two classrooms with two separate teachers. One teacher here teaches the lower grades and one teaches the upper grades."

"That does sound similar. Was there good discipline of students at your school?"

"There was excellent discipline since one teacher had to teach all grades. Students were quiet and well behaved. If not, they generally faced switching, paddling, or other corporeal punishment. Once, in first grade, I made the mistake of drawing on my wooden desk. When I was caught, the teacher made me stand on my tip toes with my nose against the blackboard. She used white chalk to draw a circle on the black board where my nose was supposed to stay. I had to stand on my tiptoes there with my nose in the circle until I was permitted to sit back down."

"Did you ever write on your desk again?"

"No," Saphah said and laughed heartily. "That taught me a lesson about not writing on my desk."

"What did your parents say?"

"Actually, I have to admit that I didn't tell them." Saphah laughed again at the memory. "Because if I had told them, they would've punished me again."

"So, the parents at that time in your world held up for the teachers if they used physical punishment?"

"Definitely! They knew there had to be good discipline so teachers could teach and students could learn. But now, according to a teacher, Daniel Buck, who spoke as part of a three-teacher panel, there's 'a trend away from discipline, standard punishments, consequences, and behavior is worsening across the country, and it's affecting everything else in education, including teacher morale.'[21] Buck claimed the trend 'is the number one reason teachers are quitting …the classroom.'[22]

"Are schools facing teacher shortages?"

"Yes, the trio said schools are 'facing growing problems with staff shortages… and moral dilemmas about politics in the classroom.'[23] A teacher from New York, Brook Ooten, told the host that 'the biggest issue we're having right now is there's a national teacher shortage. …Three-quarters of U. S. states now report that they are short on teachers. We have teachers leaving the profession in droves.'[24] But a Rhode Island teacher 'raised concern over teachers being forced to adhere to political ideologies in the classroom …and contrary to what their personal beliefs are and contrary to what is even right or true.'"[25]

"It sounds like a lot of teachers don't know what to do about these problems, so they're leaving the profession."

"That may be the case. But it seems to me the problems they face are also due to the spiritual and moral decline of America. Maybe it's also because some in our nation no longer follow God's biblical principles or commands which are intended as rules of conduct."

"Perhaps too many people in your land have turned away from God. You know what scripture says about discipline, don't you?"

"Yes, I do. For instance, it says that *whoever spares the rod hates their children, but the one who loves their children* [will] *discipline.*"[26]

"That's right. Huldah went on to elaborated. "The use of the word rod is figurative for caring discipline of any kind, because in this verse parents or teachers are encouraged to apply punishment so that young people will not follow a path of destruction."

"Another verse says to *discipline your children, for in that there is hope; do not be a willing party to their death.*[27] In other words," Saphah explained, "do not be the one who causes a child to die spiritually or physically from the unfortunate choices uncorrected children can make."

"True, and that's because *a rod and a reprimand impart wisdom, but a child left undisciplined disgraces its mother.*[28] Discipline also promotes a happy family life, because correction is rooted in love, so *if you discipline your children, …they will give you peace.*[29] Scripture states that even *the Lord disciplines those he loves as a father the son he delights in.*"[30]

"It does. And, the New Testament also notes that God disciplines His children because it says: *My son, do not make light of the Lord's discipline, and do not lose heart when he rebukes you, because the Lord disciplines the one he loves, and he chastens everyone he accepts as his son.*[31] And, *no discipline seems pleasant at the time, but painful. Later on, however, it produces a harvest of righteousness and peace for those who have been trained by it.*"[32]

"Yes, correction is beneficial, so it is far from being a reason for despair. Rather, it is a basis for encouragement and perseverance, because when applied correctly and received submissively, discipline produces righteous living."

"Thus, we need good discipline both at home and at school for the benefit of the kids. To return to our previous subject, I noticed the similarity between the educational atmosphere in the Jerusalem school and my one-room-school. Huldah, today I saw you enlist the help of some older students to help younger ones with their school work. Back in my day, when I attended a one-room-school, teachers also directed older kids to help younger students."

"It is a win, win situation for everyone."

"Right. With the small school experience, one can begin to see distinct pedagogical advantages that are quite rare in today's school systems:

> 'The students often helped with the teaching; older kids or those who mastered material more quickly would help others. Additionally, a student who was advanced in math, for example, could simply do math with the older kids. Because there was more fluidity in the learning, the one-room schoolhouse became more of a community-based education where everyone had to pitch in to some extent.'"[33]

"I think it's true students learn better when they have to teach the material to others."

"I agree. Studies have shown the strength of team or peer-based learning:

> Peer-based and team-based learning [are] quite beneficial, particularly to prepare students for success in workplaces

> where group-based work across teams of different ages and backgrounds is prevalent. Even 1st grade students providing one another feedback as part of an iterative educational process yields a profound outcome. …In the one-room schoolhouse, by design and out of necessity, these kinds of practices flourished. In today's education system, these practices are more fringe than core. …The notion of education taking place across different ages—where students are also teachers, and where team-based education proliferates—is indeed an exciting vision for the future.[34]

I can certainly vouch for the team-oriented learning experience."

"But what caused the doom of the one-room school?"

"Here's what the Tuscaloosa News wrote in 1931: 'Modern roads, modern transportation and modern minds open to the future, cannot tolerate condition that attends the one-teacher school. Their abolition is certain and every decrease in their number means increased intelligence for the children of the present and of posterity.'[35] That was the thinking back then, but now old has suddenly become new again:

> Today, the micro-school is being touted as an important model for creating innovative, personalized learning experiences. Such an environment, the thinking goes, can ease the creation of close relationships among teachers and students. It can provide an easy venue for experimentation.'"[36]

"Would the modern-day version of the one-room-school be different from the past?"

"A modern-day version of the one-room schoolhouse would look quite different, because that type of learning doesn't have to take place in a literal one-room building. Also, the atmosphere of the 'micro-school can transcend the isolation of those rural cabins of yore with digital resources, field trips, and visiting experts arriving by Google Hangout.'[37] In addition, there's no need for a cookie cutter type of accommodation to children's educational needs. So, if the micro-school makes a re-emergence in some form, it can develop in whatever direction is needed for the good of the children. That is what American parents and grandparents desire above all else."

"In the meantime," Huldah emphasized, "I hope those who care about children in your land will begin standing up to false ideology and doing everything they can to bring awareness of what's happening."

"Well, slowly I think they're beginning to stand up." Saphah was hopeful. "Huldah, I'm very happy we've had this little talk."

"Me too. Now, Saphah, let's tell Shallum that we're heading home to help Rebecca and Hannah with preparations for supper and the sleepover."

"Alright. That big goose Ebed brought home is going to make a great meal for supper tonight with Eve and Jonathan. I'm glad we're going home now to help the girls."

"Oh." Huldah suddenly remembered. "I forgot to tell you something. Shallum mentioned that King Josiah wants you to speak at the reform meeting after the celebrations."

"Really!" Saphah was surprised but honored that the king wanted her to speak at the meeting. "I'm sure glad you told me. Maybe I can begin work on a speech tonight after supper."

"Yes, you must. But if you're unable to finish tonight, maybe you can finish it when you sub at the Jerusalem school. If need be, Joel or Baruch can lead some of the recitations for you."

"Huldah, that's a good idea, because I also need to finish sewing my new sash and headwear. I'm really tired, but I'm going to try to get as much of the speech done as I can tonight, so I can sew tomorrow."

"Saphah, it'll all work out. C'mon, dear, let's talk to Shallum and head for home."

22

THE BIRTHDAY CELEBRATION

Shallum shook the shoulders of the sleeping young man. "Wake up, Ebed. It's your big day. You need to go out to your parent's camp to help them with some preparations. Ebed, wake up!"

Ebed abruptly sat upright from his bed, stretched out both arms, jumped up from the covers, and joyously sang, "Celebration time!" Shaking his hair away from his forehead, he began to loudly sing, "It's my big day, hooray! It's my birthday and wedding day all rolled into one, praise Yahweh! It's my big day, Hooray! I'm going to marry Hannah and love her forever, praise Yehweh!"

"Yes, it's your big day, but I think you've forgotten to do something important." Shallum shook his head as he reminded Ebed of his omission.

Becoming serious again, Ebed solemnly thought for a moment, then bowed his head and prayed. "Thank you, Yahweh, for sending a sweet and lovely girl, Hannah, to be my bride. And, thank you too for all your other blessings. Amen." Ebed moved around the room whistling his tune as he tidied his sleeping area, put on his clothes, and grabbed his back pack. Alright, I'm ready to go."

"Here's your water." Shallum handed a flask to Ebed and patted him on the back. "King Josiah is providing a chariot and driver for you."

"King Josiah is the best!"

There was a tapping at the door and Shallum answered it. "Your chariot is waiting," Shallum announced to Ebed. "God's speed, young man, and we'll see you later."

"Shallum, see you later. ..." Ebed trailed off as he ran out the door.

~

It was still dark when Saphah awoke, opened her eyes, and then remembered it was Hannah and Ebed's wedding day. *Oh my,* she thought, *I need to get right up. I'm subbing today at the Jerusalem School while Huldah attends the birthday festivities.* She quietly slipped out of bed, entered the washroom, cleaned up, and dressed in a new garment Huldah had sewn for her to wear when she subbed. *This is really a nice outfit and such a pretty color!* Saphah smoothed her long skirt. *Now, after I finish subbing today, I can return here to change into my nicest robe with my new sash and headwear before I travel out to the camp for the wedding festivities.*

Huldah stuck her head in the door. "Good morning, Saphah. You're up bright and early."

"Good morning, Huldah. Thank you for sewing this lovely garment for me. I really like it."

"You're welcome. I'm glad I could sew it for you."

"The reason I'm up early this morning is because it's my first day of subbing for you, and I want to have plenty of time to get prepared. Huldah, I thought things went well with Eve and Jonathan being with us for the baked goose supper and the sleepover, didn't you?"

"I did." Huldah was pleased with her recollection of events. "While you and I were doing the dishes, I was happy that the two girls took Eve under their wings by going to Rebecca's room where they all visited and got to know one another. And, Shallum told me that he and Ebed got better acquainted with Jonathan too. The three of them share a lot in common since they all work at the palace. Ebed even told Jonathan that he and Hannah are betrothed."

"Is baby Abigail's burial today?"

"Yes. They left our home early to be with family before Abigail is buried this morning," said Huldah. "Then late this afternoon, they'll be traveling over to the Rechabite Camp for the reform meeting. Although King Josiah told the couple they weren't required to come, the two decided it was important for Jonathan to attend so he'd be prepared when the actual reforms begin. Also, Eve wants to come so she can be with her husband as much as she can."

"Well, after the reform meeting is over, it would be nice if Eve could come stay with us for awhile. Huldah, what do you think?"

"Yes, Jonathan will be going back to supervise in the palace kitchen soon, so I think it would be better for Eve if she could be with us more. I just can't imagine her having to go back to live with her unfriendly in-laws right now."

"Me either."

"Let me talk to Shallum. Maybe we can figure something out."

"Good idea." Saphah smiled and grabbed her backpack. "Alright, I'm ready for school and so glad I got to train one day with you. Now I already know your students, your schedule, and my responsibilities. Did you leave me sub notes and a roster for today at school?"

"Yes, plus I left the names of responsible older students who can be your helpers. You don't know how much I appreciate your help with my youngsters. I'm thrilled that I'll be able to attend the birthday celebration and watch Ebed open his gifts. After that, I'll travel back here so I can get a good night's sleep and teach again tomorrow."

"Well, I'm really glad I could sub for you today. After all, I won't miss everything at the celebrations. After school, I can quickly change clothes and travel over by palace chariot, so there'll be plenty of time for me to see the birthday gifts and then attend all the wedding events. It was so nice of King Josiah to offer the transportation for all of us."

"Yes. Ebed and Hannah plan to escort you around in the afternoon. Then, after the wedding supper and gift opening, you'll have the pleasure of being with the group as they send off the newlyweds. They'll be traveling this evening back here by chariot to our home. Since they'll be in the guest bedroom now, we've made arrangements so you can room with Rebecca. The carpenters have set up a bed for you in her room and built you a new storage box."

"That's great! Thank you so much."

"You're welcome. I hope you have a great day. Here, I've packed you a lunch."

"Oh, that's so sweet. Thank you again." Saphah gave Huldah a kiss on the cheek. "See you later."

~

Rebecca entered the guest bedroom. "Hannah, wake up," she whispered into Hannah's ear. "It's your wedding day."

"Oh, Becca." Hannah opened her big brown eyes and looked up at her friend. "This is the happiest day of my life."

"Yes, it is. Guess what?"

"What?"

"I finished the embroidery on your veil last night."

"That's wonderful! I noticed that your lamp was still lit before I went off to sleep last night. Thank you so much for finishing it."

"I wanted to do my part to help make you a lovely bride. I think you'll like the embroidery on the veil. The flowers pick up on the pale rose color of your dress. It was so wonderful of Zephaniah to buy you such a special wedding garment."

"Yes, it was. And, I really love the slippers Shallum and Huldah got me"

"Did you know that Saphah also made you an embroidered hanky for your wedding? She cut it from the extra white linen material left over after she cut out the lining for her headgear."

"Awww. That was so sweet of her."

"Good morning, ladies." Huldah cheerfully leaned into the room from the doorway. "I've made a light breakfast for us this morning and brought it over on a tray so we can enjoy it here. It's cereal and apples cooked together, along with warm bread and butter. Shallum is going to eat at the palace, and Ebed is on his way to the camp."

"Oh, thank you so much!" Hannah was appreciative of Huldah's hospitality.

"Yes, that's great!" Rebecca chimed in. "That means we can relax and talk here. Now, everyone, let's say our private prayers." They all bowed their heads to pray.

"To tell you the truth, Becca, I'm somewhat nervous about the Rechabite wedding." Hannah explained. "I've never been to one."

"Don't be nervous, dear." Rebecca patted Hannah on the shoulder. "Huldah and I'll help you get ready here for the birthday celebration, and I'll also fix your hair in a casual style. Then, at the camp after the birthday festivities, my mother, Miriam, and I'll help you get dressed just before the wedding supper, and I'll fix your hair in an elaborate style."

"I'm so glad you ladies are going to help me." Hannah sighed with relief. "Now, Rebecca, would you please fill me in on the series of events that'll happen today?"

"I will. Just remember that Rechabite birthday and wedding events are celebrated differently than Judean ones. Anyway, first there'll be the birthday luncheon and the gift opening. I think Ebed will be happy with his presents."

"Me too." Hannah was greatly looking forward to the event. "I can't wait to see his reactions to his gifts! What happens next?"

"Everyone will relax, visit, or do whatever until late in the afternoon. Ebed will want to show you around and introduce you to some of the guests. Just before the wedding supper begins, you and Ebed will change into your wedding clothes. Then, there'll be a pre-supper gathering in the dining tent with important messages, music, and so forth. And after that, the wedding supper will be served. That'll be followed by the opening of the wedding gifts, but I'll be there to assist. Now quit worrying, Hannah. Everything will be just fine."

"Alright, I'll try," Hannah sighed.

~

"Samuel, we're almost there," Ebed said. "Turn to the right after that big tree and you'll see the Rechabite encampment. Thank you for bringing me here this morning. Look, my father and mother are coming out of their tent now."

"It was my pleasure. It's nice to get out in the countryside and away from the palace once in a while. Well, here we are." Samuel pulled back on the reins to stop the horses near Ebed's parents.

"Sam, where are you off to now?"

"I'm off to the palace to recheck my schedule with King Josiah. I think my next chariot trip will be bringing Shallum and Huldah here. Then, I'll go back to pick up your lovely bride and your sister for your birthday celebration. After that, I think I'm supposed to transport Zephaniah and Jeremiah. And, my last trip before lunch will be to pick up King Josiah."

"Well, I sure appreciate everything you're doing to transport all of us." Ebed stepped down from the chariot.

"Thank the king," Samuel answered. "He's helping out because he wants everything to turn out well for your big day." Sam shook the reins and the chariot took off.

"Well, he's fortunate to have you as his driver." Ebed watched as Samuel sped away.

~

"Son!" exclaimed Ebed's father in his happiness to see his son. "You're just in time for breakfast. Your mother began working at first light to prepare you a great meal." Levi and Miriam broke into a fast walk as they approached their son.

"Oh, Ebed, it's so wonderful to see you today. You look great." Miriam gave her son an emotional hug.

"It's because I'm so happy, mother. God has given me a wonderful girl to marry. I loved her at first sight, and I think you will too."

"I'm sure we will," Miriam and Levi shook their heads in mutual agreement.

"Well, come on in, and let's visit while we eat," said Levi. "We're having fresh fish I caught late yesterday and flat cakes."

"That smells so good! I'm glad you invited me to come early for breakfast. Where are the children?"

"They're over at grandma's tent," Miriam explained. "She's taking care of them since we had so much to do today."

"King Josiah's men have already set up the tents he provided, along with tables and seating. Now, all we men need to do is carry over the decorations and the women will set all of that up. Yesterday, the men and I started roasting all the meat and the women did all the baking. But this morning they're cooking the side dishes."

"Great! You don't know how thankful I am to have such a wonderful family. I love you all. Thank you for doing this for Hannah and me."

"Don't forget," Miriam reminded Ebed, "we're doing it for your baby too. Just think, God is blessing us with both a new child of our own and with our very first grandchild."

"Yes," Levi recalled a pleasant memory from the past. "It seems like just yesterday, Ebed, that I was bouncing you, my firstborn, on my lap. But soon, God willing, I'll be holding my new child on one arm and my first grandchild on the other. Praise be to God!"

"That's right!" Ebed was well aware of what God had done. "You have no idea what it means to me that you're welcoming my wife and my child."

"Son, we wouldn't have it any other way," said Miriam. "Now let's eat breakfast and get some preparations done."

~

"Huldah, you look so nice." Hannah was happy her relative would get to go to the birthday celebration. "That emerald green dress looks wonderful with your red hair."

"I agree." Rebecca was thrilled too. "And those gold earrings look perfect with your outfit. I'm so pleased you're getting to attend Ebed's birthday celebration."

"Thank you both." Huldah was overjoyed. "I can hardly believe that I'm actually getting to go!"

"It's about time for the arrival of the chariot. But I have something I want to show you Hannah."

"What is it?"

"You'll see," Huldah slipped out of the room.

"Look what I found." Huldah reentered with a smile on her face.

"Oh, what a lovely gown." Hannah moved over to touch the tiny pleats in the silk garment."

"Well, it's for you to wear to the birthday party." Huldah smiled at Hannah as she held out the beautiful garment.

"Oh, my goodness, that is just gorgeous. Where did you find it?"

"A merchant from Egypt was at the market, but he'd sold all his wares except this gown made for a tall, thin girl. When I saw it, I immediately thought of you, Hannah. I couldn't resist buying it, but look what else I found." Huldah held up a lovely pair of dangling pearl earrings. "When I was trying to get the merchant to reduce the price for the gown, he wouldn't budge, so I left his stall. But as I was walking away, I heard the tall Egyptian man suddenly yell out that he would throw in these pearl earrings and all for the same price. Hannah, they'll look lovely with this gown."

"Huldah, that is such a lovely thing you've done for me. Thank you." Hannah reached over and hugged her.

"You're welcome. I wanted to do something nice for you for your special day."

"That gown will look fabulous on you, Hannah." Rebecca was happy that Hannah had received the garment. "I can't wait to see you in it. Hurry and bathe so you can dress for the birthday party. I'll get ready too, and then I'll fix your hair."

There was a tap on the door before it opened and Shallum stepped into the room. Catching a glimpse of Huldah, he stopped and smiled widely. "Take a look at my beautiful wife!" Shallum stepped over, gently kissed her on the cheek, and whispered in her ear. "You look lovely in that dress. I'm so glad you're getting to go today."

"Me too." Huldah crooked her arm in his and they walked out the door toward the chariot. "You look dapper yourself, my handsome husband."

"Wow, is that your wife?" Samuel asked Shallum before turning back to address Huldah. "You look really nice today, madame."

"Thank you." Huldah smiled at Samuel. "Thank you so much for transporting us."

"Yes, she does! It's not every day I get to take my beautiful wife somewhere special."

The two girls stood watching from the courtyard gate. "I'm so happy to see Huldah and Shallum getting to attend the birthday celebration together today." Rebecca smiled as her eyes lingered on the departing couple. "I love them almost as much as my own parents."

"I greatly admire them as well. They work so hard to help others, but seldom get a chance to enjoy life themselves."

"They're obeying God's call on their lives and desire to be faithful to Him, so they wouldn't have it any other way." Rebecca understood the intensity of their faithfulness to Yahweh.

"No, they wouldn't."

"Well, they both care so greatly about the needs of others. That's why I love them so much."

"Come on Becca, lets hurry. It won't be long before Samuels back to pick us up too."

~

"Ebed, let's get ready now," Levi reminded his son. "I saw your mother earlier. She and the other ladies are already dressed for the birthday luncheon, and the guests are beginning to arrive now."

"Oh, look." Ebed glanced upward. "The sun is high in the sky so it must be almost noon. Where did the morning go?"

As Levi and Ebed entered the wash tent carrying their clothing and supplies, they noticed other men leaving dressed in their nicest clothes. "Let's hurry." Ebed took his new garb out of his basket.

"Yes, you wash up first so you'll be ready when Hannah and Rebecca get here, and I'll go next."

"Father, thank you for buying the fine material for my clothes." Ebed held out and admired each article of clothing tailored from the rich fabric Levi had purchased.

"You're welcome son. It was nice of Shallum to offer to sew your new clothes. He did an awesome job. Here." Levi handed Ebed a little jar with a stopper.

"What's this?" Ebed unplugged the jar and tried to look inside.

"Take a smell." Levi smiled as his son took a sniff of the jar.

"That really smells good!" Ebed took another sniff and chuckled. "I better be ready, because Hannah is really going to like this. Thanks father."

"You're welcome. Your mother made you something to wear to the wedding supper. Want to see it?"

"I sure do!"

Levi handed him a long, thin box. "Open it."

Ebed opened the box, spread apart the parchment his mother had wrapped around the gift, and touched the stripped material of a handsome scarf with fringe on each end. "Oh, that is a really nice scarf. When did mother have time to make it?"

"Miriam knew you'd probably be getting married one of these days since you're turning sixteen. She had already been working on it and almost had it done when we found out you were betrothed to Hannah, so she hurried to finish it."

"That's my mother! And, I couldn't love her more."

Ebed and Levi stepped away from the wash tent and began walking toward the big tent where the birthday luncheon would be served. "It looks like everyone is already here. Oh look, grandmother and the kids are over there. Hello, grandma Ruth," Ebed called out. "Hi, kids."

"Hello, Ebed and Levi." Grandma Ruth herded Ebed's siblings toward them. "You look so handsome Ebed." Grandma hugged her grandson and he hugged her back. "It's difficult for me to believe my oldest grandson is celebrating his 16th birthday and getting married all on the same day."

"I'm really happy, Grandma Ruth." Ebed was very pleased to see his grandmother. "As soon as Hannah gets here, I'll bring her over so you can personally meet her."

"Yes, please do. I'm really looking forward to meeting her." Grandma Ruth reached for Ebed's hand and gave it a squeeze. "I love you."

"I love you too." Ebed squeezed her hand in return and kissed her on the cheek.

"Ebed's getting married! Ebed's getting married!" One of his little brothers rattled off and then giggled.

"Where's your girlfriend? I want to know. Where's your girlfriend?" A curly headed little sister demanded an answer as she jumped up and down.

"Hold me, Ebed. Please! Please!" His youngest sister held out her fat little arms toward him.

"Alright, children, give your big brother some breathing room now. You'll be able to see him again after lunch this afternoon. But we need to go get seated now." Grandma Ruth guided Ebed's little brothers and sisters away from him and toward the tent.

"Zephaniah and Jeremiah are standing over there." Levi motioned toward the two. "It's been a long time since I've seen Jeremiah. Son, have you met him yet?"

"No, I haven't. I'm glad he could come and look forward to meeting him. He's going to attend the reform talks tonight, but I won't be able to be there. Perhaps he can fill me in with information on the reform plans later at the palace. I would like to be a part of the movement and I assume he does too. Maybe I'll get a chance to talk to him sometime today."

"Yes, perhaps you will. I'm so proud of you son and happy that you stand up for your faith in Yahweh. Jeremiah stands strong for the Lord too, so I think you'll like him."

"Yes, I think I will too."

~

"Levi, Ebed," a woman's voice called out, and she waved her hand high. "Over here."

"Hello, dear," Levi said. "How's everything going?"

"Well, I think almost everyone is in the tent now and I hear King Josiah is on the way," Miriam informed them. "So, we're supposed to wait here for him to arrive."

"Have you seen Hannah or Rebecca yet?"

"No, but I'm sure they'll show up any minute. I've heard most of the guests from Jerusalem, along with our friends and relatives, are already seated, so I think we're all set, thank goodness. I'm looking forward to sitting for a while and enjoying this day."

"You've done a wonderful job of getting everything ready, so why don't you let the other ladies take care of the rest." Levi smiled at his wife and gave her a kiss.

"Yes, mother, you need to take care of yourself." Ebed smiled at her and took her hand, "By the way, the scarf you made for me is really nice. Thank you so much."

"I was worried I wouldn't get it done in time. I'm glad you like it."

"Well, I sure do." Ebed leaned over and kissed her on the cheek.

"Here they come! It's King Josiah and his group riding in chariots." Levi was happy the king and his entourage had arrived.

One by one each chariot came to a halt and the guests disembarked, lined up, and headed for the tent. A herald appeared at the main entrance to the tent and loudly announced to those inside: "Men and women, boys and girls, please stand for the arrival and entrance of the guest of honor." Palace musicians already stationed in the tent began playing entrance music with wind and percussion instruments.

The music stopped and a palace spokesman standing on his spot in the tent spoke out: "On behalf of King Josiah and all those here today, I'm happy to present the guest of honor, Ebed, the Rechabite, who is 16 today and his parents Levi and Miriam."

"Come on son, stand up straight and hold your head high," Levi whispered to Ebed. The music resumed playing as the trio walked into the tent and stood by their seats. Ebed was pleased to see that although Hannah and Rebecca weren't present yet, the rest of his immediate family members, including his siblings and grandparents, were already standing in the same area. Several brothers and sisters cheerfully waved at him, and he smiled in recognition and nodded his head.

Trumpets began blowing loudly, then stopped, and the herald appeared once again at the entrance and shouted: "Now, everyone please remain standing for the arrival and entrance of the King of Judah, the highest official in the land, who is subject only to Yahweh, the Lord of all."

Trumpets briefly sounded again and the palace spokesman inside the tent loudly proclaimed: "I present to you King Josiah and retinue." Everyone clapped as the tall, handsome king entered the tent with a smile on his face, walked over to Ebed and his parents, shook their hands, then stepped over to Zephaniah to shake his hand too, before sitting down at the head table and motioning for others to sit.

"I can't believe this is happening," said Ebed. "King Josiah actually came! I still don't see the girls though."

The servers entered the tent from an opening near the head table with Rebecca and Hannah just ahead of the group. "Rebecca and another girl are walking over here," said Miriam. "Don't the girls look nice?"

"Mother, the other girl is Hannah. Isn't she beautiful?" Ebed proudly eyed her from the top of her head to the tip of her toes.

"Yes, Hannah is gorgeous," Miriam admired Hannah's beauty. "And, she looks adorable in that yellow dress and pearl earrings."

"Do you think it would be alright for me to introduce her to the crowd?"

"Of course, son," Levi said. "It's both your birthday and marriage day, so it would be completely appropriate. Please introduce your beautiful bride to the crowd."

Ebed stood and motioned to Hannah and Rebecca to join them and welcomed each girl with a kiss on her cheek. "You're the two prettiest girls in the room," he said. "I'm going to introduce Hannah to the crowd, Becca, so please go ahead and take your seat."

"Could I get your attention?" The crowd became quiet and turned their attention to Ebed. "Thank you, everyone, for being here today. And, my special thanks to King Josiah who has honored us with his presence." Ebed motioned toward King Josiah. "Most of you already know my family—my parents Levi and Miriam, my grandparents, my brothers and sisters, along with my aunts, uncles, and cousins." Ebed motioned in turn toward the various areas his family was sitting. "But I would also like to introduce you to my second parents, Shallum and Huldah." Ebed motioned toward them and gave each a little wave. Also, I want to introduce you to Prophet Zephaniah, the uncle of my betrothed." Ebed nodded toward him.

"But now it is my pleasure to introduce all of you to a very special lady." Ebed smiled at his betrothed, placed an arm around her, and gave her a kiss on the cheek. "This is Hannah, and she will become my wife today." Everyone arose and the crowd erupted in cheers and applause.

Levi motioned for the crowd to sit down. "Thank you everyone for welcoming Hannah into our Rechabite clan. Most of you already know the circumstances of how Ebed and Hannah became betrothed and have expressed your thankfulness for the providence of Yahweh in bringing this couple together and in saving their unborn child, a gift of God. This is a glorious day to celebrate Ebed's birthday and marriage to Hannah."

Next Levi supplied the order of events for the day: "The birthday luncheon will be served first, followed by the opening of the birthday gifts. It will be a time of fellowship and feasting, accompanied by music provided by the palace musicians. Later this evening, the wedding supper will be served and wedding gifts will be opened. Then the couple will be traveling back by chariot to Jerusalem where they'll be living at the home of Huldah and Shallum. Ebed plans to continue his schooling until he graduates with scribe credentials, but he'll also continue his training with Shallum working toward Keeper of the Wardrobe status. Ebed, do you have anything to add?"

"Yes, I do. I want to say a huge thank you to everyone who has worked so hard to make this a great day for Hannah and me. I sure appreciate it. Is anyone hungry?"

"I'm starving," one of Ebed's little brothers piped up and everyone laughed.

"Well, I certainly agree with my little brother about being hungry." Ebed laughed in enjoyment at what his little brother had said. "But on a more serious note, Uncle Zephaniah, would you please say the prayer over our food?"

"I would be greatly pleased to say the prayer over this bountiful feast," Prophet Zephaniah answered in his rich voice. "But first, I will begin with an introductory call to praise for Yahweh from Scripture:

> *Give thanks to the Lord, for he is good; his love endures forever. …For he satisfies the thirsty and fills the hungry with good things. …Let the one who is wise heed these things and ponder the loving deeds of the Lord. …Let them give thanks to the Lord for his unfailing love and his wonderful deeds for mankind.*[1]

Therefore, Lord, we give thanks for your provision of food and drink on this special day of celebration for my young friend Ebed on the occasion of his sixteenth birthday. Please bless this food and drink to our bodies we pray. Amen."

Ebed arose and turned to thank the prophet. "Thank you, Uncle Zephaniah, for that beautiful quote from scripture and for your prayer of thanks. And now—let the celebration begin."

The musicians began playing their wind and percussion instruments, the serving ladies began passing trays of food at the tables, and the young men bearing jars of cool spring water and fresh juice began pouring drinks.

Ebed took Hannah's hand under the table and leaned toward her for a kiss. "Darling, I love you so much."

"Oh, Ebed, I love you too."

23

THE JERUSALEM SCHOOL

Saphah mused as she walked over to an un-shuttered window at the Jerusalem School and glanced up toward the sun high in the sky. *Oh, my goodness,* the substitute suddenly realized, *the sun is straight up, so it's time for lunch. I bet the big tent at the Rechabite camp is already filled with guests, and everyone is seated for the birthday luncheon.* "Alright students, it's just about time for lunch. Please finish what you're working on now, and we'll go to the lunch room shortly."

~

What a great morning this has been! Saphah's recollection of how her day had gone so far was basically good. Of course, her walk alone to school that morning had been a little lonely without the company of Huldah or the girls. Then, when she'd opened the door to Huldah's office, everything had been eerily quiet inside, so she assumed she'd arrived before anyone else. She grabbed her basket to get her supplies for the day, but soon heard the steps of someone else walking in the hallway. *Oh good, someone else is here too.*

"Good morning, Mrs. Saphah." Caleb, the other Jerusalem School teacher, appeared at the office door to welcome her.

"Good morning Mr. Caleb." Saphah was happy another person had arrived at the otherwise empty school. "I'm glad to see you. It sure is quiet when no one else is here."

"Listen, I hear someone else coming now. Good morning." Mr. Caleb turned to cheerfully greet the young man walking toward him. "This is one of Huldah's best students, Baruch. He was absent the day you trained."

"Hello, Saphah. I'm very pleased to meet you." Baruch nodded his head and then bowed toward her.

Saphah's jaw dropped in shock. Is this who I think it is? Is this the future scribe for the soon to be Prophet Jeremiah? Retaining her composure, she spoke: "Baruch, I'm pleased to meet you as well. Are you planning to become a scribe?"

Baruch was surprised. "Well, …yes, but how did you know?"

"Don't worry. I'll tell you about it sometime." Saphah had a wry smile on her face.

"Well, I hear you're a watchwoman?" Baruch stated matter-of-factly.

"I am. …But who told you?"

"Huldah, of course." Baruch laughed at her surprise. "I'm going to be one of your helpers today."

"Oh, that's great!" Saphah nodded her head.

"Huldah also wants me to read to the students after lunch to give you a break."

"Sounds good. Thank you, Baruch."

"I need to get back to my classroom." Mr. Caleb turned to leave. "My students will start arriving any moment now. Saphah, please remember I'm here for you. Just whistle if you need me."

"Good idea," Saphah laughed. "I'll just whistle." She pursed her lips and whistled a little tune for practice.

"Good whistling!" Then Caleb whistled a little tune of his own.

"You too!" Saphah chuckled at the spontaneous whistling from the teacher.

Baruch and Saphah arrived back in Huldah's classroom and began preparations for the day. Soon the rest of the students all arrived and Baruch assisted with taking the role. Joel, her other assistant, said the morning prayer and the school day began. Saphah was happy that the rest of the morning went well and pleased with the good behavior of the students. At the beginning of the day she'd warned them that any misdeeds would be reported to Huldah later. And, evidently, that was enough to persuade the young men to behave.

~

"Alright students, put away your things and we'll go to lunch now."

"Could we eat outside?" One of the boys politely inquired.

"Since you've all been well-behaved this morning, and now I know you'll follow my rules, I don't see what it'll hurt for us to go outside. We can stop by the dining area to pick up our drinks on the way. However, please remember that I expect you to walk out to the lunch area quietly and to sit down in groups of four. If anyone misbehaves or causes a distraction in any way, the entire group will have to return inside, and you'll miss the rest of your lunch. Do you understand?"

"Yes, madame." The students grabbed their lunches and followed Saphah, first to get their drinks and then out to the shade of some trees. They all sat down in groups of four and spread out their food.

One young student turned to another and asked, "Could I trade my cheese and bread for your boiled eggs?"

"Sure, I haven't had cheese in a long time." He handed two boiled eggs to the other little boy and grabbed the cheese."

Saphah opened her lunch sack. *Wow, Huldah sent me a great lunch!* Saphah pulled out a nicely browned dove breast, a fresh slice of rye bread, some herb cheese, and a ripe apple. *Awww, that was really nice of Huldah.* She relaxed and enjoyed her meal while the boys finished their own lunches. The peaceful atmosphere at the school had a calming effect on her after the hectic pace she'd experienced since her arrival in the parallel time and place. Finally she announced to the group of boys: "Young people, it's time to go back into the school now. Would you like for Baruck to read to you for a while after lunch?"

"Sure, we would like that," answered an older student as they walked back to the school house. "Mrs. Huldah pushed us to get ahead on our lessons so we could have an easy day."

They all arrived back to their classroom. "Baruch, what are you going to read to us today?" Saphah asked.

"Huldah has written some information for me to read today on the history of the Rechabites. Ebed and his sister Rebecca are members of that group, but they both work for Shallum and Huldah, and are like family to them. Therefore, Huldah wanted to attend Ebed's sixteenth birthday celebration, so she enlisted Saphah to teach in her place today. Since most of us personally know Ebed and Rebecca, Huldah thought perhaps you might like to hear about the history of their group."

"That sounds good. I would love to hear more about the Rechabites myself. But what do the rest of you think? Everyone, please raise your hand if you want to hear about the group."

"I'd really like to hear about Ebed and Rebecca's people," a student said, and the rest raised their hands.

"Alright, Baruch, there's consensus—let's hear about the Rechabites!"

"Well, to learn about the Rechabites, we'll need to know more about
Ebed and Rebecca's ancestor Jehonadab and his association with
a man named Jehu who became the 10th king of the Kingdom of
Israel. Baruch opened Huldah's scroll and began to read what she'd
written, along with quotes from scripture.

The Rechabites

Here's how events transpired when Jehu was anointed
King of Israel:

> *The prophet Elisha summoned a man from the company of
> the prophets and said to him, …Look for Jehu son of
> Jehoshaphat, …Then take the flask and pour the oil on his
> head and declare, …I anoint you king over the Lord's people
> Israel. You are to destroy the house of Ahab your master,
> and I will avenge the blood of my servants the prophets and the
> blood of all the Lord's servants shed by Jezebel. The whole
> house of Ahab will perish.*[1]

Thus, God anointed King Jehu to enact judgment against the
house of Ahab for its wickedness, which Jehu fully carried
out.

The reason for the purging commanded by God was Ahab's
extremely wicked reign, his debased Baal worship, and
because *there was never anyone like Ahab, who sold himself to do evil
in the eyes of the Lord, urged on by Jezebel his wife. He behaved in
the vilest manner by going after idols, like the Amorites the Lord drove
out before Israel.*[2] After Ahab *married Jezebel daughter of Ethbaal
king of the Sidonians,* [he] *began to serve Baal and worship him. He
set up an altar for Baal in the temple of Baal that he built in Samaria.*[3]

After carrying out the first part of the Lord's order that 'the
whole house of Ahab [should] perish,' Jehu was traveling

toward the Baal temple to confront the false priests. It was at this same time when Jehonadab, son of Rechab, first appeared in events:

[Jehu] *came upon Jehonadab …who was on his way to meet him. Jehu greeted him and said, 'Are you in accord with me, as I am with you?' Jehonadab answered, 'I am.' Jehu said, 'If so, give me your hand.' So he did, and Jehu helped him up into the chariot. Jehu said, 'Come with me and see my zeal for the Lord.' Then he had him ride along in his chariot.*[4]

Hence, as King Jehu was on his way to confront the priests of Baal in their high temple, he saw Jehonadab, a man considered to be one of the most righteous men in Israel. 'Jehonadab was the leader of a conservative movement among the Israelites that was characterized by strong opposition to Baalism, as well as opposition to various practices of a settled agricultural society, including the building of houses, the sowing of crops, and the use of wine. His followers still adhered to these principles years later and were known as Rechabites.'[5]

King Jehu may have invited Jehonadab to ride along because public association with the Rechabite gave him added credentials among the rural populace as a follower of the Lord. But it is also possible that King Jehu felt the need for the support of a faithful follower of God who recognized the danger that Baalism posed to the worship of the One True God. Jehonadab, a true follower of Yahweh, knew that the Lord says in scripture: *I am the first and the last, apart from me there is no God.*[6]

When Jehu and Jehonadab came to Samaria, Jehu ordered the guards and officers to overcome the Baalists and then they *entered the inner shrine of the temple of Baal. …they demolished the sacred stone of Baal and tore down the temple of Baal, and people have used it for a latrine to this day.*[7]

The sins of Ahab, Jezebel, and their followers were serious. Scripture says that Elijah said to the Lord that *the Israelites have rejected your covenant, torn down your altars, and put your prophets to death with the sword.*[8] Nevertheless, Ahab and Jezebel refused to repent of their wickedness. So, he and his house, along with the unrepentant Baal worshipers, caused the consequences they themselves received. It was their own sin that brought about their demise. Only in this manner could the life-giving worship of the true God be maintained.

It must be remembered, however, that although *Jehu destroyed Baal worship in Israel,*[9] after that time *he was not careful to keep the law of the Lord, the God of Israel, with all his heart.*[10] Although Jehu was God's instrument to bring judgment on the house of Ahab and on the Baal worship, for which he was commended, he was still a sinful man. But even imperfect rulers are established by God and used for his purposes.

God anoints who he chooses and uses who he will for his plans and purposes regardless of their inadequacies. Who he chooses may not necessarily be those we admire, envision, or look to in times of trouble. Although sometimes they are used to bless God's people, other times they are used as instruments of judgment to correct us. But all leaders are accountable to God in the end.

Yet, the Rechabites, of whom Jehonadab was a wise leader, have stood firm against accepting the false religions of the nations around them. It was from Jehonadab's father Rechab that the Rechabites derived their name as noted in scripture, where it also says that they're identified with a section of the Kenites,[11] and Moses' family by marriage.[12]

Thus, the Rechabites, a nomadic group known for their strict rules, have been faithful to abide by these rules through the generations, beginning with the time of Jehu. They are an example of steadfastness in living in obedience to God.

Baruch rolled up the scroll and walked back to his seat.

"Baruch, thank you very much for reading Mrs. Huldah's work to us. I would like to add a possible takeaway from what you've read. King Jehu was anointed by God to enact judgment against the house of Ahab and the Baal worshipers. But the man, Jehu, was zealous, cunning, and even bloodthirsty by reputation. Nonetheless, God used Jehu to reform Israel and eradicate Baal worship from the nation despite Jehu's personal shortcomings. So, we must remember that God often uses far from perfect earthly rulers to judge people, reform nations, and lead the hearts of people away from idols and back to him, if only for a season. That serves as a reminder to us that God alone is sovereign, God alone is just, and God alone is King. Now, do any of you have additional comments?"

"Yes." A tall boy arose to speak. "I think that the wickedness of Ahab and Jezebel proves that the way of sin can never be the way of peace, because there are consequences to disobedience. Mrs. Huldah told us that scripture says that *there is no peace for the wicked.*"[13]

"True," Saphah said, "Those who persist in sin will never find peace or be at peace with the Lord. On the other hand, peace is reserved for those who fear the Lord and obey His commandments."

A younger boy raised his hand. "Could I ask you a question?"

"Sure, go ahead."

"Why didn't God do something about Ahab and Jezebel sooner?"

"Well, God hadn't forgotten about those who were suffering from the actions of Ahab and his family. He hadn't forgotten his servants like Elijah or Elisha, nor had he forgotten his other prophets. He had a plan to cleanse Israel of sin and bring justice to its rulers. However, God's timing is always his own and always best."

Another student raised his hand. "Well, I'm really impressed with Ebed and Rebecca's family and their obedience to God."

"I am too. And, don't forget that Tamara is also a Rechabite." Saphah wanted the young men to realize she was from the same group.

"Well, it's time for geography. Baruch, do you want to get the Ethiopian map and tell us some things about that country? I'm sure the map is different from the map of my time."

"Sure," Baruch retrieved a hand drawn and framed Ethiopian map from the map cubbyhole and placed it on an easel at the front of the room. "Today, we're going to talk about the peoples in the northern part of Ethiopia."

"Students, I'm looking forward to hearing about this myself. Ebed's betrothed, Hannah, has a parent who came from that land. Baruch, please tell us more about that part of the world."

"It will be my pleasure." Baruch began telling interesting facts about the foreign place.

Saphah thoroughly enjoyed Baruch's talk on Ethiopia, and the rest of the day passed quickly. Before she knew it, it was time for her to dismiss the students. "Young men, I want to thank you for a very good day. I hope I can fill in for Huldah again sometime. Please have a good evening. You are now dismissed."

24

THE RECHABITE CAMP

Saphah said, "Look, Samuel, there stands Huldah waiting for us to arrive so she can make the trip back to Jerusalem. Doesn't she look nice?"

"Yes, she does," Samuel agreed. "Thank you for filling in at Jerusalem School for her so she could be here for Ebed's birthday celebration."

Samuel stopped the chariot near Huldah and Saphah stepped off. "Hello Saphah, how did your day go at school?" asked Huldah.

"It went well. The students were quiet and well-behaved all day. We had a picnic out on the grounds, and after lunch Baruck read to the students from your Rechabite scroll. So, how did your day go here?"

"It was wonderful. The birthday luncheon was delicious, and Ebed was very happy with his gifts. He received a lot of presents, but he was especially happy with the bow and arrow set from Rebecca and the knife and scabbard set from Hannah. Since Shallum had informed King Josiah what Rebecca and Hannah's gifts would be, the king got him a target set. So, Ebed is all ready for target practice now. But I also want you to know that both Ebed and Hannah were thrilled about the art colors you purchased for the mural. They're really looking forward to painting it since it'll be for their bedroom."

"I'm so glad they're pleased with the colors. Before I forget to ask, are Eve and Jonathan here?"

"No, not yet, but I hear that Jonathan, Eve, and some other trusted individuals from the palace staff will be at the meeting."

King Josiah's traveling tent camp is set up near the spring, so that means he and his palace personnel will be staying overnight."

"Huldah, how did the group pass their time this afternoon?"

"Shallum and Zephaniah spent the afternoon with the men in Ebed and Rebeccas's family, and I was pleased to spend my time with their female relatives and children before they were put down for naps. I got to be with Miriam for most of the afternoon. She is a dear lady, and I'm so glad I had the opportunity to get to know her better. That's all because of you Saphah. Thanks again, dear, for subbing for me today. I really appreciate it." Huldah gave Saphah a departing hug.

"Huldah, it was my pleasure. I enjoyed being with your students."

"Alright now, it's time for me to return home so I can get the house cleaned and ready for Ebed and Hannah. Oh, and that reminds me. Ebed and Hannah wanted me to tell you that a table is set up so Zephaniah, Shallum, and you can join the family for the wedding supper. Also, Rebecca and Tamara are planning to accompany you to the reform meeting."

"Oh, that's great! Thanks for letting me know."

"Alright. Sam is waiting so I must leave. now."

"Goodbye, Huldah. I guess I'll see you tomorrow. Do you know if the rest of the Jerusalem guests will be staying overnight here?"

"Yes, as far as I know, the rest of you'll be staying over." Huldah climbed into the chariot. "I don't know the plans after that."

"Alright, have a good night." Saphah waved goodbye. "And, God willing, I'll see you tomorrow."

"See you tomorrow." Huldah held on to the rim of the chariot with both hands as she rode off with Sam toward Jerusalem.

"Saphah," a woman's voice rang out. "I'm so glad you're finally here!"

"Hello, Hannah. I'm really thrilled I could be here for the wedding supper and events. Young lady, that lovely dress fits you very nicely. You look wonderful," Saphah complemented her friend.

"Thank you. Look at this." Hannah giggled, slowly twirled, and the tiny pleats in her skirt billowed out in one direction. Then she twirled the opposite way and the pleats billowed out the other way. "I must quit doing that." She laughed at her own antics. "It's just I'm so thrilled about becoming Ebed's wife that I'm acting a little silly." She became serious once again as she touched the embroidery work on Saphah's headwear and sash. "Saphah, you're official clothing really turned out nice. You look great. In what language is your creed embroidered and what does it say?"

"Hannah, I'm glad to see you happy again. The creed is embroidered in English, the language most people in America speak, and it says, 'In God we trust.'"

"So, the people in America believe in Yahweh, right."

"Well, when our country was founded, a majority of people believed in God, the Creator of heaven and earth, but I'm not sure that's still the case," Saphah explained. "Just as some of the people in Judah turned to other gods, many people in the United States worship other gods too. They may not worship idols made of wood, clay, or stone, but they have something they worship, whether it is riches, fame, power, or anything else that distracts them from the worship of God Almighty."

"So, is that why you're here in Judah?"

"Yes, I think the main reason I'm here is to learn more about the spiritual decline of both Judah and America and to observe the reform efforts of King Josiah. So I'm glad I'll get to attend the meeting later tonight. Rebecca and Tamara have also been invited."

"Hello, Saphah," Ebed spoke up from a distance. "I'm so glad you made it for the wedding celebration."

"Me too! Something smells so good." Saphah inhaled a whiff of mingled, but delicious smells. "What's for supper?"

"C'mon Hannah." Ebed gave his betrothed a kiss on the lips. "Let's go show Saphah the meat cooking method of the Rechabites."

"Yes, let's show her." Hannah used her other hand to take Saphah's and the trio walked to where a group of Rechabite men stood.

"Hello, Ebed and Hannah," one of the Rechabite men said and the others became quiet. "Who do you have with you?"

"Hello, Uncle Micah." Ebed turned toward his relative. "Everyone, this is Saphah, a lady from America. She is wondering what you're cooking that is giving off that wonderful aroma."

"Hello, Saphah." Uncle Micah stepped toward her. "Would you like to learn about the Rechabite method of cooking meat that we call pit cooking? We use the method to roast large animal meat, both tame and wild, for events such as weddings, feasts, and so forth. We cook a variety of meat such as fatted oxen, sheep, goat, and beef in this way, in addition to wild deer and antelope."

"Yes, I would. How is pit cooking done here?"

"Here pit cooking is done by roasting a gutted, well-seasoned animal in a large hole dug in the ground and lined with flat stones. A fire is built in a pit three feet deep with wood equal to around two or three times the volume of the pit and according to the size of the animal to be cooked. The wood is allowed to burn until the pit is half filled with red-hot coal, which can require a half day or more of burning time. Hot rocks are placed in the body cavity of large animals and the meat is firmly tied to secure it together. Large wet leaves are placed around the carcass and wet, strongly woven cloth covers the leaves. Dirt is shoveled back on top which prevents air from getting into the pit, keeps the leaves and woven material from burning, and maintains a constant temperature perfect for roasting tender, juicy meat."

"That sounds like a lengthy process. How long does it generally take to cook, for instance, a large deer?"

"The cooking time is generally 12 hours, more or less, depending on the size of the pit and the animal. Since the meat is tightly wrapped and covered, it won't dry out and can tolerate a little overcooking." Micah explained. "We've already unearthed a few pits, and some men are cutting up the meat over there on cutting boards."

"Well, Micah, that smells so good it's making my mouth water. Thank you for explaining your pit cooking method."

"You're welcome."

A woman shouted from across a field. "Grandson, over here. Grandson, …"

Ebed turned to search for his relative. "Look, Grandma Ethel is over there in the meadow! She's my dad's mother. Hannah and Saphah, did you know the definition of her name is noble in Hebrew? Oh, and grandma Ruth is over in another part of the meadow too!"

"Well, I'm glad I'm finally going to get to meet these two women you've spoken of so highly," said Hannah.

"Hello, Ebed." Grandmother Ethel, standing in front of a group of youngsters in the field, waved her hand again. "Grandma Ruth and I are taking care of your siblings and some other young relatives. They're clamoring to see you and Hannah. Why don't you bring your betrothed and your other friend over here so we can meet them?"

"Let's go." said Hannah "I'm so glad I'm going to meet them all."

"Me too." Saphah was happy about the prospect of meeting some of Ebed's closest relatives. "I can't wait to talk to your grandmas and your siblings too. They're so cute."

"Alright," Ebed said, "I'm anxious to see them myself. It seems like an eternity since I've been with my little brothers and sisters."

Grandma Ethel met them halfway and led them to a meadow with abundant wild flowers blooming everywhere. Rebecca and Tamara were sitting with some little girls under a tree bordering the meadow as they constructed flower crowns to wear at the wedding supper. And Grandma Ruth was supervising some little boys, all standing in line, as they took turns using their slingshots to strike targets set up at different distances according to the ages of the boys.

"Hello, guys," shouted Ebed as he spied his little brothers slinging stones at targets. "I'm so glad to see you. Where are the girls?"

"Here we are! Here we are!" Some girls jumped up and down. One girl was petting her tame bird as it sat on her forearm. Several other little girls were standing in a big circle throwing a ball to each other.

Grandma Ethel instructed the ladies and girls to sit down together in one area, but grandma Ruth told the boys to sit down in another. Ebed stood in front of the two groups as they expectantly waited to hear what he'd say.

"Hello everyone." Ebed greeted his younger brothers and sisters, along with the rest of the group. "I'm so glad to be here with you today for my birthday and the wedding celebration. At this time, I would like to introduce all of you to my future wife Hannah, and to American Watchwoman, Saphah." As Hannah and Saphah stood up, everyone else stood and clapped. "Now, these two ladies are going to do a walkabout to personally greet those who don't know them. Please stand in two rows, and the walkabout will begin."

Oh my, how wonderful, Saphah thought. *I'm going to meet and talk to all of Ebed and Rebecca's siblings and their grandmas. And Hannah is going to become acquainted with them too.*

"Saphah, why don't you greet grandma Ethel and the girls on one side and Hannah and I'll greet grandma Ruth and the boys on the other, and then we'll switch sides."

After the walkabout was finished, grandma Ethel came forward to speak. "Now that you've all met Hannah, do you feel the same way I do? I don't know about you, but I'm very pleased to welcome her as the newest member of our Rechabite clan." They all broke out in applause to show their agreement.

"Thank you everyone," Hannah said. "I'm very pleased to be gaining such a wonderful family."

"And now, I want to tell you more about Saphah," said grandma Ethel. "As I said earlier, she's a watchwoman from America."

"Really!" said an older girl. "Saphah, I've heard that watchpersons in Judah are male, so how did you, a female, get to be a watchwoman?"

"Women in America do many of the same tasks that men do. For example, girls can enter the military, participate in sports, and engage in most vocations that're available to men."

"But aren't men better equipped to be watchpersons than girls?"

"Well, God is the one who called me as a watchwoman, and that's a spiritual role either a man or a woman can fulfill."

"Really, but how could that be?"

"God empowers men and women to do His spiritual will. Therefore, they aren't accomplishing things on their own, but God is helping them, so it doesn't matter if they're male or female. In other words, although there are differences in the physical capabilities of men and women, they're alike in their capacity for spiritual accomplishments. There are many stories of women in God's Word that you can read."

"But I don't know how to read," another girl loudly spoke up. "I wish I could read."

"That's why Rebecca and Tamara have been attending Jerusalem School," said Saphah. "When they finish school, they're planning to come back here to teach all of you how to read. Isn't that right, Rebecca?"

"Yes." Rebecca was pleased to explain to the youngsters the good news. "Our parents wanted both Ebed and me to be educated. Ebed is planning to become a scribe so he can write down the thoughts of adults in our group who don't know how to read and write. These adults want their ideas written down so others can read them. And Tamara and I are going to become teachers so we can teach young people how to read. Then in the future you can read for yourselves God's written Word. One of God's prophets named Zephaniah is here at our celebration. God speaks to Prophet Zephaniah and he writes on a scroll what God tells him since he can read and write."

"Well then, after you teach me to read and write, will I get to read what Zephaniah has written some day?"

"Prophet Zephaniah is Hannah's uncle, so he is attending all the events. You can ask him yourself."

"Yes, I'm going to do that." The girl looked toward Zephaniah's niece. "Hannah, since Prophet Zephaniah is your uncle, will you introduce me to him some time?"

"Of course. In fact, I'll be happy to introduce all of you to him."

"All right, children. It's time for everyone to get all dressed up for the wedding supper." Grandmas Ruth and Ethel trooped off with their own grandchildren, and the other grandmothers who'd been helping with food preparations retrieved their grandkids as well.

"Saphah and Hannah, do you want to see the reform meeting tent?"

"Yes," Saphah said. "Huldah told me that King Josiah has a traveling tent camp set up somewhere too."

"Yes, and the tent is readied for the reform meeting in that same area. It's nearby so we can show it to you. But then Hannah and I need to get back so we can get dressed for the wedding supper."

"I hear that some of Josiah's palace personnel will stay overnight here after the reform meeting. Is that true?"

"Yes, and some close associates of King Josiah will be staying here too. But you, Saphah, plus Shallum and Uncle Zephaniah, will be staying at the Rechabite camp with our family."

"Ebed, is there anything you'd like for me to tell King Josiah at the reform meeting?" inquired Saphah.

Ebed thought for a minute. "Yes, there is. I talked to King Josiah today at the birthday celebration. Please tell him I've consulted with

Hannah and our answer to his question is yes. Also, please inform him that we'll meet him at the designated location tomorrow."

"Alright, I'll tell him." *That's strange*, Saphah thought. *The couple will consummate their marriage tonight in Jerusalem, and King Josiah will be staying here at the tent camp. But, for some reason, tomorrow the couple will interrupt their honeymoon and meet the king at a designated location. Hum. …That's odd.*

"Hannah suddenly spoke up. "Ebed, it's getting late. We need to leave now so we can change into our wedding clothes."

Ebed quickly checked the sun's location in the sky. "You're right. C'mon, Hannah and Saphah, let's go.

"You two go on ahead," Saphah replied. "All I need to do is tidy up a bit. Hannah, please tell Rebecca that I'll be back shortly."

25

EVE

As Saphah strolled along furher in the open meadow vegetated by grass and flowers and surrounded by woodland, she thought, *It is so beautiful and peaceful here.* A flowing stream, with a deep pool of water on one side, banked with grass and shaded with trees, beaconed her to sit down for awhile.

This reminds me of the walks I used to take as a kid. Saphah's recollections of life growing up on a farm were very pleasant. She took off her sandals to dip her feet in the tinkling water and watched little fish as they dashed here and there in the flowing liquid.

"Saphah," a voice softly said.

"Eve," Saphah raised her head and was surprised to see the grieving mother standing right there by her. She patted the grass with one hand. "Please, won't you sit down here beside me."

"Yes, I'd like to cool my feet too." Eve pulled off her own sandals, sat down by her new friend, and stuck her feet into the cooling liquid.

The ladies sat quietly several minutes without speaking. Suddenly a doe with her fawn approached the stream from the opposite side. Eve and Saphah still didn't move or speak. With her head held high, the doe stared at them for several moments. But then, sensing no danger, she thrust her head down and took a long drink.

Saphah took Eve's hand and squeezed it, and Eve squeezed her hand back. They turned to look at each other. Tears streamed down Eve's cheeks as she whispered, "I'm glad she still has her sweet little fawn."

"Me too." Saphah managed to stifle the tears in her own eyes.

"Oh, Saphah." Eve began to cry softly. "Everything seems to remind me of my loss."

"I know. That was my experience too after I lost my daughter. It was even difficult for me to go shopping without my daughter. I'd see other moms with their daughters and feel happy for them, but it would remind me of my own loss. But then I'd feel guilty for feeling that way."

"Me too." Eve wiped her eyes. "Seeing the doe and fawn was bittersweet. It was sweet seeing the fawn but bitter to know I'm without my own offspring. It hurts."

"Yes, it hurts—deeply. But, as you noted earlier, it helps to remember what Huldah told you about King David and what he said after he lost his child. Similar words from scripture about King David's loss were included in the obituary written by a relative for my own daughter: *I shall go to her, but she shall not return to me.*[1]

"Those words were in the obituary for your daughter?" Eve was surprised.

"Yes, they were. Thus, through what King David said, as recorded in scripture, you and I both know that someday we can be reunited with our own little girls. But, in the meantime, Eve, perhaps God has plans for your life."

"Do you think God caused our daughters to die, if he has plans for our lives."

"No, your daughter's death was from natural causes. In my world we call it 'crib death.'"

"But, what about your daughter?"

"She died from injuries in an accident."

"God didn't cause their deaths then?"

"No, in our cases, I don't think so. Of course, I don't know for sure. But I do know that sometimes God uses the circumstances of our lives to bring about good."

"What do you mean?"

"Scripture says that *we know that in all things God works for the good of those who love him, who have been called according to his purpose.*[2] Thus, if we love God, He works things together for good in our lives, whatever they may be, because we are called according to His purpose. We can all play a part in his eternal purpose for mankind. Perhaps even King Josiah was called for God's purpose."

"Do you really think so?"

"Maybe. Scripture says God sent a prophet from Judah to Bethel to give a prophetic announcement of the rule of King Josiah, who came to the throne in Judah nearly 300 years after the division of Israel into northern and southern kingdoms. Here's how it came about."

"Good, I'd like to hear how it all occurred."

Saphah got her bible. "This happened when God tore *the kingdom out of Solomon's hand*[3] [and gave Jeroboam] *ten tribes* [but gave Solomon] *one tribe.*[4] The northern kingdom of ten tribes was called Israel and the southern kingdom of one tribe was called Judah. It was given to Solomon *so that David my servant may always have a lamp before me in Jerusalem, the city where I chose to put my name.*[5] The Lord told Jeroboam he would *be king over Israel.* [And] *if you do whatever I command you and walk in obedience to me and do what is right in my eyes by obeying my decrees and commands, as David my servant did, I will be with you.*[6]

"So if Jeroboam was obedient to God and did what was right in His eyes, God would bless him?"

"Yes, but Jeroboam wasn't confident in God's promise, so he forfeited his theocratic kingship. He did this by making *two golden calves*[7] *and one he set up in Bethel and the other in Dan. And this thing became a sin.*[8] Then *Jeroboam built shrines on high places and appointed priests from all sorts of people, even though they were not levites.*[9] He also exceeded the limits of his prerogatives as king and assumed the role of a priest:

> *As Jeroboam was standing by the altar to make an offering, …a man of God* [who] *came from Judah to Bethel, by the word of the Lord … cried out against the altar* [saying] *Altar, altar! This is what the Lord says: A son named Josiah will be born to the house of David. On you he will sacrifice the priests of the high places who make offerings here, and human bones will be burned on you.*[10]

Thus, the man of God foretold King Josiah's role as a reformer who will rid the land of the false priests of the high places, and this reform would happen as far north as Bethel."

"Really!" Eve was amazed at the implications of what Saphah had said. "A prophet predicted all those years ago that 'Josiah will be born to the house of David' and that he will become a reformer. And you and I've been invited to go to King Josiah's reform meeting tonight. Are we witnessing fulfillment of prophecy right before our eyes?"

"Yes, I think so. And perhaps we'll both be able to observe what King Josiah will do to bring about reform in this land. But, I want to tell you something else exciting. Archaeologists in my world have found actual high places from the time of Solomon, that are evidence of the events of those times. [And] a raised platform (high place) and shrine archaeologists found at Dan may be the actual 'high place at Dan, where Jeroboam set up one of the golden calves.'"[11]

"Astounding," Eve said. "One thing about it, I know from personal experience that Josiah is a good king. King Josiah told Jonathan that I can work with my husband in the palace kitchen. I think it will help me a lot in my grief for me to be with my spouse."

"I think it'll help too. I'm really happy to hear you're going to be working there. Are you coming to the wedding supper?"

"No, Jonathan and I talked about it, and we're not up to that yet."

"I don't blame you. After I lost my daughter, I wasn't up to social engagements either. Not for a really long time. But what about the reform meeting. Will you be there?"

"Well, Jonathan and I both want to be in attendance. We're grateful for what King Josiah has done for us, so we want to do everything we can to support him in his reform efforts."

"Good, we'll probably see each other there. In fact, that reminds me, I probably need to leave now so I can tidy up for the wedding event." Saphah gave Eve a hug and then turned to go to the Rechabite camp. "Bye, Eve. See you tonight at the reform meeting."

"Saphah, see you later. Oh, and could I sit by you at the meeting?"

"Of course. Perhaps you, Rebecca, Tamara, and I'll all sit together."

"That'll be nice." Eve replied. "I look forward to seeing you again later tonight." With that, she began walking toward King Josiah's tent camp.

26

THE WEDDING CELEBRATION

"Hello, Prophet Zephaniah. I hear you're attending the meeting."

"Yes, I'll be sitting together with dignitaries from the King's regime."

"Saphah, do you have your speech ready?"

"Yes, I wrote most of it the evening Jonathan and Eve came over."

"I'm looking forward to hearing it. I'll give my speech after you."

"Oh, good. I'm looking forward to your speech too. Zephaniah, I hate to leave good company so soon, but now that I'm back at the Rechabite camp, I must go tidy up for the wedding supper. I look forward to seeing you later."

Zephaniah gave Saphah a kiss on the cheek. "Yes, see you later."

~

Saphah felt tired and her hair was disheveled by the time she reached the family tent. "Anybody here?" She yelled her question as she stood by the tent opening.

"Come on in, Saphah. I'm glad you're back. I was just about ready to go out looking for you. Come over here and wash up, and then I'll wash and fix your hair. We can talk as I style it."

"Alright. Rebecca, you look so nice in that light blue frock, and your hair looks adorable with that white flower on the side. Who fixed your hair?"

"Mother styled it. I was hoping it looked nice since I'll be singing. a solo tonight."

"Well, it does. Guess what happened earlier?"

"What?"

"I saw Eve by a stream in the woods and I got to talk to her."

"Good! I'm glad you saw her. Are Jonathan and Eve coming to the wedding supper?

"No, they're not up to that yet, but they're both coming to the reform meeting later. Guess what else?"

"What?"

"King Josiah told Jonathan that Eve could be one of his assistants at the palace kitchen."

"Oh, wonderful! I'm relieved to know she's going to be with Jonathan each day. I've been terribly worried about her."

"Me too. I'm thankful King Josiah cares so deeply about the welfare of his people."

"Yes, Judah is fortunate God has sent us this good man for a leader."

"Agreed. I just hope and pray the Lord will provide a leader like that for my own country."

"I hope so too." Rebecca towel dried Saphah's hair, created a large braid across the front, and then fluffed out her long, naturally wavy hair. "Your hair turned out really nice and your cap fits perfectly behind the braid."

"Thank you. C'mon now, we must hurry. We don't want to be late."

"No, we don't."

Levi approached Rebecca and Saphah as they walked into the big tent. "Hello, ladies. I've been waiting for you. Let's go join our family sitting over there. Saphah, you may take a seat by Shallum, and Rebecca, you may take the seat across from her by Zephaniah. Miriam is sitting at that end."

"Are we late?" asked Saphah.

"No, you're not late. The musicians are still warming up, so you've arrived just in time."

The three took their seats and greeted those around them. "Miriam, everything looks so nice." Saphah was admiring the beautiful flower blossoms decorating the tables. "The flower arrangements are just beautiful. Where did you find such a gorgeous variety of flowers?"

"Judah is no stranger to endless fields of beautiful wildflowers," Mirium observed. "Since we've just experienced a few weeks of rainy season these gorgeous flowers are abundant. The red poppies you see are Kalanit and many songs have been written about them. The direct translation of their name in Hebrew means bride. We love these flowers because they're considered to be as beautiful as a bride on her wedding day. The chrysanthemums and purple anchusa can be found perched on hilltops in Jordan Valley and the tall, elegant yellow mustard flowers can be found throughout the countryside. Some of our young women went out with their donkeys and carts to collect flowers for the arrangements."

Suddenly everything became quiet as the musicians halted their warmup, and Levi, sitting at the other end of the table arose. "Good evening, King Josiah and honored guests. Again, I'm Levi, father of

the groom and I want to welcome everyone to the wedding supper
of Ebed and Hannah. Now, I'd like to present Prophet Zephaniah,
uncle of Hannah, who'll sing the opening song."

Zephaniah arose, walked to the front of the group, and began to sing
the lyrics in his deep voice:

> Come to a wedding supper,
> Come to a banquet of love,
> Come on a day when happiness reigns,
> Celebrate love and all it brings.
>
> Thanks for the love abiding,
> That holds us as one in grace,
> Parent and child, bride and groom,
> Thanks to our God, love without end.
>
> Come to this wedding supper,
> Requesting a blessing,
> For all the years that living will bring,
> Now to you both, we give our love.

Zephaniah returned to the family table to the sound of greatly
deserved applause for his beautiful rendition and took his seat.

Palace musicians began playing the harp and viol, the taboret and
pipe, as little Rechabite girls, with floral crowns on their heads and
flower baskets on their arms, strewed flower petals on the pathway.
Everyone arose as the betrothed couple, all aglow and dressed in their
wedding finery, followed them to the front of the tent.

The couple looked so nice and so happy that it almost took Saphah's
breath away. "Oh Rebecca," she whispered. "You did a fabulous job
on Hannah's veil."

"Thank you," Rebecca whispered back with a smile.

The young couple walked to the family table and sat down with their grandparents. Levi arose again to announce the recitations of the grandparents: "And now the betrothed will receive admonitions to honor God in marriage as found in scripture, and each grandparent will quote one verse in each one." The maternal grandparents, Isaac and Ruth, and the paternal grandparents, Joseph and Ethel, all arose to begin reciting.

> Isaac began, "Hannah, *blessed are all who fear the Lord, who walk in obedience to him.*"[1]

> Ruth continued, "Hannah, *you will eat the fruit of your labor; blessings and prosperity will be yours.*"[2]

They stepped back and the paternal grandparents stepped forward.

> Joseph went on, "Ebed, *your wife will be like a fruitful vine within your house; your children will be like olive shoots around your table.*"[3]

> And Ethel finished, "Ebed, yes, *this will be the blessing for the man who fears the Lord.*"[4]

"Thank you, grandparents." Levi said. "And now, I'd like to introduce to you my beautiful daughter Rebecca, who'll be singing a solo."

Rebecca, walked to the front and began her solo in her soprano voice:

> There's something I know, I plainly can see, So gently it comes and it settles on me; God made it in heaven, it comes from above, A beautiful something, the wonder of love.

The wonder of love to me is made known, God's mercy and pardon so freely are shone; Like rays of warm sunshine, it comes from above, It touches me now, the wonder of love.

It touches my heart, its warmth I can feel, It shines on my path, I see it is real. It's cause for great changes, for miracles wrought, This God given wonder of love in my heart.

The wonder of love is made known, God's mercy so freely shown; Like rays of the sun from above, It touches me now, oh the wonder of love, God's love.[5]

Rebecca returned to her seat amidst applause from one and all. Levi and Miriam both arose and walked toward the couple and Levi announced: "Now, Miriam and I would like to share admonitions for the couple to honor each other in marriage."

Levi began, "Ebed, as you and Hannah pledge before the Lord the union of your love—please remember always love must be patient, love must be kind, and love must hold fast."

Mirium continued, "Hannah, we pray that God will guide you and Ebed through all the years to be, and that your lives will be shaped by faith, courage, and serenity."

Levi spoke again, "Ebed and Hannah, we also pray that through joy and celebration, through grief and pain, that compassion, tenderness and loyalty will remain."

Finally, Mirium said, "Hannah and Ebed, if you share the blessing of love that cannot cease, you must walk the path of meekness into the place of peace."

The couple stood up and Ebed began speaking. "Hannah and I want to thank our grandparents and parents for the words of admonition.

And, now, my betrothed and I want to pledge our love to one another using scripture. Ebed took Hannah's hands in his own.

> Hannah, *you have stolen my heart, my sister, my bride; you have stolen my heart with one glance of your eyes.*[6]

> Ebed, *I* [have] *found the one my heart loves.*[7]

> Hannah, *place me as a seal over your heart, like a seal on your arm.*[8]

> Ebed, *many waters cannot quench love, rivers cannot sweep it away.*[9]

> Hannah, *my beloved is mine, and I am* [hers].[10]

> Ebed, *my beloved is mine and I am his.*[11]

> Hannah, scripture tells us *a man leaves his father and his mother and is united to his wife, and they become one flesh.*[12] Hannah, I place this bracelet on your arm as a token of our love.

> Ebed, scripture also says *marriage* [is a] *covenant* [and] *the Lord is the witness.*[13] Ebed, I place this bracelet on your arm as a token of our covenant of love.

The guests at the wedding supper broke out in applause. "Kiss the bride," someone spoke up.

Ebed raised Hannan's veil and kissed the bride. "Darling, I love you."

"Dear, I love you too." Hannah and Ebed sat back down.

Levi stood back up. "What a beautiful pledge of marriage, Ebed and Hannah. Congratulations! Now, Shallum, would you please say the prayer so the feast can begin."

Shallum stood to say the wedding supper prayer. "Father in heaven, you ordained marriage between a man and a woman and it is good. Your Word says: *If two lie down together, they will keep warm. But how can one keep warm alone. One may be overpowered, two can defend themselves.*[14] You also said, *It is not good for man to be alone. I will make a helper suitable for him.*[15] We have just seen a most beautiful example of a pledge of love between a man and a woman. And you are a witness of their fidelity, not only to each other but also to you, their Lord and God. Please bless this marriage. And, please bless this food to our bodies we pray. Amen."

"Thank you, Shallum." Levi said. "Please remember, everyone, that although young Rechabite men and women will serve courses of food and drink at this banquet, a variety of other food is available on the side tables. The regular menu lists what you will be served for the main courses. But a separate menu lists the meats, sides, fruits, breads, and drinks also available at the buffet tables."

The musicians resumed the music as the young Rechabite men and women served the food and drink. Saphah picked up the two hand written menus with delicate patterns of colored art decorating their edges. "Who did these beautiful menus?"

"Tamara and I wrote out the menus, but some other ladies did the art work," said Rebecca.

"Well, they're just lovely." Could I take these home to give to Huldah?

"Of course. I've also written out the recipes for the main courses for you to take to her."

"Here comes the first course," said Miriam. "Sweet Cucumber Salad, flatbread, and Kaymak."

"Please tell me about the cucumber salad."

"The ingredients are small crisp cucumbers sliced, pomegranate seeds separated, mint and cilantro to taste. The dressing is composed of mustard seeds lightly pounded, dates roughly chopped, pomegranate molasses, olive oil, vinegar, and salt to taste. It's refreshing, sweet, and full of fresh flavor, the perfect appetizer for a wedding banquet."

"Tell me about the flatbread too."

"You need to know this flatbread is heaven. It's shaped in a classic grooved shape with a glaze and a vibrant topping of spices which give the bread a beautiful, crispy sheen. It's served with Kaymak which is a cousin to butter, only creamier and with a deeper, toastier flavor because it's made in an outdoor oven."

"I can't wait to taste this cucumber salad, flatbread, and Kaymak." Saphah stuck her eating utensil into the salad and took a bite, along with a bite of the bread and condiment. "Oh, my goodness. This is wonderful! I need these recipes."

"Wait until you taste the next course, Rechabite herb and meat stew," Rebecca added. "It's a flavorful stew with cooked herbs, meat and a legume. The recipe combines lots of parsley, coriander, mint, and green onions, along with goat meat and chickpeas. It tastes great with this flatbread and kaymak. You'll want that recipe too."

The group ate their way through all the courses, with each dish tasting more delicious than the one before, until Saphah finally said, "I'm giving a speech tonight. I'm going to have to slow down eating or I won't be able to stay awake at the reform meeting."

"Me too," Rebecca said in agreement. "I need to stay alert to take meeting notes. I must quit eating now."

"I need to quit too," Zephaniah added. "I'm giving my speech after you. Could I talk to you about our speeches before the meeting?"

"Of course, maybe we can talk a bit during the break between supper and the meeting."

"Don't forget, everyone, we'll be sending food home with all of you tomorrow," Miriam said.

"Oh, good. Huldah will be able to taste some of this great food."

"Saphah," Levi said, "Ebed and Hannah wanted me to ask you something special. Do you have a hymn from your world in mind you could sing for the recessional tonight after the supper and gifts?"

Saphah thought for a few moments. "I do. It's called 'Great is Thy Faithfulness.' However, I only remember the first verse. Would just one verse be enough? I could repeat it as many times as necessary'"

"I think the one verses would work just fine. And if need be, you can repeat it. Will you sing it as we send off Ebed and Hannah back to Jerusalem tonight? I know they'll be greatly pleased if you do."

"It would be my pleasure. Just let me know when to sing."

"I will." Levi looked toward Ebed and Hannah's table and noticed the two seemed to be finished eating. The father of the groom arose once again. "Everyone, please give me your attention. It looks like Ebed and Hannah are finished eating, so now we'll present the wedding gifts. Please continue to enjoy your food while we do the gifts."

Two men toting a wooden chest approached toward couple. Rebecca joined them and began speaking. "Ebed and Hannah, father made you a wooden chest for your wedding present. He already had a chest started, so he hurried to complete it before the wedding. This is your wedding present from our family. All your Rechabite relatives and friends made small wooden or clay articles for your future home and placed them in the chest. But your Jerusalem relatives and friends made other types of articles or included money. For instance, Shallum and Huldah's gift is a table runner, to which Saphah applied an embroidery pattern. She included embroidery supplies so Hannah can embroider it herself."

Rebeccah stepped over to her sister-in-law and hugged her. "Hannah, are you ready now to open the chest?"

Hannah came forward and opened the lid of the beautiful wooden chest Levi had made. It was brim full of articles such as clay dishes and wooden utensils, with the beautiful handsewn table cloth and napkins on top and numerous sacks of money too. "Oh, Ebed, come and look!"

"How wonderful! I see there's a list of the gifts everyone gave us. Becca, are you going to read that to us?"

"Yes Eb, I will." Rebecca began reading the list and holding up all the gifts for everyone to see.

"Hannah and I want to thank everyone here for all these wedding gifts," said Ebed.

"Yes, thank you for the gifts," Hannah added. "But we also want to thank you for all you've done to make this the most memorable day of our lives."

"Wait a minute," a male voice said. "You have another gift." King Josiah came walking up with a half-grown, greyhound puppy on a leash. "Hannah, this gift is especially for you and your protection at home when family members are away."

The playful puppy, tail wagging, ran straight to Hannah, who reached down to pet and hug her. "You're the sweetest thing." As Hannah bent over to pet her again, the animal quickly gave her a lick on the face.

"Hannah, why don't you walk around a little with your Egyptian greyhound so she can get to know you?" King Josiah asked.

"Alright, I will." Hannah took the lease from the king and began walking her new pet. Suddenly, she stopped walking and gave the dog a command. "Sit," she said and the pup immediately obeyed."

A person in the crowd spoke up. "I think you've got a keeper."

"I think so too!" Hannah was thrilled with her gift. "Thank you, King Josiah! Have you already trained the pup and what is her name?"

"You're welcome. Her name is Lady. And, someone at the palace has already trained her."

"Oh, Lady is the perfect name for her." Hannah admired her new pet. "She looks like an elegant lady standing with her head held high."

King Josiah, I don't know how to thank you enough." Ebed bowed to the king. "I've been worried about Hannah's welfare when the rest of us are away. This is a perfect solution to that problem."

"Alright, everyone," Levi announced. "Get ready. Here come Ebed's brothers and sisters and little friends to begin the Rechabite circle dance."

As the musicians began playing lively music, Ebed and Hannah arose and stood in the middle of a large open area beyond their table. The first participants were the little sisters of the groom who formed a circle around the couple and danced their choreographed steps in one direction around them. The brothers followed them forming their own circle and performing their own dance steps in the opposite direction.

"Alright, ladies and gentlemen, everyone who wants to dance and is able, form more circles, family first." Levi took Miriam's hand as they danced their way toward the grandparent's table. Rebecca, who'd grabbed Shallum's hand, who'd grabbed Saphah's, who'd grabbed Zephaniah's—caught up with the circle of relatives, now joined by aunts and uncles.

Each new group, laughing and dancing gaily to the fast music, flowed in an opposite direction from the one before. A different circle began after that with King Josiah at the lead and Jerusalem guests joining him, all dancing their hearts out to a fast moving beat.

"Oh my." Saphah whispered to Shallum, "I hope I don't fall down in these slippery sandals."

"You'll be alright," Shallum laughed. "If you fall down, I'll help you right back up."

The music changed to a different tune and everyone stopped dancing. "Hannah, do you have a handkerchief ready?" Levi asked.

"Yes, Saphah made me a beautiful embroidered one with leaves and flowers all around the edge."

"Alright then, as you and Ebed dance, you'll need to each hold one end of the kerchief to signify your union."

"Here goes," Ebed grabbed one end of the dainty cloth and Hannah grabbed the other. They whirled and twirled and happily danced in a circle as the crowd clapped along. Then the clapping stopped and other couples joined them, all dancing in their own styles, laughing and joking as they danced along to the quick music, until the melody changed again and everyone changed partners.

The dancing continued, but soon most older couples dropped out. The younger couples on the floor continued merrily dancing until one by one they began dropping out too. Finally, Ebed and Hannan also took their seats and the music stopped.

"Oh, what a beautiful and joyous day this has been." Levi said. "Thank you all for your attendance at the glorious event of this wedding celebration. Remember that the reform meeting will commence shortly after a short break. But right now, it's time for us to send off Ebed, Hannah, and Lady to Jerusalem. Our new friend, Watchwoman Saphah from America, will sing the recessional." Levi turned and nodded at Saphah to let her know it was time.

Young Rechabite men formed an arch on each side of the aisle with lit torches raised high for the newlyweds to walk under. Then, Saphah sang the recessional as Ebed and Hannah, with Lady's leash in hand, walked hand-in-hand toward the chariot and their new life together.

> Great is Thy faithfulness, O God my father, there is no shadow of turning with Thee; Thou changest not, Thy compassions, they fail not; As Thou hast been Thou forever wilt be.

> Great is Thy faithfulness! Great is Thy faithfulness! Morning by morning new mercies I see; All I have needed Thy hand hath provided—Great is Thy faithfulness, Lord unto me![16]

27

THE ALREADY & THE NOT YET

Rebecca said, "Saphah, I see Tamara sitting over with her family. Would you like to go with me to fetch her so we can all walk together to the reform meeting tent?"

"Well, I think Zephaniah and I are going to walk together because he wants to talk to me briefly." Saphah turned toward Zephaniah with a questioning look. "Zephaniah, is that right?" The prophet shook his head yes. "So, Rebecca, why don't you and Tamara go on ahead and save two seats? Eve asked me earlier if she could sit with us."

"Of course, see you there."

"Alright, Saphah." Zephaniah turned to her and offered his arm. "Let's go." Saphah crooked her arm in his, and the two friends began walking together on a path leading to the meeting tent.

"Saphah, I need to ask you a question."

"Zephaniah, go ahead. I'll try to answer as best I can."

"After our speeches, Jeremiah is going to share ideas about the need for Josiah's reforms. In addition, I'm planning to suggest to King Josiah that women should take part. If females are an integral part of the spying, it might be possible to avoid notice of the covert nature of the spy operation."

"That makes sense." Saphah shook her head in agreement. "Also, if the king agrees that women should take part, we girls could help with clothing and disguises to conceal the spy group's identity."

"True. That brings me to my question. If women were to join the spy missions, would you be willing to be a participant?"

Saphah stopped walking. "I think I should, don't you?" She shook her head up and down as she asked.

"Yes, I do," Zephaniah said, and they began walking again. "The primary concern of God's first commandment, *You shall have no other gods before me,*[1] is exclusive loyalty to the Lord. Obviously, idolatry undermines God's plans and purposes for mankind, which in the end involves the salvation of the world. That's why God so vehemently hates false religion. So, you need to be aware that if temples or high places of false gods are discovered, serious conflict might ensue between the spy group and presiding false priests. You and the other ladies might be in danger at that time."

"Even if danger is involved, I think it's still my duty to take part in the spying that may result in reform. After all, I think one reason for my being in Judah is to observe possible reforms."

"Saphah, I'm pleased to hear that. Well, here we are. Best wishes on your speech."

"Thank you. Zephaniah, I'm looking forward to hearing your speech too."

Zephaniah and Saphah separated and made their way toward their respective seats. "Hello, ladies," Saphah took her seat by Eve. She noticed King Josiah was standing up to speak. *Whew! Zephaniah and I made it just in the nick of time!*

King Josiah stood and everyone hushed. "Good evening, honored guests. Thank you for being here at an important time in the history of our nation. I think we're witnessing a turning point in Judah, and that's why we have a guest from Jerusalem who'll be speaking to that subject later. But I also have another guest who thinks her own nation, America, is experiencing a turning point too. Therefore, I want to introduce you to our first speaker who'll be giving a two-part speech with a brief intermission. After Part 1, you're welcome to help yourself to the refreshments and drinks provided outside. Now everyone, this is Watchwoman Saphah from America. Please join me in welcoming her."

Saphah arose to applause, adjusted her posture, and walked forward. Placing the scroll containing her speech on the podium, she paused first to nod at the king and then to survey her audience. After that, she opened her scroll, smiled widely, and began her delivery.

The Already & The Not yet

Thank you, King Josiah, and good evening, everyone. I never thought I'd be so pleased to be speaking these words: 'The Already & The Not Yet.' But that is the title of Part 1 of my speech to you tonight.

I can tell from your faces that you're questioning in your minds: What is that woman, Saphah, talking about? What is 'The Already & The Not Yet?'

Well, I'll explain what the title of Part 1 means. 'The Already & The Not Yet,' is a valid statement about God's Kingdom, which unfolds in three stages. And, I'll return to the stages later. But right now, I want to tell you that a writer from my time, Oscar Cullman, wrote, 'It is already the time of the end, and yet it is not the end.'[2] He could say this because Christ the Messiah's first coming marks the *beginning* of the last days. But, Christ's second coming will mark the *end* of the last days.

Thus, Christians from the time of Christ to my day find themselves already living in the last days, since *the Spirit clearly says that in later times some will abandon the faith and follow deceiving spirits and things taught by demons.*[3] Here, in the New Testament, when the apostle Paul talks about 'later times,' he is referring to 'the time beginning with the first coming of the Messiah. 'That Paul is not referring only to the time immediately prior to Christ's second coming is obvious from his assumption that the false teachings were already present at the time of his writing.'[4]

Therefore, Christians of my time live in the overlapping of the ages. Salvific benefits are ours already but not yet fulfilled in their entirety. Cullman offered an analogy:

> 'God has revealed himself in history through a series of redemptive acts. For the Old Testament believer [that is, for you here tonight], the midpoint of history [is] in the future. But for the New-Testament-era disciples [that is, for those who were witnesses of the Messiah's redemptive acts] and succeeding peoples [that is, for me and my generation], this midpoint now lies in the past. The first coming of Jesus [Messiah] is the great midpoint in history, it lies behind us.'[5]

Thus, from the perspective of you sitting here in the audience, the midpoint of history is defined as follows: (1) through the coming of the eschatological Davidic Messiah; (2) through the latter-day outpouring of the Spirit; and (3) through the general resurrection of the dead.

First, according to Old Testament scripture, the midpoint of history is defined as the coming of the Davidic Messiah as God foretold to King David:

The Lord declares to you that the Lord himself will establish a house for you. When your days are over and you rest with your ancestors, I will raise up your offspring [Solomon] to succeed you, your own flesh and blood, and I will establish his kingdom. He is the one who will build a house for my Name, and I will establish the throne of his kingdom forever. …Your house and your kingdom will endure forever before me; your throne will be established forever.[6]

The covenant with David is grounded in God's firm and gracious purpose and fulfilled in the kingship of Christ who was born of the tribe of Judah and the house of David. In Jesus Christ this promise comes to ultimate fulfillment.

Second, the midpoint is defined in your scripture as the latter-day outpouring of the Spirit: *And afterward, I will pour out my spirit on all people. Your sons and daughters will prophecy, your old men will dream dreams, your young men will see visions. Even on my servants, both men and women, I will pour out my Spirit in those days.*[7] The New Testament agrees with the Old when Peter quotes these very verses and interprets them as referring specifically to the new covenant in contrast to the old covenant.[8]

Hence, he proclaimed the arrival of the age of Messianic fulfillment when numerous people of all ages and genders would prophesy by the power of the Spirit, Jesus would be accredited by miracles, wonders and signs, and everyone who calls on the name of the Lord will be saved.

And, third, the midpoint of history for you is prophesied in your scripture as the general resurrection from the dead: *And, after my skin has been destroyed, yet in my flesh I will see God; I myself will see him with my own eyes—I, and not another. How my heart yearns within me!*[9] Here the writer of the Book of Job senses that a disease afflicting his skin will eventually bring about his death. But he is certain that death is not the end of existence and that someday he will stand before his redeemer and see him with his own eyes. And the New Testament agrees about the reality of resurrection: *But we know that when Christ appears, we shall be like him, for we shall see him as he is.*[10]

This is also spelled out in scripture when the apostle Paul said:

> *I worship the God of our ancestors as a follower of the Way,*
> *…I believe everything that is in accordance with the Law and*
> *that is written in the Prophets, and I have the same hope in*
> *God as these men themselves have, that there will be a*
> *resurrection of both the righteous and the wicked.*[11]

And here, Paul states that he shares the same hope as the Jews—resurrection and judgment. But after Paul became a follower of Christ, he saw this age and the age to come much differently. He could now clearly see that the redemptive-historical line had been divinely reconfigured.

Paul notes that now Israel's hope of general resurrection and salvation hangs on the resurrection of Jesus Christ:

> *I stand here and testify to small and great alike, I am saying*
> *nothing beyond what the prophets and Moses said would*
> *happen—that the Messiah would suffer and, as the first to rise*
> *from the dead, would bring the message of light to his own*
> *people and to the Gentiles.*[12]

Brandon Crowe writes 'that the resurrection is not simply one event among many but is the quintessential way that scripture is fulfilled and is the means by which Jesus as Messiah is Lord of all. The resurrection, in short is the hope of Israel, and this hope has broken into history through

Jesus of Nazareth.'[13] So, whereas once the general resurrection of the dead was the turning point of time, now Jesus's resurrection is the decisive turning point.

Christ's death and resurrection is the central event that launched the latter days—an eschatological event beginning the new creation and moving us into an overlapping of the ages. The reason for the shift in perspective in my age is profound: the resurrection of Christ is closely united and connected with our own resurrection. Specifically, our future resurrection is determined by our present, spiritual resurrection with Christ.

In the New Testament, Jesus said, *I am the resurrection and the life. The one who believes in me will live, even though they die; and whoever lives by believing in me will never die.*[14] Jesus presents himself here as the full embodiment of Israel's hope. But he is not only the resurrection, he is life itself. He conveys life to believers so that death will never triumph over them. Faith and life are connected because the decisive actions of Christ's life, death, and resurrection have taken place, and the believer no longer belongs to the realm where death reigns supreme but to the realm of life.

Those who believe in him will live even though they die. They have already been spiritually resurrected, but they will be raised from the dead at the end of time:

> *Do not be amazed at this, for a time is coming when all who are in their graves will hear his voice and come out—those who have done what is good will rise to live, and those who have done what is evil will rise to be condemned.*[15]

Believers are already members of His kingdom, and our future is certain because Jesus, the hope of Israel, is our hope.

Anthony Hoekema gave a helpful summary by saying the nature of New Testament eschatology is summarized by three observations:

> (1) the great eschatological event [i.e., resurrection] predicted in the Old Testament has happened; (2) what the Old Testament writers seemed to depict as one movement is now seen to involve two stages: the present age and the age of the future; and (3) the relation between these two eschatological stages is that the blessings of the present (eschatological) age are the pledge and guarantee of blessings to come![16]

Cullmann offered a second analogy. We've had two world wars in our world. And the distinction between D-day and V-day in our second World War is a common analogy of the already, not yet tension. Historians generally agree that World War II was decided in the Battle of Normandy that began June 6, 1944 and was referred to as D-Day. The Allied Forces struck a fatal blow to Germany at that time that rendered its defeat inevitable. But it took another year for Germany to surrender in what was referred to as V-Day. Therefore, between D-Day and V-Day, the victory the Allied Forces had in principle already won was not yet manifested as an actual fact.

The dynamic of 'The Already & The Not Yet' is captured by that illustration. The decisive battle may occur in early conflict, yet the war continues. The already won battle means victory even though the war goes on for a time. When Jesus completed his work by dying on the cross and rising from the dead, the powers of the devil were defeated in principle. As a result, Jesus is seated on his rightful throne, *for God has rescued us from darkness and brought us into the kingdom of the Son he loves, in whom we have redemption, the forgiveness of sins.*[17]

This victory has occurred. Because of what Jesus has accomplished, our position as God's viceroys on earth has been restored. But we do not yet see everything subjected to us because the dark powers still battle. Christ in principle defeated death, nonetheless we continue to die because V-Day lies in the future. But we do experience Jesus, *the firstborn among many brothers and sisters*,[18] who is already everything we shall be when V-day arrives.

We see Him in the fulness of kingdom power when souls are saved, miracles are performed, and bodies are healed. Eventually at Christ's second coming, there'll no longer be a need for evangelism and salvation. But that time is not yet here in the history of the world. We need, as Jesus prayed, *Your Kingdom come, your will be done, on earth as it is in heaven.*[19]

Therefore, theologians see the Kingdom of God as unfolding in three stages—the preparation, the establishment, and the consummation. We could refer to it as the kingdom narrative in three acts.

The first act, the preparation of the kingdom, began when God created Israel as a theocratic nation under the eternal monarch, and said, *I am the Lord, your Holy One, Israel's Creator, your King.*[20] *Although the whole earth is mine, you will be for me a kingdom of priests and a holy nation.*[21] But his call to be a holy nation was conditioned on whether they'd obey the king's laws which flowed out of consecration, holiness, and devotion to him. They were warned to avoid the profaneness of the surrounding nations, including the worship of false gods, and to honor God's commandments. But throughout Israel's existence, the people chose to forsake God's ways. Then God promised the Messiah:

> *For to us a child is born, to us a son is given, and the government will be on his shoulders. And he will be called Wonderful Counselor, Mighty God, Everlasting Father, Prince of Peace. Of the greatness of his government and peace there will be no end. He will reign on David's throne and over his kingdom, establishing and upholding it with justice and righteousness from that time on and forever. The zeal of the Lord Almighty will accomplish this.*[22]

And God promised a new covenant: *This is the covenant I will make with the people of Israel after that time, declares the Lord. I will put my law in their minds and write it on their hearts. I will be their God, and they will be my people.*[23]

Therefore, the Old Testament time, in which you sitting here tonight live, is a time of preparation. So far, the kingdom hasn't come in the mode it was intended to come because many of the people in your land have forsaken the laws of the kingdom. A change is needed so that's why God promised through your prophets the Messiah, who will establish his kingdom by transforming people. In the meanwhile, believers in your time and place look forward in faith to the saving grace of the coming Messiah.

The second act, the establishment of the kingdom, begins with the birth of the baby Messiah. The angel Gabriel declared to Mary: *You will conceive and give birth to a son, and you are to call him Jesus. He will be great and will be called the Son of the Most High. The Lord God will give him the throne of his father David, and he will reign over Jacob's descendants forever; his kingdom will never end.*[24] The Messiah is also Savior. An angel announced to shepherds near Bethlehem, the birthplace of Jesus: *I bring you good news that will cause great joy for all people. Today in the town of David a Savior has been born to you; he is the Messiah, the Lord.*[25]

The Lord Jesus announced the fulfillment of the establishment period: *The time has come, he said. The kingdom of God has come near. Repent and believe the good news!*[26] Ever since Jesus came, men and women who surrender to the Lordship of Jesus can enjoy the reality of the kingdom in their lives, because 'the kingdom of God has come near.'

However, the Jewish nation—the establishment representing the people—rejected their true Messiah. Thus, Jesus announced that *the kingdom of God will be taken away … and given to a people who will produce its fruit.*[27] Now, the kingdom that Messiah established belongs to those who surrender to Jesus as king. He has made us, both Jews and Gentiles, *to be a kingdom and priests to serve his God and Father,*[28] which emphasizes these blessings as present possessions already enjoyed by believers. Christ is presently reigning over his people who've received *God's abundant provision of grace …and who reign in life through the one man, Jesus Christ.*[29]

The third act, the completion of the kingdom, still awaits future fulfillment. We inherit it now, but it will be fully revealed at the return of Christ. At the present time, the kingdom does not reveal itself to the outward eye— the kingdom of the world still exists alongside of the kingdom of God. The kingdom is mixed with the unregenerated (unsaved), and the regenerated (saved). Jesus told the parable of the weeds:

> *The kingdom of heaven is like a man who sowed good seed in his field. But while everyone was sleeping, his enemy came and sowed weeds among the wheat, and went away. When the wheat sprouted and formed heads, then the weeds also appeared. The owner's servants came to him and said, 'Sir, didn't you sow good seed in your field? Where then did the weeds come from? …Do you want us to go and pull them up.'*[30] 'No,' he

> *answered, 'because while you are pulling the weeds, you may uproot the wheat with them. Let both grow together until the harvest.*[31] *...The weeds are the people of the evil one, and the enemy who sows them is the devil. The harvest is the end of the age.'*[32]

And only God, the Creator of the Universe, can sort them out at that time. So, that finishes the first part of my speech entitled 'The Already & The Not Yet,' which describes the kingdom of God as unfolding in the three stages of the preparation, the establishment, and the consummation. Those of you in the audience tonight live in the preparation stage—the Old Testament era, but the people of my land live in the establishment and consummation stages—the New Testament era.

~

"We will now take a short break. As King Josiah noted, please help yourself to the refreshments and drinks, and when the meeting resumes shortly, I'll speak on the subject of the second part of my speech, 'America's Spiritual Condition.'"

Saphah and the other ladies all arose to get refreshments. As they stood in line to get their choice of a variety of little dried fruit and nut cakes, along with fruit juice, Saphah spied Zephaniah talking to a man she'd never met. "There's Prophet Zephaniah, but who is that young man talking to him?"

"I don't know." Rebecca said. "I've never seen him before." The others shook their heads in uncertainty.

Prophet Zephaniah glanced their way and discretely waved a raised hand to acknowledge them. Then he said something to his friend and the two began walking toward them. "Hello, ladies. I want to introduce you to a special person. Saphah, Rebecca, Tamara, and Eve, this is Jeremiah, who I just learned is also going to briefly speak to us tonight."

"Oh, I'm pleased to meet you," said Saphah. "Are you Jeremiah, *the son of Hilkiah, one of the priests at Anathoth in the territory of Benjamin?*"[33]

"Yes, I'm a son of Hilkiah of Anathoth. It sounds like you've already heard of me."

"Oh, believe me, I've already heard a great deal about you." Saphah couldn't help but chuckle under her breath at the thought of all she'd learned about Jeremiah from scripture. Saphah curtsied toward the man. "I'm pleased to become acquainted with you Jeremiah."

"As I am to become acquainted with you, Watchwoman Saphah, and your friends." Jeremiah bowed at Saphah and then at the other three ladies in turn.

"By the way, I greatly enjoyed the first part of your speech and found it very informative."

"Thank you, Jeremiah. I'm pleased to hear that you'll be speaking briefly tonight in addition to Prophet Zephaniah."

"Yes, as I told Prophet Zephaniah, earlier today I talked to the King. I wanted to let him know that recently I spoke with some priests in Anathoth who shared some insights on spiritual conditions in Judah. Therefore, the king suggested that I share details of what the priests told me with everyone here tonight."

Saphah thoughtfully considered. *The fact that Jeremiah has talked about spiritual conditions in Judah to priests in the Levitical town of Anathoth shows that he 'sympathize[s] with and support[s] [Josiah's] attempts at spiritual reform and renewal.*'[34]

Saphah was drawn out of her reverie by the sound of Zephaniah's deep voice. "Saphah, I also thought the first segment of your speech went well." But then Prophet Zephaniah spotted King Josiah walking back with associates toward the tent. "I see the king is going back inside, so perhaps we should too."

"I agree. I think we'll need to keep on schedule so our meeting can finish before it gets too late, don't you?" asked Saphah.

"Yes," Jeremiah said. "This is a very important meeting and results of what we say tonight could have implications not only for Judah, but also for America, and in the end, even for the entire world."

28

AMERICA'S SPIRITUAL OUTLOOK

Saphah stood at the podium again to continue her speech. "Alright, men and women of Judah, I hope you enjoyed the break. Thank you, King Josiah, for providing the refreshments. And now, I'd like to share Part 2 of my speech:

America's Spiritual Outlook

To begin my talk on the spiritual condition of America, I'll turn to Revelation 12, which some consider to be the centerpiece of the book's review of history. There we read about a woman:

> *She was pregnant and cried out in pain as she was about to give birth. She gave birth to a son, a male child, who will rule all the nations with an iron scepter. And her child was snatched up* [the ascension] *to God and to his throne. The woman fled into the wilderness to a place* [of spiritual refuge] *prepared for her by God, where she might be taken care of for* 1,260 *days.*[1]

Here, the 1,260 refers to the concluding days of the period of tribulation occurring in the final days before Jesus returns and corresponding to the time of intense persecution of the saints. It is called the 'Great Tribulation.'

Revelation then shifts to a heavenly perspective:

> *Then war broke out in heaven. Michael and his angels fought against the dragon, and the dragon and his angels fought back. But he was not strong enough, and they lost their place in heaven. The great dragon was hurled down—that ancient*

serpent called the devil, or Satan, who leads the whole world astray. He was hurled to the earth, and his angels with him.[2]

Here, Christ's victory over the dragon and his angels on earth is envisioned in terms of heavenly combat between God's and the devil's forces, with the devil's forces inevitably losing. The dragon was hurled to earth—not the original casting out, but his final exclusion—which explains his intense hostility in the last days against God's people. Then John writes:

I heard a loud voice in heaven say: Now have come the salvation and the power and the kingdom of our God, and the authority of his Messiah. For the accuser of our brothers and sisters, who accuses them before our God day and night, has been hurled down. They triumphed over him by the blood of the Lamb and by the word of their testimony; they did not love their lives so much as to shrink from death. Therefore rejoice, you heavens and you who dwell in them! But woe to the earth and the sea, because the devil has gone down to you! He is filled with fury, because he knows that his time is short.[3]

Again, scripture confirms that Jesus has already won the victory, for 'now have come the salvation and the power and the kingdom of our God, and the authority of his Messiah.' The Crucial battle has been fought and won in the death and resurrection of Christ. But the cease-fire is yet future. Christ is already the victor, but 'the devil, or Satan, who leads the whole world astray was hurled to the earth and his angels with him.' Therefore, 'woe to the earth and the sea, because the devil has gone down to you! He is filled with fury since he knows his time is short.' Revelation 12 ends by telling us:

When the dragon saw that he had been hurled to the earth, he pursued the woman who had given birth to the male child. The

> *woman was given the two wings of a great eagle, so that she might fly to the place prepared for her in the wilderness, where she would be taken care of for a time, times and half a time* [1260 days], *out of the serpent's reach. …Then the dragon was enraged at the woman and went off to wage war against the rest of her offspring—those who keep God's commands and hold fast their testimony about Jesus.*[4]

Now, Satan and his demons, enraged with believers in general, as contrasted with Christ, the male child, rage off to 'wage war' against the saints.

Jesus has won the main victory, but many unbelievers remain in deception and spiritual warfare continues. The battle is *against the devil's schemes. For our struggle is not against flesh and blood, but against the rulers, against the authorities, against the powers of this dark world and against the spiritual forces of evil in the heavenly realms.*[5] So, Satan's defeat in heaven doesn't mean an end of earthly suffering, but an escalation of it. But Christians continue to triumph over the devil by the blood of the Lamb, by the word of their testimony, and by boldly proclaiming Christ regardless of the cost.

The final hurling out of Satan and his demons (spiritual beings in league with him) is an explanation of their intense hostility against God's people throughout history, but this anger and hostility will intensify even more in the final days just before Jesus' return. But the fact is that Satan and his demons are already exerting an extremely evil influence on human affairs at the present time in my world.

Switching back to a passage in Revelation 9, John speaks of a vision depicting horses and riders. And the power of the horses *was in their mouths and in their tails, for their tails were like snakes, and having heads with which they inflict injury.*[6] Snakes with tails which had heads show 'the demonic origin of the horses.'[7] Scripture informs us unbelievers who were not killed by these plagues still didn't repent: *They did not stop worshiping demons, and idols of gold, silver, bronze, stone, and wood— idols that cannot see or hear or walk. Nor did they repent of their murders, their magic arts* [sorceries in KJV], *their sexual immorality or their thefts.*[8]

These five sins, present even now in my modern society after the Coronavirus Pandemic, seem to indicate the spiritual decadence in my world at the present time. The world system is vile and degrading over the course of history further and further away from God. Following are some reasons for such a conclusion.

In the rebellion of unbelievers in Revelation 9, the first sin involved refusal to stop worshiping demons. Worship of demons is mentioned in 1 Corinthians where the apostle Paul referred to Old Testament scripture from Moses' time. First, he referred to the golden calf in Exodus 32 where the people ate a ritual meal sacrificed to an idol. And, second, to Israel's participation in the worship of Baal of Peor in Numbers 25, where the Israelites disgraced themselves in sexual rites associated with Baal worship. Israelite men had unmarried sex with Midianite women, who were acting as cultic prostitutes. Thus, they incurred the wrath and punishment of God.

Therefore, Paul was warning the Corinthians:

[Do] *not be idolaters, as some of them* [in Moses' time] *were; as it is written: 'the people sat down to eat and drink and got up to indulge in revelry.' We should not commit sexual immorality, as some of them did and in one day twenty-three thousand of them died.*[9]

According to scripture, when these people worshiped idols they actually sacrificed *unto devils, not to God; to gods whom they knew not, to new gods that came newly up, whom your fathers feared not.*[10] Thus, the downfall of Israel took the form of idol worship *when they provoked him to jealousy with strange gods, with abominations provoked they him to anger.*[11] In spite of God's great provision for them, the people scorned Him and made sacrifices to something they created.

Since God forbids idolatry, Paul wanted the Corinthians to take heed because of the consistency of God as judge of Israel and the church. He wanted the men and women to know that when people offer sacrifices to false gods, they actually offer sacrifices to demons. Of course, man-made idols are not gods, but there are 'many invisible spirit beings in the world and these devils (demons) can indwell idols made by men as objects of worship. These evil spirits do have certain powers, which can be used to impress their worshippers with the ...insights and abilities of the [indwelt] images.'[12] That's why Paul told the Corinthians to *flee from idolatry.*[13]

Demon worship is 'a serious problem today, not only in lands where images and animalistic spirits abound, but even in the Christian west, both in the proliferating New Age cults and in mainline churches that have diluted sound Bible teaching with humanism and ritualistic pantheism.'[14] Scripture also warns: Whatever belongs to your earthly nature: *sexual immorality, impurity, lust, evil desires and greed is idolatry. Because of these, the wrath of God is coming.*[15] In fact, covetousness of money or power or anything else which takes us away from God is idolatry.

Recently, demon worship reared its head in a profound way in our southern state of Louisiana: 'A priest and two women were arrested after allegedly engaging in a sexual act on a Catholic church's altar, one of the most sacred sites in the Catholic tradition.'[16] At the Saints Peter and Paul Catholic Church in Pearl River, a town just northeast of New Orleans, a passerby saw the church's lights on later than usual and decided to check things out. Looking through windows and glass doors, the person saw the priest 'half naked—but still wearing his priestly attire—having sex with two women on the altar. …The eyewitness took a video and called … police, who arrived at the scene and viewed the recording.[17]

Archbishop Gregory Aymond of the Archdiocese of New Orleans said the acts of the perpetrator, the (former) Rev. Travis Clark, were 'demonic. His obscene behavior was deplorable, his desecration of the altar in church was demonic. I am infuriated by his actions. When the details became clear, we had the altar removed and burned.'[18] And, 'the archbishop then consecrated a replacement altar.'[19]

The two women, 'Melissa Cheng and Mindy Dixon, allegedly told police they were at the church with Clark's permission and were recording themselves in role play. …Dixon is an adult film actress and works for hire as a dominatrix, according to public records. …A social media account associated with Dixon includes a post …saying she was on her way to the New Orleans area to meet another dominatrix and defile a house of God.'[20]

In the instance of the priest having sex on the altar, his demonic act is symbolic of the failure by some false priests and pastors in all Christian denominations in the modern age, to live up to spiritual duties. Worship of demons has been a problem throughout human history. It was a problem in the day of Moses, in the time of Paul, in the era of you sitting here, and in the present era in the world in which I live.

The other verse I quoted in Revelation 9 informed us that after the mentioned plague, the unbelievers also refused to repent of other evil deeds such as their murders, magic arts or sorceries, sexual immoralities, and thefts. This follows a pattern clearly stablished in scripture that unbelievers, in general, are willful in their disobedience and cling to their sinfulness even when facing consequences.

Thus, the second example of the defiance of mankind against God's authority in America is shown in the numbers and types of murders committed:

'There are more murders with no apparent motive than ever before, murders that are an afterthought. Somebody goes to commit a crime and as an afterthought they kill everybody who happened to be around the situation. …There are more gang murders of rival gang members and of bystanders who are shot simply while sitting in their house watching television because they get caught in the crossfire. …[Also], more drug and prostitution-related murders. …[And], there are more multiple murders in a shorter period of time than before.'[21]

Third, in Revelation 9, the unrepentant also refused to abandon their magic arts or sorceries. Magic arts or sorceries are terms evoking the idea of a spell-caster or magic-user which is also a part of man's rebellion against God. When Paul preached at Ephesus, Jewish exorcists there invoked the name of the Lord Jesus over the demon possessed. …

> *One day the evil spirit answered them, 'Jesus I know, and Paul I know about, but who are you?' Then the man who had the evil spirit jumped on them and overpowered them all. He gave them such a beating that they ran out of the house naked and bleeding.*[22]

So, this came to be known to the Jews and Greeks living in Ephesus:

> *They were all seized with fear. …Many of those who believed now came and openly confessed what they had done. A number who had practiced sorcery brought their scrolls together and burned them publicly. When they calculated the value of the scrolls, the total came to fifty thousand drachmas.*[23]

Interestingly, 'such documents, bearing alleged magical formulas and secret information have been unearthed.[24]

In Deuteronomy 18 we see that sorcery is listed along with several other abominations to God:

> *Let no one be found among you who sacrifices their son or daughter in the fire, who practices divination or sorcery, interprets omens, engages in witchcraft, or casts spells, or who is a medium or spiritist or who consults the dead.*[25]

In the biblical context, sorcery also refers to magical arts and the usage of drugs for spiritual and ceremonial purposes. So, just as the Canaanites were using cannabis to worship their god, Ashera, today there are pagan religions in the world that have been using drugs for spiritual purposes to worship demons they think are deities. In some forms of Hinduism, they use high doses of substances, such as liquid cannabis to contact demons they worship.

In fact, three drugs are still used today, in a similar way to how they were used in the ancient world to try and contact the spiritual or know the purpose of life. 'Many people are actively involved in this and it is considered sorcery. [The drugs are] Marijuana (Weed/Cannabis), …Magic Mushrooms (Psilocybin), …[and] Ayahuasca (DMT).'[26]

People are not to engage in occult practices employing the use of drugs for spiritual/ceremonial purposes. However, the Greek root word translated in Revelation 9 as sorceries is *pharmakeia* from which we get the modern English words pharmacy and pharmaceutical. And as such, this is a reference to our illicit drug culture.

According to the Substance Abuse and Mental Health Services Administration, drug use and substance abuse 'are on the rise in the United States among adults, young adults, and adolescents. Substance abuse includes illicit drug use (such as cocaine use and marijuana use), as well as prescription drug (including opioid) misuse.'[27]

Drug use, abuse, and trafficking have reached epic proportions in our modern day. Matthew J. Strait, on behalf of the Drug Enforcement Administration and the Department of Justice, said:

> 'Americans today are experiencing the most devastating drug crisis in our nation's history. This is because one drug—illicit fentanyl—has transformed the criminal landscape. Illicit Fentanyl is exceptionally cheap to make, exceptionally easy to disguise, and exceptionally deadly to those who take it. It is the leading cause of death for Americans between the ages of 18-45, and it kills Americans from all walks of life, in every state and community in this country. …From February 2022 through January 2023, 110,000 people lost their lives to drug poisonings in the United States. …These poisonings are a national crisis.'[28]

Strait added that the availability of these drugs is primarily due to two Mexican cartels—the Sinaloa Cartel and Jalisco

Cartel. They are extremely violent cartels that rely on a global supply chain to manufacture, transport, and sell illicit fentanyl, and on a global illicit financial network to pocket billions of dollars in revenue from those sales."[29]

However, the main reason drugs are so freely flowing into our country is the fact that our southern border with Mexico remains open. Our federal government, headed by our current president, is allowing the free flow of dangerous drugs into America.

Fourth, the next category of sin mentioned in Revelation 9 is sexual immorality or fornication. The Greek word *porneia* which translates into fornication refers to all sexual sins, beginning with unmarried sex, and including adultery, homosexuality, lesbianism, incest, prostitution, pornography, and all forms of biblically unlawful sexual intercourse. Despite all evidence that God looks unfavorably on those who indulge in illicit sexual sins, those involved refused to repent.

And, finally, those who engage in thievery likewise failed to repent of their crimes. In the large cities of my nation, roving bands of thieves invade retail stores and rob them of their merchandise. At other times, thugs steal, loot, burn and riot without any punishment because of negligent prosecutors and inadequate laws. Instead, lawbreakers are turned loose to commit crime over and over again, and even to murder without repercussion in many instances.

So, in some cases in large American cities, there is a general lack of law enforcement and prosecution of crime. And, the lawlessness and violence continue because some city and state governments are run by a minority of the elite class who are pushing hard on a woke agenda that leaves out God. Presently, the agenda also dominates our federal government and has infiltrated parts of our military, corporations, medical field, school systems, news media, and other organizations.

The scary part is that this destruction of our country by crime, lawlessness, and disorder is intentional. It is a form of the political, economic, and social principles promoted by an evil man named Karl Marx. Marx noted that without a structure of law and order, people will devour each other like animals. So, to gain control over people, the far left who follow Marxist teachings want to break the systems, such as law enforcement, that people rely on and replace them with systems controlled by their own form of communism.

Until now, our country has always had systems of law and order and government that worked well, but now our systems are broken and dysfunctional. This is all by the design of those who want to take over and turn America into a communist country.

Sadly, another reason this bad agenda continues is because a segment of society, especially in large cities, keeps voting for corrupt politicians. These voters seem unable to connect the dots that the increase in big city crime is due in part to the failures of the leaders they vote into office. Some of the voters are non-working men and women who, though able-bodied, are dependent on the government for welfare. Therefore, they keep voting for the political candidates who push for both the social welfare and the criminal leniency which allows for the disruptive behavior of people who commit crime on a repeated basis.

Yet, in 2 Thessalonians, Paul tells the people there that *some among you are idle and disruptive.*[30] Then Paul gives warnings

against idleness when he says that those who *are not busy,
...such people we command and urge in the Lord Jesus Christ to settle
down and earn the food they eat.*[31] Thus, scripture commands
Christians, if they are physically and mentally able, to work
and earn their own way. Another time, Paul tells fellow
believers to *warn those who are idle and disruptive,*[32] that they
should continue working to earn a living.

I've just shared with you some internal strife, lawlessness, and
other evil affecting my nation in a detrimental fashion. The
five sins of Revelation 9—the idolatry, the murders, the
sorceries, the fornications, and the thefts—which are
symbolic of the general depravity of humanity have not let
up. These internal dangers result from the fact that more and
more people have unrepentant hearts. Scripture says they
are storing up wrath against [themselves] for the day of
God's wrath, when his righteous judgment will be revealed.[33]

But we also face external threats to our nation's security from
China, a country which has expressed an intent to dominate
the world. Recently, our federal government began trying
to find malware it believes is hidden within networks.

The networks control power grids, communications systems,
and water supplies that support U.S. military bases. ...The
detection of the malicious malware 'has raised fears that
Chinese hacker have inserted it to disrupt U.S. military
operations in the event of a conflict, such as Beijing invading
Taiwan. ...The malware is basically a ticking time bomb that
could allow China to slow or stop American military
deployments or resupply operations by cutting power,
communications, and water at U.S. military bases.'[34]

U.S. officials fear the impact could be much more widespread,
however, because that same infrastructure often supplies the

homes and businesses of average Americans. 'There is debate over whether the operation's goal is to disrupt the military or civilian life more generally in the event of a conflict …with disruptions to our critical infrastructure, …water systems, pipelines, rail and aviation systems. …[Also,] the president has mandated rigorous cybersecurity practices for the first time.'[35]

Additionally, other nations, such as Russia, Iran, and North Korea want to harm us militarily or through terrorism in our homeland.

To sum up the spiritual condition of America, a rundown of the five sins of Revelation 9 have made it obvious that my country is in serious decline from internal evil. But external threats of war from wicked adversaries now threaten my nation as well. It is my hope that Zephaniah and Jeremiah, who both will be speaking tonight, can help you, the citizens of Judah and me, a citizen of the United States, to unravel the puzzle of what is in store for our nations as we face the consequences of increasing sin in both countries.

~

"Thank you once again, King Josiah, for allowing me to speak to your group on this important subject. And thanks to your audience, as well, for listening in such a gracious and attentive manner." Saphah rolled up her scroll and walked to her seat as the audience gave her a round of applause. She nodded appreciatively, mouthed her thanks, and took her seat again beside Eve.

29

A PRIESTLY OUTLOOK ON SIN

King Josiah said, "Thank you, Watchwoman Saphah, for your informative speech about the spiritual outlook of America, the land that you cherish. You and I have much in common in our concerns over the people we love in our respective nations. It is my prayer that God will give us success in reforms in Judah and that our efforts will provide guidance for reforms in your nation as well. Now, audience, please welcome our next guest, Jeremiah, from the priestly line of the household of Hilkiah of Anathoth. Jeremiah, would you please come up to offer insights on the spiritual outlook of Judah?"

Jeremiah arose and walked toward the podium to the applause of those in the crowd. "Thank you, King Josiah. As most of you know, I'm from a priestly family, so the expectation is that I'll become a priest at age 30. Therefore, due to my association with the priests at Anathoth, I possess information related to your reform efforts I'd like to share. Thus, I'm here tonight to represent the portion of Levitical Priests who remain faithful to God. Unfortunately, other priests have gone astray from the Lord and led the people astray as well. Now, as best I can, I'll attempt to relate the situation to you."

A Priestly Outlook on Sin

As you know, Israel's religious worship is organized around the work of priests at the temple. The Levitical Priests are responsible to slaughter, prepare, and roast animals brought by the worshipers as proper sacrifices to God and to carry out other types of offerings as well. But the roles of the good priests go far beyond the mere physical work of dealing with thousands of animal or other types of sacrifices to the Lord. Although many see the role of the priest as being primarily that of a mediator between the people and God in the temple sacrifices, a larger duty is to teach the people *all the decrees and laws the Lord has given them through Moses.*[1] So the priests are responsible to be the spiritual and moral guides for the people.

But another role of the priests is to oversee judges and officials in every town so they'll *judge the people fairly.* They mustn't *pervert justice or show partiality…*[or] *accept a bribe, for a bribe blinds the eyes of the wise and twists the words of the innocent.* [They're to] *follow justice and justice alone.*[2] In addition, because of the danger of idolatry, the priests are warned *not to set up any wooden Asherah pole beside the altar you build to the Lord your God, and do not erect a sacred stone, for these the Lord your God hates.*[3]

However, if a person in authority such as a king, judge or priest discovers:

> *A man or a woman living among you in one of the towns the Lord gives you* [who] *is found doing evil in the eyes of the Lord …contrary to* [God's] *command,* [and who has] *worshiped other gods, bowing down to them or to the sun or the moon or the stars in the sky, and this has been brought to your attention, then you must investigate it thoroughly. If it is true and it has been proved that this detestable thing has been done in Israel, …You must purge the evil from among you.*[4]

And, another scripture specifies that when there are reports of idolatry, then you must inquire, probe, and investigate it thoroughly [to see] if it is true and it has been proved that this detestable thing has been done among you.[5] So, for this reason, I recommend to King Josiah, the highest authority in Judah except for God, that he spy out the land to investigate reports of idolatry throughout the nation.

In addition, regarding law cases, if a case comes before your courts that is too difficult to judge, whether it is a bloodshed, lawsuit, or assault case, people are to:

> *Go to the Levitical priests and to the judge who is in office at that time. Inquire of them and they will give you the verdict. …Act according to whatever they teach you and the decisions they give you. Do not turn aside from what they tell you, to the right or to the left. [If] anyone …shows contempt for the judge or for the priest, …you must purge the evil from Israel.*[6]

Again, I want to inform King Josiah, that reports of evil carried out by our citizens against our judicial system should be investigated for the sake of our nation.

Sadly, despite the stringent rules God set forth in scripture for priests, some of them have turned away from the true worship of God and led their people into idol worship. These priests have turned a blind eye to the despicable actions of rulers such as Judah's King Ahaz, the great-great-grandfather of King Josiah, and have departed from God's ways just like the kings.

Listed in the biblical account about Ahaz are some common practices of idolatrous worship. Scripture says:

> *King Ahaz made idols for worshiping the Baals. He burned sacrifices in the Valley of Ben Hinnom and sacrificed his children in the fire. …He offered sacrifices and burned incense at the high places, on the hilltops and under every spreading tree. Therefore, the Lord his God delivered him into the hands of the king of Aram. …[and] he was also given into the hands of the king of Israel, who inflicted heavy casualties on him.*[7]

God delivered Ahaz into the hands of both the king of Aram and the king of Israel. His sins were so heinous, retribution fell on him immediately as a result of his disobedience. Forsaking the Lord led to defeat in war with great slaughter and being given into the hands of his enemies. This tells us that 'defeat in war is one of the results of disobedience.'[8]

God himself carried out the punishment on the king, the priests, and the citizenry. Hence, I want to report to King Josiah that these charges of corrupt places of worship such as 'at the high places, on the hilltops and under every spreading tree,' should be investigated thoroughly.

Another way Judah's corrupt priests led the citizens astray was by failing to give them guidance for living as a holy and distinct people. When God's precepts aren't taught by the priests, this results in many forms of oppression such as the unjust or cruel exercise of power by those in authority and the elite class.

Rulers, business leaders, lawyers, tax collectors, and others overturn God's standards resulting in corruption such as extortion, taking bribes, influence peddling, and all sorts of dishonest gain. The elite, who lack concern for the poor, the widow, and the fatherless, often oppress those who are in greatest need.

So, instead of enriching the land, ungodly leaders and priests, by their morally degenerate practices, cause the downfall of nations such as Judah and America, and if reform doesn't occur, God himself has no choice but to carry out judgment. Again, I'm informing you, King Josiah, about these false priests so you can take appropriate action to address both this issue and the others I've mentioned.

It is my hope that you here tonight, along with King Josiah, are now more aware of the disobedience of secular rulers, spiritual leaders, and the people themselves toward God's moral standards and the worship of Him. Good leaders in Judah pull the people back from sin and corruption, but evil ones reverse the good that has been done.

Most recently, good King Hezekiah—son of evil King Ahaz—was replaced by evil King Manasseh, whom scripture says that he did evil in the eyes of the Lord. *…He rebuilt the high places his father Hezekiah had destroyed, he also erected altars to Baal and made an Asherah pole, as Ahab king of Israel had done. … He did much evil in the eyes of the Lord, arousing his anger.*[9]

Manasseh reversed the religious policies of his father, Hezekiah, and reverted to those of King Ahaz, from the northern kingdom, Israel. But we also note that earlier in history Israel was exiled, and *all this took place because the Israelites had sinned against the Lord their God.*[10]

Thus, from a theological standpoint, it's easy to see the reason for Israel's downfall. It pertains to her repeated rejections of the Lord's gracious acts, her refusal to heed the warnings of various prophets about impending judgment, and her failure to keep covenant obligations. Hence, the covenant curse of Deuteronomy was implemented exactly as it had been presented to the Israelites by Moses.

But now, because of Manasseh's evil ways, Judah is in the same boat as Israel, unless there are reforms. Fortunately for Judah, the evil King Manasseh and King Amon have been followed by good King Josiah who arranged this meeting because he already suspects cases of idolatry in Judah.

But followers of God in America, according to what Saphah and Zephaniah have told me, are also hopeful that reform efforts can take place there as well. However, the situation in America is somewhat different from Judah's. Throughout Old Testament history, whenever a large part of secular rulers, religious leaders, and the people have distanced themselves from Yahweh, the Lord has called men and women like Prophet Zephaniah and Prophetess Huldah to speak God's Word to the people. The prophets are like preachers warning the people to repent or face God's wrath.

But in Saphah's world in New Testament times, especially when a large part of a society or a nation or even the entire globe has turned away from God either by commission (intentional apostasy) or omission (unintentional apostasy) or through neglect, God may need to use different tactics to reach the people.

The modern society where Saphah lives already possesses God's completed Word in a book called the Holy Bible, but many people fail to consult it, so God may want to use other means to get people's attention. But since God's Word in its entirety is available to people in New Testament times, the Lord doesn't need to speak through prophets. Instead, he can call watchpersons to sound an alarm by quoting scripture from His Holy Word.

In ancient Israel, 'trumpets made of metal or ram horns (shofars) were used for various purposes like giving warnings, calls to battles, and announcing feasts. ... [But in the future] the blowing of the trumpet will signal the day of the Lord and announce the return of Jesus.'[11] But the trumpet can also be symbolic of the method of warning that the Watchman Ezekiel used in Old Testament times, because God told him:

Son of man, I have made you a watchman for the people of Israel; so hear the word I speak and give them warning from me. When I say to a wicked person, 'You will surely die [spiritually],' and you do not warn them or speak out to dissuade them from their evil ways in order to save their life, that wicked person will die for their sin, and I will hold you accountable for their blood. But if you do warn the wicked person and they do not turn from their wickedness or from their evil ways, they will die for their sin; but you will have saved yourself.[12]

Thus, according to the bible, the Lord can use watchpersons in future eras such as Saphahs time and place, and they'll be held responsible to give people warnings from God of coming judgment on nations such as America. At that time, when the Lord calls people to ministries such as Watchman Ezekiel held, they'll hear the word God speaks to them and give their citizens warnings from Him. They're the last voices in a future time calling people back to God and to a right relationship with Him before coming calamity.

"This ends my discourse on the spiritual condition of Judah as it pertains to the role of those who have precipitated her fall. Apostate rulers, priests, elite and ordinary citizens alike have all played a part in Judah's idolatrous downfall and apostasy. And, we have already heard Saphah's discourse on her own nation, America. But, what does this all mean in a practical sense for Judah and America?"

~

Jeremiah turned to look at Prophet Zephaniah. "Next, to help answer that question, Prophet Zephaniah will share God's Word as it was given to him by the Holy Spirit. But before he does, I would like to take this opportunity to introduce my faithful scribe, Baruch."

Baruch stood up and bowed to the crowd as they gave him a round of applause. "Thank you, thank you." The scribe gave a big bow and returned to his seat.

"Alright," Jeremiah said, "I want to thank King Josiah again for allowing me to bring you this speech on a priestly outlook on sin. And now, I'll turn the podium back to him."

30

LAST CHANCE TO REPENT

King Josiah said, "Jeremiah, thank you for your talk on a priestly outlook on sin. The info will be helpful in my reform efforts for Judah. Now, I'd like to introduce a man who speaks to you by divine revelation from the Holy Spirit. The first part of his speech is prophetic warning, but the second is practical info for Judah and the U. S. Please welcome, Prophet Zephaniah."

Zephaniah arose, picked up a lit lamp, and proceeded toward the front as the audience applauded. "Thank you, dear friends, thank you!" Zephaniah motioned for them to quit clapping. "And, thank you, King Josiah, for allowing me to share God's Word at this point in the affairs of two nations." Zephaniah stepped up to the podium and immediately proclaimed in a booming voice:

Be silent before the Soverign Lord.[1]

~ Saith the Lord.[2]

Then, Prophet Zephaniah quit speaking and stared straight ahead in silence. Everyone else was quiet too as they all stared forward. Not a peep could be heard in the room. Saphah thought, *I think this would be a good time to finish my last paragraph on Jeremiah's talk so I can be ready to begin on Prophet Zephaniah's speech.*

She dipped her pen in ink to continue writing. But when she glanced up to recall what to write next, she was startled to see Jeremiah's scribe Baruch, right in front of her and glaring directly into her eyes. "What!" she said in alarm as Baruch reached both arms toward her and shoved a sheet of papyrus at her face. It read: 'Be silent before the Sovereign Lord.'

Then Baruch walked back to his seat and sat down. Saphah carefully laid down her pen and placed her hands on her lap. She was almost afraid to breathe. Zephaniah was looking straight at her from the podium, but the expression on his face didn't change. *Why the silence?*

She thought for a few seconds. *Oh my, I think I know why. I remember reading about the fact that in prophetic discourse, the going forth of the Almighty in judgment is introduced over and over by a reference to silence. Habakkuk does it. As does Ezekiel. In Revelation, John mentions a time of silence to prepare us for the terrible character of the judgments that will follow. Oh my, perhaps Zephaniah's prophecy is similar! So fearful and awesome is the thought of God's coming retribution that it causes humanity to be spellbound, lost in silent, reflective amazement!*

Saphah sat in silence for what seemed like an eternity, wondering what God's Word spoken through Zephaniah would reveal. She didn't dare to look to the right or the left, for now she knew to remain silent before the Sovereign Lord. But finally, after what seemed to her like an agonizingly long time, Saphah was startled to hear Zephaniah's title for his speech which he finally announced in his deep voice. Her stomach tightened and her hand shook as she transcribed the title of Zephaniah's speech:

Last Chance to Repent—Judah and America

These words are for you, Josiah, King of Judah, as you guide your nation in reform efforts. Likewise, these words are also for you, Saphah, Watchwoman from America, as you consider sounding your shofar to warn your nation of temporal chastizement to come. Listen carefully!

The Future of Jerusalem and Washington:

> *Woe to the city of oppressors, rebellious and defiled! She obeys no one, she accepts no correction. She does not trust in the*

*Lord, she does not draw near to her God. Her officials within her are roaring lions; her rulers are evening wolves, who leave nothing for the morning. Her prophets are unprincipled; they are treacherous people. Her priests profane the sanctuary and do violence to the law. The Lord within her is righteous; he does no wrong. Morning by morning he dispenses his justice, and every day he does not fail, yet the unrighteous know no shame.[3]
~ Saith the Lord.[4]*

Jerusalem and Washington Remain Unrepentant:

*Of Jerusalem [and Washington] I thought, surely you will fear me and accept correction! Then her place of refuge would not be destroyed, nor all her punishments come upon her, but they were still eager to act corruptly in all they did.[5]
~ Saith the Lord.[6]*

The Future of Judah and Jerusalem—Temporal Judgment:

*I will stretch out my hand against Judah and against all who live in Jerusalem. I will destroy every remnant of Baal worship in this place, the very names of the idolatrous priests—those who bow down on the roofs to worship the starry host, those who bow down and swear by the Lord and who swear by Molek, those who turn back from following the Lord and neither seek the Lord nor inquire of him. …On that day, declares the Lord, a cry will go up from the Fish Gate, wailing from the New Quarter, and a loud crash from the hills. Wail, you who live in the market district; all your merchants will be wiped out, all who trade with silver will be ruined.[7]
~ Saith the Lord.[8]*

Zephaniah picked up the lit lamp and searched around in the room.

At that time, I will search Jerusalem with lamps and punish

those who are complacent, who are like wine left on its dregs, who think, 'the Lord will do nothing, either good or bad.'[9]
~ Saith the Lord.[10]

The Future of America and Washington—Temporal Judgment (Later, Eschatological Judgment):

The cry on the day of the Lord is bitter, the Mighty Warrior shouts his battle cry. That day will be a day of wrath—a day of distress and anguish, a day of trouble and ruin, a day of darkness and gloom, a day of clouds and blackness—a day of trumpet and battle cry against the fortified cities and against the corner towers. I will bring such distress on all people that they will grope about like those who are blind, because they have sinned against the Lord. Their blood will be poured out like dust and their entrails like dung. Neither their silver nor their gold will be able to save them on the day of the Lord's wrath.[11]
~ Saith the Lord.[12]

America and nations summoned to repent:

Gather together, gather yourselves together, you shameful nation[s], before the decree takes effect and that day passes like windblown chaff, before the Lord's fierce anger comes upon you, before the day of the Lord's wrath comes upon you. Seek the Lord, all you humble of the land, you who do what he commands. Seek righteousness, seek humility; perhaps you will be sheltered on the day of the Lord's anger.[13]
~ Saith the Lord.[14]

America and Nations unrepentant:

Therefore, wait for me, declares the Lord, for the day I will stand up to testify. I have decided to assemble the nations,

to gather the kingdoms and to pour out my wrath on them—
all my fierce anger.[15]
~ Saith the Lord.[16]

Eschatological Judgment on the Earth:

'I will sweep away everything from the face of the earth,'
declares the Lord. 'I will sweep away both man and beast; I
will sweep away the birds in the sky and the fish in the sea—
and the idols that cause the wicked to stumble. When I destroy
all mankind on the face of the earth.'[17]
~ Saith the Lord.[18]

Judgment of Entire World Is Near:

The great day of the Lord is near—near and coming quickly.
…In the fire of his jealousy the whole earth will be consumed,
for he will make a sudden end of all who live on the earth.[19]
~ Saith the Lord.[20]

After Temporal Judgment, Judah and America Restored:

The Lord your God is with you, the Mighty Warrior who
saves. He will take great delight in you; in his love he will no
longer rebuke you, but will rejoice over you with singing. I
will remove from you all who mourn over the loss of your
appointed festivals, which is a burden and reproach for you.
At that time, I will deal with all who oppressed you. I will
rescue the lame; I will gather the exiles. I will give them praise
and honor in every land where they have suffered shame. At
that time I will gather you; at that time I will bring you home
I will give you honor and praise among all the peoples of the
earth when I restore your fortunes before your very eyes.[21]
~ Saith the Lord.[22]

After World Judgment, God's People Restored:

> *The remnant of Israel* (all God's people) *will trust in the name of the Lord. They will do no wrong, they will tell no lies. A deceitful tongue will not be found in their mouths. They will eat and lie down and no one will make them afraid. The Lord, the King of Israel, is with you; never again will you fear any harm.*[23]
> ~ *Saith the Lord.* [24]

~

"Good friends, that concludes the prophecy part of my speech which the Lord gave me regarding forthcoming temporal judgment on Judah and America. But the prophecy also warns of universal judgment on the entire world at a later time. Therefore, as Josiah noted, I think it is important now for me to focus on the practical aspects of the prophecies for Judah and America."

"Of course, you've learned from Saphah and Jeremiah's speeches of the declining spiritual conditions of both nations. So, most likely, you're aware that a time of temporal reckoning is in store for Judah and the U. S. too, if she doesn't change her ways. In addition, you probably realize that national reform in these two nations will only delay the inevitable prospect of God's judgment. But, the prophecy I just delivered also contains a warning of a different world catastrophe reminiscent of Noah's flood, except it will be by fire, not by water."

Prophet Zephaniah glanced toward the American woman, picked up his lit lamp again, began walking toward her, and as he drew near, he loudly announced in a booming voice: "Watchwoman Saphap, coming world judgment is also imminent." Saphah's entire body began trembling, shaking so badly she couldn't keep a grasp of her writing pen. She dropped her pen on the scroll, where a single drop of ink made a big splat like a drop of blood.

"Saphah, God is warning your world of both a temporal judgment on your nation and a universal judgment on your world that will one day descend upon earth and involve every living creature that dwells on the land, air, and sea. It's a statement that echoes God's warning to Noah just before the flood. At that time, *the Lord saw how great the wickedness of humans had become on earth, and that every inclination of the thoughts of the human heart was only evil all the time,*[25] which is a profound statement of the total depravity that provokes God's wrath."

Zephaniah continued, "But the future destruction described in the prophecy of end time events will exceed that of the flood, because fish and other sea creatures will also feel the brunt of God's wrath. So, all creation will suffer as a result of human sin. The destruction will begin with humans who have denied their Creator and therefore involved in their sin every living thing that inhabits the earth. And, that is grim indeed!" Prophet Zephaniah sighed heavily. "Mankind's sin at that time will be so weighty that it involves not only humanity but also the total environment."

Zephaniah gazed around at the audience of men and women in the room. "In summation, I want to emphasize to the citizens of both Judah and America that temporal catastrophe is 'near and coming quickly' for both nations. And this is the last chance for the people of Judah and America to repent. Thankfully, God sent Josiah to Judah to become a reforming king and to provide a temporary respite before coming disaster. Hopefully, the Lord will also send a reformer to America so your nation can also enjoy a reprieve too. Everyone, please pray that God will send a reformer or reformers to America. Now, I'll turn the program back to King Josiah."

~

King Josiah approached the podium. "Prophet Zephaniah, thank you for sharing prophecy for both the Judah of our time and the America of Saphah's era. Watchwoman would you like to add anything?"

"Yes, I would," Saphah said. "The prophetic messages Zephaniah shared tonight are extremely important. Prophecy, which comes directly from God, is profitable to all who read or hear it. And, that is because we know that *no prophecy of Scripture came about by the prophet's own interpretation of things. For prophecy never had its origin in the human will, but prophets, though human, spoke from God as they were carried along by the Holy Spirit.*[26] In prophecy, God makes *known the end from the beginning, from ancient times, what is still to come. I say, 'My purpose will stand, … what I have said, that I will bring about; what I have planned, that I will do.'*[27] So, if God gives us a prophetic warning, we definitely need to listen and to take to heart to what the Lord says."

"Yes, I've definitely taken it to heart," King Josiah said. "And I hope everyone else here tonight has too. Now, I think it's a good time for us to take another short break. Please help yourselves to the snacks and drinks, and we'll pick up again on this important meeting shortly."

31

LADY ZEBIDAH

King Josiah said, "Prophet Zephaiah, thank you again for delivering God's Word of hope and judgement. Earlier in history, another man, Prophet Joel, gave divinely inspired revelations warning the Jews that invaders were coming. He predicted that a foreign nation would erase the northern Jewish nation of Israel from the world map. And, we know that prophecy came true in 722 B.C. when a vast army from Assyria overthrew Israel. But Joel warned Israel ahead of time to turn to God. He noted that the Lord wanted people to return to Him with all their hearts and with fasting, weeping, and mourning: *Rend your heart and not your garments. Return to the Lord your God, for he is gracious and compassionate, slow to anger and abounding in love, and he relents from sending calamity. Who knows? He may turn and relent and leave behind a blessing.*"[1]

Sadly, King Josiah noted: "Israel didn't listen."

But then, King Josiah became optimistic. "It is my prayer that Judah and America will heed Jehovah's call, because sincere repentance can bring blessings such as revival and reprieve, at least as long as a majority of people stay faithful. For Prophet Joel also foresaw another day of the Lord in the more distant future. He forewarned a future generation that on that day God *will show wonders in the heavens and on the earth, blood and fire and billows of smoke. The sun will be turned to darkness and the moon to blood before the coming of the great and dreadful day of the Lord. And everyone who calls on the name of the Lord will be saved.*"[2]

"Again, we see bible prophecy working on more than one timeline. A day of judgment is a future reality for Saphah's world. But, as both Zephaniah and Joel noted, it's a good day for those who've turned to God for salvation."

"I want you to know, Watchwoman Saphah," King Josiah said as he turned to look toward her, "that although Prophet Zephaniah warned of a final judgment on your world in the future, he also explained there's still time for your people to be sheltered from forthcoming temporal judgment too, if only they'll repent: *Seek the Lord, all you humble of the land, you who do what he commands. Seek righteousness, seek humility; perhaps you will be sheltered on the day of the Lord's anger.*[3] American Watchwoman Saphah, do you share the same opinion?"

"King Josiah, I do! I believe the prophecies of both Zephaniah and Joel! After all, it's an historical fact and an archeological certainty that Joel's prophecy happened to Israel. For generations God had spared Israel from doom, over and over giving them one more chance to repent. But then the nation reached a point of no return and God's judgment fell on them. Likewise, as Zephaniah noted, God is giving the people of America one last chance to repent—to turn to Him in faith, to submit to Him in repentance, and to reciprocate His love with joy and faithfulness. For He is Christ the Lord, the Sacrificial Lamb who takes away the sins of the world, once and for all."

"Yes, indeed!" Josiah exclaimed. "Watchwoman Saphah, I'm happy to know you agree that repentance and reform are necessary in America and Judah in the perilous times in which we live. But what about the rest of you? Is there anyone here tonight who disagrees that reform efforts are needed in Judah? If so, please raise your hand, and you'll be dismissed without reprisal. Anyone?" King Josiah's eyes searched the room for a dissenter. "Anyone?" But then, Judah's young leader sighed in relief and nodded his chin up and down at his recognition of total agreement in the room. "Thank you all! I'm certainly pleased that everyone here is in accord!"

A messenger walked forward from the tent's entrance toward King Josiah and whispered something in his ear. In response, the king beamed in joy and announced: "Everyone, please stand for our next guest." As a trumpet sounded, a lovely woman, tall and slender, dressed in a royal robe with a jeweled crown upon her head and a scepter in her hand, approached the king. "Now, it is with great pleasure that I present to you a very special person. Everyone, please welcome Zebidah, queen of my heart and Judah's first lady!"

The audience broke out in loud applause and someone in the crowd exclaimed in approval: "Long live Lady Zebidah!"

As the crowd continued in applause, the royal lady responded by repeating over and over, "Thank you, everyone! Thank you! Thank you!" She turned toward different areas of the room and nodded her head in acknowledgment.

"Thanks, everyone, for your support of my beautiful wife." King Josiah put his arm around his Queen Consort, drew her near to him, gently kissed her on the cheek, and then motioned for the crowd to take their seats. "I'm delighted to inform you that Lady Zebidah, who is a follower of Yahweh and in agreement on the need for reform in Judah, has volunteered to join our movement as a leader and helper of the women's group. As some of you may know, I'm greatly in favor of women joining with men in the work of God whenever they can and as appropriate."

Upon hearing the good news, Saphah and the other women sitting in the audience were overjoyed. "That's just wonderful!" Tamara exclaimed, and the other ladies all smiled and shook their heads in agreement.

Rebecca noticed Zebidah was looking toward the little group. "Thank you, Lady Zebidah!"

Zebidah responded by giving Rebecca a nod. But after King Josiah whispered something in her ear, her eyebrows raised and she turned back toward the young lady. "King Josiah tells me you're Ebed's sister. Becca, I'm so pleased I'll be working with you and the other ladies."

Rebecca smiled widely and nodded her head in agreement. "Lady Zebidah, me too!"

King Josiah said, "I want everyone to know that Lady Zebidah has just arrived at the meeting because she had another commitment at the palace to finish before she could join us. But now that my lovely Queen is here, she would like to briefly speak to the women's group tonight."

Message of Welcome to the Ladies

Thank you, King Josiah. I'm pleased to be here to personally let all of you know I'm greatly in favor of steering our nation toward a closer relationship with Yahweh and away from idolatry. Hopefully, I can be of assistance to the brave women in the audience who've offered to help in this effort. Ladies, thank you for being here tonight. Please stand for us."

The small group of females all stood to a round of applause from the men gathered in the tent.

We're greatly indebted to all the women in history who've allied with men in support of God's work. So, thank you Watchwoman Saphah, Rebecca, Tamara, and Eve, along with Hannah who is not here tonight but will also be helping. We're greatly pleased with your offers of help. I also want to thank the members of my palace staff who've worked so hard to help us get supplies ready and transported here to the king's travel camp. Staff members, please arise."

A big group of people arose and Eve stood as well to another round of cheering and applause.

I want you to know that since Eve came to work at the palace, she's been very helpful to me. She and I've been busy forming plans on how we can help the movement. For example, we want to work together with the other ladies on appropriate costumes to hide the identity of those who spy out the land. Therefore, we gathered a large supply of garments from the palace wardrobe for both men and women. In addition, we purchased a few items of foreign clothing to help disguise the spies as worshipers of foreign gods.

Eve and I also raided the cosmetic supplies left by a former queen. As some of you may know years ago a foreign woman named Athaliah, the daughter of King Ahab of Israel and his wicked wife Jezebel, appointed herself leader of Judah and then ruled for around six years. She was eventually executed, but a large quantity of her cosmetics and foreign jewelry are still present at the palace. In addition, we found a perfume dispensary in the same location which yielded a huge supply of foreign fragrances for women and colognes for men.

We also brought shawls and other types of clothing which can be draped to help hide the identity of spies. And, to disguise some of the spies as elderly people, we have items like canes and walking sticks, wigs, and similar items. We even have a baby doll collection, from which women spies may choose a 'baby' to carry on certain missions. Another way I hope to help is to oversee the travel camp kitchen when Eve and Jonathan are spying. Eve, thank you again for your help.

"Lady Zebidah, you're welcome," Eve said. "Actually, I'm thankful to both you and King Josiah. I'm thankful to the king for giving me the opportunity to work in the palace kitchen, and I'm thankful to you for allowing me to help with the disguises." Eve bowed toward both.

The First Lady then turned toward Saphah.

> Watchwoman Saphah, I'm glad you're joining us to learn
> about our reform efforts. I look forward to assisting you any
> way I can to help make this a good learning experience for
> you.

"Thank you, Lady Zebidah," Saphah said. "I'm very grateful you'll be
leading the women in our endeavors as a spy team. I want you and
everyone here to know that I'm appreciative of your hospitality and
gracious acceptance of me into your efforts at reforming Judah. I'm
excited and hopeful that revival and reform will occur in both your
nation and mine. Of course, our countries differ culturally, but we
both worship the same God, and we can depend on him to guide us
in both Judah and America."

> I'm grateful as well to have this opportunity to work with you
> and the other women. And, I'm looking forward to seeing the
> difference we females can make in the spiritual life of our
> nations.

Queen Zebidah took her seat to a loud round of applause. "Thank
you very much, Zebidah," King Josiah said. "Now we're ready for
another important segment of our meeting. Representative Levi of
the Rechabite Clan, please come forward to give us your thoughts
about what we should do to help bring about reform in Judah."

"Thank you, King Josiah," Levi said. "I really enjoyed the speeches of
Saphah, Jeremiah, Prophet Zephaniah, and Lady Zebidah. I found
the messages to be helpful. Now I'll give a talk on recommendations
for bringing reform and correction in Judah and America."

"Of course, reform methods in America will differ greatly from
those in Judah because our societies differ so much. Reforms will
need to be according to the mores—the binding customs and

proprieties of each land. In other words, there must be conformity to what is acceptable in conduct or speech in the two different times and places, but according to God's moral standards. Following is my speech:

Comply with God's Instructions

Jeremiah mentioned in his speech that the priests of Anathoth told him about suspected places of false worship throughout Judah and Israel. These priests also said God has provided detailed information in Deuteronomy of actions to be taken when worship of false gods is suspected in Old Testament times. And since our ancestor, Jehonadab, was present to witness most of King Jehu's reform efforts back in that day, the members of our clan are quite aware of what strategies need to occur.

Therefore, we highly recommend that the reform team, led by King Josiah and Lady Zebidah, should faithfully follow all instructions in scripture that God has provided for Old Testament leaders. I'm telling you this for a reason. Although King Jehu started out fairly well in his reform efforts, he failed to faithfully carry out what God had said to do, as I will now attempt to explain in detail.

When Jehu was a commander in the Israelite army, a prophet sent by Elisha anointed him to become the king of Israel and to eliminate the house of Ahab known for its idolatry and wickedness. So, Jehu proceeded to launch a coup against Joram, the king of Israel, and Ahaziah, the king of Judah, who was allied with the house of Ahab.[4] Then Jehu eliminated the House of Ahab's family, and thus fulfilled the prophecy against Ahab's wicked reign.[5]

At that time, our ancestor Jehonadab became a witness of Jehu's reform activities: *After he [Jehu] left there, he came upon Jehonadab, son of Rekab, who was on his way to meet him. Jehu greeted him and said, 'Are you in accord with me, as I am with you?'*[6] [Jehonadab answered in the affirmative.] *Jehu said, 'Come with me and see my zeal for the Lord.' Then he had him ride along in his chariot. When Jehu came to Samaria, he killed all who were left there of Ahab's family; he destroyed them, according to the word of the Lord spoken to Elijah.*[7]

Jehu's mission was ordained by God to purge Israel of the corrupting influence of Ahab and his wife Jezebel and their promotion of idolatry and especially the worship of Baal. Jehu's destruction of the temple of Baal in Samaria and purge of its priests marked a notable effort to rid Israel of foreign influences of Idolatry.[8]

However, Jehu's religious zeal was dramatically incomplete, as he continued to allow *the worship of the golden calves at Bethel and Dan as had been established by Jeroboam I.*[9] Therefore, despite Jehu's early efforts to rid Israel of the worship of Baal, his failure to fully restore Israel's worship of God led to the continuing spiritual decline of the northern kingdom. Additionally, *he was not careful to keep the law of the Lord, the God of Israel, with all his heart.*[10]

Some think Jehu's actions occurred because Jehu sought to keep his power as king by perpetuating calf worship, because he thought political independence from Judah required religious separation. This could be an expression of his selfish desire to keep his position as king of Israel. Also, it is believed that Jehu spilled blood beyond the proper execution of Jehovah's judgment, thereby displaying his callousness and selfishness in gaining and keeping his position as king of Israel. Thus, the kingdom of Israel was eventually destroyed.

I think we can conclude from what I just recounted, that reform efforts in a nation must, of necessity, comply with God's true intents and purposes. Therefore, I recommend a two-step procedure in your efforts to comply with everything God has instructed you to do in His Word.

First, you'll need to thoroughly spy out various locations to verify that false worship of foreign deities exists in those places. If so, then you'll be justified to fully carry out all God has commanded as set forth in Deuteronomy. Of course, there may be instances when further actions need to be taken at the time of spying. But other times it may be best to return to base camp to plan actions and then proceed later with complete destruction of the places of false worship.

All this activity to destroy places of idolatry will take a lot of time, perhaps years, because of allowances for the following: time to travel back and forth, time to construct and maintain demolition equipment, and time to thoroughly complete all requirements. But all of this must be done to fully carry out what God expects you to do. King Josiah, you must not waver! Thank you for allowing me to speak.

"Thank you, Representative Levi!" King Josiah said. "I believe everything you've said to be true, and I want you and the others here tonight to know I'll comply with God's instructions to the best of my ability. Now, everyone, we've had a long day with the birthday and wedding celebrations, along with this reform meeting, so it's time to finish up and start fresh tomorrow."

"Our friend Jeremiah," King Josiah continued, "has noted some nearby locations we should spy out for idolatry first. But knowing the meeting would run late and everyone would be tired, Lady Zebidah and I decided we should wait until tomorrow morning to discuss the time, the place, and the main preparations for our first mission."

"Remember, you're not allowed to share what's said at any meeting, including the one tonight, not even with a spouse or your dearest friend. Our plans are secret! We can't compromise the safety of the spies or the guards or the success of our missions. Deviations from the rule of secrecy, if discovered, will be handled with imprisonment or worse, according to the breach. And now, Lady Zebidah, would you please close our meeting with prayer?"

"Thank you. Yes, I will. My closing prayer will be a psalm read in prayer for you, King Josiah, and by extension for those who listen to your voice of clarity in a degenerate land."

> *Hear my cry, O God; listen to my prayer. From the ends of the earth*
> *I call to you, I call as my heart grows faint; lead me to a rock that is*
> *higher than I.*
>
> *For you God, have heard my vows,*
> *you have given me the heritage of those who fear your name.*
>
> *Increase the days of the king's life,*
> *his years for many generations.*
>
> *May he be enthroned in the Lord's presence forever,*
> *appoint your love and faithfulness to protect him.*
>
> *Then I will ever sing in praise of your name*
> *and fulfill my vows day after day.*
>
> *But the king will rejoice in God;*
> *all who swear by God will glory in him.*[11]
>
> Amen.

"Thank you, Queen Zebidah, for that special prayer for myself and those who follow me. For we greatly need God's help, guidance, and protection for everything we plan to do. Reform group, I want all of you to always remember that we have Yahweh on our side. Please look to the Lord and earnestly pray that he will give us wisdom and strength that we might go forward successfully in this work of reformation."

"Everyone, thank you for being here tonight." King Josiah began his closing remarks. "It's time to dismiss, but I look forward to seeing you again first thing tomorrow morning. The Rechabite women will be graciously serving a breakfast buffet consisting of various leftovers from our celebrations yesterday, along with other fresh items. You may all be dismissed."

SPYING OUT THE LAND

Miriam stood at the opening to the tent area where Rebecca and her sisters all slept. "Ladies, you need to wake up now. I'm going over to King Josiah's tent camp to help with breakfast preparation and I must leave shortly.

"Becca, may I sleep with you now?" Little sister Lilly kissed her big sister's cheek. The toddler gave her sis a tender hug and crawled under the covers with her.

"Lilly, just for a minute, honey."

"Rise and shine, girls." Levi stuck his head through the tent flap opening. When he saw no immediate response from the ladies, he sternly barked, "Get up, RIGHT NOW! This is an important day and we need to get right over to King Josiah's tent camp!"

Rebecca and Saphah wasted no time getting up. Rececca sat up on her mat, momentarily stretched her arms and legs, and then quickly jumped up. Saphah grunted a little as she navigated getting up from her mat on the ground, but she got up as quickly as she could. "Oh, my body's so stiff this morning!"

But Tamara just turned over and went back to sleep. "Tamara wake up." Rebecca warned her recalcitrant friend who was still lounging on her mat. "Start getting up right now or I'll have to tell father."

"Alright, alright," Tamara moaned as she finally got up despite her grumbling. Consequently, all three ladies were soon up from their mats and off to the wash tent to finish getting ready.

When they came out of the tent all tidied up for the day, Levi was standing outside waiting to join the three for the trek to the travel camp. "Good job, girls. We mustn't be late to arrive for any of these meetings."

"You're right," Saphah agreed. "The welfare of your nation and mine is in the balance, and we ignore it to the peril of our people."

"I'm sorry, Levi and Saphah," Tamara apologized. "I'll do better from now on."

"Thank you, Tamara," Levi said. "No harm done this time. But just remember, it's important to do just as you're told in important situations such as the upcoming reforms for our nation."

"Alright, I'll remember."

~

The group soon reached their destination and walked into the tent which was filled with the aroma of delicious breakfast foods. A line of people had already formed beside tables covered with a variety of meats, along with freshly boiled eggs, flat cakes, cereals, and fruits.

King Josiah, Lady Zebidah, and their tablemates already had plates of food and were headed to seats. When Josiah reached the table, he remained standing while others sat down. "May I have your attention please?" Everyone became quiet and the king began speaking. "Good morning. Thank you for being here on our first day of spying out the land. Jeremiah of Anathoth, I'm very pleased you're accompanying us on our first venture at spying as well. I'm also pleased to hear you've a special announcement regarding God's call on your life. Therefore, Jeremiah, at this time would you please say a word of thanks?"

"King Josiah, I'd be honored." Jeremiah stood and began his prayer:

"Yahweh, we thank you for this bountiful provision of food the Rechabite women have prepared and set before us. We also thank you for our present ruler, King Josiah, who inherited the rule of a nation led astray, yet he's chosen a different course. Please watch over and protect the king and his group today in their first mission. Also, I thank you for placing a call on my life, because *the word of the Lord came to me, saying, 'Before I formed you in the womb I knew you; before you were born I set you apart; I appointed you as a prophet to the nations.'*[1] Please show me your will for my life and grant me perseverance for my call. We thank you for all your blessings and praise you forever. Amen."

"Jeremiah, thank you for your prayer. We're so pleased God has called you to be a prophet and that you'll be traveling with us today." Josiah smiled and nodded his head at Jeremiah. "And, Rechabite ladies, thank you again for this wonderful breakfast. And now, everyone, please remember the two most important things Zephaniah said last night. First, He prophesied forthcoming judgement on Judah and America which cannot be avoided long-term. second, he announced the opportunity God has provided short-term for the personal repentance of the wayward in Judah and America. Therefore, as king of Judah, I'm determined to do all in my power, as derived from God, to bring about reform for the benefit of my citizens."

"However," Josiah admitted, "I realize the immense task set before me. When I hear stories of the wickedness of my people, I almost feel discouraged before I begin. The evil nature of our society has been increasing throughout the kingdom for years. My grandfather Manasseh worshipped the idols of heathen nations and led his people to do the same. And, my own father, Amon, did likewise. Scripture says that *Manasseh led them astray, so that they did more evil than the nations the Lord had destroyed before the Israelites.*[2] And, Amon *did evil in the eyes of the Lord, as his father Manasseh had done.*[3] Conversely, I want to be a good and faithful king, as was our ancestor, King David."

"Since the authority over Judah has now fallen into my hands," Josiah emphasized, "I'm ready to begin right away the destruction of idolatry throughout the whole kingdom. To do this effectively will be a difficult task I'm sure. But I've prayed to God for direction and support, and with Him at my side, I know I can endure any labor and overcome any adversity. Scripture informs me that it is not only in my power and authority to break up sinful practices, but also my solemn duty to comply with what God has commanded his rulers to do as directed by His Word."

"You do need to know," King Josiah noted, "that some think a part of scripture has been misplaced or lost. If so, hopefully it will soon be found. But in the meantime, the Rechabites told me they possess certain parts of scripture written out in abstract form and other parts orally summarized. This happened because their ancestor Jehonadab wanted the people to retain knowledge of God's law even though they didn't possess the actual written Word of God. These writings and oral summations can serve to direct me to know the course I should follow in fighting idolatry. Likewise, Jeremiah says that certain priests of Anathoth in the past have written out portions of scripture from the original copy that will be helpful to let me know God's will regarding Old Testament reform."

King Josiah added, "Watchwoman Saphah has a printed copy of the entire scripture. However, it's written in English, a language we cannot read, but it'll serve to let her know that the actions we take are verified by her copy of God's Word. I'm told that her bible exists because over time God, by his providence, directed events so all of scripture would be preserved, both for the benefit of the people of our era and of all succeeding generations. Original copies of God's Word exist in the modern world from the times when the different parts were written, but compiled into one book and translated into world languages. Now millions of copies exist in Saphah's time and place. Saphah, please raise your bible to show attendees you possess a copy and then pass it around so everyone can admire it?"

"Here is my Holy Bible printed in English." As Saphah held up her copy of the Word of God, she heard exclamations of wonderment from those in the room.

"Oh, look!" A short young man was standing on his tiptoes to see Saphah's book. "She's actually holding up a copy of God's Word!"

"Praise God! Praise God!" An elderly Rechabite man using a cane began walking toward her. "Oh, Watchwoman Saphah, could I please examine your scripture?"

"Of course." Saphah handed her bible to the gray-haired man. He laid down his cane, solemnly took the book into his trembling hands, and began crying like a child.

"Oh, thank you, Yahweh!" the old man sobbed. "Thank you for letting me touch this book!" He slowly ran his hand over the smooth, leather cover, carefully opened the book and kissed the pages, and then turned to Saphah. "My dear, would you please read to me from your bible?"

"Yes, I'd be honored to read to you Psalm 23 written by King David, and translate it into Hebrew as I read:

> *The Lord is my shepherd, I lack nothing. He makes me lie down in green pastures, he leads me beside quiet waters, he refreshes my soul. He guides me along the right paths for his name's sake. Even though I walk through the darkest valley, I will fear no evil, for you are with me, your rod and your staff they comfort me. You prepare a table before me in the presence of my enemies. You anoint my head with oil; my cup overflows. Surely your goodness and love will follow me all the days of my life, and I will dwell in the house of the Lord forever.*[4]

I think the 23rd Psalm is absolutely beautiful!"

"Yes, it is. Thank you so much, Watchwoman Saphah," the old man said gratefully. "I'm going to hand this book to the next person in line so everyone here can see this Holy Bible." He carefully handed the scripture over to another man. Turning to Saphah again, he asked, "The people in your land are fortunate to have a large number of bibles, but how did it come about that you have so many copies?"

"We possess many copies because in a certain era in history the printing press was invented," Saphah explained. "In Judah, your time and place, scripture must be copied by hand, which is tedious, but in America, my time and place, scripture is mass produced using machines, which is efficient. Thus, most of the people of my day have one copy or more of scripture. It's sad though, that many folks don't read the Holy Bible, although it is the Word of God and abundantly available. In fact, the Lord's preservation of the entire bible is one proof it is the Word of God. So, we owe a debt of gratitude to our loving God for giving us a book more valuable than any other which shows us the way to life everlasting."

"Yes, it's extremely sad that many precious souls in America don't read God's Word when you possess so many bibles and most people there evidently know how to read." The old man found it difficult to comprehend the situation. "We Rechabites don't possess a copy of scripture and most of us haven't learned to read. Thankfully Ebed, Rebecca, and Tamara know how to read now that they've attended Jerusalem School. Maybe someday Ebed can copy a part of scripture and read it to me."

"Elderly man, what's your name?" Saphah asked.

"Kind lady, my name is Joshua."

"Well, Joshua, I'm sure Ebed would love to read to you from scripture. When I get a chance, I'll ask him about it."

"Oh, thank you so much! You've made an old man very happy with your promise."

King Josiah spoke up. "My Rechabite friend Joshua, I want you to know that I'll personally set up an opportunity for Ebed to use his talents as a scribe to copy portions of scripture from the Psalms and the Proverbs for your clan. As faithful followers of Yahweh, you and your clan greatly deserve to have these copies."

Joshua bowed low and tears came into his eyes again as he spoke. "King Josiah, I can't thank you enough for allowing Ebed to write out parts of the Psalms and the Proverbs just for our clan. Thank you again."

"You're welcome, Joshua," King Josiah said. "And now everyone, thank you for joining me here today to be a part of our quest for reform in Judah. It is my belief we should complete our preparations and get started immediately. But first, I want to personally pray for our reform group efforts: Yahweh, we come to you in thankfulness and praise for who you are and for your love for mankind. Lord, we pray you'll supply us with direction and guidance in our efforts at reform, help us to possess moral courage and determination to complete our tasks, assist us to endure any adversity encountered, and help us to have long-term commitment and success. Amen."

"Alright, I think we possess what we need—the personnel, the resources, and the plans to begin this work. Our spy team will be composed of four couples: Eve and Jonathan; Tamara and Solomon; Rebecca and Caleb; Saphah and Ebed. Hannah will not participate at this time, but will be a helper instead. Each spy team will have two guards disguised as an elderly couple for extra protection. Also, my guards and I'll be riding in chariots in the background, hidden from sight as the spies carry out the mission. However, we'll be observing what happens, and if conflict erupts, we'll quickly come to your aid."

King Josiah continued, "Now, we're going to the disguise tent where Lady Zebidah and her personal assistants will dress us in gaudy foreign clothes, apply makeup to our faces to hide our identity, and perfume us until we all smell like pagan idolaters. Ladies, I also want you each to please choose a baby doll wrapped in a blanket to carry."

"Next, we'll go to the supply tent so you can pick up weapons such as light spears, javelins, and swords disguised as walking sticks or canes. Also, everyone will carry an appropriate knife in a sheath hidden under their clothing. Later we'll meet at a designated spot with Ebed and Hannah, who'll both be leading donkeys from the palace stables for the ladies to ride. Bows and arrows will be hidden in leather cases built into the sides of saddles. Our spy team can grab the bows and arrows from them if needed."

Lady Zebidah and her helpers worked quickly to get everyone in disguise. and then the entire group walked over to get their weapons. After that, King Josiah spoke to them again. "Remember, you must try to stay incognito as you spy. Try not to allow anyone to see your full face. Also, remember that if circumstances demand you to take action, you must proceed despite the possibility of danger to yourself or to others in our group. Evil idolatry must be stopped!"

"Well, people, I don't know about you, but I'm devoted to pleasing God and reinstituting the observance of faithfulness to Him. I want our reform efforts to be successful and to be a great example for our guest Saphah in her hopes for revival in her own land. Everyone, are you with me?"

"Yes!" Someone arose and clapped. Then others arose until the whole assemblage was on their feet clapping.

"Praise, Yahweh!" King Josiah shouted. "let's get this reformation started. We're headed to the Hinnom Valley, since Prophet Jeremiah has received word that idolators are worshipping Molek there."

Tamara echoed, "Yes! C'mon, ladies, let's get this reformation going!" She resembled a beautiful, but worldly, foreign woman with her eyes heavily lined in kohl, her ears ornamented with earrings, her dark hair plaited in elaborate braids, and her arms circled with bracelets.

"Let's go!" Rebecca was pacing in a gorgeous, embroidered garment, her sun-bleached hair completely covered with a scarf and topped with a jeweled head band. Each of her ankles sported a golden chain with tiny bells attached which tinkled as she paced.

"Let's do it, ladies!" Eve, dressed to the hilt in an elaborate robe with layers decorated with fringes, pulled up her skirt a bit to keep from walking on it and tucked it into her sash. Her hair was covered by a heavily embroidered scarf, and a head band held it in place.

Saphah glanced down at her dark hands. *Wow, they've disguised me as a black person. What does my face look like all blackened with kohl?* She rearranged the shawl on her head and repositioned her turban over it. Then she straightened the numerous golden chains and beaded necklaces dangling down from her neck onto her lovely blue garment. *Anyway, I really don't think anyone will recognize me.*

"C'mon, Saphah," Eve grabbed her hand and the two walked briskly toward the trail. Rebecca and Tamara followed.

"Alright men, are you going to let these ladies get ahead of you?" Josiah shouted. "Get going!" The men hustled to catch up with the women.

Jonathan caught up with Eve. "Honey, I've never seen you as excited about anything as you've been about this spy mission. Why?"

Eve turned to look at her husband. "Jonathan, I think God has called me to be a member of this group."

"But, Eve, do you really believe Yahweh would call a women to assist in the work of spying for Judah?"

"Yes, I do. I know for a fact that God has called women in the past to help with spy efforts. Look at Rahab. She demonstrated her faith in God and was *considered righteous for what she did when she gave lodging to the spies and sent them off in a different direction.*[5] And look at Prophetess Huldah. Rahab is one of her ancestors and Huldah is a woman of great vision. She receives revelations from God just as Zephaniah does. In this case, God is using both a male and a female as recipients of His Word. So, if God so chooses, why wouldn't he use someone like me, Rebecca, Tamara, Hannah, Saphah, or even Lady Zebidah, the same way He uses the men?"

"Eve, I think you may be right. But I'm just worried you might get hurt out here spying like a man!"

"Jonathan, don't you trust Yahweh to take care of me?" Eve was perplexed at her husband's lack of faith.

"But you're so young!"

"Consider David who was young when he killed the Philistine, Goliath." Eve retorted. "King Saul considered David too young when he wanted to go up against the giant man and said:

> *'You are not able to go up against this philistine and fight him; you are only a young man.'*[6] But Saul finally relented after David persisted. So, David approached Goliath with *five smooth stones …in the pouch of his shepherd's bag, and with his sling in his hand.*[7]
>
> *Goliath looked David over and saw that he was little more than a boy …And the Philistine cursed David by his gods* [and said]: '*Come here,* [and] *I'll give your flesh to the birds and the wild animals.*'[8]

But David said to the Philistine, 'You come against me with sword and spear and javelin, but I come against you in the name of the Lord Almighty, the God of the armies of Israel, whom you have defied. This day the Lord will deliver you into my hands, and I'll strike you down and cut off your head.'[9] David, reaching into his bag and taking out a stone, slung it and struck the Philistine on the forehead. The stone sank into his forehead, and he fell face-down on the ground.[10] Thus, all who gathered there knew that it is not by sword or spear that the Lord saves; for the battle is the Lord's.[11]

Rebecca, what do you think about women spying?" Eve turned to her friend for support.

"Well, I think that God can use anyone he chooses, whether male or female, young or old." said Rebecca. And Tamara shook her head in agreement. "Ladies, we can do this because God is the one in control and he possesses the power to give all of us success in the work he calls us to do, if only we'll trust and follow Him."

"Amen," Saphah said. "Praise be to God for great things he has done in the past and great things he'll do for Judah in your time and for America in mine if only we've faith in Him. Ladies, I know an old hymn about the faith of our fathers, but I think we should sing about the faith of our mothers too. What do you think?"

"I definitely agree," Tamara said. "Let's sing the hymn about both, beginning with a verse about the faith of our fathers and then of our mothers."

"Alright, I'm going to sing the verses once so everyone can hear the words." Saphah sang the words for the first time. "Now, everyone, please join in and we'll sing again:

Faith of our fathers! Living still, in spite of dungeon, fire, and sword: O how our hearts beat high with joy when-e'er we hear that glorious word! Faith of our fathers! Holy Faith! We will be true to thee till death!

Faith of our mothers! We will love both friend and foe in all our strife, and preach Thee too, as love knows how, by kindly words and virtuous life; Faith of our mothers! Holy Faith! We will be true to thee till death![12]

"Come on men, join in with us and sing loudly for both our fathers and our mothers."

Then the male spies, the guards, and even King Josiah and Jeremiah all joined in to belt out the hymn about males and females of faith as they marched along on their journey.

Finally, King Josiah's chariot pulled ahead and then stopped. "All right spies," King Josiah announced. "No more singing. We may see other travelers now so we need to be quiet. We're going next to meet up with Ebed and Hannah who'll be leading donkeys for the women to ride the rest of the way. Then Ebed will be joining us, but Hannah will be riding her donkey back to camp to assist Lady Zebidah today. Just over that ridge is the Hinnom Valley and Jeremiah has told me that historically the idolatry practiced in a certain place there is far beyond all the evil you could ever imagine."

"The Valley of Hinnom," said King Josiah, "is where kings of Judah burned their sons and daughters as sacrifices to local gods. King Ahaz, my great, great grandfather introduced Molek worship and *burned sacrifices in the Valley of Ben Hinnom and sacrificed his children in the fire, engaging in the detestable practices of the nations the Lord had driven out before the Israelites.*"[13]

Josiah added, "But my grandfather King Manasseh not only *sacrificed his children in the fire in the Valley of Ben Hinnom,* [but also] *practiced divination and witchcraft, sought omens, and consulted mediums and spiritists.*

He did much evil in the eyes of the Lord, arousing his anger.[14] And, my father, Amon, *did evil in the eyes of the Lord, as his father Manasseh had done. Amon worshiped and offered sacrifices to all the idols Manasseh had made.*"[15]

"Therefore," Josiah warned, "if the deeds are still occurring here, this valley is a very wicked place. It's a location for sorcery, necromancy, obsession with the dead and with trying to learn about the future from the souls of the departed. And, rumor is that a high place called Topheth, an evil place of false worship, still exists somewhere near the Potsherd dump, a location where cracked pottery is thrown away. Isn't that right, Jeremiah?"

"Yes, and the previous inhabitants of Canaan, who were here when the Israelites returned from slavery in Egypt, had been sacrificing their children to the god Molek for centuries, a detestable way of treating human beings in the eyes of our Creator who made heaven and earth and everything in it. Hence, scripture forbids you *to give any of your children to be sacrificed to Molek, for you must not profane the name of your God.*[16] If anyone blatantly violates God's revealed will, as in child sacrifice, they desecrate his name because they fail to honor his holiness."

"Previous inhabitants were also guilty of deviant sexual sins as listed in the scripture which forbade child sacrifice. The Israelites were told *not to do as they do in Egypt, where you used to live, and you must not do as they do in the land of Canaan, where I am bringing you. Do not follow their practices.*"[17]

Josiah listed off some of the deviant sins: "*No one is to approach any close relative to have sexual relations.*[18] *Do not have sexual relations with a man as one does with a woman, that is detestable;*[19] *Do not have sexual relations with an animal and defile yourself with it.*[20] *Do not defile yourself in any of these ways, because this is how the nations that I am going to drive out before you became defiled. Even the land was defiled; so I punished it for its sin, and the land vomited out its inhabitants. But you must keep my decrees and laws.*"[21]

"Hence, scripture informs us God destroyed the nations that had previously lived in Israel and Judah because of their sexual sins and their evil worship of false gods which included child sacrifice. It is no wonder these people needed to be destroyed. It is difficult to imagine any culture on earth becoming so depraved. However, as I've already told you, Ahaz, Manasseh, and Amon, my own flesh and blood, were guilty of sacrificing their children. It's a wonder I'm still alive and that my father, Amon, didn't sacrifice me to Molek. And yet, Saphah tells us her own world is depraved now too. Many babies are murdered there by abortion and sexual deviations exist there as Deuteronomy mentions. Saphah, is that true?"

"It's true. And scripture gives us the same answer in Ecclesiastes when it says: *The thing that hath been, it is that which will be; and that which is done is that which shall be done; and there is no new thing under the sun.*[22] Those are the words of King Solomon, who made the point that there really is nothing new under the sun. As noted, many people in Judah in your time have offered up their children on the altars of idols. But 'what country could kill 63 million babies over the last fifty years? What country would be so deviant in its sexuality, that it encourages parents to take kids to drag shows or somehow pretend they can change their gender. What country's artists would proudly worship Satan on live tv for the world to see?'[23] Here is the answer to all three questions: It's America."

"Again," Saphah explained, "it's nothing new. The gods in your world are like the gods in mine, they just have different names. Instead of an altar to Molek, we have an altar to abortion. Instead of an altar to fertility goddess Asherah, we have an altar to LGBTQ and any aberrant sexual act is encouraged there. For years now, America has worshipped gods such as these, until now, as Zephaniah warned, America faces judgment if we don't abandon our wicked ways."

"Yes," Josiah said. "it's sad to think how far Judah and America have fallen. Apart from a small remnant of people, Judah has become as pagan as the nations around it, and from what you've said, apart from a segment, much of America has become pagan too. It looks like Judah and America are in for a winnowing."

"Sadly, it does!"

33

RUIN UPON THINE HABITATION

"King Josiah, I agree with you that it looks like Judah and America are in for a winnowing. Earlier, the Lord let me know that the next thing to happen in America after the Covid Pandemic will be that God will winnow my country. But recently one morning, the Lord seemed to reaffirm that fact with a different statement."

"What was God's statement?"

"Here is what the lord said."

"I will bring down ruin upon thine habitation."

Saphah turned toward Prophet Jeremiah. "Sir, If I may ask, what do you think that means?"

Prophet Jeremiah looked sadly at Saphah and said in a sympathetic tone: "My American friend, I think the meaning is the same for both Judah and the United States. The Lord said of Judah: *Thine habitation is in the midst of deceit; through deceit they refuse to know me, saith the Lord.*[1] But from what you've told us so far, Saphah, I think your country is in the same situation."

"I think you're right." Saphah shook her head in agreement. "So, what do you think God is going to do?"

The prophet looked at Saphah thoughtfully. "My dear, this is what the Lord Almighty says: '*See, I will refine and test them, for what else can I do because of the sin of my people?*'[2] In other words, the Lord will refine Judah and America by invasions from their foreign adversaries. He will winnow both nations because of their sins."

"But, what exactly do you think God will do to refine and test them?"

"The Lord will test Judah and America *in the furnace of affliction,*[3] as Isaiah referred to it in his writings. Judgment will happen because the ungodly in Judah and America live in deception and in their deceit they refuse to acknowledge God. So, the main reason for the refining is the falseness of such people."

"Yes, I think I understand what you mean. The corruption of woke people in America has affected all segment of society, but especially some out of the elite class, the big-city educators, and the federal and state leaders. Many of them have completely inverted the truth, causing others to believe the lie that God is not against wickedness. Because of this lie they call evil good, and good evil. And, the lie has allowed most of society to think that anything goes and evil is alright. In fact, some of these people seem incapable of anything else but deceit."

"Sad to say, the picture you've painted of America now seems to be the opposite of a society that is built on God's morality," Jeremiah commented.

"True. The Lord's purpose as set forth in scripture is for people to be sustained by integrity and love for God and for one another. Instead, some of the citizens of my land have formed a corrupt society where God's purposes have been frustrated. And, where God's purposes are thwarted and His plans for mankind are foiled, there is no choice but for Him to call a formal end to the situation. The only thing that can cause postponement is revival and reform. Evil must be stopped, so if the people can't or won't stop it, God will!"

"Jeremiah added, "That's why the Lord said: '*I will make Jerusalem a heap of ruins, a haunt of Jackals; and I will lay waste the towns of Judah so no one can live there. Who is wise enough to understand this? Who has been instructed by the Lord and can explain it? Why has the land been ruined and laid waste like a desert that no one can cross?' The Lord said, 'It is because they have forsaken my law, which I set before them: they have not obeyed me or followed my law. Instead, they have followed the stubbornness of their hearts; they have followed the Baals, as their ancestors taught them.'"*[4]

"But I'm wondering if the refining process will bring results? Some of our elite, educators, and leaders have completely inverted the truth. So, will the people be able to recognize the problem and to turn back to God?"

"Saphah, I don't know. Most certainly there will be a remnant, but who knows how large or small it will be. Did the Lord say anything else to you at that time?"

"Well, yes," Saphah said, "Here is what the Lord proclaimed."

"Look to the east, look to the west, your nation will be cut off. There will be pillaging and destruction, and the land will be laid bare. Upon these ruins I will rebuilt my church. And, the glory of the Lord will reign there. I will rebuilt my church, and no one will stop me. You have my solemn word."

"Saphah, I think the Lord is letting you know that your land will lay in ruins, but God is also promising he will rebuild the church in your nation upon the ruins. And, that's something for which to be grateful! In his writings Prophet Joel noted that *the day of the Lord is at hand, and as a destruction from the almighty, it will come.*[5] But the Prophet also mentioned the possibility of revival."

"Oh, I'm so thankful!" Saphah agreed. "The commentary in my bible notes that 'specific historic events are associated with the day of the Lord, including Israel's fall to Assyria and Babylon's subsequent conquest of Judah,'[6] which are both temporal judgments. So, does that mean the coming attack on the United States by foreign enemies is temporal judgment such as befell Israel and will befall Judah in your era? Likewise, doesn't this mean that God can still judge nations in New Testament times as he did in Old Testament history?"

"Indeed," Jeremiah answered. "In the Psalms we read that the *Lord has established his throne in the heavens, and his sovereignty rules over all.*[7] Therefore, as sovereign God, he judges the world in righteousness according to his will and purposes in all times and places. He rules over the kingdom of light."

"But Satan rules over the kingdom of darkness." Saphah observed. "He is a fallen angel who has created a kingdom of darkness, so he desires world control, and to a certain degree, he has attained it in my land. Scripture informs us that Satan *is the god of this world* [and] *hath blinded the minds of them which believe not, lest the light of the glorious gospel of Christ, who is the image of God, should shine unto them.*"[8]

"True, but Satan cannot force people to do his will, so he operates by deceit or deception, tempting individuals, groups, cities, and nations to follow him rather than God, thereby placing themselves under God's judgment. All this is true of Judah. And, when individuals, cities, and nations turn away from God, he has the right to judge them according to his righteous character and his moral laws: *You are righteous, Lord, and your laws are right.*[9] Whatever the righteousness of the Lord requires, his justice executes to either approve or reject, to bless or condemn, because God is a righteous judge."[10]

"Therefore, it's unimaginable to serve a God who cannot or will not judge sin."

"That's right, but though God judges, he is not one to judge quickly for it is written in the Psalms that *you, Lord, are a compassionate and gracious God, slow to anger, abounding in love and faithfulness.*"[11]

"And, in the New Testament, Peter reveals that God *is patient with you, not wanting anyone to perish, but everyone to come to repentance.*"[12]

"Thankfully, in this way God is quick to warn but slow to judge," Jeremiah agreed. "But the Almighty is not patient forever, and there are multiple accounts of judgment throughout scripture. God has judged people in the past and he will judge individuals, groups, cities, and nations in the future."

"But Jeremiah, on what basis does God judge?"

"In Old Testament times, Israel as a nation is unique in human history because it's the only nation created by God as a theocracy: *For the Lord is our judge, the Lord is our lawgiver, and the Lord is our king.*[13] Therefore, God gave Israel specific laws and the Mosaic Law was the standard by which Israel lived rightly before God and the basis for reward for obedience or punishment for disobedience."[14]

"Well," Saphah noted, "reading through all Old Testament scripture, one can see a consistent pattern of God blessing or cursing his people depending on whether they obeyed or disobeyed His written law. And, the trend throughout all of history was that of rebellion. However, God was extremely patient with His disobedient people, repeatedly warning them of His coming judgments. But, what about the Gentile nations in Old Testament times?"

"During the old covenant, Gentile nations didn't possess the Mosaic Law as Israel did, but a Gentile nation could be blessed or judged according to two factors. First, God would bless or curse a Gentile nation according to how it treated Israel: *I will bless those who bless you, and whoever curses you I will curse; and all peoples on earth will be blessed through you.*[15] Second, a Gentile nation could be blessed or cursed according to whether they pursued godly virtues or wickedness. God has placed within each person a moral sense of right and wrong."

"Right. Scripture says that *the requirements of the law are written on their hearts.*[16] The moral nature of Old Testament Gentiles, enlightened by conscious, functioned for them as the Mosaic law functioned for the Jews. So, since each person has a sense of right and wrong, and can choose how they behave, God *accepts from all nation the one who fears him and does what is right.*"[17]

"But how people behave collectively has results or consequences upon their city or state or nation," Jeremiah added. "Here is what happened when Jonah preached that God was going to judge the Ninevites: *The word of the Lord came to Jonah son of Amittai: 'Go to the great city of Nineveh and preach against it, because its wickedness has come up before me.' But Jonah ran away from the Lord and headed for Tarshish.*[18] Jonah was trying to escape his divinely appointed task by sailing the opposite direction, but then he was thrown into the sea and *the Lord provided a huge fish to swallow Jonah. …From inside the fish Jonah prayed to the Lord his God.*"[19]

"After that, the Lord commanded the fish to vomit Jonah out on dry ground: *Then the word of the Lord came to Jonah a second time: 'Go to the great city of Nineveh and proclaim to it the message I give you.' Jonah obeyed the word of the Lord and went to Ninevah. Now Nineveh was a very large city; it took three days to go through it, Jonah began by going a day's journey into the city, proclaiming, 'Forty more days and Ninevah will be overthrown.'*"[20]

"Wow, it took a lot of bad consequences for Jonah to finally realize the futility of trying to run away from God." Saphah laughed at the stubbornness of the man.

"Yes, it did. But now, to get back to what happened in Ninevah after Jonah's proclamation:

> *The Ninevites believed God. A fast was proclaimed, and all of them from the greatest to the least, put on sackcloth. When Jonah's warning reached the king of Nineveh, he rose from his throne, took off his*

royal robes, covered himself with sackcloth and sat down in the dust. This is the proclamation he issued in Nineveh: …Let everyone call urgently on God. Let them give up their evil ways and their violence. Who Knows? God may yet relent and with compassion turn from his fierce anger so that we will not perish. When God saw what they did and how they turned from their evil ways, he relented and did not bring on them the destruction he had threatened."[21]

"The case of Ninevah reveals that God will judge any nation, but it also shows there is hope for any country if the leadership and the people there turn to God and pursue righteousness in conformity with his character. Right, Jeremiah?"

"Yes, you're right. God can judge America or relent if people there turn back to him. But to bring up another aspect of God's judgment of nations, also remember that the divine principle is still true: *From everyone who has been given much, much will be demanded.*[22] And, from what you've told us, over the course of its history America has been greatly influenced by Christianity and blessed by God. Also, you've talked about the abundance of bibles in your land, so I assume the quantity of Christian literature is great too. Therefore, it seems that the light of divine revelation is greater in America than in pagan nations that haven't had such influences. Therefore, God will judge your country more severely than pagan societies if your people keep turning away from the divine message of the bible."

"So, let me get this straight. God blesses or judges nations utilizing two factors: First, according to how the country treats Israel. And, second, according to whether the country pursues either godly virtues or wickedness. But God has greatly blessed America. Thus, because of our continued sinfulness we may be tested 'in the furnace of affliction.' Is that right?"

"That's right. But I also want to share with you something additional the Lord told me in regard to my recent call into prophetic ministry for Judah. The Lord said: *See, today I appoint you over nations and kingdoms to uproot and to tear down, to destroy and overthrow, to build and to plant.*[23] Thus, when the Lord called me, he stressed that I would be both a prophet of doom and a prophet of restoration. First, the Lord said I was called 'to uproot and to tear down, to destroy and overthrow.' But my commission didn't end with destruction, because the Lord also said I was called 'to build and to plant.'"

"Wow! That's similar to what the Lord said to me about America: 'The land will be laid bare.' But then, the Lord also said, 'Upon these ruins I will rebuild my church.'"

"Yes, and the same power with which God will bring judgment upon Judah and America is the power by which he promises to eventually rebuild what is broken in both nations. The Lord also assured me regarding my people, the nation of Judah: *I will rejoice in doing them good and will assuredly plant them in this land with all my heart and soul.*"[24]

"And, praise God, He promised to rebuild the church in the nation of America: 'I will rebuild my church, and no one will stop me. You have my solemn word.'"

"Praise God, praise God! The Lord has promised to rebuild in both Judah and America. So, just as he will prove to be a powerful judge of justice and righteousness, he will likewise prove to be an equally patient, compassionate, and merciful rebuilder."

"Jeremiah, thank you so much for sharing that information with me. Now, I'm keenly aware that as a watchperson God has given me a sure word that I'm to give warnings from God of both negative and positive events that will soon transpire in my land, America."

"Yes, Saphah, I think *the day God visits* [America] *has come, the day your watchmen sound the alarm,*[25] to announce in advance the coming of events to affect America. One event the Lord wants you to reveal is negative: 'The land will be laid bare.' But the other event God wants you to reveal is positive: 'Upon these ruins I will rebuild my church.'"

"The scripture I quoted above is from Micah, a prophet from King Hezekiah's time. Micah's warnings were instrumental in Hezekiah's reformation. But Micah forewarned of Jerusalem's destruction a century earlier, and I'm quoting verbatim from Micah 3:12: '*Zion will be plowed like a field, Jerusalem will become a heap of rubble, the temple hill a mound overgrown with thickets.*'[26] So, Micah not only gave warnings for his own nation, the Northern Kingdom or Israel, but he also gave future warnings for the Southern Kingdom or Judah. Yet his message from God can also serve as a warning for modern America, because it states that 'the day your watchmen sound the alarm,' has arrived and that fact is pertinent to the United States too."

"That's incredible!"

"Yes, it is!" Jeremiah was amazed too. "Micah even noted he was speaking to both Israel and Judah, because he said in a salvation message of deliverance promised by God: *I will surely gather all of you, Jacob; I will surely bring together the remnant of Israel. I will bring them together like sheep in a pen, like a flock in its pasture; the place will throng with people. The One who breaks open the way will go up before them; ...the Lord at their head.*[27] Although Israel and Judah will both be carried into captivity, a remnant will return from each land."

"Oh, how wonderful! Do you think that America will rise again too?"

"Again, what did God say to you about it?"

"He told me that 'upon these ruins I will rebuild my church. And the glory of the Lord will reign there. I will rebuild my church, and no one will stop me. You have my solemn word.'"

"You believe God's word, don't you?"

"Definitely! Praise God!"

"Well, you might be interested to learn that Micah also revealed 'a prophetic liturgy made up of four subunits: an expression of trust; a promise of restoration; a prayer and the response; and a hymn of praise.[27] I think it applies to all three nations, Israel, Judah, and America. Would you like to hear it?'"[28]

"Of course!"

"The first part could be called: Israel, Judah, and America Rise:

> *Do not gloat over me, my enemy! Though I have fallen, I will rise. Though I sit in darkness the Lord will be my light. Because I have sinned against him, I will bear the Lord's wrath, until he pleads my case and upholds my cause. He will bring me out into the light; I will see his righteousness. Then my enemy will see it and will be covered with shame, she who said to me, 'Where is your God?' My eyes will see her downfall.[29]*

A name for the second part might be: Building and Restoration

> *The day for building your walls will come, the day for extending your boundaries. In that day people will come to you …from sea to sea and from mountain to mountain. The earth will become desolate because of its inhabitants, as the result of their deeds.[30]*

An apt description for the third section would be: Prayer and Wonder

> *Shepherd your people with your staff, the flock of your inheritance, … As in the days when you came out of Egypt, I will show them my wonders. Nations will see and be ashamed, deprived of all their power. They will put their hands over their mouths and their ears will become deaf. …They will turn in fear to the Lord our God.[31]*

A good name for the last section may simply be: Hymn of Praise:

> *Who is a God like you, who pardons sin and forgives the transgression of the remnant of his inheritance? You do not stay angry forever but delight to show mercy. You will again have compassion on us you will tread our sins underfoot and hurl all our iniquities into the depths of the sea. You will be faithful to Jacob, and show love to Abraham, as you pledged on oath to our ancestors in days long ago.*"[32]

"Oh, Jeremiah, I'm glad you shared Micah's prophetic liturgy of hope and comfort. The citizens of America need to realize that God's actions regarding America's corporate sins and disobedience are meant for our good. It's essential for men and women to know that God will be merciful and gracious to us if we turn to him for pardon and forgiveness of our sins. They also need to note that when God promised Abraham he had *made him a father of many nations,*[33] it meant all believers are ultimately included in that promise. Additionally, it means we are included in the Lord's pledge by oath to show love to Abraham."

"Yes, and when God makes a pledge or an oath, He always keeps his promise!"

"Yes, He will! Praise God! Praise God!"

King Josiah, who'd been listening, spoke up. "My friend, Saphah, I agree with what Prophet Jeremiah shared with you. And I believe God is letting you know it's time for you to sound a warning on your shofar. After this spy mission, I think you should return to America to check out what is occurring in the U. S. and to compose your book to this point. Then, after you get your book mostly written, you can come back to catch up on happenings here. What do you think?"

"I think you're right."

"Alright then, Saphah, after our reconnaissance at Topheth today, we can escort you back to Jerusalem and drop you off at the gate where Shallum will be greeting visitors to the city. Later, he can guide you to their residence at the Jerusalem school where you can stay the night with Huldah and then leave from there tomorrow to return home. After that, the rest of the reform team, along with myself, will all head back to the travel camp to get ready for our next excursion. Would that work for you?"

"Oh, thank you, King Josiah. Yes, that'll work fine. Since the Lord spoke to me again, I feel concerned about my people, and think I should return home to see what's happening there."

"Now everyone, gird up your loins and get prepared for this mission, because just over that ridge is the Hinnom Valley."

~

Suddenly, dark clouds arose on the horizon and darkened the sky, and the wind came up and blew clumps of tumble weeds across their pathway. Saphah shivered as the cold breeze blew her warm shawl away from her neck and a vulture circled high above them. *Oh, this place is beyond eerie!*

34

TOPHETH

The spy team neared the top of the ridge which led down into the Hinnon Valley. But fear gripped the American Watchwoman's heart. *What kind of abomination of the Lord exists in the Hinnom Valley?* Saphah wondered. *And, what type of secret rituals do the people practice in their worship of idols there?* She glanced around at the surrounding area. *The path we are traveling right now looks safe enough, but what will we encounter just over the next ridge?*

"Alright," King Josiah shouted from his chariot. "Just a little further on is the Potsherd Gate where we're supposed to meet up with Ebed and Hannah and fetch the donkeys for the ladies to ride." The group passed over the rocky ridge and began walking down a steep slope into the valley, crossed a stream by walking on rocks scattered in intervals, and then began the climb upward toward the Jerusalem Wall and the Potsherd Gate.

"Oh, here come Ebed and Hannah." Rebecca, joyful to see her brother and his new wife, picked up her pace.

"And they've brought Hannah's dog Lady with them," Tamara happily observed as she tried to catch up.

"Look, they're waving at us." Saphah waved back, as did the others.

Hannah, with Lady's leash in hand, began running toward the female spies. "Oh, you all look great dressed in that foreign finery." Hannah checked everyone out, but laughed when she came to the American Watchwoman. "Saphah, is that really you?" Hannah stared at her quizzically. "No one is going to recognize you for sure!"

"I think they tried to make me look beautiful like you and failed."
Saphah laughed and gave her friend a big hug.

"Well, you look nice anyway."

"And you look wonderful, Hannah! Both of you do!"

"Ebed and I are so happy!" Hannah's big pup jumped up and licked
her on the face. "Even Lady is happy."

King Josiah and Prophet Jeremiah arrived in their chariot near the
spies, and the driver pulled back the reins to stop. Jeremiah turned
toward the ruler. "King Josiah, would it be alright if I go over to the
area where the potters are working? The lord just spoke to me and
said: *Go and buy a clay jar from a potter.*[1]

"Of course, my friend." He glanced toward the chariot driver. "Please
take Prophet Jeremiah over to where the potters are working their
clay. I'll stay here and visit with Ebed, Hannah, and the others."
Everyone visited until Jeremiah returned with his jar, and then King
Josiah signaled for the group's attention. "Alright, female spies, there's
a donkey for each of you. Go ahead and mount up and we'll get on
our way. Hannah, I want you to know that Lady Zebidah is waiting
for you at the travel camp and looking forward to getting acquainted.
I'm glad you brought Lady along so she can guard you on your trip
back to camp. Take care and we'll see you later."

"Thank you, King Josiah." Ebed and Hannah tenderly kissed each
other goodbye, the new bride jumped astride her donkey, and then
she and her greyhound headed in the direction of camp kicking up a
trail of dust behind them.

The members of the spy operation separated from Josiah, Jeremiah,
and the guards and began their approach back to the Hinnom Valley.
But Saphah started to ruminate again. She was having a difficult time

controlling her emotions. The *clomp, clomp, clomp* of her donkey's hooves beneath her reverberated in her ears and caused her to feel anxious. *I hope King Josiah brought along enough personnel and especially guards,* Saphah thought. *But what if there are more idolators worshipping their false god than our little group can handle?* She turned to look back toward Josiah and reminded herself that he and his men would help if the need arose.

The group descended into a steep, craggy valley scarred by shallow caves and hollowed out places where burial chambers were located. Saphah shivered. *I wonder what kind of people are buried in this weird place? Criminals, indigents, lepers?* Dark clouds had completely blotted out the sun midway up in the sky by this time. Then the wind picked up a bit more and Saphah had to grab her turban with one hand to keep it straight on her head. Several crows circled in the sky above them.

Lord, I'm afraid. Please give me courage to do your will in this dark valley. And, please be with me and help me to know what to do when we reach this place of wicked idolatry.

Saphah's thoughts turned to the Psalm she'd read to the old man, Joshua, back in camp, the part she'd quoted about a valley: *Even though I walk through the darkest valley, I will fear no evil, for you are with me, your rod and your staff they comfort me.*[2]

Oh, Lord, Saphah silently prayed again, *thank you for bringing that verse to my mind. I don't have to worry because you are with us through this ordeal, just as Rebecca pointed out back in camp. I only need to put all my faith and trust in you!*

"Saphah, are you alright?" Eve inquired. "You seem lost in thought."

"I'm okay now," said Saphah. "I'm just a little tired from yesterday, aren't you?"

"Yes, I am. I think we could've used a little more sleep this morning."

"Well, I think we'll all sleep well tonight."

"I just hope we get to rest more tomorrow morning," Tamara added. "Becca, do you think your parents will let us sleep in?"

"I doubt it," Rebecca said. "But hopefully we can get more sleep by going to bed earlier tonight."

The group began a descent into a deeper, rockier ravine and rode along eastward for a bit before beginning an ascent from the area again. A whiff of smoke entered Saphah's nostrils and choked her. She grabbed her hanky and held it over her nose. Some of the others were coughing as they breathed in the acrid smoke. "Where is that smoke coming from?"

"Look over there." one of the guards pointed out where to look. "See that plume of black smoke coming from the east. The strong wind this morning is blowing it straight over here."

Ebed, who was wearing a fake beard for a disguise, noted, "It looks like it's coming from some kind of chimney, but I can't really make out much else because of all the smoke. Let's travel south for a bit to get out of this smoke and then approach it from a different angle."

The gray clouds overhead and the scent of the smoke in the air sent an ominous message, as if revealing some impending doom awaiting them ahead. The group traveled along for quite some time in the bottom of the valley along a dry stream bed with high banks on each side. Suddenly Saphah pulled up hard on the reins of her donkey at the sight of a billowing cloud of smoke appearing around the bend. Then the other ladies likewise pulled up too, and their donkeys abruptly skidded to halts. Ebed and the other men all took the reins of the donkeys being ridden by the women.

Ebed narrowed his eyes and guided Saphah slowly forward on her donkey as he tried to make out the source of the huge, black plume of smoke. They were some distance away from the smoke, but Ebed could just make out a crowd of dozens of people gathered opposite the side of the billowing smoke. Other people were hovered over drums and their hands held sticks poised over the percussion instruments as if to begin beating them. Still others held trumpets up in front of their mouths as if to start blowing the horns. Some of the people were on their knees chanting and rhythmically waving their arms up and down but then they all arose from the ground and began rocking back and forth, chanting:

"Molek, Molek, Molek!"

The crowd of people seemed unaware of the nearing presence of the spies. As they drew closer, Saphah perceived a large statue and felt her heart drop. *This place must be Topheth*, Saphah thought in horror. *And… that is the statue of the pagan god Molek*. The monstrosity had the head of a bull with two horns, the body of a man with outstretched arms, and a hollow stomach which held a furnace. Belching flames shot out of a protruding chimney along with dark smoke.

The watchwoman searched the crowd to see who was standing there. Couples composed of men and their spouses holding babies, were standing around everywhere. *Dear Lord, are these couples planning to sacrifice their own infants to the demonic idol with outstretched arms? Oh, what a hideous thing to do! And are the people with drums and horns planning to drown out the sound of the babies crying by beating the drums and blowing the horns?* Saphah glanced over at Ebed who was shaking his head in dismay and horror.

Suddenly Ebed's brows furrowed in disgust and he shouted in fury. "It's Jude! And he's a false priest now!"

Saphah saw a man dressed in a foreign robe with a priestly turban crowning his head and the vest of a priest covering his torso. "Oh, Ebed," Saphah shouted in horror. "It *is* Jude! And, I think he's planning to sacrifice that baby to Molek."

Ebed immediately reached over, grabbed the startled Saphah by the waist with both hands, pulled her off her donkey, and set her on her feet. "Run Saphah! You grab the baby and I'll take care of Jude!"

Saphah ran as hard as she could toward Jude, whose hands held the baby, but whose arms were poised to place the infant onto the searing hands of Molech. "Jude, stop!" Saphah shrieked as loudly as she could.

The false priest switched his attention to Saphah. "Who are you?" Jude bellowed and swung around toward her with the baby still in his hands.

Ebed tackled Jude to the ground with a thud, but the tiny baby slipped out of the fake priest's hands as he went down and landed at Saphah's feet. She quickly picked up the infant and handed it back to Eve, who was standing right behind her.

But Jude wrestled off Ebed, shoved him away, and plunged again toward Saphah, angry that she'd rescued the baby. He jerked off her turban, which released her long blonde hair onto her shoulders, then pulled himself up short to glare in her face. A look of recognition came over his countenance as he suddenly realized with whom he was dealing. "I know who you are! You're that friend of Hannahs from Jerusalem!" He quickly pulled back his fist to punch her.

Saphah closed her eyes in anticipation of a punch and stepped back, but tripped and fell backwards. Almost immediately, something heavy landed on her and she opened her eyes. Jude's face was right above hers and his eyes were staring straight into hers. Saphah screamed.

"It's alright, Saphah," Ebed's consoling voice assured as he pulled Jude's limp body, with an arrow piercing his heart, away from hers and tossed it to the ground. Ebed turned toward Eve's husband. "Whew, fine shot, Jonathan! That was just in time!"

At that moment Saphah heard for the first time the precious cry of the baby as Eve snuggled the little one in her arms. "There, there, it's alright baby girl," Eve was laughing and crying all at the same time as she soothed the tiny infant with her tender voice. Suddenly she began to proclaim loudly, "Yahweh, thank you for saving this baby! Praise God! Praise God! Praise God!"

"Yes, Yahweh, thank you for saving this baby!" shouted King Josiah, who was running up on the scene, crying hot tears of horror and bitterness, as he considered the evil deeds happening in Topheth. Then, Judah's ruler began shouting in rage at the crowd still milling about. "What are you wicked people doing? Where are the parents who were ready to sacrifice their innocent infant by burning it to death in the fire? His eyes searched in different directions until he saw a couple fleeing the scene. "Capture them," he yelled and two guards jumped aboard his chariot to dash after them. The guards soon arrived back with the couple in tow, shackled together for restraint.

King Josiah yelled at the people standing around, "Get out of here you degenerate people and don't ever come back! I will not have this in my kingdom! *I will desecrate Topheth …in the Valley of Hinnom, so no one can use it to sacrifice their son or their daughter in the fire to Molek.*[3] Remember this and mark my words, you disgraceful bunch, I will come back to completely desecrate this abominable place."

"Now, guards, I want half of you to stay here tonight to guard this place until I can come back. You have your supplies with you. Remaining guards, I want you to take this evil couple and the false priests as captives. I'm going to have them cast into Jerusalem

Prison until I can find out exactly what God wants me to do with them. Therefore, get ready because we're going to travel back now to the Potsherd Gate. Prophet Jeremiah tells me he's received another word from God."

"Yes, and this is what the Lord said: *Go out to the Valley of Ben Hinnom, near the entrance to the Potsherd Gate. There proclaim the words I tell you.*"[4]

"Thank you, Prophet Jeremiah. Now, guards, please form a column and begin marching toward the Potsherd Gate taking the captives with you. Jeremiah and I'll catch up with you later."

King Josiah turned toward his best friend and requested his presence. "Ebed, I need your assistance. Please escort this group of spies back to Jerusalem. When everyone gets to the Potsherd Gate, the entire assemblage, including the spies, the captives, the guards, and those already in attendance at the gate need to hear Jeremiah's prophecy. Therefore, when you see Shallum at the gate, please tell him to make an announcement of what's happening so the elders, leaders, and others there can listen and observe everything Prophet Jeremiah says and does."

"Alright, King Josiah." Ebed bowed to his ruler. "My king, what else would you like for me to do?"

"Afterward, please inform Shallum about Saphah's situation so he can escort her to the housing at the Jerusalem School. She's planning to stay overnight with Huldah and then leave from there to go back to America."

"Isn't Saphah going to keep spying with us?"

"Saphah recently received a new message from God, so she wants to return to her land to write on her book and to check out what's happening there. When she gets back we can fill her in on what has occurred since she's been gone."

"Oh, I see. But what about Jonathan, Eve, and the baby?"

"Let's go talk to them now," said King Josiah. The two men walked to the group of spies and stopped near the young couple. "Jonathan and Eve, I think God has blessed you today."

"King Josiah, I think so too," Jonathan said. "And, I also think my young wife has been right all along."

"What do you mean?" Ebed stepped in to ask.

"Eve thinks that God has called her to be a spy and now I think so too. Look at what God has done for us."

"Yes, I agree," Ebed said and then smiled. "It seems that God is working all things together for good in your lives."

Eve was sitting on a boulder still holding the tiny baby God had rescued from sacrifice. "Isn't she beautiful?" Eve gently touched the tiny infant's face and spoke to her. "You're so pretty, my little one, in your lovely dress." The tiny baby girl looked up at her and smiled. Eve glanced toward King Josiah. "My king, did you see this baby smile at me?"

"Indeed, I did!" King Josiah wiped the tears still lingering in his eyes and smiled. "Eve and Jonathan, this is your baby now. God has given you the gift of a baby girl."

Eve started crying and so did everyone else. There was nary a dry eye in the bunch. "These are tears of joy, you know." Eve cried and smiled all at the same time.

"Yes, I'm thankful beyond words for God's gift to us of a baby daughter." Jonathan's voice broke as he spoke.

Eve handed the baby to Jonathan as tears escaped from his eyes and ran down his face. He brushed aside the tears, sat down by Eve on the big rock, and held the tiny infant out in front so he could see her face. With a smile he began talkng to her. "Hey, little girl, I'm going to be your new father." The wee girl seemed to study his face as she intently listened to him speak. "Are you my favorite girl?" he asked as if she could understand him.

Then he used his spare hand to draw circles in the air as he moved his hand ever closer to her chin. "I'm going to get your chin." Then he drew more circles again with his hand. "I'm going to get your chin." As he touched the baby's chin the second time, she let out a sweet giggle. "Oh, you're the cutest thing," he said to her and she smiled back. With tears still in his eyes, he hugged the chubby baby and handed her back to her new mother.

"Eve and Jonathan, what are you going to name her?" Rebecca asked.

Eve cradled the child up to her chest and thought for a few seconds. "Jonathan, what do you think about naming her Mattea, which means 'gift of God' in Hebrew?"

"Mattea." Jonathan listened to the sound of the name as he spoke it. "Mattea." He repeated the name again and briefly thought about it. "Eve, I think that is a beautiful name and an appropriate choice. Alright everyone, her name is Mattea!"

"Perfect name, Mattea," said King Josiah. "Eve, are you still going to continue to spy with us?"

"I want to, but who would care for Mattea while I spy?"

"Ebed and Becca, do you think your mother would take care of Mattea while Eve is spying?" King Josiah asked.

"I think she would," answered Rebecca. "And then Mattea could be a playmate for my new little brother or sister mother is expecting."

"Yes," Ebed agreed. "And when Hannah has our baby, all three of the babies can play together."

"Alright, Eve and Jonathan, we'll ask mother when we get back to camp," said Rebecca.

"Everyone, let's get going now," King Josiah instructed. "We don't want to miss Jeremiah's prophecy. Ebed, as we were saying, you can escort the spy team, but Jeremiah and I'll ride on ahead to catch up with the guards and their deplorable captives."

35

THE TWO JARS

The spy team arrived at the Potherd Gate shortly after King Josiah's group. Ebed immediately located Shallum and informed him about Jeremiah's forthcoming prophecy.

Shallum spoke loudly to get the attention of those at the gate. "Travelers, Jerusalem citizens, secular leaders, religious leaders, and everyone else assembled here at this gate, please give me your attention. I'm happy to announce that Jeremiah has been called as a prophet, a spokesman for God, and he is present here to give you a message from the Lord. He's planning to go out to the Valley of Ben Hinnom, near the Potsherd Gate entrance, to proclaim a word from God to you. By the command of King Josiah, ruler of Judah, everyone here at this gate must follow Prophet Jeremiah out to the spot in the Valley of Ben Hinnom."

The crowd followed Prophet Jeremiah to a ridge overlooking the Valley of Ben Hinnom. "Now, everyone, I present to you Prophet Jeremiah, who has an important message from God to share with you today."

"Thank you, King Josiah," said Prophet Jeremiah. "The following two-fold message of the Lord came to me in the place where potters make earthen vessels. First, the Lord spoke to me about a clay jar a potter was forming which was still moist and pliable, making it possible to reshape and rework. But the second message the Lord delivered to me concerned a clay jar that was hard and unsuitable for the owner's use, so it had to be destroyed. Now, here is the prophecy as God delivered it to me:

The Two Jars

The first message:

> *He said, 'Can I not do with you, Israel, as this potter does?' declares the Lord. 'Like clay in the hand of the potter, so are you in my hand, Israel. If at any time I announce that a nation or kingdom is to be uprooted, torn down and destroyed, and if that nation I warned repents of its evil, then I will relent and not inflict on it the disaster I planned. And if at another time I announce that a nation or kingdom is to be built up and planted, and if it does evil in my sight and does not obey me, then I will reconsider the good I had intended to do for it.' Now therefore say to the people of Judah and those living in Jerusalem, 'This is what the Lord says: Look! I am preparing a disaster for you and devising a plan against you. So turn from your evil ways, each of you, and reform your ways and your actions.' But they will reply, 'It's no use. We will continue with our own plans: we will all follow the stubbornness of our evil hearts.'*[1]

I think you'll all agree with me that the meaning of the illustration is clear. God can form and reform nations as he pleases: *'Can I not do with you, Israel, as this potter does?'*[2] This affirmation of the sovereignty of God shows his power over the people he has formed. It implies that wholehearted repentance on the part of any nation can avert the judgment that looms over them. The last verse, however, puts a quote in the mouth of the people that they will *'follow the stubbornness of our evil hearts.'*[3] This quote is based on their actions and non-reception of the prophecy from God.

The second message:

> *Hear the word of the Lord, you kings of Judah and people of Jerusalem. This is what the Lord Almighty, the God of Israel, says: Listen! I am going to bring disaster on this place that will make the ears of everyone who hears of it tingle. For they have forsaken me and made this a place of foreign gods: they have burned incense in it to gods*

*that neither they nor their ancestors nor the kings of Judah ever knew,
and they have filled this place with the blood of the innocent.*[4]

*They have built the high places of Topheth in the Valley of Ben
Hinnom to burn their sons and daughters in the fire—something I
did not command, nor did it enter my mind. So beware, the days are
coming, declares the Lord, when people will no longer call it Topheth or
the Valley of Ben Hinnom, but the Valley of Slaughter, for they will
bury the dead in Topheth until there is no more room. Then the carcasses
of this people will become food for the birds and the wild animals, and
there will be no one to frighten them away. I will bring an end to the
sounds of joy and gladness and to the voices of bride and bridegroom in
the towns of Judah and the streets of Jerusalem, for the land will become
desolate.*[5]

Here, the Kings of Judah—past and future—are symbolically allowed
in absentia to hear of God's coming judgment relevant to the Valley
of Ben Hinnom, and the acts of human sacrifice committed there.
This is because the message wasn't actually for the reigning king,
Josiah, but for the entire dynasty that was responsible for the
apostasy. Kings Ahaz, Manasseh, and Amon were all guilty, as was
even King Solomon, as follows:

*On a hill east of Jerusalem Solomon built a high place for Chemosh
the detestable god of Moab, and for Molek the detestable god of the
Ammonites. He did the same for all his foreign wives, who burned
incense and offered sacrifices to their gods.*[6] *For Solomon's idolatrous
worship, the Lord tore the kingdom away from him …[except for]
one tribe [Judah] for the sake of David my servant and for the sake of
Jerusalem, which I have chosen.*[7]

The Lord also promised great catastrophe to come upon this place
associated with idolatry and child sacrifice. Then God said to me:
Break the jar while those who go with you are watching.[8]

Jeremiah picked up the earthen jar and threw it down on the ground, where it smashed into little bits and pieces.

> *This is what the Lord Almighty says: I will smash this nation and this city just as this potter's jar is smashed and cannot be repaired. They will bury the dead in Topheth until there is no more room. This is what I will do to this place and to those who live here, declares the Lord. I will make this city like Topheth. The houses of Jerusalem and those of the kings of Judah will be defiled like this place, Topheth—all the houses where they burned incense on the roofs to all the starry hosts and poured out drink offerings to other gods.*[9]

Here is what God will do to Judah because of their heinous sin:

> *In this place I will ruin the plans of Judah and Jerusalem. I will make them fall by the sword before their enemies, at the hands of those who want to kill them, and I will give their carcasses as food to the birds and the wild animals.*[10]

God will use Judah's enemies to cause the Judeans to fall by the sword and to be food for the birds and the wild animals. Thus, here in the Valley of Ben Hinnom where Topheth, the place for human sacrifices is located, God has indicated the irrevocable judgment to come on Judah by telling me to smash the earthen jar which cannot be repaired.

Yet for those with ears to hear and eyes to see, God's word of judgment is not unalterable, because sincere repentance will still bring salvation to any individual who seeks the Lord with all their heart. And that's why reform efforts are so important in Judah and America. Although judgment is irrevocable for Judah, and perhaps for America too, individual salvation can still be a reality for all those who sincerely turn back to the Lord. Also, as Prophet Zephaniah pointed out in his recent speech when he summoned the people of Judah to repent:

> *Gather together, gather together, you shameful nation, …before the day of the Lord's wrath comes upon you. Seek the Lord, all you humble of the land, you who do what he commands. Seek righteousness, seek humility; perhaps you will be sheltered on the day of the Lord's anger.*[11]

As Zephaniah explained, the call to a future remnant to gather themselves together means for them to join in genuine repentance and submission to the will of God. They must do this in order to effect shelter both for themselves and for others who will unite with them in salvation before the day of God's judgment. The plea is urgent because God's decree is settled and will soon be put into effect, therefore reform efforts should occur right away.

Prophet Zephaniah also stressed that people should stay positive:

> *Do not fear Zion; do not let your hands hang limp. The Lord your God is with you, the mighty Warrior who saves. He will take great delight in you; in his love he will no longer rebuke you, but will rejoice over you with singing.*[12]

The physical manifestation of fear, limp hands, is something to be laid aside. God, in His might as a Divine Warrior, is powerful enough to save us. As he acted on behalf of his people in the past, he will again, both today and tomorrow. Gentleness and power are combined in a figure who is like a good parent, delighting in the return of a lost child and quieting their fears.

~

"Thank you, Prophet Jeremiah," said King Josiah. "I appreciate your endorsement of our reform efforts. I agree with you that Judah is beyond the line of hope, which is very sobering indeed. God's judgment is coming and certain for both Judah and America. Yet we must press on in fidelity to God and commitment to Him, because individuals can still be saved, a remnant can still be protected, and the Lord can still be honored in righteousness. Therefore, it is important we move forward with our reform efforts in Judah and America."

The king added. "It is vital, Saphah, for you to return to your nation to finish your book up to this point and to check on the happenings in your time and place. Shallum is going to escort you in Jerusalem to spend the night at their home before you head for America. So, I want to take this opportunity to thank you for all your help up until now and to tell you I look forward to seeing you again, hopefully soon."

"Thank you, King Josiah, for your hospitality, for your acceptance of me as a woman in your group, and for all the experience I've gained helping so far with reforms. I too look forward to seeing you and the others again soon. King of Judah, farewell."

Saphah walked down the line of reformers to speak with her friends and to wish them all well. After many hugs and kisses, Saphah joined Shallum and those guarding the false priests to walk toward the Potsherd Gate. "Farewell to all." She turned to wave and they all waved in return. But the reform group, headed up by King Josiah, began their departure toward the spy camp.

36

A NATION ON THE BRINK

Where am I and how did I get here? Saphah glanced all around the room in confusion because she wasn't recognizing her own bedroom. *Oh,* she finally realized, *this is my bedroom! Why didn't I recognize it sooner?* She stared up at the ceiling above her bed and thought a bit. *I seem to remember a dream I had last night about an angel who came to get me to transport me somewhere. But I can't remember much about it.*

The watchwoman sat up on the side of her bed and began putting on her slippers. She reached into her pajama pocket to get a tissue to blow her nose. *What's this?* She felt a small, triangular object in her pocket with a pointed tip. She pulled the object out of her pocket to examine it, and that's when she realized it was an Indian arrowhead. *Where did I get this arrowhead and why is it in my pajama pocket?* Suddenly the disoriented woman began remembering. *Oh, my, what I experienced last night wasn't a dream! It really happened! I picked up this arrowhead in the cave where the angel Malak took me! This was the same cave my cousin Ben used to explore!*

Saphah walked into her kitchen, sat down on a chair, placed the arrowhead on the table, and just stared at it. *This is unbelievable! The events beginning last night weren't a nightmare! The arrowhead I found in my pajama pocket is my proof.* But still she struggled to remember exactly what had happened. *How did I get back here? The last thing I remember is being in the Aperture of Process. I think I went to sleep in there as I twirled around and around processing back into my normal body. Evidently, the angel named Malak must have gathered me up asleep from the Aperture and deposited me into my own bed here at home.*

Staring around the room, the sleepy lady tried to recollect more about her journey to Jerusalem. Her eyes locked on her back pack hanging from a different chair. *Oh, there is my satchel with the notes on the prophetic speeches I listened to at the reform meeting and other material for my book. Now I'm starting to remember everything that happened. She reminisced briefly about the events which occurred while she was in Judah.* Then, she opened the case to look for the scrolls and dug them out. "Thank you, Lord," she prayed after finding them. "I've retrieved all the written material from my backpack to assist me in writing my book."

After she made a pot of coffee, Saphah poured herself a cup and went back to the desk in her bedroom where she usually said her morning prayers. "Precious Lord and Savior, thank you for safely guiding me to the Holy Land and back again to my home in America. I fervently thank you for all your blessings and pray for forgiveness for my sins. Now, I earnestly pray for guidance as I do research on the state of America's affairs, share truth that'll resonate in the ears of those who hear it, and catch up on my writing to the present. Also, please help me to stay strong amidst the trials and tribulations our once great nation faces in the days ahead. I pray these things in the name of Jesus. Amen."

Alright, the watchwoman thought. *I need to go online to check out various news outlets to see what's happening in the U.S. and the world.* The first thing she found was an article about an unexpected attack by Hamas on Israel's citizens. She read aloud: "At 6:30 a.m. on Saturday, October 7, Hamas, the Iran-backed terror group controlling Gaza, launched an unprovoked and vicious surprise attack on Israel. Using rockets, paragliders, boats, motorcycles, other vehicles, and whatever other means they could, terrorists infiltrated Israel with one goal—to murder and kidnap Israelis."[1] After searching for updated news, she learned that Hamas terrorists massacred over 1,400 Israelis and foreign nationals and held hostage more than 241 people.

Staring at her computer in horror after reading more news, the researcher mouthed loudly: "Oh my, this is serious! The Hamas attack on Israel is far bigger than a war limited to Israel and Gaza. It threatens the peace of the whole world!" Then she read another article which stated that not only Israel, but also the entire globe was surprised by the attack. Her mind pondered the implications of these facts: *Reaction to the Hamas surprise attack reminds me of American denial which occurred before the Japanese attacked Pearl Harbor during our second World War. They thought the nation of America would never be attacked. But my uncle was actually on a U. S. ship in Pearl Harbor when the Japs attacked.*

Hum! This is interesting! Saphah read to herself from a different article:

> In 1941, two months before the Japanese surprise attack on Pearl Harbor plunged America into war, only 17% of Americans overall, favored a declaration of war. …The West, And particularly the U.S. cannot fall into the same trap again. Today we need a clear stance recognizing Hama's October 7 massacre as the latest round in the 21st century's war of good against evil. The values and liberties the West holds dear must defeat the darkness that comes with Islamic extremism. …Hamas might …claim to be fighting for Palestinian freedom, but that is clearly not the case when it burns babies and cuts off limbs of children in front of their parents— before slaughtering young and old alike.[2]

These murderers aren't just terrorists, Saphah mulled over the information in horror. *They're evil personified!*

The American Watchwoman turned back to her reading. But then after reading more, she paused with her elbows on her desk, her fingertips on her temples, and her eyes firmly closed to contemplate what she'd just read. *My goodness, how terrible!* She opened her eyes and shook her head back and forth in dismay. *Large groups of protestors, many of them college students, are demonstrating in favor of evil Hamas rather than Israel.*

The millions marching in support of Hama's crimes in New York, London, Paris and Sydney prove that the terrorist group enjoys sympathizers worldwide. Today, the attacks target Israel, but tomorrow any democracy could be targeted. Regrettably, much of the world remains ensnared in an illusion we recognize from the early 2000s … that this is an isolated battle. … Tragically, what happened to Israel [has come] true again and again. In 2001 Al Qaeda terrorists struck New York and Washington on 9/11. In 2002, Jemaah Islamiyah's bombings murdered 202 people in Bali. … Islamic terrorists attacked Madrid commuter trains in 2004, the London Underground and bus system in 2005, and the Charlie Hebdo offices, a Jewish supermarket, and a music concert in Paris in 2015.[3]

I can clearly remember when all these events happened, Saphah reflected. Aren't universities in the U.S. teaching this important history to their students so they'll know what's occurring in the world? If so, then why are large numbers of people, including students, protesting in favor of Hamas instead of backing Israel? Of course, I know that many on the Left have attempted to revise history and to assert that Jews are simply occupiers of the land of Israel.

Continuing her search online, the researcher found something that piqued her interest. She came across some information about the deceit being perpetrated by those trying to rewrite history:

With the October 7, 2023 Hamas Massacre, …there've been renewed attempts to rewrite history and assert that Jews are 'foreign occupiers' with no ties to the land of Israel. Among lies being spread is an effort to undermine Israels' legitimacy by accusing it of being a settler-colonial state. Those [telling] this lie argue that Jews have no historical connection to the land of Israel. …But here are some facts about the long history of the Jewish people's ties to the land of Israel.[4]

Wonderful Saphat enthusiastically thought. *The article gives a summary of the biblical info that a continuous presence of Jews has always existed in Israel.* She read on:

> Jerusalem has been the spiritual, religious, and national center of the Jewish people for thousands of years. …In the book of Genesis, God promised the land of Israel to Abraham, the first Jew, and then reaffirmed the promise to Abraham's son Isaac and grandson Jacob. In fact, the name Israel is another name for Jacob. In the book of Exodus, Moses leads the Israelites out of slavery and oppression in Egypt with a promise to take them back to the land of Israel, the land of their forefathers.[5]

Oh good, here are more of the details:

> Approximately 3,000 years ago under the rulership of King David, Jerusalem became the capital of Israel. Jerusalem was the site of two great Temples. …The first Temple was built by King Solomon during the tenth century BCE and destroyed by the Babylonian Empire in 586 BCE. …The second Temple was built less than a century later, and destroyed in 70 CE by the Romans, who also destroyed the Jewish capital and forcibly exiled most of the Jewish inhabitants. …[But] while the Romans expelled the majority of Jews in 70 CE, the Jewish people have always been present in the land of Israel. A portion of the Jewish population remained in Israel throughout years of exile while the rest settled around the world and became the Jewish diaspora. Jewish communities existed …[mainly] in the Four Holy Cities: Jerusalem, Hebron, Safed (Tzfat), and Tiberias.[6]

This article proves that remnants of Jews never left Jerusalem from the time of Genesis until now! The article succinctly states that although many Jews are 'scattered throughout the world during various points in history, …

Jews have had a constant presence in the land of Israel.'[7] *But, while other Jews have been in exile, they've never stopped yearning to return to Israel, the land God gave them as noted in scripture. And, their enduring hope of eventual return came to fruition with the establishment of the State of Israel in 1948. Finally, the Jews had realized their* 'long-held dream of a Jewish homeland, and it has since become the center of Jewish identity and culture for millions of Jews worldwide. Israel is seen as a place of refuge, a place of cultural renaissance, and a symbol of Jewish self-determination.'[8]

Saphah mentally noted, *It says here that a way exists to defeat the culture of death as presented by the Hamas terrorists.* 'It begins by standing with Israel in its time of need, while making it clear that calls for Israel's destruction or support of Hamas and its actions will not be tolerated. The world has an opportunity to stand on the right side of history. It should not be missed.'[9]

Well, up until recently, our American presidents have all stood on the right side of history. The lady reminisced. *I remember in 1973, when I was just 30 years old with a husband and two young children, that gas prices averaged 35 to 40 cents per gallon. But late in the fall that year, gas prices started going up sharply, and then we all heard on the news that Saudia Arabia was enforcing an oil embargo against the U.S. This economic hardship to our nation had occurred because our president at that time, Richard Nixon, had provided help to Israel after Syria and Egypt invaded them with the assistance of the Soviets.*

Saphah recalled it quite well. *All this happened after the Arab Nations had threatened to use oil as a weapon against any country that aided Israel. Therefore, when former Israeli Prime Minister Golda Meir appealed to European nations for military support, her appeal failed. So, it was our current American President at that time who decided to help the country of Israel despite financial hardship it would bring our nation. President Nixon, already embroiled in a scandal that would lead to the loss of his presidency, had nevertheless made the decision to stand on the right side of history.*

Saphah remembered that *one night Nixon received a phone call from Prime Minister Meir pleading for assistance. One source quoted the president as saying: he could almost hear his mother's voice:* She would tell me stories and read to me from the Old Testament [about] the heroes of the Bible. And one afternoon, she said, 'Richard, someday you're going to be in a position where you can help save the Jewish people. And when that day comes, you must do everything in your power.'[10]

Saphah knew that the president's mother, Hannah, was known to have heavily influenced her son, and he affectionately described her as a Quaker Saint. *By God's providence,* Saphah thought, *the Lord had let this godly lady know in advance that her young son would someday 'help save the Jewish people.' And when he became president of the United States, he remembered what she'd said and did 'everything in his power,' as exhibited by the details of the airlift for Israel:*

> At first, the United States attempted to provide material assistance to Israel by loading equipment on EL Al airliners, so that American aircraft would not be seen providing obvious support. However, it became obvious that a much more extensive airlift would be necessary, and President Nixon ordered the U.S. military to 'send everything that can fly.' Only one European nation, Portugal, allowed the U.S. airlift to refuel on their soil. But the United States delivered a massive amount of materials and fighter aircraft to Israel over about a month. The U.S. support helped Israel survive the invasion and effective ceasefire was eventually implemented.[11]

And so, Saphah mentally noted, *that is how America's 37th Commander in Chief, Richard Milhouse Nixon gained* the satisfaction of being allowed to assist Israel, the 'Apple of God's Eye,' at a crucial time [in history], a reward in itself and a lasting testament to American character.[12] *And all this happened because his Christian mother had taught him that the nation of Israel was important to God because through them all nations would be blessed.*

The Lord said to Abram, 'Go from your country, your people and your father's household to the land I will show you. I will make you into a great nation, and I will bless you; I will make your name great, and you will be a blessing. I will bless those who bless you, and whoever curses you I will curse; and all peoples on earth will be blessed through you.'[13]

Saphah remembered that when speaking of the nation of Israel, Prophet Zechariah had warned: *Whoever touches you touches the apple of his eye.*[14] *In other words,* she thought, *Israel is so precious to God, that anyone who harms that nation is harming Him:* 'In practical terms the phrase speaks of God's awareness of all abuse and harmful actions against the nation of Israel. The Lord is extremely sensitive to how countries over the centuries have treated His chosen people …God's watchful care guarantees Israel's survival and ultimate deliverance from every aggressor outside His will who seeks Israel's annihilation.'[15]

Additionally, the watchwoman recollected that Prophet Jeremiah had foretold that Israel will be preserved as long as the world exists: *This is what the Lord says, he who appoints the sun to shine by day, who decrees the moon and stars to shine by night, who stirs up the sea so that its waves roar—the Lord Almighty is his name: Only if these decrees vanish from my sight, declares the Lord, will Israel ever cease being a nation before me.*[16]

However, Saphah thought, *we're just finding out that our 44th Commander in Chief, Barack Hussein Obama, who served an eight-year term, reneged on his duty to back the Jewish people. Here is what Harvard Law professor emeritus and author Alan Dershowitz a said:*

> [Dershowitz] expressed outrage over former President Barack Obama's call for an end to Israeli 'occupation.' He said about Obama: 'I think he always had a deep hatred of Israel in his heart. He hid it very well. …And finally, his true feelings have come out now that he's no longer president and doesn't have to be elected. He has contributed enormously to the problem because he is respected among young people. And

> if he says the occupation is unbearable and that anything can
> be done to stop it, he is encouraging young people to engage
> in their antisemitic, anti-Israel and anti-American attitudes.
> He should be ashamed of himself.'[17]

But then, continuing her research, Saphah also read in amazement from another article about Hamas' attack in Israel on Saturday:

> [It] shines a glaring spotlight on the failures of the Biden
> administration's foreign policy. …What's alarming is the
> extent to which [the Iran and Hamas] alliance has been
> fueled by the Biden Administration's billions in aid to Iran. …
> and the recent reports that suggest that Iran has successfully
> placed agents of influence within the Biden administration.
> This is not just a breach of national security; it's a chilling
> testament to the level of Tehran's ambitions and a direct
> contributor to the emboldening of Iran and its proxies
> like Hamas.[18]

Research work on Saphah's computer revealed a shocking headline about spying in the capital: 'High-Level Iranian Spy Ring Busted in Washington: The trail that leads from Tehran to D.C. passes directly through the offices of Robert Malley and the International Crisis Group.'[19] *Well, I'm not really surprised,* she thought sadly. *America's government is chock-full of deceit just like Prophet Jeremiah suggested.* 'The Biden administration's now-suspended Iran envoy Robert Malley helped to fund, support, and direct an Iraniah intelligence operation designed to influence the United States and allied governments, according to a trove of purloined Iranian government emails.'[20]

Oh, my goodness! Saphah thought. *Now it looks like our 46th Commander in Chief, Joseph Robinette Biden, is implicated in assisting Israel's enemies. New political leadership in America is urgently needed—people from top to bottom who'll amend our foreign policy, purge out foreign influence, and stand firmly in support of allies, and especially Israel. If we fail to do so, the consequences will impact our globe far beyond the borders of Israel and Gaza, as this article points out:*

> As the crisis unfolds, Chinese Communist Party leader Xi Jinping is observing America's response closely. Any sign of American indecisiveness or weakness will be analyzed as a factor in China's own geopolitical calculations, particularly concerning Taiwan. In a world increasingly defined by great power competition, how America responds to Israel-Hamas crisis will resonate far beyond the Middle East.[21]

Saphah went on with her search and was disheartened by info titled: Israel's UN Ambassador Erdan Warns of US Terrorism:

> 'We Are on the Brink of a Catastrophe.' …On CNN's 'State of the Union,' Erdan emphasized the situation right now is shocking. We see thousands of people chanting, 'Death to Israel, death to the Jews.' We see Jewish students all across the United States on college campuses that are threatened not only by other students, [but] by their professors, and presidents of universities who cannot even condemn the terror attacks. …The ambassador stressed that 'if we accept the modus operandi of Hamas, Western civilization societies can never win and destroy terrorist organizations. It will inspire all terrorist organizations across the globe, because that's the way now they attack our democracies.'[22]

Saphah thought: *Goodness, it's no wonder God recently spoke to me, saying: 'I will bring down ruin upon thine habitation.' And that UN Ambassador Erdan Gilad warned about the possibility of terrorism coming to America, saying: 'We're a nation on the brink of catastrophe.' The reason is because, like he noted, terrorism is the 'Modus Operandi' of terrorist organizations. It's their kind of warfare, and they're likely planning to attack the United States.*

37

LEARNING TRUTH

Saphah racked her brain. How did this state of affairs happen? How did American universities become places where so many students are throughly antisemitic and against Christian principles? Then she found an article with answers:

> University campuses nationwide are under siege by students celebrating Hamas' attack against Israel on October 7. … [calling] for wiping Israel entirely off the map, [chanting] 'from the river to the sea'—a reference to the Mediterranean Sea and the Jordan River, with Israel in between. …How did American universities become places where so many students are viciously and passionately antisemitic and proudly stand with Hamas terrorists? When did it become acceptable to support terrorists beheading babies and murdering them in ovens, raping women and girls, and mass murdering civilians? The answer is simple and sobering: The radical left has taken over our universities and turned them into indoctrination camps.[1]

But how did all this begin? Saphah questioned. She continued reading the piece about Ted Cruise's new book, *Unwoke*, where he explains how Cultural Marxists have systematically taken over major U. S. instititions and educational facilities. It all started in the 1960s, she realized, when members of the New Left tried to uproot American society by tactics like lighting city blocks on fire and planting bombs in restaurants. But these extreme tactics caused public opinion to turn against them. Since the United States is different from nations like Russia, North Korea, China, or Vietnam, where violent communist overthrows are possible, the Leftists had to change approaches in their efforts to erode the values of America, the greatest nation on earth:

> Universities became hotbeds for terrorist sympathizers …[by
> shifting] to a new tactic: They would launch their revolution
> by slowly infiltrating the institutions that form the foundation
> of western society. Left-wing activists embarked on a mission
> to take over government, boardrooms, Hollywood, academia,
> and they have been effective. …At universities, Cultural
> Marxism has been able to metastasize with minimal outside
> scrutiny—until these past few weeks. Americans across the
> country are now shocked to find out just how radical those
> beliefs are. They are learning that college students have
> become so radicalized they chant slogans calling for the
> annihilation of Israel.[2]

Things like this happened in Nazi Germany. Saphah remembered what
had happened because she learned about it as a child in school, heard
about it from her dad—a World War II veteran, read about it in
magazines like Life and Look, and in books like *Anne Frank: The
Diary of a Young Girl. But*, Saphah thought, *I never thought a similar kind
of thing could happen in America. How terribly sad!*

She read aloud: "The despicable marches we are seeing on college
campuses represent the future of American society unless good and
decent people on both sides of the isle step up to stop it. …Even
more people need to confront this vile rhetoric, defeat the toxic
woke ideology indoctrinating students on college campuses, and
ensure that our country resembles the one we grew up in."[3]

How true, Saphah reflected. *The older generation in my land realizes we need
to support Israel.* Actor Jon Voight [age 84] expressed disgust in his
daughter Angelina Jolie's attacks on Israel. Voight responded to the
words of his daughter after she attacked Israel and accused the
country of turning Gaza into a 'mass grave':

> 'I am very disappointed that my daughter, like many others,
> has no understanding of the glory of God, of the truths

of God,' Voight said in a video he posted on his social media pages. 'The issue here is the destruction of the history of God's land, the Holy Land, the land of the Jews.'

He continued: 'The Israeli army has to protect the Land of Israel and its people - this is war. It will not be as the Left thinks it will be; it will not be cultural. Israel was attacked through inhumane terrorism [against] innocent children, mothers, fathers, grandparents. And you fools say that Israel is the problem? You need to look at yourselves and ask: 'Who am I? What am I?'

He also read in the video: 'Ask God: Am I learning the truth: Or am I being lied to and I do like everyone else?' - because friends, those who understand the truth see the lie. They see Israel was attacked, and these animals want to wipe out the Jews [and] Christianity.

'We all want justice and love, but this cannot happen with these animals, who want to wipe Jews and Christians off the face of the earth.' Voight continued in the video. 'It is a lie that Israel kills innocent people, but they all have the free will to leave. They are prisoners of the barbaric state that uses them as human protectors. The children on the land of Palestine are being exploited by these animals, to make everyone think that Israel is taking these lives - and this was actually the plan of Hamas. To create the war of good against evil.'[4]

It was like a light bulb lit up Saphah's brain: *While people like Jon Voight are standing up for truth, others, like our 44th and 46th presidents, aren't holding up for what is good and true. Hence, our nation is moving toward antisemitism and away from what is right. Our values are distorted, our country is destabilized, and our principles are moving away from God's truth. Things are moving fast, and we're soon going to reach a point of no return. But God sees, and He will move if things don't change. And, that's why we need reform now—rather than later!*

Saphah reiterated in her mind what actor Jon Voight had mentioned: *Voight asked if people today are 'learning truth.' But the sad fact is that some folks in my day and age seem unable to even define truth.* She shook her head in dismay. *Instead, they may say something like the following:*

"There is more than one truth. I have my truth, and you have your truth. But, the person over there has his or her truth."

But, that kind of talk only illustrates the fact they've forgotten the definition of truth. So, what does it take to learn truth and where can we find it?"

'Learning Truth'

In the Word of God, Jesus informs us: *I am the way and the truth and the life. No one comes to the Father except through me.*[5]

First, Jesus explained that he is 'the way.' A way is a path to a destination for which there is no other route to that place. Jesus is telling you and me to follow him since there is no other way to the Father: *Salvation is found in no one else, for there is no other name under heaven given to mankind by which we must be saved.*[6] *The exclusive nature of the only way to salvation is emphasized by Jesus' words 'I am the way.'*

Second, Jesus said, I am …*'the truth.'* Truth can be defined as the authoritative standard of righteousness for mankind from God. As the incarnate Word of God, Jesus is the author and source of truth. Regarding Jesus, scripture explains: *Your righteousness is everlasting and your law is true.*[7] It also notes, *In the beginning was the Word, and the Word was with God, and the Word was God.*[8] 'In the beginning' stresses the *eternality* of Jesus as God; 'The Word was with God' shows the *distinctiveness* of

Jesus as Son of the Father; and 'The Word was God' states his *deity*. The real truth is seen in Jesus' words 'I am the truth.'

Third, Jesus said, I am …'the life.' Jesus is the source of both physical and spiritual life. In the Book of John, Jesus gave the promise that because I live, you also will live.[9] Jesus was declaring himself as the great 'I am,' the true source of life everlasting. The reality of life without end is spotlighted by Jesus' words 'I am the life.' Jesus is the only 'path' to heaven, the only 'standard' of righteousness, and the only 'source' of physical and spiritual life. He is the God of Creation.

But how do we follow Jesus today? We follow Him the same way the disciples did long ago: We hear the words of Jesus, accept His words as truth, and obey them as the authoritative Word of God. We believe that He died to take the punishment for our sins and arose from the dead to give us new life. We confess our sins to Jesus and accept Him as our Lord and Savior. We follow his example and we tell others the truth about sin, righteousness, and judgment.

There is only one God, but the Godhead consists of three distinct persons—Father, Son, and Holy Spirit—and all are equally omniscient, omnipotent, omnipresent, eternal, and unchanging. But each member of the Godhead has a specific role.

God the Father designed a plan of how mankind would be redeemed: *But when the set time had fully come, God sent his Son, born of a woman, born under the law, that we might receive adoption to sonship.*[10] God the Son, carried out the plan by coming down to earth, *not to do my will, but to do the will of him who sent me.*[11] *For my Father's will is that everyone who looks to the Son and believes in him shall have eternal life, and I will raise them up on the last day.*[12] God the Spirit, administers the plan by being our Helper.

Jesus said that *the Advocate, the Holy Spirit, whom the Father will send in my name will teach you all things.*[13] He will transform the heart and lives of all those who receive salvation through Jesus Christ.

Thus, we learn truth from the source of truth, the Supreme Being—Father, Son, and Spirit—God Almighty, in all His nature and attributes.

38

HAUNTED FOREVER

The watchwoman was sound asleep. Suddently she felt warm drops of water falling on her face. *Is the roof leaking?* Saphah wondered. *But it has only been a few years since the roof was re-shingled.* She wiped off her skin with the palm of her hand and opened her eyes. *Oh my!* she thought in wonder. *I'm in the Aperture of Process and gentle showers are raining down on my head again.*

The American woman continued to twirl in the Aperture several times until her body slowly stopped swirling and her feet gradually settled to the ground at the gate to ancient Judah. The gate opened with its groaning sound and angel Nahal appeared.

 "Saphah, I'm so glad to see you again." Nahal's blue eyes twinkled as as he stood in the glow of the Aperture and graciously welcomed her back with a smile. "So how are you?"

"Oh, I'm fine, but the moral state of my world is declining fast."

"Please, Saphah, you must tell me about it, but why don't we get everything ready for your travels, and then we can talk as we walk?"

"Great! It'll be wonderful to have company while I walk." Saphah happily retorted before giving him a big frown. "But don't you need to guard the Aperture of Process?"

"Well, a different angel will be guarding the gate while I'm walking with you. He is talking with Malak right now, but he'll be here shortly. Right now, I just need to tell you about the food I've prepared for you. But since you've just arrived, I'm going to put the little fresh loaves, the hunk of cheese, and the raisin cakes into your satchel for later." Nahal placed everything in the backpack, gave Saphah her flask of water, and helped her strap her satchel back on. "Now, please inform me about the situation in your world."

Saphah tied the flask to her sash and turned to Nahal. "Alright. But I want to ask you something first. Since you're an angel, do you know about modern items like videos, cameras, electronic equipment, etc.?"

"Actually, I do." Nahal wanted to reassure Saphah he'd understand the concerns she was about to divulge. "The Lord filled me in on such matters before I met you. Of course, God is omniscient, so He was able to inform me about everything I needed to know."

"I'm so thankful, because I need to talk to someone about the events that happened in Israel. But would graphic descriptions of mankind's inhumanity to mankind be too much for you?"

"In the various assignments God has given me throughout history, I've observed many instances of man's inhumanity to man, so I think I can handle it. Now let's just travel toward Jerusalem, and we'll visit as we go." Nahal handed Saphah a lit lamp. "Now, please tell me more."

"A terrorist group called Hamas attacked Israel's citizens on October 7, 2003. It was unprovoked and their goal was to terrorize, murder, and kidnap Israelis. The entire globe is in a turmoil since it happened because the event threatens the peace of the whole world."

"So, are people worldwide supporting Israel?"

"Although some support Israel, others support Hamas, which carried out their attack on the citizenry of Israel in a barbaric and evil way. Here is a headline and story of recent news of what happened:

'Israel's Horrific Video of Hamas Atrocities Leaves Viewers Shocked and Sickened.' Fox [New's] Lawrence Jones spoke with individuals who watched Hamas footage of 'Repeating of Isis' to get their initial reaction to Hama's brutality.

Jones spoke about watching from Israel as the 43-minute film of footage of the Hamas terrorists' massacre [was shown worldwide]: 'The extreme, horrified reactions of Congress, the United Nations, and even Hollywood to the film—a compilation of body cameras worn by Hamas terrorists, dashcams, traffic cameras, closed-circuit TV, mobile phones, and social media accounts of victims, soldiers, and emergency medical workers—haven't surprised me. I will be haunted forever.'[1]

This is the nightmare Israelis have been living ...since Hamas and other Palestinian terrorists from the Gaza Strip infiltrated Israel on that Saturday morning—now referred to as 'Black Saturday'—attacking 20 civilian communities, army bases and a music festival. More than 1,200 people were murdered in the attack, and another 200-plus taken hostage, including nearly 40 children and a dozen mothers. Even the headiest of individuals struggle to stomach this compilation of horror.[2]

[A spokesman says] raw footage taken by the terrorists shows graphic images seen by diplomats, international organizations, influencers and decision makers at highest levels, shared by Israel in more than 60 of its embassies and consulates. It is a difficult film to watch. ...Not everyone can stay and watch the movie. I've seen people shocked to see such atrocities committed against human beings by monsters from Hamas.[3]

In Congress, footage was seen by about 300, reportedly including 'Squad' member Rep. Alexandria Ocasio Cortez. While she's been vocal with criticism of Israel, she doesn't seem to have made comment, but reactions from other Congress members were similar to when I saw it in Israel.[4]

'I've seen decapitation and I've seen just beating and beating on both dead and alive bodies,' said California Rep. Darrell Issa, who spoke with Fox News after watching footage. 'And, quite frankly, I'm just sick to my stomach.'[5]

New York Rep. Ritchie Torres who saw the film at a different screening, wrote on X, 'I find myself haunted by the cries of two children witnessing their father die from an explosion after a Hamas terrorist throws a grenade inside their shelter. Suffering the savagery of Hamas feels like a fate worse than death. The fatherless child is seen crying in agony 'Why am I still alive?'[6]

Indeed, that scene, captured on a family's private webcam, is particularly upsetting, but not the only stuff of nightmares. A selection of still photographs taken as forensic evidence shows unidentifiable human bodies, including babies in pajamas, beaten, burned and unimaginably mutilated, with evidence of gender-based crimes, which Fox News has detailed in previous stories.[7]

Equally horrific is footage taken from cellphones of victims who likely did not survive or were taken hostage, including a group of young female soldiers in a bomb shelter seconds before a gun-wielding terrorist walks calmly inside and begins shooting. In another clip, blood-dripping partygoers from the festival are seen blown to bits by the terrorist's grenades.[8]

Another aspect …is footage taken by terrorists themselves. Many who carried out the barbaric attack wore bodycams to document their atrocities. …In a particularly awful moment, a group of elderly people is gunned down and mutilated on the pavement next to their minibus. In another scene, we see a Hamas terrorist screaming 'Allahu Akhbar,' as he relentlessly hacks the head off a Thai laborer with a hatchel. Also, …we see snippets of exhilarated terrorists celebrating heinous acts, including joyous celebrations as they dragged decapitated bodies of Israeli soldiers and civilians through Gaza streets.[9]

In [a] journalist screening …the question of how humans could do this to other humans hung heavy in the air in an auditorium. …Maayan Hoffman, The Jerusalem Post's deputy CEO, who was at that screening told Fox News she believed more people should see the footage. 'It is important for more people to see the film because it's difficult to understand the barbaric behavior and the joy these terrorists had while they were hurting others. …It also gives us a better understanding of what victims and families of hostages suffered that day.'[10]

"Saphah, I see why you need to talk to someone about the atrocities." Nahal compassionately smiled at her and shook his head in sympathy. "The behavior of these terrorists is monstrous! I agree with Maayan Hoffman, that the film should be released to the public so people can see for themselves the crimes the cruel terrorists committed."

"I believe likewise. After the liberation of the Nazi concentration camps following World War II, American forces made the local German people tour the camps to see the crimes their own government had perpetrated. They also insisted officials, journalists, and others go to liberated camps to witness and document atrocities:

On April 4, 1945, the US 5th Armored Division and 89th Infantry Division of the Third US Army came upon horrors of Nazi brutality. They discovered Ohrdruf, a Nazi labor camp and subcamp of the Buchenwald system. …Ohrdruf was the first Nazi camp to be liberated by US forces. On April 12, Generals Dwight D. Eisenhower, George S. Patton, and Omar Bradley toured the site. …German citizens from Ohrdruf were forced to view the camp and bury the dead, a practice that was later repeated in other camp liberations.[11]

> Afterwards, Eisenhower …cabled General George C.
> Marshall, head of joint Chiefs of Staff, Washington D.C.
> requesting members of Congress and journalists be sent to
> liberated camps to witness and document horrific scenes US
> troops were uncovering. The liberation of Ohrdruf opened
> the eyes of Americans, soldiers and civilians, to the barbaric
> conditions innocent people faced under Nazism, including
> Dora-Mittelbau, Dachau, Mauthausen, and Buchenwald. …
> As more camps were uncovered by Allied forces, it became
> evident that the Third Reich had committed unprecedented
> atrocities everywhere the regime had reigned.[12]

> Following the discovery of Ohrdruf, Eisenhower stated: 'We
> are told the American soldier doesn't know what he is
> fighting for. Now, at least we know what he's fighting
> against.[13]

"Yes, evil must be fought wherever it is found and Eisenhower knew
that truth. Saphah, would you share more about the atrocities?"

"Yes, Nahal, I'd be glad to. I've been so disturbed about the cruel
things done to the Israelites and especially the women, children, and
elderly. So, it really helps to be able to speak about it to you."

"Here, let's both sit down for awhile on this ledge as you
share more about these crimes against humanity." Nahal patted the
outcropping and then they both sat down with their legs stretched
out in front. "Now, Saphah, please continue."

"Alright. It's painful to consider what they endured, but here is more
of what the Israeli people experienced. Nahal, it's graphic:

> Two short videos …emerged showing groups of cheering
> Palestinian men, …around half-naked and bloodied young
> Israeli women. In one clip, a woman later identified as

German-Israeli citizen Shani Louk, 22, is seen barely clothed lying unconscious in an unnatural position on a pickup flatbed. In another video, 19-year-old Israeli soldier Na'ama Levy is pulled from a jeep by an armed gunman, hands bound behind her and thick blood stains between her legs, as Palestinian men jeer. Louk is counted among the 1,200 people murdered that day and Levy is thought to be one of 240 hostages, including babies and children, held by the terror group[4]

[An eye] witness, identified only by the initial 'S,' recounted that while she was hiding from the terrorists, she saw a group pass a woman with long brown hair among them. 'S' then described how one terrorist sliced off the woman's breast and began playing around with it. Another, the witness said, shot the woman in the head while still penetrating her. 'He did not even lift up his pants and shot her in the head,' 'S' said, adding she spied another terrorist haul a naked woman over his shoulder and walk off. Another cut off someone's head and was walking around with it like a trophy.[15]

Videotaped interrogations of some captured terrorists show them confessing they had orders to murder, rape and kidnap Israeli civilians. One suspect told Israeli interrogators he and his men received religious permission to kill children 'because they'll grow up to be soldiers' and decapitate 'to sow fear among the Israelis.'[16]

First responders from Israeli military and civilian services described in detail the disturbing brutality and atrocities carried out by estimated 3,000 Hamas and other Palestinian terrorists who entered Israel October 7. … In [one] case, a soldier from the army's special forces sent to search for survivors on a kibbutz told a media outlet he found dead bodies of two young girls together in one room. There was a teenage girl, 14 or 15, lying on the floor, on her stomach, her pants covered in blood. 'It was like a slap in the face,' the soldier said. 'It was the first time I realized we are not acting against terrorists here, we are acting against savages.'[17]

Elkayam-Levy, legal expert from Hebrew University noted, 'We established a commission …as more and more evidence of gruesome crimes against women and children emerged.' She said that though some Hamas' crimes …'showed clear violations of international law and brutal crimes committed against women and children,' there was little international condemnation. Therefore, we took it upon ourselves to call for recognition and action.[18]

"Thankfully, they're calling for an accounting!" Nahal commended the fact that a commission had been established. "There may be little international condemnation, but God knows about and condemns these crimes against humanity. In the meantime, I'm glad legal experts are planning to bring this to the attention of the international community."

"Me, too." Saphah said. "And I'm also going to write about this in my book because more people need to know. Nahal, I want to ask you something else. When I first met you and Malak here in the cave, you informed me that as I travel back and forth between America and Judah, I could ask you or Malak questions as I pass through on my way. Is that still the case?"

"Certainly, you may ask Malak and myself any questions you wish."

39

I Desire Worship, Not Conflagration

Saphah said, "Nahal, I've received two more messages from the Lord for America. In the first message for my nation, the Lord said: 'I will bring down ruin upon thine habitation, thus saith the Lord.' Then in the second, the Lord elaborated: 'Look to the East, look to the West, your nation will be cut off. There will be pillaging and destruction, and the land will be laid bare. Upon these ruins I will rebuild my church and the glory of the Lord will reign there. I will rebuild my church and no one will stop me. You have my solemn word.' Previously I'd talked about these messages when I was in Jerusalem. Then God gave me another message when I was back in America, saying:

"I desire worship, not conflagration."

"That sentence was the entirety of God's recent message. So, I researched conflagration on Merriam Webster's website where one definition of the word is: 'conflict/war.'[1] But the website also gave an example of the word in a sentence, which read: 'With the Middle East primed for a *conflagration*, American policy-makers must recognize two realities.' The source for the sentence was an online article in National Review, where I found the original source titled, 'It's Looking Like the 1930s,' which likened what happened before World War II with what's now happening in my world: 'Russia, China, and Iran have forged an entente with clear resemblance to the Axis of the mid-20th century.'[2] Germany's invasion into Poland on September 1, 1939, began World War II. But now, the article says that present-day circumstances in the world resemble the pre-war scenario of the 1930s."

"Therefore, since I've received a new message, I've interpreted that to mean that in my role as a watchwoman, I'm to share the message with my fellow citizens quickly. So, I plan to make my stay in Judah brief and to return to the U. S. to finish and publish my book as soon as I can. But Nahal, would you please answer some questions?"

"Of course, I'll be pleased to answer your questions."

"Well, I know that according to Old Testament history, God judged or disciplined many different nations in the past. But, does the bible confirm that God might also discipline individual nations in my era?"

"Saphah, I know it seems like a new idea that God is planning to discipline America, but God's plan regarding your nation really isn't anything new. God has been disciplining nations throughout history."

"Nahal, would you please give me more from scripture about what happened to nations that turned away from God."

"God makes it clear in scripture that he judges or disciplines people, whether individuals, cities, or nations. In Genesis, the biblical record says that God pronounced judgment, not only on Adam and Eve, but also on the entire human race by virtue of the sinful inclinations they all share. But God also judges groups such as cities and nations according to how they honor or dishonor Him. So, the bible says that God placed judgments on numerous city states or countries."

Saphah reached into her backpack, pulled out her bible, and flipped through some pages in Genesis. "Early in Genesis it says that God judged the entire human race of that time with a worldwide flood due to mankind's rebellion against God. In one of the most vivid descriptions of total depravity, scripture says:

> *The Lord saw how great the wickedness of the human race had become on the earth and that every inclination of the thoughts of the human*

heart was only evil all the time. …So, the Lord said, 'I will wipe from the face of the earth the human race I have created—and with them the animals, the birds and the creatures that move along the ground—for I regret that I have made them.' But Noah found favor in the eyes of the Lord.[3]

So, God destroyed mankind and began fresh with Noah and family."

"That's right," Nahal said. "But then the Lord also destroyed two cities, Sodom and Gomorrah, for their wickedness and evil doing."

Saphah flipped through Genesis again. "Well, here it says: *The people of Sodom were wicked and were sinning greatly against the Lord. …then the Lord rained down burning sulfur on Sodom and Gomorrah—from the Lord out of the heavens. Thus, he overthrew those cities and the entire plain, destroying all those living in the cities—and also the vegetation in the land,*[4] So, the Lord completely demolished the two cities plus every bit of vegetation growing there, but left Lot and his daughters alive."

"But what happened in Nineveh when God sent Jonah there?"

"Prophet Jeremiah and I talked about this earlier." Saphah turned pages to the passage. "The introduction says that 'in this story of God's loving concern for all people, Nineveh … is representative of the Gentiles. …Thus, the book depicts the larger scope of God's purpose for Israel: that she might rediscover the truth of his concern for the whole creation and better understand her own role in carrying out that concern.'[5]

Well, here scripture reveals that the Lord was attempting to send the Jewish Prophet Jonah to the Gentile city of Nineveh with a warning to repent or be destroyed. However, the recalcitrant Prophet didn't want any part of helping to save Gentiles. Nevertheless, after being swallowed by a fish and almost losing his own life, Prophet Jonah decided to do it God's way: *Jonah began by going a day's journey proclaiming, 'forty more days and Nineveh will be overthrown.' The Ninevites believed God.*[6] Nahal, did you hear that? Wonder of wonders, the Ninevites believed God's message as delivered by the Prophet Jonah!"

"Yes, praise God! Saphah, this is an example of a city that received a message from God telling them to repent, and they believed God!"

"How wonderful! So, Nineveh is a city that heeded God's warning to repent, and therefore the Lord did not destroy them."

"Although the Lord is a God of justice, He is always fair," Nahal pointed out. "And that's why His warnings precede his discipline or judgment. But God's warnings don't always avert His judgment, because sometimes people fail to pay attention to His warnings. There are many examples in scripture of nations and cities failing to heed God's warnings to repent."

"In Jeremiah's book of the bible this is spoken of in hindsight after Judah's downfall. I think I know where to find it." Saphah searched her bible. "Here is the word of God which came to Jeremiah: *Again and again I sent my servants the prophets, who said, 'Do not do this detestable thing that I hate.' But they did not listen or pay attention; they did not turn from their wickedness or stop burning incense to other gods. Therefore, my fierce anger was poured out.*[7] And there are other passages that speak of the Lord's warnings to various cities or nations that they were in danger of judgment, yet they didn't believe God."

"I've been told that an attentive search of the Holy Bible will reveal a long list. But in the New Testament, Jesus himself foretold He would judge the Jewish nation for their unrighteousness, and it happened in 70 AD. Saphah would you please read that for me?"

"Yes, here is Luke's account: Jesus said, '*As for what you see here* [the adornment of the temple], *the time will come when not one stone will be left on another; every one of them will be thrown down.*[8] And historically this aligns well with Jesus' statement because it was 'fulfilled in AD 70 when the Romans took Jerusalem and burned the temple.'[9] Also, 'the Romans under Titus destroyed Jerusalem and the temple buildings. Stones were even pried apart to collect the gold leaf that melted from the roof when the temple was set on fire. …excavations in 1968 uncovered large numbers of these stones, toppled from the walls.'"[10]

"Jesus also foretold the Jewish genocide at the hands of Rome:

> *Jesus turned and said to them* [women followers], *Daughters of Jerusalem, do not weep for me; weep for yourselves and for your children. For I say the time will come when you will say, 'Blessed are the childless women, the wombs that never bore and the breasts that never nursed.' They will say to the mountains, 'Fall on us,' and the hills, 'Cover us.'*[11]

It seems 'the most reasonable interpretation is that the genocide and destruction of the temple were prophecies fulfilled in AD 70.'[12] Jesus foretold that Jerusalem, the temple, and the jews would all fall and they did in AD 70. This reveals that God has judged or disciplined nations in both Old and New Testament times. Thus, if God were to discipline the U. S., that wouldn't be contrary to biblical teachings."

"That's correct. Again, just remember that God always warns before He disciplines. So those who fail to heed divine warnings can only blame themselves. Saphah, do you remember what Ezekiel said?"

"I do. Here is the word of the Lord which came to Ezekiel:

> *Son of man, speak to your people and say to them: 'When I bring the sword against a land, and the people of the land choose one of their men and make him their watchman, and he sees the sword coming against the land and blows the trumpet to warn the people, then if anyone hears the trumpet but does not heed the warning and the sword comes and takes their life, their blood will be on their own head. If they had heeded the warning, they would have saved themselves.*[13]

On the other hand," Saphah continued "the next verse points out that *if the watchman sees the sword coming and does not blow the trumpet to warn the people and the sword comes and takes someone's life, that person's life will be taken because of their sin, but I will hold the watchman accountable for their blood.*[14] Nahal, I think I'm definitely responsible to warn my fellow countrymen/women that danger is near. Right?"

"Right." Nahal shook his head in agreement. "When God is planning to discipline a nation or nations, He may use certain people to fore-tell coming disaster for multiple timeframes of history. For example, Zephaniah in his prophecies seemed to speak to the citizens of Judah and other nations living in one timeframe, to those of America living in another, and to the people of the entire world living in the time of the end."

"So, Zephaniah, Jeremiah, Huldah, Ezekiel, and other prophets or watchpersons are all examples of those who forewarned people in Old Testament times," Saphah said. "But sometimes they also warned people of future generations and especially the generation living just before the second return of Christ. They all foretold coming disaster upon a nation or nations as revealed to them by God for the people."

"Correct. However, in New Testament times, including your era, God wants watchpersons in your time and place to do the same thing. You're to warn the citizens of the U. S. of their need for repentance before God's hand of discipline falls on your nation. But keep this in mind, sometimes God gives prophets or watchpersons additional roles. For example, although both Jeremiah and Ezekiel each received spiritual training for the priesthood, God also called both of them to be prophets. Huldah likewise received spiritual training to be a morah (female spiritual teacher), but God called her to be a prophetess too. Ezekiel was also called to a be watchperson, as were you, Saphah. So, here's what you should do in your era."

"Watchwoman Saphah, you've been called to warn your citizens of coming danger by figuratively blowing your shofar to proclaim either negative or positive messages from God to your people. But you're also to deliver spiritual truth from God's Word to them, such as Morah Huldah delivered to her people, by quoting scripture."

"So, my role in the New Testament era is similar to that of those who were called by God to deliver messages in Old Testament times?"

"Yes, you're similar in some ways and different in others."

"Alright, let's begin walking again, and we can talk as we go."

The two continued walking in the cave. "Nahal, here is a question. From what we just discussed, we know that when the Jewish nation reached the zenith of its rebellion, God sent the Romans in 70 AD to destroy Jerusalem and many of the Jews. And, according to historian, Josephus, more than a million were slain and thousands were made slaves. But does the New Testament say God is still working to raise up and overthrow powers, consistent with his will for mankind?"

"In the New Testament, the apostle Paul contends that God is still working in this way. Saphah, let me hold your lamp so you can read from Acts 17 on this subject. It's right after the verse about God giving everyone life and breath and everything else."

"Alright." Saphah opened her bible again, and Nahal held the lamp over it so she could see. "Here it reads that *from one man God made all the nations, that they should inhabit the whole earth; and he marked out their appointed times in history and the boundaries of their lands.*[15] Oh, wow! The commentary on this verse, referring to the fact that God 'marked out their appointed times,' says that God 'planned the exact times when nations should emerge and decline,' and the 'boundaries of their lands.'[16] Thus, the orchestration of God's providence of international history is revealed in this verse."

"So, the principle still prevails that God can discipline nations today."

"Well, now that the Holy Spirit has helped us to figure that one out, would you please answer my last question? What do you think God meant when He said: 'I desire worship, not conflagration?'"

"The meaning of 'I desire worship, not conflagration' is the Lord loves the citizens of America, but He desires reciprocation of that love and affection in return. The United States has a long history of being a Christian nation devoted to God, but recently evil forces have entered your culture and God has been left out."

"Yes, God has been left out of much present-day culture in America. So, when scripture says—*Blessed is the people whose God is the Lord, there will be no breaching of walls, no going into captivity, no cry of distress in our streets.*[17]—that passage rings untrue for the U. S. at the present time."

"Saphah, that seems to be the case. Wickedness has ensnared your country like a boa constrictor and won't release its grip. In fact, evil is so pernicious in some areas of your nation, especially your big cities, that something urgently needs to be done to stop the decline. If not, your nation will quickly reach the point of no return. Much prayer and reform are needed to put on the brakes and to postpone the inevitable. God Himself doesn't want war to come against 'the land of the free and the home of the brave,' but unless there's revival and reform, he'll have no choice. And that means conflagration—war! God will winnow America by allowing foreigners to invade your country. It's not too late—yet. But soon it will be."

"In other words, God's desire for my people is that they worship him in spirit and in truth. He desires worship, not conflagration, but war may be necessary to refine America."

"Well, it says in scripture that *God disciplines those He loves, just as a father, the son he delights in.*[18] The writer of Proverbs recognizes that as children need discipline from their father or mother, people likewise need discipline by God their Father."

"But, Nahal, if I tell people God disciplines, 'just as a father,' there are those who'll question the love of God. Some will ask: 'If God is so loving, why would he judge or discipline a nation by sending war?' People like that struggle to reconcile a loving God with one who judges His own people."

"Before people cast God into the role of an angry disciplinarian, they should begin by asking, 'Who is God?' Their understanding of God's judgment should be grounded in the attributes of who He is. You've already set forth God's attributes in your previous chapter. And, God is all those attributes and more, all the time. But we must separate God's actions from His attributes. Are judgment and wrath a part of God's attributes?"

"Of course not. They're actions or responses born of His character."

"You're right. In the face of injustice and evil deeds, a just God casts judgment. Confronted by the unholiness of sin, the Lord must respond in the holiness of justice. Judgment is the necessary response of a holy God to the injustices and sins of a fallen world."

"In other words, when God is faced with extreme sin, he responds with extreme punishment. He doesn't just give us a slap on the wrist. Faced with the wreckage of human evil, God responds in kind."

"True, but through it all, He offers mercy. He is a God gracious and just. He judges evil even while offering mercy to the perpetrator."

"God offers a perfect blend of love and justice by the death of Jesus on the cross. His judgment for mankind's sin came down on Himself in the person of Jesus Christ who was condemned so we might have eternal life. But through it all He tenderly calls his people to himself."

"And there is the answer to the question you asked, Saphah. God isn't wielding his justice as some kind of punishment, but as an invitation. God's purpose in discipline is grace and reconciliation, not revenge or destruction. He 'desires worship, not conflagration.'"

"And that is why the Lord says: *Those whom I love I rebuke and discipline. So be earnest and repent. Here I am! I stand at the door and knock. If anyone hears my voice and opens the door, I will come in and eat with that person, and they with me.*[19] Here is a picture of Christ knocking on the door of an unbeliever's heart. Also, the Lord says: *To the one who is victorious, I will give the right to eat from the tree of life, which is in the paradise of God.*[20] In the battle against evil, the challenge is to be victorious, to win the battle, and to enter the eschatological state in which God and believers are restored to the state of fellowship that existed before sin entered the world."

"Yes, I agree!"

"Well, Saphah, we've getting close to the area where a wall divides the cave from the Gihon Spring and Hezekiah Tunnel area. So, I think I should tell you that you'll be entering Jerusalem in a later timeframe. You can catch up on details of what happened while you were gone by hearing the accounts of Huldah and others who lived through it. Alright then, Saphah, I'm going to take my leave now and return back to guard the Aperture of Process. I wish you well in the final leg of your journey and I look forward to seeing you again."

"Thank you so much, Nahal, and I too look forward to seeing you again soon."

40

JOSIAH'S REFORMS

Saphah knew she was near the Pool of Siloam. She'd already passed the inscription on the wall which described construction of the Hezekiah Tunnel. Turning the last bend in the tunnel before the Siloam Pool, she suddenly stopped and listened. *What's that muffled sound from afar?* She intently listened again. *Boom, boom, boom* came the faint, rhythmical noise. Continuing to walk forward, Saphah heard two women talking nearby as they filled their jars with water. The watchwoman stopped and focused her eyes on the women and their dog at the far end of the pool. *That looks like Hannah's greyhound, Lady,* Saphah thought, *but I don't see Hannah anywhere.*

The two women, perhaps a mother and her daughter, both stared intently at the watchwoman as if startled by her sudden appearance. Saphah decided to speak up to calm their concerns. "Good morning, ladies. I'm a traveler from the United States here to visit Jerusalem."

"Oh!" The middle-aged woman's mouth gapped open as she turned to the girl who looked to be near twenty. "I think that's the American watchwoman I told you about." She returned her gaze to the visitor. "Saphah, is that you?"

"Yes, but who're you?"

"Saphah, I'm so glad to see you. It's me, Eve. But, guess who this is?" Eve put her arm around a dark-haired girl.

"Oh, my goodness, Eve, I'm thrilled to see you too! But I don't think I know your young friend."

"Do you remember the gift God gave me at Topheth?"

"Well—yes." The wheels started turning in Saphah's brain. "Oh, my goodness, but this couldn't be Mattea?"

"Yes, it's my daughter Mattea that you helped rescue, and she's all grown up now. But where have you been all this time?"

"Oh, Eve, only a few months have passed in my world since I've been gone. Angel Nahal in the cave told me I'd be entering Jerusalem in a later time frame, but I didn't realize it'd be years later." Saphah quickly waded across the pool and ascended the steps toward the two. Eve introduced Mattea to Saphah, and they all exchanged hugs.

"Saphah you look wonderful! You haven't changed at all."

"But Eve, you're so thin. Have you been sick?" Saphah noticed that both Eve and Mattea's arms looked bony. "Are you two alright?"

"No, we're not," Eve lamented as both shook their heads. "Jerusalem has been under siege for so long the food supply is low. People like me who work for the king receive some rations daily from the palace storeroom, but other poor souls don't have much food left to eat."

"Please tell me about it."

"Saphah, we can't talk now. It's dangerous to even be out on the streets. But it's Mattea's turn to fetch water for Huldah's household where she lives, so I came from the palace to escort her and brought this dog for protection. We need to go now, but we can talk later."

Boom, boom, boom continued the rhythmic sound, but now louder. Two unsavory men appeared around a corner on the descent to the pool. "Yes, let's go," Saphah agreed. But then some women also descended the steps, serving to relieve Saphah's anxiety.

Reaching the landing, the three immediately broke into a brisk walk toward Huldah's residence. A small number of other people were also out, with everyone in a hurry to reach their destinations. A woman and boy had stopped to glance in different directions as if to locate someone following them. But then the two abruptly set out on a side street. *The atmosphere of this place is totally different from when I first visited here. There is definitely a palpable mood of fear in the air. And what is that horrible smell? I've never smelled anything quite like that before.* Saphah involuntarily shuddered. *Something is terribly wrong in this place, but what is it?* She heard a scream. "Shouldn't we investigate to see if someone needs help?"

"No, Saphah, in our current environment it's better for a man to check out such matters. Hurry, we're almost to Huldah's quarters."

"But what is that repeating *boom, boom, boom* that I hear?" Saphah jumped in fear as a person ran up beside her and wrapped an arm around her shoulder from the side. "Help!" She spontaneously yelled before turning to see who it was. "Oh, Hannah, you almost scared me to death! I'm shaking like a leaf!"

"Saphah, is that really you! I didn't mean to frighten you!" Hannah put both arms around the woman and hugged her close. "We've been to the palace to see Ebed, but then I saw you. I'm so glad to see you!"

"I'm glad to see you too!" Saphah stared up and down at her. "My goodness, Hannah, you're expecting a baby. Are you doing alright?"

"Yes, thanks to Ebed bringing extra food for me from the palace, I'm doing fairly well. But now I want to introduce you to someone. Saphah, this is my sweet daughter, Anna."

"Anna, what a pleasant surprise," Saphah hugged the ebony girl who was an exact image of her mother. Then she saw the dog Anna held by a leash. "Hannah, is this your greyhound named Lady?"

"No," Hannah replied, "it's Lady's granddaughter named Lily."

"Well, she's a beauty." Saphah petted Lily's head. "How is Ebed?"

"He is doing great and excited about our new baby who is due soon."

"Hurry everyone," Rebecca yelled from the gate.

"Yes, quit talking and get yourselves in here right now," Huldah said.

Saphah covered the distance in a run to Huldah's outstretched arms, and Eve closed and securely locked the gate. "Let me take a look at you, dear." The matron put a hand on each of her shoulders, looked her up and down, and then gave her a big hug. "You look just great!"

"Yes, she does." Rebecca hugged Saphah too. "I'm happy to see you!"

"I'm happy to see all of you too!" They began walking to the living area. "Oh, your court looks nice," Saphah noticed everything had grown, including several trees. "You even have shade trees out here."

"When Ebed planted the trees, I didn't realize what a life-saver they'd be. We harvest crops from these fig and nut trees every year. Produce from them has been our main source of food to keep us alive."

"Please tell me more about the food shortage in Jerusalem."

Huldah held an arm around the watchwoman as they continued walking side by side to the door. "Jerusalem is under siege, my dear, so everyone here is lacking food, but it's worse for some than for others. We've all lost weight, but we're doing alright because Shallum and Ebed work at the palace, so they can bring home rations for us." The matron tried to reassure Saphah of the well-being of the group. "Come on inside where it's warm, and we'll get reacquainted."

Rebecca gave their guest another hug. "Are you alright, Saphah. You're shaking."

"I'm feeling stressed because everything seems different here now."

"Yes, things have changed, and we'll tell you all about it later." As the ladies all piled inside and closed the door, the traveler breathed a huge sigh of relief. Then she spied an extremely beautiful lady sitting on a cushion near the fire.

"Who's this?"

"Saphah," Huldah said, "I want to introduce you to someone very special. This is Yafa, the wife of Ezekiel, who is training to become a priest. But this lady recently completed her training to be a midwife. Ezekiel doesn't want her to be alone at home while he's gone each day, so he brings her here."

The lady arose and walked toward Saphah. "I'm so pleased to meet you, Yafa." Saphah grasped her hand with one of her own. "It's wonderful you've received training to be a midwife. And, I've heard a lot about your husband too."

"Well, I've also heard a great deal about you, Saphah," Yafa retorted. "And, I'm glad I'm getting to meet you now."

Alright, ladies," Huldah said. "Please sit down on a cushion, make yourselves comfortable, and then we can talk. Rebecca, would you please assist me in getting some hot tea poured for everyone."

Eve entered the conversation. "Huldah and Rebecca, please don't fix tea for us, because we're returning to the palace. Mattea is going back with me so we can spend family time with Jonathan this evening."

"Oh, how wonderful. How is Jonathan?" Saphah asked.

"He is doing fine. We're both still working in the palace kitchen, but during the siege food is in short supply, so now we're preparing just one scant meal a day. Therefore, both of us have the remainder of the day off, so we want to spend the time with our daughter."

Mattea turned toward Saphah. "I'm so glad I finally got to meet you. Mother is planning to bring me back tomorrow, so I look forward to visiting with you then."

"I also look forward to talking to both of you."

"As do I," Eve said as she gave Saphah a goodbye hug. "Mattea, we must leave now to get back to the palace before it gets late."

"Yes," Huldah agreed. "I'm glad you have Lily with you. Now, both of you take care, and God willing, we'll see you tomorrow."

"Yes everyone, we'll see you tomorrow, God willing."

Rebecca served the tea, then she sat down on a cushion with Saphah and began a conversation. "American friend, we've really missed you, and we're so glad you're back. Much has happened in our ancient land since you've been gone, so we want to fill you in on details, but first, please tell us about your return home. Do you have family?"

"Yes, I do. I'm a wife, mother, mother-in-law, and grandma to three grandsons. In addition, I'm a doting mom figure to our mixed greyhound/labrador. However, while I was away visiting your world, time didn't pass back home, so my family didn't even know I was gone. When I came here the first time, the angel Nahal informed me time wouldn't pass in my world while I was away. He was right too, because that's what happened! However, I did catch up on my book."

"Well, I'm happy you got caught up on your writing. But now, please tell us more about conditions back in your modern world."

"The spiritual condition in the U. S. has deteriorated. I won't go into detail, except to say apostasy has increased, the incidence of wars and rumors of wars has escalated, and antisemitism has proliferated. It is for these and other reasons God has revealed to me His plan to 'bring down ruin' upon America by temporal warfare. In other words, at a future time America will be attacked by enemies."

"Later," Saphah continued, "God also revealed to me the following: 'I desire worship, not conflagration.' For me as a watchperson, that means God not only wants me to warn folks in advance of his plan to bring down ruin on apostate America, but also to inform them postponement is possible, because the God of the Universe desires worship, not war. Simply put, sincere repentance and contrite worship will postpone war but only as people remain faithful to God."

The watchwoman finished, "Since Josiah's reforms in your age are meant to provide an opportunity for repentance to occur in your land and to forestall judgment, I'm anxious to learn about the events that will provide the reprieve. Therefore, I'm looking forward to hearing a brief recap of Josiah's reforms. So, I think all I need is a summary of the happenings and a briefing of the applications."

"Saphah, I think you're right," Rebecca concurred. "I don't see any need for wordy explanations. What do you think, Huldah?"

"I agree. Rebecca and Hannah, I'll rely on you two to lay out the main highlights of early reforms since you were present. But I'll speak to the dual application of reforms as they apply to Judah and America."

Hannah turned to Yafa and Anna. "What would you young ladies like to do while we older adults have our discussion?"

Anna shot a questioning look at Yafa. "What should we do?"

"Well, maybe we could sew or embroider or paint?"

"Mother, would you mind if Yafa and I each made a dish towel to embroider? I think enough white cloth is left for us to make two."

"Good idea. You might check the amount of embroidery thread left in different hues. Then you could each pick out the pattern to use by considering the amount left of the various colors."

"Oh, I'd love to make a nice embroidered towel like that," said Yafa.

"Alright," Hannah said. "That will be a productive use of your time."

"C'mon Yafa, let's go pick everything out," Anna said. "And then we can sit in here to work while we listen to them talk over ancient and modern events in our parallel worlds, as they refer to it."

"Great idea," said Yafa, "I'd really like to hear their conversations to be better prepared to discuss it later with Zeke."

Rebecca began her account on reforms in Judah. "Saphah, after you left, it took six years for King Josiah to complete early reforms. He knew what to do because my clan, the Rechabites, had memorized scripture and passed it on to him orally. He destroyed altars used for worship of false gods, burned human bones to desecrate them, and got rid of sacred poles, graven images, molten statues and so forth."

"Saphah," Hannah said, "The king's efforts extended from Judah to the former ten-tribe kingdom of the northern region desolated by the conquest of the Assyrians and the subsequent exile It happened *in the towns of Manasseh, Ephraim and Simeon, as far as Naphtali, and in the ruins around them,* [where] *he tore down the altars and the Asherah poles and crushed the idols to powder and cut to pieces all the incense altars throughout Israel. Then he went back to Jerusalem.*"[1]

"Well, it is admirable that King Josiah and group were able to do early reforms all the way up to the former ten-tribe kingdom!" Suddenly she had an idea. "I think I'll get my writing gear so I can make notes on Josiah's efforts point by point. Alright, here's the first one:

> Point 1: Reforms can take much effort and time. So don't get discouraged but stick to the plan by consulting God's Word and getting guidance from Him through prayer. Remember that reforms needed in modern America may differ from those needed in Judah. Thus, adjust your reforms to meet the requirements of your own era.

"Saphah, I think it's a good idea to write down points," Hannah said. "I'm pleased to tell you we ladies continued to assist in the mission. The Rechabite camp traveled along with King Josiah's camp to assist in the campaign. I gave birth to Anna there and Miriam delivered her baby Mary about the same time. It was great to be at the camp, along with Ebed's family, and for him to join Anna and me at times. Miriam did a great job caring for the babies so we women could continue to help. Of course, all the destruction, the grinding and crushing of the idols, altars, and high places, was done by the men."

> Point 2: Any capable person can help with reforms, whether young or old, male or female. The main requirements for spiritual work of this type are fidelity to God, allegiance to His cause, and dedication to His will. Other workers can join the cause by giving assistance to those on the front lines through practical support, financial aid, and fervent prayer.

"We all think Zephaniah and Jeremiah had positive influences on King Josiah's actions," Prophet Huldah said. "Because of their strong denunciations of idolatry and their pronouncements of doom for Judah unless reforms occurred, Josiah was made aware of the need to purge idolatry. Josiah's battle against idolatry should resonate with the people of all times. Throughout history, the nature of idols may differ, but the human drive to worship that which isn't divine endures in all times. The willingness of Josiah to serve God's cause in his opposition to the worship of idols should be an inspiration to leaders in all places of habitation and all eras of time."

> Point 3: Good spiritual leaders can influence secular leaders such as those in federal and state governments. When he was alive, Reverend Billy Graham was a spiritual leader who influenced our presidents and other government officials. It is vital to the well-being of our nation that godly leadership be made available to advise those who lead our government.

"Here is what happened after Josiah's return to Jerusalem," Rebecca said. "After all that grueling work of destroying idolatry in Judah and the former northern kingdom of Israel, King Josiah began a clean-up and repair campaign on the temple. At that time, High Priest Hilkiah found a *Book of the Law of the Lord that had been given through Moses,*[2] which was possibly the original copy. *Shaphan the secretary informed the king, 'Hilkiah the priest has given me a book.' And Shaphan read from it in the presence of the king. When the king heard the words of the Law, he tore his robes*[3] in alarm and distress."

> Point 4: America's leaders need to stay in God's Word, because deviance from His will is what got Judah into trouble. The Book of the Law became lost in Judah, so the leaders just before Josiah's time didn't follow the law. King Josiah was pleased the Rechabites, who memorized parts of God's Law, could orally share it with him. However, the Holy Bible, God's complete revelation to mankind, is abundantly available in America. Yet our leaders often fail to consult or follow it. It is of utmost importance our people elect leaders who consult the Bible and follow its principles.

"Saphah," Hannah said, "Eve reported to us that she could hear the commotion Josiah was making that day all the way in the kitchen where she was cooking. She said Josiah was so upset when he heard the words of the Law, he didn't even eat the food they'd prepared.

Instead, he sent a delegation to *'go and inquire of the Lord for me and for the remnant in Israel and Judah about what is written in this book that has been found.'*[4] Basically, Josiah was so upset because he realized the intensity of the Lord's anger against Judah, since *those who have gone before us have not kept the word of the Lord; they have not acted in accordance with all that is written in this book.'*[5]

> Point 5: Josiah took God's will seriously and realized the kings before him had not acted in accordance with God's Law. American leaders need to take seriously God's will for our country before it's too late!

"When the delegation brought me a copy of the Law," Huldah explained, "God revealed to me that the material I received was the Book of the Law of the Lord. And, I told them to tell Josiah:

> *'This is what the Lord says: I am going to bring disaster on this place and its people—all the curses written in the book that has been read in the presence of the king of Judah. Because they have forsaken me and burned incense to other gods and aroused my anger by all that their hands have made, my anger will be poured out on this place and will not be quenched.'*[6]

However, I also told them to tell Josiah, as God revealed to me, that since he was humble and repentant, he would die and *be buried in peace before the disaster God was going to bring on this place and on those who live here.'*[7]

> Point 6: When Huldah told Josiah God was 'going to bring disaster on this place and its people,' Josiah took it to heart. The leaders of government in America need to remember our God, the Creator of the Universe, is still in power and can discipline nations who greatly displease Him. They also need to remember that 'to whom much is given, much is required.'

"Huldah," Saphah added, "you might be interested to learn that my bible commentary refers to Josiah being 'buried in peace,' and it says:

> [Prophetess Huldah's] 'prediction refers to Josiah's death before God's judgment on Jerusalem by Nebuchadnezzar and so is not contradicted by his [earlier in history] death in battle with Pharoah Necho of Egypt. [Therefore], Josiah was assured that the final judgment on Judah and Jerusalem would not come in his own days.'[8]

I thought you'd be glad to hear the commentator got it right."

"Yes, I'm grateful the commentator gave a correct interpretation." Huldah continued, "To finish what happened after the discovery of the Book of the Law and my prophecy, King Josiah responded with more reforms. Josiah then gathered the people of Judah:

> *And he read in their hearing all the words of the Book of the Covenant. ...The king stood by the pillar and renewed the covenant in the presence of the Lord—to follow the Lord and keep his commands, statute[s] and decrees ...Then he had everyone in Jerusalem and Benjamin pledge themselves to it.[9]*

King Josiah provided an example of what the people should do by renewing the covenant and pledging himself to it, and then the people followed him by pledging themselves to it as well."

> Point 7: Just as Josiah provided a good example to emulated, perhaps America's leaders need to resolve to do the same. We also need secular leadership that'll return to God's Word and to its principles and laws as did our forefathers. But the only way to have good leaders is for our people to vote for responsible, godly people who run for office. We also need spiritual leadership that continues to follow God and His laws. Apostasy—a rejection of truth once believed and

proclaimed—is rife in some of our denominations in America. These churches have forgotten their foundations and turned away from their glorious beginnings.

"Now," Rebecca said, "I'm going to lay out from scripture details of Josiah's later reforms. At this time the king also launched a more intensive campaign against idolatry:

> [He removed] *from the temple of the Lord articles made for Baal and Asherah and all the starry hosts. …He also tore down quarters of the male shrine prostitutes that were in the temple of the Lord,* [and] *the quarters where women did weavings for Asherah. …He removed from the temple of the Lord the horses that the kings of Judah had dedicated to the sun. …*[and] *burned the chariots dedicated to the sun. …He pulled down the altars Manasseh had built in the two courts. …The king also desecrated the high places that were east of Jerusalem on the south of the Hill of Corruption—the ones Solomon …had built for Ashtoreth the vile goddess of the Sidonians, for Chemosh the vile god of Moab, and for Molek the detestable god of the people of Ammon.*[10]

Of course, earlier King Josiah had also gone back, as he said he would, to desecrate *Topheth, which was in the Valley of Ben Hinnom, so no one could use it to sacrifice their son or their daughter in the fire to Molech.*"[11]

> Point 8: Josiah's actions to prevent child sacrifice set an example Americans should emulate by voting for responsible leaders promoting laws which uphold God's moral standards, such as banning abortions. Otherwise, they risk inciting God's anger for the choice of abandoning God's moral mandates.

"Josiah also removed false priests and disqualified Levite priests who'd engaged in improper worship from serving at God's altar.

> *Even the altar at Bethel, the high place made by Jeroboam son of Nebat, who had caused Israel to sin—even that altar and high place he*

demolished. . . . Then Josiah looked around, and when he saw the tombs that were there on the hillside, he had the bones removed from them and burned on the altar to defile it, in accordance with the word of the Lord proclaimed by the man of God who foretold these things.[12]

In 1 Kings, the bible sets forth the event of the man of God who came from Judah to Bethel as Jeroboam was standing by the altar to make an offering. *By the word of the Lord he cried out against the altar. 'Altar, altar! This is what the Lord says: A son named Josiah will be born to the house of David. On you . . . human bones will be burned.'*"[13]

> Point 9: This was 'a prophetic announcement of the rule of King Josiah, who came to the throne in Judah nearly 300 years after the division of the kingdom,'[14] and it was fulfilled in the mentioned passage. Perhaps God also has a person in mind for America, who could bring about reform as Josiah did. The American people need to pray that the Lord will send a person like Josiah to bring about reform in our land.

"I agree," Rebecca observed. "And then, after everything else he did, Josiah held a Passover celebration that surpassed any other: It had not been observed like this in Israel since Prophet Samuel's day. And *none of the kings of Israel had ever celebrated such a Passover as did Josiah, with the priests, the Levites and all Judah and Israel who were there with the people of Jerusalem.*[15] To top this off, *Josiah got rid of the mediums and spiritists, and the household gods, the idols, and all the other detestable things seen in Judah and Jerusalem.*[16] And, the reason he did all this was to fulfill the requirements of the law written in the book that Hilkiah the priest had discovered in the temple of the Lord."

> Point 10: King Josiah was a wonderful leader, a righteous ruler, and a faithful servant of God. And, this godly man has provided a template for any leader of any country or any church who desires to follow the Lord. *Neither before nor after Josiah was there a king like him who turned to the Lord as he did—*

with all his heart and with all his soul and with all his strength, in accordance with all the Law of Moses."[16]

"We all miss King Josiah and Lady Zebidah, who both died early. But at least," Prophetess Huldah added, "Josiah and Zebidah didn't have to live to see what is occurring right now in Judah."

"I'm glad," Hannah said. "We all loved the king and queen so much. *Jeremiah composed laments for Josiah, and to this day all male and female singers commemorate Josiah in laments. These became a tradition in Israel.*"[17]

"It is a blessing that Josiah didn't have to see all this after *his acts of devotion in accordance with what is written in the Law of the Lord.*[18] But please tell me, who became king after that?"

"Well," Rebecca began, "The people took Jehoahaz son of Josiah, and *made him king in the place of his father. ...*[and] *he reigned in Jerusalem three months* [in 609 BC]. *He did evil in the eyes of the Lord ...Pharoah Necho put him in chains at Riblah in the land of Hamath. ...*[and later he] *took Jehoahaz and carried him off to Egypt and there he died.*"[19]

"So, who ruled after the short reign of that ungodly king?"

Hannah answered, "Well, the Egyptian Pharoah Necho made Josiah's son Eliakim king:

> [He] *changed Eliakim's name to Jehoiakim* [and] *he reigned in Jerusalem eleven years* [in 609-598 BC]. *...And* [Necho] *imposed on Judah a levy of a hundred talents of silver and a talent of gold. ... Jehoiakim paid Pharaoh Necho the silver and gold he demanded. In order to do so, he taxed the land and exacted the silver and gold from the people of the land according to their assessments. ...And he did evil in the eyes of the Lord.*"[20]

"In the third year of the reign of Jehoikim king of Judah," Huldah added, *"Nebuchadnezzar king of Babylon came to Jerusalem and besieged it.*[21] The deportation in 605 BC had included Daniel and his friends, Hananiah, Mishael and Azariah, who were all students I'd taught at the Jerusalem School. I'm really sad that these fine students were all exiled. During the reign of Jehoikim he became subordinate to Nebuchadnezzar:

> *Nebuchadnezzar king of Babylon invaded the land, and Jehoiakim became his vassal for three years. But then he turned against Nebuchadnezzar and rebelled. The Lord sent Babylonian, Aramean, Moabite and Ammonite raiders against him to destroy Judah, in accordance with the word of the Lord proclaimed by his servants the prophets. …Jehoiakim* [died and then] *rested with his ancestors."*[22]

"So, did another son of Josiah rule after King Jehoikim?"

"No," Rebecca replied. *"After that, Jehoiakim's son Jehoichin succeeded him as king. …He reigned in Jerusalem three months* [from December 598 to March 597 BC]. *He did evil in the eyes of the Lord, just as his father had done. At that time the officers of Nebuchadnezzar king of Babylon advanced on Jerusalem and laid siege to it."*[23]

"Saphah, we are in the third month of that siege of Jerusalem right now." Huldah said. "The booming sounds you're hearing in the back ground are caused by the siege-works pounding the Jerusalem walls. When the pounding ceases, we'll all know the Babylonians have broken through the wall." The lady raised her eyebrows and sighed. "Of course, as you may know, it's expected that the current siege in 598/597 BC will probably result in a second deportation."

"Oh my, the invasion of Jerusalem and Judah is happening in stages," Saphah observed. "How frightful! No wonder there is such terror in this place. Rebecca, are you people unable to leave Jerusalem?"

"Yes, there's no escape," Rebecca said. "Jerusalem is surrounded by Babylonian troops, so there's no way to leave the city. And, there's no way to cart off trash or dispose of waste beyond the city gates."

"Is that why there's such a strange smell in Jerusalem?"

"It is. But that may not be the only factor," answered Huldah.

"What do you mean?"

Huldah hated to tell Saphah the gruesome facts, but finally she spoke: "Jeremiah's writings report that cannibalism happens sometimes during a siege: *Those killed by the sword are better off than those who die of famine; racked with hunger, they waste away for lack of food from the field. With their own hands compassionate women have cooked their own children, who became their food when my people were destroyed.*[24] None of us have observed a treacherous act such as this happening. But the strange smells in this place cause us to suspect horrible acts such as that are occurring during this siege. And, if people could commit such an atrocity against their own children, who can be safe here?"

"Oh, that's true!" Saphah exclaimed.

Huldah spoke as she looked out the window and saw the position of the sun. "It's about time for Ezekiel to arrive here from his priestly training. Rebecca, please go out with Yafa to watch for him. We don't want him standing alone outside the gate waiting for us to open it."

"C'mon Yafa, let's go wait for Ezekiel."

"Alright," Yafa immediately jumped up and the two hurried outside.

"Mother, we've finished hemming our towels and we need to pick out our patterns. Which embroidery patterns do you like best?" Anna placed all of them on the low table so Hannah could choose.

"I like the ones with animals, but you two need to make your own choices."

The door opened and the ladies reentered the room followed by a handsome young gentleman. "Saphah, I'm pleased to introduce you to my husband, Ezekiel."

41

APOSTATE JUDAH & AMERICA

Saphah reached out her hand to the young man, "Ezekiel, I'm very pleased to meet you."

Ezekiel took her hand into one of his and patted it with the other. "I'm so pleased to make your acquaintance too. How are you and how was your journey here from America?"

"My journey was fine, but I'm sorry to hear Jerusalem is under siege."

"Yes, we're under siege, but talk at my priestly training is that the wall will be breached soon." The man walked to his wife, embraced her with one arm, and kissed her on the cheek. "That reminds me, Yafa, I need to tell you something. We didn't get our ration of food today."

Huldah spoke up, "Please stay and have supper with us. Lentil soup is simmering on the fire, and there's enough for a serving for all."

"Oh, thank you for inviting us," Yafa said. "Zeke, could we stay."

"Yes, please stay." Saphah turned toward Ezekiel to entreat him to stay. "Back in the cave before I began walking to Jerusalem with the angel Nahal, he placed a cloth sack filled with little loaves of bread, a hunk of cheese, and tiny raisin cakes in my backpack, so there's extra food in there to share." Saphah took off her satchel, opened the flap, pulled out the cloth bag, and held it up. "Here's the bag of food."

"Well, that sounds wonderful," Ezekiel responded. "Yes, we'll stay."

"Good!" Huldah was happy they were staying. "Rebecca would you please help me set out the hot soup and other food? We even have olive oil to dip our bread in. Then we can all enjoy this great meal."

"Of course," Rebecca answered as the two set everything out, poured more hot tea, and took their seats again on a cushion.

"Ezekiel," Huldah noted, "Since you have spiritual training, perhaps you can give Saphah input on applications from Josiah's reforms. But first, would you please say a word of thanks for our meal."

"I'd be pleased to give thanks," Ezekiel replied as he bowed his head. "Heavenly Father, thank you for the food you've provided for us on a day of uncertainty about whether we'd have a single morsel to eat. Yet on this special day you've given us food sent by an angel. Thank you, Lord, and we praise your name forever. Amen."

"Oh, this is so yummy," Yafa savored the flavor of the hot soup and the bread dipped in oil. Everyone was enjoying the fare so much that no one uttered a single word for several minutes.

"Ezekiel," Saphah finally broke the silence, "the ladies have told me all about King Josiah's various reforms and about the kings who ruled after him. However, I'm wondering about something. Why did the succeeding rulers—two sons and a grandson of Josiah so far—return to the old evil ways of those who ruled before him? Why was there immediate apostasy?"

"For one thing, since Josiah's wife Zebudah died young, his sons were influenced instead by his wife, Hamutal, an apostate in her faith."

"Oh, I remember reading about the princes in scripture." Saphah grabbed her bible from her satchel, searched it, and began reading:

> *Take up a lament concerning the princes …'What a lioness was your mother among the lions! She lay down among them and reared her cubs. She brought up one of her cubs and he became a strong lion. He learned to tear the prey and he became a man eater. The nations heard of him, and he was trapped in their pit. They led him by hooks to Egypt.*[1]

What does it mean that he became a man eater?"

"Well, Saphah, laments are sometimes used sarcastically by prophets, as in this case. The first cub in lioness Hamutal's pack was Jehoahaz, who reigned only three months and was a man-eater, a reference to his oppressive policies. And, he was taken by hooks to Egypt."

"After that, scripture mentions more about the lioness and another one of her cubs:

'When she [the lioness] *saw her hope unfulfilled, her expectation gone, she took another of her cubs and made him a strong lion. He prowled among the lions for he was now a strong lion. He learned to tear the prey and he became a man eater. …Then the nations came against him, those from regions round about. They spread their net for him, and he was trapped in their pit. With hooks they pulled him into a cage and brought him to the king of Babylon. They put him in prison, so his roar was heard no longer on the mountains of Israel.'*"[2]

"Again, are these words said in a sarcastic manner?" asked Saphah.

"You're right. 'Another of her cubs' can refer to Jehoiachin who'll likely be taken to Babylon after the current siege. But it might also refer to a prophecy about Zedekiah as a future king who'll be deported later to Babylon. Whatever the case, the scripture reveals the fall of the royal family after Josiah's death. Kings are too busy with matters of state to spend time in instruction of offspring. Hence, in the case of Josiah, after his wife Zebudah' death, his sons and even his grandsons, were spiritually instructed by Queen Hamutal. Apostate in her faith, Hamutal led the youngsters astray."

"I'm surprised that Hamutal was apostate."

"Actually, she wasn't the only one who was apostate, and that is my second point. Although the people of Judah outwardly followed King Josiah during his reign, inwardly many were still apostate in their hearts. Therefore, when Josiah and Zebudah died, many of those in the palace household, as well as many of the citizenry of Jerusalem, returned to their old evil ways of idolatry. This included not only the lioness and her cubs, but also most of the elite and upper class, who never experienced a change of heart."

"Oh, I see. So, do you think the reform movement was a good idea?"

"Yes, I do. The movement gave Judah more time. God wanted the people to have every opportunity to return to their Maker, and wisely some people took advantage of that period to turn to Him. But now that Josiah is dead, many of those who never knew God in their hearts have returned to their wicked ways. However, a portion of the people from both the city and rural areas remained true to Him."

"Please tell me, Ezekiel, what exactly does it mean to be apostate?"

"Apostasy is a rejection of truth once believed and proclaimed, a falling away from God's truth."

"When you talk about apostasy are you speaking to the people of Judah alone, or are you also speaking to the citizens of America?"

"Saphah, I'm speaking to both nations. Huldah and I've discussed what's happening in your world, so what I'm saying isn't just meant for Judah, but for America too. It's a dual application. Old Testament prophecy can have a dual application both for now in my world, and for then in yours."

"Come to think of it, Paul also says in the New Testament that truths from your age can be of a dual nature: *These things happened to them as examples and were written down as warnings for us, on whom the culmination of the ages has come.*[3] And when scripture speaks of 'the culmination of the ages to come,' it's referring to 'the period of time inaugurated by Christ's death and resurrection and continuing into the future until

Christ's second coming and beyond. It is the period of fulfillment when all that God has been doing for his people throughout all previous ages comes to its fruition in the Messiah.'"[4]

"In that context," said Ezekiel, "the prophecy I'm about to reveal is clearly a truth disclosing God's will when his people fall into apostacy. So first, in regard to the people of Jerusalem, the siege we're under is about to end. Some will go into captivity, but others will remain:

> *This is what the Sovereign Lord says: As I have given the wood of the vine among the trees of the forest as fuel for the fire, so will I treat the people living in Jerusalem. I will set my face against them. Although they have come out of the fire, the fire will yet consume them. And when I set my face against them, you will know that I am the Lord. I will make the land desolate because they have been unfaithful, declares the Sovereign Lord.'"[5]*

"My commentary talks about: 'Although they have come out of the fire,' and says it is a reference to the siege of Jerusalem in 597 BC which resulted in exile.' But here's what the phrase, 'the fire will yet consume them,' means. It is a 'prophecy threatening a devastating siege,'[6] which will consume those living in Jerusalem."

"That's right," Ezekiel said, "That's exactly what it means."

Yafa jumped up from her cushion and questioned in a quivering voice, "Oh goodness, Zeke, are we really going into captivity? I'm so frightened!"

"Yes, Yafa, I afraid so." Ezekiel immediately walked toward his young wife, gently stretched an arm over her shoulder, placed his free hand on her cheek, and tenderly kissed her lips. "Darling, please look at me." Tears streamed down her face as she stared into her husband's eyes. "My dear, God will take care of us, so don't be afraid."

"Thank you, Zeke," Yafa managed to stifle her tears and put a smile on her face for her beloved husband. "Prayer will help too."

"Yes, it will. Are you alright?" He gave her a big smile and motioned toward a cushion. "Come over here with me and we'll sit together."

"Yes, I'm alright." The two walked over to the cushion to sit together.

"Saphah, now I would like to ask you a question. In the past, did God ever give you a hint of what he might want you to do in the future?"

"Yes, he did provide a hint. When my current husband and I first met around 20 years ago, one day we were out for a drive and the two of us were discussing our Christian faith. Then the subject changed to my writing and he asked me about the number of books I planned to write. I told him I didn't really know. At that point, he stared straight ahead for a time as if listening, and then he said:

"You have two, maybe three, more books in you and then it will be the end."

"I told my future husband I felt God had used him as a mouthpiece to speak to me. That's when I first realized God wanted me to write two, maybe three, more books besides the three books I've already written, and I would write them before the end of the age."

"So how many of the additional three books have you written?"

"This is the first, and I'm almost finished, so I know God wants me to write at least one or maybe two more, but I suspect it'll depend on how history unfolds. I really have no idea how this will play out. But what about you? Has God given you a hint of expectations for you."

"Well, because of Josiah's reforms, the kingdom of Judah received a temporary reprieve from the destruction God had in store for us.

But now God's winnowing of Judah has begun and is apparently occurring in stages. The first deportation happened when Daniel went into exile, and from what we just discussed, presently it looks like there'll be a second deportation soon. But then the Lord seemed to impress on my heart: *Son of man, confront Jerusalem with her deplorable practices.*[7] Actually though, I don't really know what that means at this time. Presently I'm studying to be a priest, but soon the wall will be breached and many of us will go into exile. Thus, I'm confused about how and when God expects me to confront Jerusalem."

"Ezekiel, it's alright." Huldah gently reassured him. "When the time comes God will let you know details of what you're to do. In the meantime, I think we should help Watchwoman Saphah. There is a pattern happening in both ancient Judah and modern America. Reform has already happened in Judah, but Saphah is here to learn more about it. And, God has already informed her of approaching ruin to come down upon her habitation—the United States of America—unless reform happens there too."

"I agree one hundred percent," Ezekiel said. "Let's help Saphah."

"Thank you. But first, I need to confirm what is actually going on. Do you think both Judah and America have already set their courses?"

"Yes, the course is set for Judah, because the people are already too far gone. And, from what you've told us, it appears America may be too. Although God withheld his judgment on Judah during Josiah's reign, he hasn't reversed His intent to eventually discipline us."

"But I'll tell you one thing," Ezekiel was emphatic. "I truly think Josiah can be viewed as the greatest king in Judah's history.: *He did what was right in the eyes of the Lord, …not turning aside to the right or the left.*[8] The king did what was right in an apostate nation and the result was heart stirring. Judah experienced something so encouraging that it was applicable not only for my generation, but also for your later generation as well. On a route toward inevitable destruction, Judah was given a stay of execution for a time, but America was also given a reform pattern to follow. And, this happened because King Josiah was faithful to God, 'not turning aside to the right or the left.'"

"However, God is still angry with Judah even after Josiah's reforms." Saphah noted. "Is that right, Ezekiel?"

"Yes, after the Book of the Law became lost, apostacy became so prevalent no one showed concern about God's warnings in his Word. If you remember, Prophet Zephaniah declared that the people of Jerusalem had become so complacent *they are like wine left on its dregs, who think, 'the Lord will do nothing, either good or bad.'*"[9]

"That is an accurate depiction of the arrogance of apostate people."

"Saphah, do you have examples of apostacy occuring in your world?"

"Yes, I do. But first I want to share a new survey from the Pew Research Center, 'About 80 percent of U.S. adults think religion is losing its influence on American life. …Nevertheless, a combined 57% of U.S. adults—a clear majority—express a positive view of religion's influence on American life.'"[10] So, '8 out of 10 Americans believe religion's influence in U.S. life is declining.'"[11]

"Yet," Saphah went on to explain, "the pattern of such polls seems 'to show Americans turning away from organized religion while still seeking spiritual meaning in their lives. …And the trend mirrors a sharp decline in Americans who identify as Christians. According to a 2022 Pew Report, as many as 90% of U.S. adults and children identified as Christian in the early 1990's. That share fell to just 64% of Americans who said the same in 2020. Pew predicted that if this trend continued and accelerated with Christians under 30 in the U.S., Christianity could become a minority religion by 2045.'"[12]

"How many years is it from the present time there until 2045?"

Saphah calculated the figures in her mind, but then opened her mouth wide in alarm and dismay. "Oh, no! Presently, we're in the year 2024 in America, so it is only 21 years until 2045."

"Well, things don't look good in the U.S.A., unless there's reform in your land. Now, please give me examples of the apostasy there."

"Alright, I'll give you some prime examples of the apostasy on my globe. For one thing, our world has become politically correct. So a person who doesn't conform to a so-called 'politically correct notion', such as approval of same-sex marriage or transgenderism, may be disqualified from getting or keeping a job. Sadly, in America from the White House down, people are celebrating untruthful things God has condemned in His Word. But God's truth is what we need to hear."

"Yes, I agree, but in both Judah and America, some people don't want to hear truth."

"Another thing that is happening on my globe is that Islamic Sharia Law is taking over in some European countries. And they've become completely paralyzed by political correctness. Sadly, because of lack of immigration law and the birthrate among immigrants there, the game is over for them. Unfortunately, it looks like the same thing is beginning to happen in America too!"

"Yes, America should definitely take heed now before it's too late."

"Another apostasy in my world has to do with churches, such as:

> 'The Episcopal church, [which] has regularly made headlines for some years now. It is one of the oldest and largest denominations in the world, a church whose origins were solidly rooted in biblical teaching. It preached the gospel of

a risen Savior and its pulpits were blessed with holy
preachers. Indeed, the godly influence of the Episcopal
church spread throughout the world, from Europe to Africa
and the Americas. Now, however, this once-devoted church
has fallen into apostasy.'"[13]

"Please tell me what is happening in that church."

"This once faithful denomination has moved from its beginnings.
The Episcopal church 'is one of the first to ordain a homosexual
bishop, …to try to debunk the divinity of Jesus, …to state that the
church's dioceses could interpret the Trinity however they pleased,
to [say that] God can be a she, Jesus a loving thought, and the Spirit
an individual's choice."[14]

"I would like to hear about other churches that have drifted."

"An example is the Anglican Church in England:

> That denomination has dwindled to such small numbers that
> church buildings which stood for centuries are now closing
> permanently. …These magnificent structures once were
> packed with zealous believers. But the Anglicans' condition
> has grown so apostate that they've had to sell off numbers of
> their church buildings, some of which are being turned into
> nightclubs, occult museums, and even mosques."[15]

"Oh my," Ezekiel remarked, "It sounds like that church is far gone in
their apostasy. Soon there may be more mosques than churches."

"Evangelist Franklin Graham, eldest son of the late Billy Graham,
chastised the Methodist Church in the U. K. for a 'language guide'
that falsely instructs ministers and church-goers to shun what
they say are 'hurtful terms like husband and wife.'

Graham, president and CEO of Samaritan's Purse and the Billy Graham Evangelistic Association, slammed the U.K. church for trying to edit what the Word of God says:

> 'Shame on the Methodist Church,' Graham wrote on a Face book post last week. 'These are biblical terms—and marriage between a man and a woman is biblical truth.' … The same church in 2021 voted overwhelmingly to redefine marriage to include homosexual couples and officiate same-sex weddings. …Last month, Graham also rebuked Pope Francis' document allowing priests to bless same-sex couples, declaring it 'has no meaning' because 'we're still going to have to stand before God.'"[16]

"Are there other categories of apostacy happening in your world?"

"Apostacy exists at some bible-based colleges in the U. S. and other places. Consider Harvard and Yale which started as bible schools:

> Today these renowned universities are hotbeds of atheism, unabashed deniers of the divinity of Christ. They have become apostate institutions, moving far from their biblical roots. The same is true of Columbia in New York and Princeton in New Jersey. …Even in Christian colleges and evangelical seminaries worldwide, the leaven of apostacy has become embedded. It is now a losing battle for these schools to try to stay the course of the old paths, because apostatized professors no longer hold to biblical truth. The new gospel they present dismisses the divinity of Christ, the reality of hell and judgment, and biblical standards of purity and morality."[17]

"My goodness," Ezekiel said, "It is terribly arrogant of some of the these religious schools to dismiss 'the divinity of Christ, the reality of hell and judgment, and the biblical standards of purity and morality."

"Yes, it takes an awful depth of pride to remove the divinity of the One who died for us. All of this has resulted in a lukewarm gospel of half-truths spreading to the detriment of the real gospel."

"True, Isaiah warned of a non-offensive or smooth gospel, which people are clamoring for in your day and mine. Thus, his prophecy applies directly to both Judah and America because God said:

> *Go, now write it on a tablet for them, inscribe it on a scroll, that for the days to come it may be an everlasting witness. For these are a rebellious people, deceitful children, children unwilling to listen to the Lord's instruction. They say to the seers, 'See no more visions!' and to the prophets, 'Give us no more visions of what is right! Tell us pleasant things, prophecy illusions. Leave this way, get off this path, and stop confronting us with the Holy One of Israel.'*[18]

Then Isaiah revealed what God said about the rejection of His Word:

> *This is what the Holy One of Israel says: 'Because you have rejected this message, relied on oppression and depended on deceit, this sin will be to you like a high wall cracked and bulging, that collapses suddenly, in an instant. It will break in pieces like pottery, shattered so mercilessly that among its pieces not a fragment will be found for taking coals from a hearth or scooping water out of a cistern.'*[19]

The people used oppression and deceit to build a wall for their safety and prosperity. But Isaiah gave the true way to security and salvation:

> *This is what the Sovereign Lord, the Holy One of Israel, says: 'In repentance and rest is your salvation, in quietness and trust is your strength, but you would have none of it. You said, 'No we will flee on horses.' Therefore you will flee! You said, 'We will ride off on swift horses.' Therefore your pursuers will be swift! A thousand will flee at the threat of one: at the threat of five you will all flee away, till you are left like a flagstaff on a mountaintop, like a banner on a hill.*[20]

God told both Judah and America that 'in repentance and rest is your salvation, in quietness and trust is your strength.' But, Judah 'would have none of it.' Therefore, because the people of Judah rejected God's Word, they're suffering greatly in my day," observed Ezekiel. "But the Lord told Prophet Isaiah: 'Inscribe it on a scroll, that for days to come it may be an everlasting witness.' Saphah, you live in 'days to come,' and the Lord has given your people, 'an everlasting witness,' of what to do. So, they should take the following to heart:

> *Seek the Lord while he may be found; call on him while he is near. Let the wicked forsake their ways and the unrighteous their thoughts. Let them turn to the Lord, and he will have mercy on them, and to our God, for he will freely pardon."*[21]

"Praise God!" Saphah joyfully shouted, "'Let them turn to the Lord, and he will have mercy on them, for he will freely pardon!' The way of confession and forgiveness stands open to my people to return to the Lord in repentance:

> [They are to] *put aside the deeds of darkness and put on the armor of light, to behave decently, as in the daytime, not in carousing and drunkenness, not in sexual immorality and debauchery, not in dissension and jealousy. Rather, to clothe themselves with the Lord Jesus Christ, and do not think about how to gratify the desires of the flesh."*[22]

"Absolutely, those who turn to the Lord need to join the spiritual battle against evil."

"The New Testament says take up a spiritual sword and join the fight:

> *Be strong in the Lord and in his mighty power. Put on the full armor of God, so that you can stand against the devil's schemes. For our struggle is not against flesh and blood, but against the rulers, against the authorities, against the powers of this dark world and against the spiritual forces of evil in the heavenly realms.*[23]

Ezekiel said, "Doubters should heed Jeremiah's admonishment to Judah about what will happen if they fail to turn to Him:

> *This is what the Lord says: 'Look an army is coming from the land of the north; a great nation is being stirred up from the ends of the earth. They are armed with bow and spear; they are cruel and show no mercy. They sound like a roaring sea as they ride on their horses; they come like men in battle formation to attack you, Daughter Zion. We have heard reports about them, and our hands hang limp. Anguish has gripped us, pain like that of a woman in labor. Do not go out to the fields or walk on the roads, for the enemy has a sword, and there is terror on every side.'*[24]

Thus, Jeremiah also points out what will happen if such people fail to turn to God. The Lord will refine and test them:

> *'I have made you a tester of metals and my people the ore, that you may observe and test their ways. They are hardened rebels, going about to slander. They are bronze and iron; they all act corruptly. The bellows blow fiercely to burn away the lead with fire, but the refining goes on in vain; the wicked are not purged out. They are called rejected silver, because the Lord has rejected them.'*[25]

The people of Judah failed the test. But, again, the quoted scripture above is an 'everlasting witness' to the citizens of America too."

"Yes, and I hope my people pay attention to the 'everlasting witness,' because if they do, reform and revival will result!"

"That's right," Ezekiel enthusiastically replied. "Perhaps *God will send down showers in season; there will be showers of blessing.*[26] But your people need to remember there can be no blessing until they put away evil, purge away sins, and sincerely repent. When they look on others with love, then will he minister to the hearts of your people in blessing. He will withhold his chastisement and revive your people in that day."

"Oh, praise God! I'm encouraged, for if that happens a new day will dawn in my land: a day of gathering and repentance for my people! Ezekiel, thank you so much for your advice." Saphah was gratified by the prophet's words. "But would you please refresh me about my responsibilities as a watchperson?"

"Certainly," Prophet Ezekiel said. "In my studies to become a priest, I've learned about the practical and spiritual role of watchpersons, but I assume you want to learn more about the spiritual."

"Definitely," Saphah said. "I want to learn about my spiritual role."

"Saphah, in your function as a watchperson, you're to warn the wicked to turn from their evil ways and encourage the righteous to remain steadfast. So, scripture says for you to: *Hear the word I speak and give them warning from me.*[27] Therefore, your first responsibility is to turn the wicked from death to life:

> *When I say to a wicked person, 'you will surely die,' and you do not warn them or speak out to dissuade them from their evil ways in order to save their life, that wicked person will die* [spiritually] *for their sin, and I will hold you accountable for their blood. But if you do warn the wicked person and they do not turn from their wickedness or from their evil ways, they will die for their sin; but you will have saved yourself.*"[28]

"In this part of my role, I'm to 'warn the wicked to turn from their evil ways,' and thereby release myself from responsibility for them."

"But, your second role is to encourage the righteous to be steadfast:

> *Again, when a righteous person turns from their righteousness and does evil, … they will die. Since you did not warn them, they will die for their sin. …*[and] *I will hold you accountable for their blood. But if you do warn the righteous person not to sin and they do not sin, they will surely live because they took warning, and you will have saved yourself.*"[29]

"Thus, in the second portion of your watchwoman role, you're to admonish the righteous to stay steadfast and thus dismiss yourself from being responsible for them."

"So, the dual role of my calling is to proclaim life to the righteous and to warn the wicked from their ways. In this way, I'll be making both groups aware of their true state and releasing myself from responsibility for both."

"Saphah, you'll need to remember, however, that this may cause you suffering and persecution. When you give warnings, people may laugh at you or think you're weird. But concern for those around you, who're bound for a lost eternity unless they hear truth and respond, should be your main concern, not your own interests."

"You're right. And, I have the Messiah, Jesus Christ, as a prime example to follow. Christ has fulfilled the role of a true watchman who stood in the gap in the wall for our sakes. On the day of battle, he freely gave his own life for the good of all mankind, spilling his blood on the cross. He didn't let his own security or comfort stand in the way. *Rather, he made himself nothing by taking the very nature of a servant, being made in human likeness. And being found in appearance as a man, he humbled himself by becoming obedient to death—even death on the cross.*"[30]

"Just think about it. God has provided a way for even the vilest offender to come to him through the sufficiency of the atonement, the righteous for the unrighteous, provided in Christ's death on the cross. Thus, the greatest of sinners, or even the most wicked of cities or nations, can be reconciled with God and restored to fellowship."

"So, if a nation, such as the United States, which deserves to be judged, turns from its evil ways and returns to God in sincere repentance, even a nation such as that can receive a reprieve from calamity?"

"Yes, I assure you it can. Look at the city of Ninevah. Jonah warned them of God's message of doom by going *into the city, proclaiming, 'Forty more days and Nineveh will be overthrown.' The Ninevites believed God. …When Jonah's warning reached the king of Nineveh, …this is the proclamation he issued in Nineveh: …Do not let people or animals, herds or flocks, taste anything; do not let them eat or drink. But let people and animals be covered with sackcloth. Let everyone call urgently on God. Let them give up their evil ways and their violence. Who knows? God may yet relent and with compassion turn from his fierce anger so that we we will not perish. When God saw what they did and how they turned from their evil ways, he relented and did not bring on them the destruction he had threatened.*"[31]

"But why were animals and sackcloth involved?"

"In my time and place," Ezekiel noted, "the inclusion of domestic animals signified the urgency with which the Ninevites sought mercy from God. And, sackcloth was involved because it is a customary sign of humbling oneself in repentance. The scripture here says that the Ninevites 'believed God.' So, this might mean that all or even part of them genuinely turned to the Lord. Conversely, the belief of others may have gone no deeper. But at least they took Jonah seriously and acted accordingly."

"How wonderful!" Saphah said. "This scripture plainly lets us know that God often responds in mercy to the repentance of people groups by postponing threatened calamity. In the case of my own nation, God first gave me a message to share with my people that He is planning to 'bring down ruin upon thine habitation,' the United States of America. But then, at a later time He gave me an additional message to share, saying, 'I desire worship, not conflagration.'"

"Yes, God was letting your nation know that they can postpone war or conflagration if they will just follow the basic example of the Ninevites. They or their animals don't have to put on sackcloth or ashes, but they do need to exhibit urgency in turning to God for reconciliation. First, the Americans need to 'believe God.' Second, everyone needs to 'call urgently on God.' Third, they need to 'give up their evil ways and their violence.' Thus, if they turn to God in humble repentance, discard their wicked ways, and worship Him with thankfulness and love, there is hope for reconciliation to occur to postpone war. God extended that hope to your people when he said: 'I desire worship, not conflagration.'"

"Praise God for the awesome magnitude of what Christ has done on the cross and the impact that reality should have on our hearts. I think the wonderful hymn, 'To God Be the Glory,' by Fannie J. Crosby, says it best:

> O perfect redemption, the purchase of blood!
> To every believer the promise of God;
> The vilest offender who truly believes,
> That moment from Jesus a pardon receives.

> Praise the Lord! Praise the Lord! Let the earth hear His voice!
> Praise the Lord! Praise the Lord! Let the people rejoice!
> O come to the Father, through Jesus the Son:
> And give Him the glory! Great things He hath done![32]

42

THE MIRY CLAY

Ezekiel took his wife's hand. "My dear, I think it's time for us to go before it gets dark, don't you?" Then he addressed Huldah. "Thank you for your hospitality and for inviting us to share a meal."

"Well," Huldah responded, "I'm glad you could stay for fellowship and thankful the Lord provided food for us to share."

Ezekiel turned to the American. "Saphah, I've enjoyed talking to you, and hope my insights prove helpful to you and your people."

"I'm so glad I got to meet you both. Ezekiel, thanks again for giving me insights. And Yafa, I hope we can get better acquainted soon."

"We're glad we got to meet you too," Yafa replied. "I'd like to invite you over for a visit, but we don't have food, so we can't provide hospitality." A glimmer of tears were in her eyes.

"Yafa, it's alright." Saphah walked over and gave her new friend a hug.

"Yes, everything will be fine, Yafa." Rebecca smiled at the lovely lady. "I hope you can keep coming here to dine with us because we still have some nuts and figs and plenty of tea."

"We really must be on our way. Farewell, everyone," Ezekiel said.

"Bye, Saphah." Yafa gave her a smile, waved goodbye at everyone, and the two departed.

"I'm just thankful, Becca, that we still have some food left," Anna said. "It really worries me though that mother is pregnant, yet she lacks enough food for good health. I'm also concerned about my unborn brother or sister. I'm praying both my mother and my baby sibling will be alright." With that, Anna's eyes glazed with tears, but she held them back. "Mother, I'll just be glad when this baby arrives."

"Me too," Hannah agreed. "Besides that, I can hardly get up from this cushion." She laughed as she tried to position herself to get up. "Anna dear, would you please give me a hand getting up?"

"Sure, mother." Anna reached out her hand to pull up her mother from the pillow.

"I'm just so tired right now." Hannah stretched her arms and yawned. "If the rest of you don't mind, I think I'll go to bed early."

"Mother, I think I'll go to bed early too," said Anna. "Then we can talk a little or I can read to you before we go to sleep."

"Yes," Hannah replied. "I'd love to hear one of the stories that Becca wrote for the Rechabite children."

"Hannah and Anna, could I read one of my stories to you?"

"Oh, Becca, that would be wonderful!" Hannah exclaimed.

"Yes, please do!" Anna was thrilled Rebecca had volunteered to read.

"Alright, ladies, c'mon let's go." Hannah put her arm around Anna and whispered in her ear: "My daughter, I love you so. But, please quit worrying about me, honey. God willing, everything is going to turn out alright." Hannah turned to survey the other two women. "Good night, Huldah and Saphah, and we'll see you in the morning."

"Yes, see you in the morning," Anna and Rebecca echoed as they walked out of the room.

"Huldah, it's wonderful Rebecca is writing for the Rechabite kids."

"Yes, Rebecca's done some reading projects for them, but while we're under siege she's quit. The Rechabites are living in Jerusalem now for safety from Babylonian attacks. However, I'm worried many of us, including the Rechabites, will go into exile when the wall is breached. Right now she's substituting at school and helping me at the gate."

"So, you're still teaching and ministering?"

"Yes, thanks to the women in this household who share the cooking and cleaning duties. However, because of dangerous conditions here during the siege, we walk about in the city two by two to stay safe."

"That's good. There must be a lot of women and children drastically needing help in Jerusalem."

"Yes, many of them need practical and spiritual help. But there's only so much we can do in a practical sense, especially with food, because of the food shortage. However, we're able to help with clothing needs, mostly for the children and babies. Weekly, Shallum supplies us with a sack of discarded royal clothing from the palace wardrobe. We take old clothes apart to sew new ones for little ones. We all pitch in, including Yafa during the day. But, I also try to help by ministering to them in spiritual matters and telling them to look to the Lord rather than idols. But I really don't know how much they listen."

"It sounds like the situation in Jerusalem is dire for the people."

"Yes, the living conditions in Jerusalem are devastating! We've had drought, plague, famine, to name just a few of the things experienced during this siege, along with the emotional anticipation of warfare hanging over our heads. But we ladies in this house do the best we can to help the women and children here under the circumstances."

"The spiritual situation in America is declining too, especially after the event we call 9/11, when our nation was attacked by foreigners."

"So, when exactly was the United States attacked on your own soil?"

"The 9/11 terrorism event happened in 2001, but there was an event in 1993 called the 'World Trade Center Bombing,' an attack that some consider 'to be something of a deadly dress rehearsal for 9/11.'[1] That is because the mastermind behind the World Trade Center bombing, Ramzi Yousef, revealed it was by Khalid Sheikh Mohammed's help that al Qaeda would later return to commit the 2001 attack."

"Well, it sounds like your nation may've already experienced preludes of God's temporal judgment," Huldah pointed out. "So, how did the people of your country respond to the 9/11 attack?"

"In the beginning, some American citizens realized the spiritual aspect of the event. Some responded by putting their faith in God for the first time, and others showed a renewed interest in attending church and praying regularly. However, that reaction was temporary. Since the attack, our nation has slipped farther away from God."

"Please tell me more about the things that're happening."

"Lately, there's an increase in ungodly leadership in the branches of our federal and state governments. In fact, some leadership includes a squad of people who endorse things like antisemitism, a betrayal of the Jewish people. People are also suffering from unwise government borrowing and spending, leading to rapid inflation. And, leadership that fails to stand up to foreign adversaries has gained power. In addition, our government allows open borders, so anyone can enter the U. S., including drug traffickers and people from enemy nations. In a letter to congressional leadership, 10 retired FBI directors and counterintelligence experts gave a warning. Saphah got out a copy of a letter she'd brought along with her to Jerusalem and read:

The Biden administration's border policies have enabled a 'soft invasion' of the United States at the Mexico border. 'Military-aged men from across the globe, many from countries or regions not friendly to the United States, are landing in waves on our soil by the thousands—not by splashing ashore from a ship or parachuting from a plane but rather by foot across a border that has been accurately advertised around the world as largely unprotected with ready access granted. It would be difficult to overstate the danger represented by the presence inside our borders of what is comparatively a multi division army of young single adult males from hostile nations and regions whose background, intent, or allegiance is completely unknown.'

'In light of such a daunting, unprecedented penetration by uninvited foreign actors, it is reasonable to assert that the country possesses dramatically diminished national security at this time. The nation's military and laws and other natural protective barriers that have provided traditional security in the past have been thoroughly circumvented over the last three years.' They argue that the prevalence of these young men 'is particularly alarming in light of the Hamas terror attack on Israel last October 7,' as such attacks are often copied by other terror groups, and called on Congress to secure the borders against them. Going a step further, they said 'those already here illegally must be identified and removed without delay.'

'It is stark to say so, but having a large number of young males now within our borders who could begin attacking gatherings of unarmed citizens, in imitation of 10/7 and at the behest of a foreign terror group, must be considered a distinct possibility,' the letter stated. 'We would be remiss not to call out this potentially grave threat in the most direct terms. The warning lights are blinking.'[2]

Huldah, this article says another terrorist attack, such as recently occurred in Israel on 10/7/23, could repeat itself in the U. S."

"Oh!" Huldah was alarmed. "It sounds like America could suffer another terrorist attack soon. And if so, that might be a prelude to God allowing temporal judgment to fall on your nation."

"Oh, Huldah, I'd never thought about it that way. Regarding Judah, King Josiah's reforms gave your nation a reprieve from war while he was still alive. But after he died apostasy returned full force, and that's when the Lord began stages of temporal judgments on Judah. So, in regard to America, could reform still occur here even after we've suffered one, or maybe even two, stages of temporal judgment?"

"Presently, we know God is still open to the citizens of your nation turning to Him for salvation. But the people of America can't take God for granted. They need to return to the Lord soon before it's too late. Do you remember the last thing God said to you?"

"God said, 'I desire worship, not conflagration.'"

"For now, I think that's your answer."

"I see what you mean. The Lord doesn't want us to suffer warfare. Instead, He's trying to get the attention of the American people so they'll realize their great need for Him. And, in relation to their need for him, the Lord said something else. Here is what He said:

"Miry Clay."

"Oh, I'm so glad God gave you the words 'miry clay,' because that means the Lord is informing your people there's still a way for them to postpone war."

"So, there's still a way out?"

"Yes, the subject of miry clay is in a Psalm of King David:

> *I waited patiently for the Lord; and he inclined unto me, and heard my cry. He lifted me up also out of the horrible pit, out of the miry clay, and set my feet upon a rock, and established my goings. And he hath put a new song in my mouth, even praise unto our God: many shall see it, and fear, and shall trust in the Lord."*[3]

"Please tell me more."

"At some historical point, King David described the condition of his life as being in a horrible pit of miry clay from which he couldn't escape. Likewise, Judah and America are both stuck in very difficult places and there seems to be no way of escape."

"In other words, you're telling me the nations of Judah and America can't escape the miry pit on their own. It's like they're stuck in quicksand or miry clay and need assistance to get out! They need the hand of God to pull them out of the mire!"

"Definitely, at the present time my ancient land of Judah is trapped in abysmally dark circumstances. Nevertheless, most Judean people aren't seeking God's help."

"Why aren't they?"

"Well, here's what God says: *The wicked are like the tossing sea, which cannot rest, whose waves cast up mire and mud. 'There is no peace,' says my God, 'for the wicked.'*[4] The plight of the wicked is seen here in terms of the salvation they've refused. Their choice to reject God separates them from the peace of those who trust in God for deliverance. They're trapped in deep, soft clay, powerless to escape by their own devices."

"I'm afraid America is finding itself in similar dire circumstances, so what should my people do to escape?"

"Americans should humble themselves and acknowledge that God has provided them with the means to escape the miry clay: *This is what the high and exalted One says—he who lives forever, whose name is holy: I live in a high and holy place, but also with the one who is contrite and lowly in spirit, to revive the spirit of the lowly and to revive the heart of the contrite.*[5] God rescues the 'contrite and lowly,' and offers hope for those who return to him. He'll forgive and restore His repentant people: *I have seen their ways, but I will heal them; I will guide them and restore comfort to Israel's mourners, creating praise on their lips.*[6] And, likewise, Americans who mourn for their sins will also obtain healing and peace."

"Returning to Psalm 40, it reveals that God will also 'set our feet upon a rock and establish our goings.' So, Huldah, I think that means God has a plan for a spiritually awakened America. The Lord said: 'Look to the East, look to the West, your nation shall be cut off. There will be pillaging and destruction, and the land will be laid bare. Upon these ruins I will rebuild my church, and the glory of the Lord will reign there. I will rebuild my church and no one will stop me. You have my solemn word.' And, there we have it—the Lord will respond to repentance of my people, because they have His 'solemn word,' that He will rebuild His church and no one will stop Him. Huldah, I think that means that if the citizens of the United States are contrite, humble, and sincerely turn back to the Lord in repentance, America will regain her spiritual footing."

"Yes," Huldah said. "God will bring America out of the miry clay and set the feet of her repentant citizens 'upon a rock,' referring to a place of safety, security, and stability. The Lord will also 'establish the goings,' of your people because He has a plan for the U. S. Perhaps the last part of the quoted Psalm—'And he hath put a new song in my mouth, even praise unto our God: many shall see it, and fear, and shall trust the Lord'—has to do with God's future plans for the United States."

43

PREPARE THE WAY

Huldah asked, "Saphah, what do you think about going out to the court to continue our conversation?"

"That's an excellent idea. We can watch the sunset while we talk."

"Yes, we'll enjoy being outside." Huldah grabbed a sack of unshelled nuts and two picks. "Saphah, please grab the little empty sack, and we'll use it to store nuts we pick out. Since we don't know if we'll receive rations tomorrow, we need to pick as many as we can."

The two ladies went outside. "See those three big pots over there?" Huldah pointed to the containers. "Why don't you grab one and I'll grab the other two. We can turn them over and use two of them to sit on and the other one for a table between us as we pick out nuts. We need to use every spare minute to pick out these kernels, because soon they may be our only food along with the leftover figs."

"Oh my, that's right." Saphah was saddened to hear the news.

"The sunset this evening is gorgeous." Huldah and Saphah stood side by side in silence as they viewed the lovely hues, ranging from yellow to golden to orange to red, splashed on a celestial blue background.

"Yes, the beauty of this sunset is so gorgeous it's almost unbearable!" Saphah agreed. "To see the glorious beauty of God's creation, but then to simultaneously know the people of our nations are under God's judgment, is painful. It's the blending of opposite realities—beauty and glory on the one hand, and hurt and shock on the other. Nevertheless, as we look at the marvelous work of God's hands, we can sense God's nearness and His love for his creatures. This sunset reminds me of how I felt when my fifteen-year-old daughter died from injuries in an accident all those years long ago. One evening I went outside, saw the grandeur of a sunset, and felt God's presence calling me to Himself. Although I no longer had my youngest child, I realized God was with me and that He cared."

"Oh Saphah, I can deeply feel it too. God is with us and He cares."

Huldah is in shock too, Saphah thought. *But God is comforting both of us through the beauty of His creation. The two bent their heads together sideways until they touched, but didn't say another word—each understood what the other felt.*

The ladies finally sat down to begin their work. "I've already cracked these nuts, so they should be fairly easy to get out of the shells."

"I'm glad you've already cracked them." Saphah reached into the sack to get a portion to fill her little bowl so she could shell them. "Huldah, why do you think Psalm 40, where it says—'And he hath put a new song in my mouth, even praise unto our God: many shall see it, and fear, and shall trust the Lord'—could imply that God has a plan for America?"

"Well, after King David was rescued from the miry clay of his circumstances, God set his feet on a rock, established his goings, and put a new song of praise in his mouth. Then many people saw what God had done for the king, heard David's praise unto the Lord, and trusted in the Almighty themselves. There're similarities between what happened to King David, what's happening now in my time to Judah, and what'll happen in your time to America too. Regarding all three, deliverance is not by their doing, but by the hand of God."

"So, after Judah and America come out of temporal judgment, do you think God will have plans for good for the two nations just as He did for King David? Listen to this from Isaiah: *Comfort, comfort my people, says your God. Speak tenderly to Jerusalem* [and by inference

Washington], *and proclaim to her that her hard service has been completed.*[1] Here, after judgment, the Lord determined that Judah [and America] had [or will] learn their lessons by their punishments."

"That's right," Huldah shook her head.

"And my bible commentary says 'chapters 40-66 of Isaiah assume the exile of Judah is almost over.'[2] Then, after the previous part from Isaiah 40 we hear:

> *A voice of one calling in the wilderness, prepare the way for the Lord; make straight in the desert a highway for our God. Every valley shall be raised up, every mountain and hill made low, the rough ground shall become level, the rugged places a plain. And the glory of the Lord will be revealed, and all people will see it together. For the mouth of the Lord has spoken.*[3]

Huldah, did you know these words from Isaiah may apply to separate instances of good news down through history?"

"Yes, first they apply to the good news that God will lead his people back to their homeland on a figurative highway to Jerusalem, or in America's case Washington, after judgments of the two nations end."

"But the New Testament expands this 'good news' to state the 'gospel' or salvation that Christ (Messiah) brings to all who receive Him by faith: *that Christ died for our sins according to the Scriptures, that he was buried,* [and] *that he was raised on the third day according to the Scriptures.*[4] The New Testament also tells us John the Baptist applied that part of Isaiah 40 to his ministry of calling people to repent in preparation for the first coming: *John replied in the words of Isaiah the prophet, 'I am the voice of one calling in the wilderness, make straight the way for the Lord.'*"[5]

"Did John also focus on letting people know repentance is needed to prepare the way for the first coming of the Messiah?"

"Yes, Repentance is the crucial thing people need to do for a saving faith in Jesus Christ, because God does all the real work: There's nothing we can do to pay for our sins or remove their guilt or break their hold upon us. God does all that through Christ's death on the cross and the powerful working of the Holy Spirit in our hearts. But there is one work he commands us to share in by the Holy Spirit's enabling: *Repent and believe the gospel. Turn from sin and self to Christ and salvation.*[6] But, Huldah, what about the second coming of the Lord? Do you think repentance is necessary to prepare the way for Jesus Christ's second coming?"

"Definitely," Huldah stressed, "and that was another reason why God said 'Comfort, comfort my people.' After the discipline of judgment is over, the Lord wants to reassure His people that He'll not only deliver them, but he'll also place them in a position to tell the world of the deliverance and saving grace of God."

"Maybe that's the reason Isaiah 62 speaks of preparing a highway:

> *Pass through, pass through the gates! Prepare the way for the people. Build up, build up the highway! Remove the stones. Raise a banner for the nations. The Lord has made proclamation to the ends of the earth: Say to Daughter Zion, 'See, your Savior comes! See, his reward is with him, and his recompense accompanies him.' They will be called the Holy People, the Redeemed of the Lord; and you will be called Sought After, the City No Longer Deserted.*[7]

The gates scripture refers to are thought to be of Babylon: *I will surely bring together the remnant, …[and] the one who breaks open the way will go up before them; they will break through the gate and go out. Their King will pass through before them, the Lord at the head.*[8] In this prophetic message of deliverance, God's people will be carried into exile, and a remnant will return. Thus, in 538 BC Cyrus the Great will free the Judahites from captivity brought about by Nebuchadnezzar. The people will pass through the gates of Babylon and return home to restore Zion."

"And all this was in anticipation of the promised arrival of Messiah, the coming of the Savior promised by God!" Huldah shook her head in comprehension. "So, it is a promise of both a first and a second coming of the Lord!"

"Yes, and going back to Isaiah 62, we see this as a continuation of prophecy of future exaltation of Zion, of which this is an example:

For Zion's sake I will not keep silent, for Jerusalem's sake I will not remain quiet, till her vindication shines out like the dawn, her salvation like a blazing torch. So, the nations and kings will see their vindication; they will be called by a new name that the mouth of the Lord will bestow. *You will be a crown of splendor in the Lord's hand, a royal diadem in the hand of your God. No longer will they call you Deserted or name your land Deserted.*[9]

Here we have God's assurance of a new name Zion shall be called, and of a 'crown of splendor' and 'royal diadem' held in God's hands for the coming vindication and glory of Zion. It is truly wonderful to consider that all God's people here are symbolized to be a crown of glory in His hand. Furthermore, when the nations and kings see her righteousness, then they too will be brought to trust in the Lord. Additionally, the thought of a new name extends to Christians in Revelation: *To the one who is victorious, …I will give that person a white stone with a new name written on it, known only to the one who receives it.*"[10]

"So, going back to Isaiah 62, what else does it say?" Huldah asked.

"It says that *as a bridegroom rejoices over his bride, so will your God rejoice over you.*[11] With beautiful imagery, Isaiah sets forth the loving union between God and His bride, which Revelation foresees as *the wedding of the Lamb.*[12] But Isaiah also proclaims that the Lord promises to protect Zion: *I have posted watchmen on your walls, Jerusalem; they will never be silent day or night. You who call on the Lord, give yourselves no rest.*"[13] These Heralds, Proclaimers, Prayer Warriors or whatever you call them have a constant duty and cannot rest until they're sure people everywhere are warned of the second coming and hear of God's salvation. Recall when God says to 'Daughter Zion': 'See, your Savior comes! See, his reward is with him, and his recompense accompanies him.'"

"Yes, I recall that message," Huldah said. "Is there something similar in the Book of Revelation?"

"Yes, there's a similar verse: *Look, I am coming soon! My reward is with me, and I will give to each person according to what they have done. I am the Alpha and the Omega, the First and the Last, the Beginning and the End.*[14] Oh my goodness, Huldah, it looks like the focus of Isaiah 62 speaks to the eschatological hope of the second coming of the Lord?"

"It does! And you know what that means, don't you?"

"I do. It means that now is the time to prepare the way for the Lord's return. Lots of work lies ahead for God's people, for Christ our Savior is coming again soon!"

"Yes, Isaiah looks forward prophetically to the time for God to fulfill these promises. Now, since Christ is coming soon to your time and place, your people need to 'build up the highway' so a smooth road is ready to usher the unsaved to salvation. They must make the road accessible to all manner of pilgrims by identifying obstacles and clearing them out of the way. So too, they must 'raise a banner' or hoist road signs so the people can find the right route. Thus Isaiah 62:10 opens the gates of the city to forge a pathway to God for those who'll believe in Him:

> *Yes, blessed are those who wash their robes, that they may have the right to the tree of life and may go through the gates into the city.*[15]
> But the gates are closed for those *who do not think it worthwhile to retain the knowledge of God. ...They have become filled with every kind of wickedness, evil, greed and depravity.*[16]

But happily, the way remains open still to those who'll repent and turn to God for salvation."

"That's right," Huldah said. "Today in your world before the Lord's second coming, and in the spirit and power of John the Baptist, God desires to warn a judgment-bound world of events to take place before the reappearance of Jesus as King of kings and Lord of lords."

"Do you think we should list everything we've talked about in the order of occurrence?"

"Yes, I do. Why don't I sum up about my ancient land, and you can summarize about your modern world.?"

"Huldah, you go first."

"First," said Huldah. "we noted that Judah in my ancient time was under the threat of coming judgment. Then, reform happened with King Josiah so there was reprieve from judgement during his reign. But now Josiah is dead, so Judah is suffering stages of judgement and we're in the second siege of Jerusalem right now. Thus, we know that after the third siege, my entire land will go into exile, except for a remnant. But we also know from Isaiah that when Judah's exile is over my people will return to their own soil. But then Isaiah reports 'a voice of one calling in the wilderness, prepare the way for the Lord,' which applies to the first coming of the Messiah and John the Baptist."

"But now" Saphah noted, "America in my era is under the threat of coming temporal judgment. I know this because the Lord said to me, 'I will bring down ruin upon thine habitation,' which is the United States of America where I live. He also said 'Look to the East, look to the West, your nation shall be cut off. There will be pillaging and destruction, and the land will be laid bare. Upon these ruins I will rebuild my church, and the glory of the Lord will reign there. I will rebuild my church and no one will stop me.' But then later,the Lord gave me an additional message, saying the following:

'I desire worship, not conflagration.'

So, I think God wants my people to know that even under threat of temporal judgment by invasion, they can postpone the inevitable for a time by returning to the Lord. Thus, there may be a period of reform and revival in America such as happened in Judah during Josiah's reign. However, after the reform period is over, America will decline again which will then lead to descipline and perhaps exile."

"Sadly, exile is a strong possibility, now please set forth the rest."

"But if exile happens, Isaiah suggests that my people will return home. Again, however, Isaiah reports 'a voice of one calling in the wilderness, prepare the way for the Lord,' which in my era points to the end time event of the second coming of the Messiah. Huldah, I'm really concerned and wondering: what do you think I should do at this point?"

"Saphah, since the American people are under the threat of temporal judgment at this time, I think the main thing God presently wants you to do is to finish your book to warn them of coming calamity."

"But won't there be skeptics and doubters?"

"Yes, Prophet Jeremiah speaks to the certainty of that fact regarding my land and, by similarity, your land as well:

*'The people of Israel and the people of Judah have been utterly unfaithful to me'
declares the Lord. They have lied about the Lord; they said, 'He will do nothing!*

No harm will come to us; we will never see sword or famine. The prophets are but wind and the word is not in them; so let what they say be done to them."[17]

"So, skeptics would say God's messengers are a bunch of windbags to whom we should pay no attention, because God's 'word is not in them.' Or, in modern parlance, doubters might say these prophecies aren't real, because God isn't speaking. These 'windy' Christians talk nonsense.'"

"Are there warnings about skeptics in the New Testament?"

"Yes, for instance, Peter especially forewarned of doubters in the 'last days,' which is an expression that refers to the entire time frame introduced by Christ's first coming. In comparison to Old Testament times, which were preparatory and preliminary, these days are last and a prelude to prophetic fulfillment. However, in 2 Peter, as follows, the emphasis is on the return of Christ, but these words are certainly similar to what skeptics of any time might say:

> *Above all, you must understand that in the last days scoffers will come, scoffing and following their own evil desires. They will say, 'Where is this coming he promised? Ever since our ancestors died, everything goes on as it has since the beginning of creation.' But they deliberately forget that long ago by God's words the heavens came into being and the earth was formed out of water and by water. By these waters also the world of that time was deluged and destroyed. By the same word the present heavens and earth are reserved for fire, being kept for the day of judgment and destruction of the ungodly.*[18]

However, God doesn't view time the same way humans do, *so the Lord is not slow in keeping his promise, as some understand slowness. Instead he is patient with you, not wanting anyone to perish, but everyone to come to repentance."*[19]

"Thus, scoffers misunderstand the reason for the apparent divine delay, because they don't realize that the Lord is a long-suffering God. He is simply waiting for all who'll 'come to repentance.'"

"But what about those who are already believers in your land?"

"God wants unbelievers to repent, but He also wants believers to be ready. Jesus warned that many who claim to be believers will not be ready, for they'll be deceived. The theme of the parable of the Ten Virgins underlines the division between the ready and the unready:

At that time the kingdom of heaven will be like ten virgins who took their lamps and went out to meet the bridegroom. Five of them were foolish and five were wise. The foolish ones took their lamps but did not take any oil with them. The wise ones, however, took oil in jars along with their lamps. But, the bridegroom took a long time to come, *and they all became drowsy and fell asleep. At midnight the cry rang out: 'Here's the bridegroom! Come out to meet him!' Then all the virgins woke up and trimmed their lamps.*[20]

But the five foolish ones had no oil, their lamps went out, and they had to purchase oil."

"So, what happened to the five foolish ones?"

"The parable's theme is a wedding with virgin bridesmaids leaving the bride and going to a place of waiting for the bridegroom. The occasion of the waiting is to escort the groom in a torchlit procession as he brings his bride home. Yet the five foolish bridesmaids had to go to those who sell oil to buy some for themselves. But while they were on their way to buy the oil, the bridegroom arrived. The virgins who were ready went in with him to the wedding banquet. And the door was shut. Later the others also came. *'Lord, Lord,'* they said, *'open the door for us!'*"[21]

"So, what did the bridegroom say to them?" Huldah was curious.

"The bridegroom replied, '*Truly I tell you. I don't know you.' Therefore keep watch, because you do not know the day or the hour.*"[22]

"That is a warning to Christians in your era, isn't it?"

"Yes, the important part of the story is the delay of the bridegroom. The church must be prepared to wait for the Parousia. All ten virgins fell asleep, so it is not that we should be on constant alert, but that we must be ready with the necessary provisions for when the time comes. Here, personal responsibility is emphasized. The application is the possibility of ultimate exclusion from the kingdom of heaven."

"Thus, believers in your era must be prepared for the second coming of Christ, right?"

"Yes, we are to be prepared for the coming of the bridegroom, and we are to have faith on the earth during trouble. In the book of Luke Jesus asks: *When the Son of Man comes, will he find faith on the earth?*[23] When the Lord returns the second time, will He find faith that endures in prayer and loyalty to Him? And, particularly, will He still find perseverance that continues during a period when spiritual decline and persecution are assumed to be the norm?"

"Nevertheless, Saphah, even though the end times will be a period characterized by wickedness and fierce persecution, Christians of your era must continue to share the gospel and to prepare the way for the Lord."

"True! As Ezekiel told me, it's part of my calling as a watchperson to encourage the righteous to remain steadfast. Years ago, when I first became a Christian, my pastor's wife took me to purchase a new Bible at a local college book store. Later, the Lord directed me to a verse in that bible: *The Lord God has given Me the tongue of disciples. That I may know how to sustain the weary one with a word. He awakens Me morning by morning, He awakens my ear to listen as a disciple.*[24] Because the pronoun

'Me' was capitalized here, and because of the immediately following verses, I realized that these words referred to Christ. Yet I also realized the words clearly revealed that the Servant's obedience to the Lord will result in suffering for him:

> *The Sovereign Lord has opened my ears; I have not been rebellious, I have not turned away. I offered my back to those who beat me, my cheeks to those who pulled out my beard; I did not hide my face from mocking and spitting. Because the Sovereign Lord helps me, I will not be disgraced. Therefore have I set my face like flint, and I know I will not be put to shame. He who vindicates me is near. Who then will bring charges against me? Let us face each other! Who is my accuser? Let him confront me! It is the Sovereign Lord who helps me. Who will condemn me? They will all wear out like a garment; the moths will eat them up.*[25]

Huldah, do you think these verses which foretell Christ's sufferings, also anticipate the sufferings individual believers will suffer toward the end of the age?"

"I do." Huldah replied. "I'm familiar with Isaiah, so I'll explain."

"Yes, please do," said Saphah.

"The verse indicates the servant's 'ear' has been 'awakened' to listen as a disciple, and his 'tongue' has been 'given' so he can know how to 'sustain the weary one with a word.' Hence, the servant is to speak and not be silent, because God's revelatory Word—his message to mankind through the Holy Bible—approaches each person as a demand. So like Jesus, Christians must be 'witnesses' of that message. And they must do so even when persecution, torture, and martyrdom are possible. True Christians need to be prepared to pay the price for following Jesus and for sharing the message of salvation with others."

"That's right. Believers need to know that to speak for God is to invite abuse. Christ did nothing but obediently speak the words that

God the Father had instructed Him to speak, but the next thing that happens is He is offering His back to those who beat Him, His cheeks to those who pull out His beard, and His face to those who mock and spit. Although there is no explicit connection between what Christ said and what they did, nevertheless He was abused."

"Now, please read the follow-up part directed toward believers,"

"Alright, I found it:

> *Hear me, you who know what is right, you people who have taken my instruction to heart. Do not fear the reproach of mere mortals or be terrified by their insults. For the moth will eat them up like a garment; The worm will devour them like wool. But my righteousness will last forever, my salvation through all generations.*[26]

"How wonderful! The Lord is speaking here to His servants, the righteous, those 'who know what is right' and 'who have taken my instruction to heart.'"

"Yes, He is offering comfort to His people who live in a fallen world and who suffer insults and reproach from unbelievers. God wants them to know that the abuse spoken by those who are passing away like garments eaten by moths will soon be gone, but the righteous salvation of God will endure forever. Therefore, in the case of both the Servant and the Christian, the righteousness of God will in the end vindicate his own."

"Yes, Jesus was abused for what he said. He claimed to be the Son of God, He pronounced judgment on the religious leadership, and He said He was the Way. If He hadn't said these things, He might not have been put to death. Language and words are at the heart of God's revelation. Thus, the linguistic efforts of the prophets in former times, of witnessing believers in my time, and of Jesus Christ, the ultimate communication of God to humans, can bring about persecution in any age. But Jesus could die in confidence because He knew that the Word of God provides eternal salvation and that His Word will never pass away. Likewise, we who share this same message can endure because we have the confidence of the redeemed, for we know 'Christ's righteousness will last forever, His salvation through all generations.'"

44

DANIEL'S PRAYER

Huldah reminded Saphah it was getting Late. "My dear, It's going to get dark soon, so I think we need to go back inside."

"I agree, I'm having trouble seeing what I'm doing as I try to pick out these nuts. But when we get back inside, what do you think about using the nuts we picked out and some of your leftover figs to make a fig and nut treat for tomorrow? That is, if you have some flour, honey, and oil left."

"Well, I think I do have a little flour, honey, and oil."

"Oh, good! We can make fig and nut crisps!"

"I've never heard of that. How do you make it?"

"It's fairly simple. I'll use half of the nuts we picked out for a finely chopped bottom layer. Then I'll simmer the figs, the other nuts, the honey, and a little water together for a second layer. After that, I'll make a dough of flour, oil, and some water and crumble it on top and then bake it in the oven."

"Great idea. That'll be a good way to use the little dab of floor and oil we have left." The two ladies both went inside and rummaged around to find cooking utensils and ingredients. "Alright, I'm going to make the fire in the oven now, and you can get started by chopping the figs and nuts."

"We'll have this mixed up and ready to bake before you know it." Saphah industriously worked to chop up the main ingredients.

"While you're mixing things up, I'm going to make fresh tea, then we can get comfortable on the cushions by the table to continue shelling nuts for tomorrow while we talk."

"Sounds good. I have some things I need to ask you about."

"Go ahead, I'm listening."

Saphah began mixing the ingredients for the dough with her hands. "Well, according to my bible, there are three Babylonian invasions of Jerusalem, and the first one occurs in approximately 604 BC , the second in 597 BC, and the third in 586, BC."

"It's frightening!" Huldah interjected. "The 597 BC invasion of Jerusalem might occur any time now, because Ezekiel thinks the Babylonians will probably break through the Jerusalem wall soon!"

"Yes, that is scary!" Saphah exclaimed. "Speaking of invasions, Huldah, do you remember telling me about the young lad Daniel who went into exile in 604 BC?"

"Yes, I remember."

"Well, did you know that the Daniel who went into captivity at that time is the author of the Book of Daniel in my bible?"

"There's a Book of Daniel in your bible? And my former student Daniel is the author? I didn't know that. However, I'm not surprised to learn this information, because he is a fine and godly young man."

"Yes, that fact is readily apparent in Daniel's book." Saphah poured the simmered fig, nut, and honey mixture over the finely chopped nuts in the oiled baking pan and spread it out evenly. Then she sprinkled the crumbled dough evenly on top. "Alright, Huldah, are you ready to put this in the oven? After that, please help me remember to check the progress of the baking every little bit. I don't really know how long it'll take to bake."

"Alright, I will. Saphah, do you know anything else about Daniel?"

"Yes, I would like to share something with you from Daniel's book of the bible:

> *In the first year of Darius son of Xerxes* (a Mede by descent) *who was made ruler over the Babylonian kingdom—in the first year of his reign* [539 BC], *I, Daniel, understood from the Scriptures, according to the word of the Lord given to Jeremiah the prophet, that the desolation of Jerusalem would last seventy years.*[1]

In Babylon in 539 BC toward the end of the captivity, Daniel reads from one of Prophet Jeremiah's letters to the exiles and notes the prophet's declaration that the exile would last seventy years. Huldah, do you think Daniel knew from Deuteronomy that the true blame for the exile rested not on the Babylonians who had taken Judah into captivity, but on the people of Judah themselves? In other words, God was behind the process that had brought Judah under control of their enemy. The people of Judah had broken the covenant and that was the reason the Babylonians were victorious over them."

"Yes," Huldah said, "It's all written in Deuteronomy, and since Daniel was my student at Jerusalem School before going into exile, he studied it in a class I taught. In the Book of Deuteronomy, God's covenant not only lays out His laws for the people, but also states the blessings and curses for obedience or disobedience to those laws. If the Lord's people obey the laws, they'll be blessed, but if they disobey the laws and depart from the worship of the true God, they'll be cursed with, among other things, oppression by enemies and exile:

> *Then the Lord will scatter you among all nations, from one end of the earth to the other. …Among those nations you will find no repose, no*

resting place for the sole of your foot. There the Lord will give you an anxious mind, eyes weary with longing, and a despairing heart. You will live in constant suspense, filled with dread both night and day, never sure of your life. In the morning you will say, 'If only it were evening!' and in the evening, 'If only it were morning!'—because of the terror that will fill your hearts and the sights that your eyes will see.[2]

So, from Daniel's perspective living in captivity, he'd know that Judah is experiencing the curses of the covenant, because of disobedience."

"Huldah, do you think we should check on our pan in the oven?"

"Yes, just keep talking, and I'll check on it while I listen to you."

"But do you think Daniel realized that God is merciful and forgiving, so he knows this is not the end of the story for Judah?"

"I think he knows." Huldah agreed. "But would you please come look at this to see if you think it should be baked longer."

"Yes, it needs to brown a bit more. Let's bake it a few more minutes."

"I thought it should bake longer too." Huldah said. "Another relevant passage of scripture we studied at Jerusalem school while Daniel was a student clearly puts forth the formula for a nation's restoration with God. At the dedication of the newly built temple, Solomon offered a prayer in which he recognized a time might come when a country's sins might cause their defeat at the hands of an enemy:

When your people … have been defeated by an enemy because they have sinned against you, and when they turn back to you and give praise to your name, praying and making supplication to you …, then hear from heaven and forgive the sin of your people …and bring them back to the land you gave their ancestors.

When they sin against you—for there is no one who does not sin—and you become angry with them and give them over to their enemies, who take them captive to their own lands, far away or near, and if they have a change of heart in the land where they are held captive, and repent and plead with you in the land of their captors and say, 'We have sinned, we have done wrong, we have acted wickedly,' and if they turn back to you with all their heart and soul in the land of their enemies who took them captive, and pray to you toward the land you gave their ancestors, … then from heaven, your dwelling place, hear their prayer and their plea, and uphold their cause.

And forgive your people, who have sinned against you; forgive all the offenses they have committed against you, and cause their captors to show them mercy; for they are your people and your inheritance.[3]

Solomon's prayer sets forth that a nation's way back to reconciliation with God is through repentance, which involves acknowledgement of past transgression against Him. Without confession of sin there is no 'forgiveness' to be found anywhere in the bible."

"So, if Daniel recognizes that fact, that's why the Book of Daniel reports he *turned to the Lord God and pleaded with him in prayer and petition, in fasting, and in sackcloth and ashes*[4] for his nation."

"True, when Daniel prepared for his prayer by fasting and putting on sackcloth and ashes, that indicated his deep grief and sorrow for his nation's sins. Saphah, let's take the fig and nut crisp out of the oven."

"Yes, we don't want to burn it. Besides, it's the last of our food."

"It is! Now, let me take out the pan so you won't get burned." Huldah used a long flat utensil to carefully lift out the baking pan.

"Oh, that looks and smells good!" said Saphah. "The crisp part is a light golden brown, so it's baked just right. Now we'll let it cool."

"Alright now, please tell me more about Daniel's prayer."

"Daniel identifies with his people and confesses their sins on the basis of their covenant relationship with God, but includes himself along with them. His prayer begins with invocation and confession:

> *Lord, the great and awesome God, who keeps his covenant of love with those who love him and his commandments, we have sinned and done wrong. We have been wicked and have rebelled; we have turned away from our commands and laws. We have not listened to your servants the prophets, who spoke in your name to our kings, our princes and our ancestors, and to all the people of the land.*
>
> *Lord, you are righteous, but this day we are covered with shame—the people of Judah and the inhabitants of Jerusalem and all Israel, both near and far, in all the countries where you have scattered us because of our unfaithfulness to you. …The Lord our God is merciful and forgiving, even though we have rebelled against him; we have not obeyed the Lord our God or kept the laws he gave us through his servants the prophets.[5]*

Next Daniel speaks of God's punishment, saying God was right in what He had done, because the exile of Judah and the destruction of Jerusalem are not acts of an arbitrary God, but consequences of the sinful behavior of God's people who had been repeatedly warned:

> *All Israel has transgressed your law and turned away, refusing to obey you. Therefore, the curses and sworn judgments written in the Law of Moses, the servant of God, have been poured out on us, because we have sinned against you. …Just as it is written in the Law of Moses, all this disaster has come on us, yet we have not sought the favor of the Lord our God by turning from our sins and giving attention to your truth. The Lord did not hesitate to bring the disaster on us, for the Lord our God is righteous in everything he does; yet we have not obeyed him.[6]*

Daniel not only prays for the people as their representative, but also for himself, by confessing the sins of the nation. All had sinned, whether by commission or by omission. Now he asks the Lord to show mercy to his people and to restore the city of Jerusalem:

> *Now, Lord our God, …we have sinned, we have done wrong. Lord, in keeping with all your righteous acts, turn away your anger and your wrath from Jerusalem, your city, your holy hill. …Now, our God, hear the prayers and petitions of your servant. …Give ear, our God, and hear; open your eyes and see the desolation of the city that bears your Name. We do not make requests of you because we are righteous, but because of your great mercy. Lord, listen! Lord, forgive! Lord, hear and act! For your sake, my God, do not delay, because your city and your people bear your Name.*[7]

Although the plea for God's mercy follows the confession, and couldn't proceed without it, we'd be remiss to think the confession is the basis of His restoration. The people are still sinful. Daniel knows that if there is any hope for them, it is because of God's righteousness and grace, not because of anything they'd do on their own. Forgiveness of the people is based on the reputation of God himself."

"Indeed!" Huldah agreed. "Thanks to God's grace, the story for a nation doesn't have to end with exile. Listen to what Deuteronomy says:

> *When all these blessings and curses I have set before you come on you and you take them to heart wherever the Lord your God disperses you among the nations, and when you and your children return to the Lord your God and obey him with all your heart and with all your soul according to everything I command you today, then the Lord your God will restore your fortunes and have compassion on you and gather you again from all the nations where he scattered you. Even if you have been banished to the most distant land under the heavens, from there the*

> *Lord your God will gather you and bring you back. He will bring*
> *you to the land that belonged to your ancestors, and you will take*
> *possession of it. He will make you more prosperous and numerous*
> *than your ancestors. The Lord your God will circumcise your hearts*
> *and the hearts of your descendants, so that you may love him with all*
> *your heart and with all your soul, and live.*[8]

Just think, Saphah, since America is facing judgment because many
of your people have departed from God's ways, this message of
grace is tremendous news for your nation as well."

"It certainly is! Thanks to God's grace, the story doesn't have to end
for either Judah or the United States. Listen to what Jeremiah said:

> *This is what the Lord says: 'When seventy years are completed for*
> *Babylon, I will come to you and fulfill my good promise to bring you*
> *back to this place. For I know the plans I have for you,' declares the*
> *Lord, 'plans to prosper you and not to harm you, plans to give you hope*
> *and a future. Then you will call on me and come and pray to me, and I*
> *will listen to you. You will seek me and find me when you seek me with*
> *all your heart. I will be found by you,' declares the Lord, 'and will bring*
> *you back from captivity. I will gather you from all the nations and*
> *places where I have banished you,' declares the Lord, 'and will bring*
> *you back to the place from which I carried you into exile.'"*[9]

"Wow! As we talked before, God has a plan for Judah, and by
inference for America too!"

"Yes, but don't forget the route to reconciliation with God involves
repentance on the part of America's citizens," Huldah reminded.

"I won't forget! It's wonderful Daniel heard the voice of God from
reading the writings of Prophet Jeremiah. In this way he realized
his people had broken the Mosaic Covenant and was motivated to
respond in prayer and repentance for his nation Judah. But did you

know that in my day and time, the concept of the covenant reaches its culmination in the teaching of Jesus Christ. Just before going to the cross at the end of His life, Jesus shared a last meal with his disciples. At that point he introduced a ritual we know as the 'Lord's supper' or 'communion,' as described in Matthew:

> *While they were eating, Jesus took bread, and when he had given thanks, he broke it and gave it to his disciples, saying 'Take and eat, this is my body.' Then he took a cup, and when he had given thanks, he gave it to them, saying, 'Drink from it, all of you. This is my blood of the covenant, which is poured out for many for the forgiveness of sins. I tell you, I will not drink from this fruit of the vine from now on until the day when I drink it new with you in my Father's kingdom.' When they had sung a hymn, they went out to the Mount of Olives.*[10]

Here, Jesus seals a new covenant with his twelve disciples which reminds us of God's old covenant dealings. The new covenant is spoken of by Jeremiah in the Book of Consolation.[31]

> *'The days are coming,' declares the Lord, 'when I will make a new covenant with the people of Israel and with the people of Judah. It will not be like the covenant I made with their ancestors when I took them by the hand to lead them out of Egypt, because they broke my covenant, though I was a husband to them,' declares the Lord. 'This is the covenant I will make with the people of Israel after that time,' declares the Lord. 'I will put my law in their minds and write it on their hearts. I will be their God, and they will be my people. No longer will they teach their neighbor, or say to one another, 'Know the Lord,' Because they will all know me, from the least of them to the greatest.*[11]

In this bridge between the Old and the New Testament, we see the suggestion that there is both continuity and discontinuity between the two covenants. The new covenant has its foundations in the old covenant, but the new feature is its power to transform participants from within their hearts. However, the new feature doesn't imply a complete break with the old covenant. Jesus doesn't ignore the old covenant but rather fulfills it. Jesus Christ fulfills the covenant of law mediated by Moses because He is the one who fulfills the conditions of the law. He also fulfills the covenant of the kingdom of David because he is David's greater son who sits on the heavenly kingdom throne as opposed to David's merely political kingdom throne."

"So, what is the role of the law in the new covenant?" asked Huldah.

"Obeying the law has never been the route to a relationship with God. Salvation doesn't result from our obedience to the Law, as said in Galatians: *All who rely on the works of the law are under a curse, as it is written: 'Cursed is everyone who does not continue to do everything written in the Book of the Law. Clearly no one who relies on the law is justified before God, because the righteous will live by faith.'*[12] Nevertheless, the New Testament also indicates a role for the law:

> *Do not merely listen to the word, and so deceive yourselves. Do what it says. Anyone who listens to the word but does not do what it says is like someone who looks at his face in a mirror and, after looking at himself, goes away and immediately forgets what he looks like. But whoever looks intently into the perfect law that gives freedom, and continues in it—not forgetting what they have heard, but doing it—they will be blessed in what they do.*[13]

That language is reminiscent of the Old Testament teaching that the keepers of the law will be blessed, but the non-keepers will be cursed."

"Yes, it is. But did Jesus say that the law continues to play a role in the new covenant?"

"He does. Jesus says that the law continues to play a crucial role:

Do not think that I have come to abolish the Law or the Prophets; I have not come to abolish them but to fulfill them. For truly I tell you, until heaven and earth disappear, not the smallest letter, not the least stroke of a pen, will by any means disappear from the Law until everything is accomplished. Thus, anyone who sets aside one of the least of these commands and teaches others accordingly *will be called least in the kingdom of heaven, but whoever practices and teaches these commands will be called great in the kingdom of heaven. For I tell you that unless your righteousness surpasses that of the Pharisees and the teachers of the law you will certainly not enter the kingdom of heaven.*[14]

We know, both from our own experience and from scripture, no one keeps the law perfectly. All have broken the law. But disobedience of God's law can lead to the rupture of relationships with those close to us such as our spouse, our relatives and friends, our coworkers, and our brothers and sisters in Christ. King David is an example of how sinning against the Lord can produce a break in human relationships. When the king slept with a married woman, Bathsheba, and then saw to it that her husband would die in battle, he tore her relationship with her husband apart in a violent manner."

"True," Huldah said, "David tried to cover up his sin, but God sent a messenger, Prophet Nathan, to confront him. David's prayer of contrition and repentance for adultery and murder is set forth in a Psalm. Saphah would you read it?"

"Yes, I would be glad to read it to you. It begins this way:

> *Have mercy on me, O God, according to your unfailing love; according to your great compassion blot out my transgressions. Wash away my iniquity and cleanse me from my sin. For I know my transgressions, and m y sin is always before me. Against you, you only, have I sinned and done what is evil in your sight; so you are right in your verdict and justified when you judge.*[15]

After the king's confession of sin, he prays for pardon and purity:

Cleanse me with hyssop, and I will be clean; wash me, and I will be whiter than snow. Let me hear joy and gladness; let the bones you have crushed rejoice. David wants God to hide his face from his sins and to blot out his iniquity. *Create in me a pure heart, O God, and renew a steadfast spirit within me. Do not cast me from your presence or take your Holy Spirit from me. Restore to me the joy of your salvation.*[16]

Then David prays for deliverance and vows to praise God:

Then I will teach transgressors your ways, so that sinners will turn back to you. Deliver me from the guilt of bloodshed, O God, you who are God my Savior, and my tongue will sing of your righteousness. David wants God to open his lips, so he can praise Him. *You do not delight in sacrifice, or I would bring it; you do not take pleasure in burnt offerings. My sacrifice, O God, is a broken spirit; a broken and contrite heart you, God, will not despise."*[17]

"Thank you, Saphah, for reading from your bible. Did you notice, in the beginning of David's prayer to God, he says—'Against you, you only have I sinned and done what is evil in your sight.' Those words may seem shocking to some. But in an important sense, David is right. Our sins against other people are really sins against God, in whose likeness all human beings are created."

"I think it's important to note," Saphah said, "whether individual or corporal, our sins break our relationship with God. Therefore, we see that God calls us to repent of our sins to keep a good relationship with both him and with others. And, in Daniel 9, we saw how that works when Daniel recognized that Israel's sin had broken Judah's bond with the Lord. That's when Daniel prayed to restore Judah's relationship with God through a prayer expressing confession and repentance. Likewise in my own day, a nation's relationship with God, once broken, can be restored through repentance. But God requires that we acknowledge our sins for restoration of national relationship with Him."

"So, does that mean that repentance does not stop after an individual becomes a Christian?" asked Huldah.

"That's right. We Christians must continue to acknowledge our sin and rebellion in our association with God, both individually and as a nation. But a fundamental teaching of the New Testament helps to clarify everything. While we must repent of our sins, our personal relationship with the Lord is not based on our ability to either keep the law or to keep up with daily repentance, because our faith is not built on good works or obedience, but on the work of Jesus Christ, the perfect law-keeper, the only one who never broke the law. He is the one who died on the cross to pay for our sins. Jesus is our substitute in fulfillment of the Old Testament sacrificial system."

"Oh, I see what you mean." Huldah smiled and raised her eyebrows in acknowledgement she understood what Saphah was saying. "In the Old Testament period, the act of repentance is accompanied by an animal sacrifice. We Judahites acknowledge the depth of our sins by sacrificing an animal in our place."

"True. But in my era, the New Testament teaches that our repentance doesn't need an animal sacrifice because our high priest, Jesus Christ, has *offered for all time one sacrifice for sins. …For by one sacrifice he has made perfect forever those who are being made holy.*[18] Jesus' death and resurrection is the foundation for our faith, not our repentance. But to maintain a good relationship with God, He calls us to repent of our sins. As Paul wrote: *Godly sorrow brings repentance that leads to salvation.*[19] So, godly sorrow manifests itself by repentance and divine grace displays itself as a result."

Huldah pointed out, "In the light of Judah's sins, Daniel displayed 'godly sorrow' and was moved to say a prayer of repentance for Judah's citizens in the expectation of 'divine grace.'"

"And we, the citizens of the United States of America, will also be under obligation to do the same thing. If God proclaims a nation to be under judgment, and makes that fact known to the people of the land, and if an enemy of that nation defeats them, and takes a remnant captive to their own land, then we must follow the counsel of God. For we have the admonitions of the book of Deuteronomy, of Solomon, of Jeremiah, of Jesus, and of the apostles as examples of what we should do. In addition, we have Daniel's prayer, a template of an actual prayer that we can emulate. Oh Huldah, thank you so much for helping me to sort this all out."

"You're welcome, Saphah."

45

GOD IS IN CONTROL

Huldah asked with a twinkle in her eyes and a big smile on her face: "Saphah, do you think we should sample these fig and nut crisps now?"

"Oh definitely, we always need to make sure our baked sweets are good, don't we?" Saphah chuckled as she took a knife and cut the crisps into bars, stacked them neatly on a big tray, and set aside the last two for them to munch on.

Saphah and Huldah sat down on cushions by the low table, and then Saphah began a prayer of thanks: "Heavenly Father, thank you Lord for this food and for the blessing of your great love for mankind shown in all generations. Therefore, we come to you today thankful and with praise for your gracious offer of mercy to the citizens of Judah and America. Thank you too that our lord *Jesus Christ is the same yesterday, today, and forever.*[1] Our Savior is always the same and His Word will always be true. In Jesus' precious name I pray. Amen."

"Amen," echoed Huldah.

"Alright now, let's sample these crisps." The two ladies both took a bite of their smooth fig and nut bars with little crisps on top.

"I don't know if it's just because I'm hungry, but I think these little fig and nut bars, are superb."

"Thank you, Huldah. I'm glad you like them." The ladies finished their crisps and sipped their tea in enjoyment. Saphah finally asked, "My friend, when the devastating things we've talked about come to pass in the United States, what should I tell my people to give them hope?"

"Saphah, the Lord will guide you to know what to say. Meantime, you need to share more with them about God's sovereignty over the historical process. It is important for them to remember whatever the circumstances, God is in control and will certainly win the day. The issue of divine sovereignty and human responsibility is an extremely important subject."

"Yes, even Daniel understood that divine sovereignty and human responsibility are both operative and form a mystery. Although God is sovereign, nevertheless human being are accountable, but the bible doesn't tell us enough to allow us to understand how the two aspects work together. Therefore, the ultimate answer to the mystery may be beyond our present intellectual grasp."

"That's right, But the fact that something is a mystery doesn't mean it's untrue. It just means it's beyond our human ability to understand. That's another subject Daniel studied at Jerusalem school."

"Well, I've definitely noticed that in the bible we can see God's hand of control over history, but He leaves human responsibility intact, a factor which can be a great source of confidence for His people. I think the story of Joseph is a prime example."

"I do too," Huldah agreed. "The narrator of the story explains Joseph's movements from his homeland to Egypt, then from the house of Potiphar to jail, and finally to Pharoah's court. But he doesn't reflect on God's agency in Joseph's life."

"Thus, to the reader, it seems that the blind forces of chance are pushing Joseph around in every direction. However, Joseph doesn't interpret his circumstances that way, as shown in his final speech. Joseph speaks to his brothers who had sold him into Egyptian slavery. They're afraid of him since they surmise their brother will now take out his revenge on them. But Joseph tells them: *You intended to harm me, but God intended it for good to accomplish what is now being done, the saving of many lives* [from famine]. *So then, don't be afraid. I will provide for you and your children. And he reassured them and spoke kindly to them.*"[2]

Huldah noted, "The act of personal animosity and jealousy toward their brother Joseph, was used by God to save the lives of the Israelites, the Egyptians, and the other nations that came to buy food from Egypt during the time of famine. In addition, the events reveal that God's purpose for the nations is life and would be accomplished through Abraham's descendants."

"Isn't that wonderful?"

"Yes, it is. But a different case is Samson who was a self-absorbed man who did nothing unless it was for himself, as the narrative of his story reveals. Even the dramatic end of that story is clouded by mixed motives. After his lover Delilah's betrayal of him, Samson found himself in Philistine custody, blinded and bound to a pillar. That's when he made a final request to God."

"That's right," said Saphah. "Here is Samson's prayer:

> *'Sovereign Lord, remember me. Please, God, strengthen me just once more, and let me now with one blow get revenge on the Philistines for my two eyes.'…Then he pushed with all his might, and down came the temple on the rulers and all the people in it* [including himself]. *Thus he killed more when he died than while he lived.*"[3]

"Did you notice?" Huldah asked. "Here was a great defeat of the enemy, but Samson counted it as revenge for his own eyes, not as a victory for God's glory. Here we see that God controls history, so He can even overrule the mixed motives of others to bring about his purposes."

Saphah said, "Again, at Jericho, we see another window opened on the issue of divine sovereignty and human responsibility. There is no doubt about the outcome of a war when the Lord enters the battle, so the Israelites could have just stood back and watched as God defeated their enemies. But the Lord doesn't work that way. He commanded His people to enter the battle by marching around the city each day for six days and on the seventh to march again but to also blow their trumpets. Joshua commanded the army, '*Shout! For the Lord has given you the city.*' Earlier, the Lord told Joshua, *When you hear them sound a long blast on the trumpets, have the whole army give a loud shout; then the wall of the city will collapse and the army will go up, everyone straight in.*"[4]

"Isn't that something!" Huldah nodded her head up and down. "The Israelites participated in the battle, although they already knew with certainty the outcome and to whom the praise belonged."

"Yes, it is! Similarly, the Lord fought for Israel under Gideon."

"He sure did! God reduced the army so that Israel would know that the victory was by his power, and not their own. Here is what God said to Gideon: *You have too many men. I cannot deliver Midian into their hands, or Israel would boast against me, 'My own strength has saved me.'*[5] Thus, God commanded Gideon to pare down his troops from thousands to just 300, but the small number of troops still had a job to do because, as you commented, that's how God works."

"And we also see God's hand at work behind the scenes in Daniel's book." Saphah observed. "He and his three friends are put through extremely difficult circumstance, yet they survive every trial they endure, but their enemies are often humiliated or killed. So, yet again, we see that God is sovereign. But that isn't all. The last chapter of Daniel goes further to address the issue of justice and retribution. Here we notice that rewards for faithfulness and punishments for rebellion go beyond death. Here, Daniel is talking about a particular event."

"What event is that?"

"Daniel is talking about the time before the second return of Jesus. It will be:

> *A time of distress such as has not happened from the beginning of nations until then. But at that time your people—everyone whose name is found written in the book—will be delivered. Multitudes who sleep in the dust of the earth will awake; some to everlasting life, others to shame and everlasting contempt. Those who are wise will shine like the brightness of the heavens, and those who lead many to righteousness, like the stars for ever and ever."*[6]

"Oh, Daniel is talking about the culmination of history here!"

"Yes, and God is sovereign not only within the world, but even over death, which causes us to reflect on the significant fact that God is as sovereign in my own day in the third millennium AD as he is in your day, Huldah, in the first millennium BC. He is sovereign over all eternity. Therefore, we understand that 'whatever the circumstances, God is in control.' To Christians living over 2000 years after Jesus, it may look like Satan and evil are in control, but they aren't. God is in control, so we can have peace and optimism for the future whatever the circumstances:

> *And we know that in all things God works for the good of those who love him, who have been called according to his purpose. For those God foreknew he also predestined to be conformed to the image of his Son, that he might be the firstborn among many brothers and sisters. And those he predestined, he also called; those he called, he also justified; those he justified, he also glorified. What, then, shall we say in response to these things? If God be for us, who can be against us? He who did not spare his own Son, but gave him up for us all—how will he not also, along with him, graciously give us all things?*[7]

For those who love God, He works out everything, even acts of harm against us, for our good. What a blessing this is for our lives.

God is omniscient, so He foreknew from all eternity all those who would come to Him for salvation. And, He graciously gives us all things, including eternal life:

> *Who will bring any charge against those whom God has chosen? It is God who justifies. Who then is the one who condemns? No one. Christ Jesus who died—more than that who was raised to life—is at the right hand of God and is also interceding for us. Who shall separate us from the love of Christ? Shall trouble or hardship or persecution or famine or nakedness or danger or sword? As it is written: 'For your sake we face death all day long; we are considered as sheep to be slaughtered.' No, in all these things we are more than conquerors through him who loved us. For I am convinced that neither death nor life, neither angels nor demons, neither the present nor the future, nor any powers, neither height nor depth, nor anything else in all creation, will be able to separate us from the love of God that is in Christ Jesus our Lord.*[8]

It is our faith in the events of the cross and resurrection of Jesus Christ which gives us certain hope for our future and confidence amidst present circumstances. In spite of a troubled present, believers know that something better awaits us in the future, so we can persevere until that time comes, for nothing 'will be able to separate us from the love of God that is in Christ Jesus our Lord.'"

46

PRAYER FOR A NATION

Sleeping on a mat on the floor in Huldah's room, Saphah heard something. *What is that moaning?* She listened again. *Maybe Hannah is having labor pains.* "Huldah, wake up."

"What!" Huldah awakened in surprise and sat up in her bed. "What's wrong?"

Saphah heard the low prolonged groan again. "Did you hear that?"

"Yes, I did. Hannah's labor pains must have started. Let's go see about her."

"Alright." Huldah and Saphah headed toward Rebecca's bedroom. Rebecca was already up and slipping on her sandals. Hurrying into the guest bedroom, the three saw Anna attending to Hannah who was in the throes of a labor pain.

Anna was holding one of Hannah's hands and talking tenderly to her. "Mother, do you think you're having real labor pains this time?"

"Oh, honey, I do." Hannah lifted her other hand to wipe sweat from her forehead with her hanky.

"Huldah, Saphah, and Rebecca are here now, mother."

"Oh, thank goodness! My labor pains are getting worse, and I'd like for Huldah to go to the palace to fetch Ebed."

"Huldah, do you want me to go with you?" Rebecca asked.

Huldah thought for a minute. "No, I'll go alone. I think it would be best for you to stay with Hannah. You and the other ladies need to quickly pack up extra clothes to take along when you all head for Ezekiel and Yafa's house. We may need to spend a few nights there since Hannah might be unable to return home for awhile after the baby's birth. I'll pack up extra clothes for myself too before I go to the palace to get Ebed."

Huldah took Hannah's hand. "Sweetheart, hang in there. I'm going to the palace to get Ebed. Maybe Shallum can come back with us too. These ladies will take good care of you, and Yafa is prepared to help you with delivery of the baby when you get there."

"Thank you, Huldah. Be careful!" Hannah smiled at Huldah, but then moaned with a new labor pain.

"Please be careful, Huldah," Rebecca also advised the older lady as she turned to leave.

"You ladies take care too," Huldah's words trailed off as she rushed out of the room.

"Let's hurry," said Rebecca, "because Hannah's pains are getting more severe. Here's our plan. We each need to pack a bag with extra clothes. Anna, you pack Hannah's and Saphah you can lug it for her."

"Also, don't forget to grab my bag of clothes over there for the baby," Hannah interjected.

"I won't forget," Saphah held a bag for Anna, who was stuffing it full.

"Does everyone have their bag packed now?" Rebecca asked.

"Yes, and here is the bag of baby stuff." Saphah held up the bag and then tried to sling it on her back along with Hannah's stuff.

"Saphah, let me take the baby's bag. I think that load is a little heavy for you." Anna relieved Saphah of part of her load.

"Thanks, Anna. I need to go over to the kitchen area to get some fig and nut bars Huldah and I baked last night, along with the tea leaves we have left. Yafa said they don't have any food left at their house."

"Oh, that's a good idea, because mother will be needing food after she gives birth to the baby."

"Hannah." Rebecca gently helped her from bed. "Are you alright?"

"I think so." Hannah looked toward Saphah. "Our friend from America, would you please say a prayer for us for today?"

"Of course, I would be pleased to offer a prayer. Heavenly Father, please watch over your servants in this house, and especially Hannah who is ready to bring new life into the world today. We don't know what a day may hold, but we know that we are in your hands, because scripture says: *For I am the Lord your God who takes hold of your right hand and says to you, Do not fear; I will help you.*[1] Our Lord and our God, please have mercy on all of us this day. In Jesus' name I pray. Amen."

"Thank you, Saphah. C'mon, let's go now." Anna slipped one arm around her mother's waist and kissed her on the forehead. "Mother, please tell us when you need to stop for a labor pain."

"Don't worry, I will. I'm sure glad it isn't very far to Zeke and Yafa's."

"I'm going over to get the fig and nut bars now, but I'll catch up with you." Saphah ran across the court to fetch the baked goods.

After several stops for Hannah's labor pains, the four finally drew near to Ezekiel and Yafa's house. But then abruptly, the *boom, boom, boom* sound of the siegeworks suddenly ended. Everyone stopped in their tracks and looked at each other in wide-eyed dismay. *Oh, no!* Saphah's heart dropped but she didn't say a word and neither did anyone else. *I know what that means! The Babylonians have broken through Jerusalem's wall! Her mind started racing and her heart vigorously pumping— thump, thump, thump!* Saphah took in several deep breaths and let each one out slowly. *Dear Lord, please help me to stay calm for Hannah's sake.* Then she swiftly walked the last few steps to Ezekiel and Yafa's door and knocked loudly. After the knock, she heard footsteps and then Ezekiel's voice calmly asked:

"Who is it, and what do you want?"

"It's Saphah, Rebecca, Hannah, and Anna. Ezekiel, please let us in," pleaded Saphah. "Hannah is having sharp labor pains, and she needs Yafa's midwife assistance. Please, please allow us into the room!"

Ezekiel promptly opened the door, and the three women, along with Hannah's daughter Anna, rushed into the room. Rebecca, who clutched a bag of clothes hanging from her shoulder, swung it around and slung it to the floor, as did Saphah and Anna, each carrying shoulder bags of their own.

"Ohhhh …, ohhhh …," moaned Hannah, agonizing in pain as she folded her arms over her extended belly. Bending over, she let out a scream.

Yafa quickly spanned the space between herself and Hannah. "Zeke, you and Anna need to go outside," she brusquely instructed the two as she continued to carry out her midwife tasks. Ezekiel took the young lady's hand, and the two quickly walked out, shutting the door behind them. Anna's demeanor became pensive because she was concerned about her mother's well-being. Then she lamented in a broken voice that she was very worried because her mother was inside going through the agony of childbirth, her father was clear over at the palace, but the Babylonians were fast approaching.

"Zeke, I can hear them right now, can't you?"

"Yes, I hear them." Ezekiel sympathetically patted Anna's shoulder.

"What are we to do? I'm so scared!" Anna began crying in earnest and talking all at the same time. "What about the others? Huldah, Shallum, Eve, Jonathan, and Mattea are all at the palace. What will happen to them?" She alternated between talking and sobbing.

"Anna, I'm fairly certain those at the palace will go into exile, along with the king and his associates, including family and staff. If Huldah has reached the palace, Shallum will vouch for her, so I think she'll be taken with the palace group, including Eve, Jonathan and Mattea."

"I hope so. But what about us? I'm worried about mother and my new little brother or sister." Anna sobbed with her face in her hands.

"Anna, you know why this is happening, don't you?"

"Yes, I've heard the rest of you talking about it, so I know it is because evil people in Judah have turned away from God. But what about us? We still worship God. It doesn't seem fair that good people have to suffer along with the wicked."

"Well, the sad thing is that when evil people choose to leave the Lord out of their lives, God has to discipline them for their own good. But God's people, the righteous, have to suffer along with the wicked because we all live together in a fallen world. And, although it may seem unfair, just remember that God knows every righteous person who calls on His name. And, He will hear their prayers and help them. Of course, He also expects us to use the common sense he has endowed us with to make wise decisions for ourselves, our families, and others. "Anna, do you think you should pray now?"

"Ezekiel, I see what you mean, and I do think I should pray now."

"Well, early this morning when I first woke up, I began praying. So Anna, perhaps you would like to say a prayer now yourself."

"Yes, I would. Dear Yahweh, thank you for knowing and loving us. Please bless my little brother or sister who is being born today, my mother Hannah, my father Ebed, and me, so we can all remain family in captivity. Lord, please bless everyone else here and at the palace and keep them safe. Father in heaven, please help my country and my city Jerusalem, and the people who live here but don't know you. And, Yehweh, please help us to trust in You as Ezekiel does. Amen."

"That was a beautiful prayer, Anna."

"Wahhh, wahhh, wahhh," cried the newborn baby.

"I hear the baby crying!" Anna wiped her eyes with her fists in her excitement. "Do you think it's a boy or a girl?"

"I don't know, but it won't be long now before we find out."

Shortly, they heard Yafa's voice again: "Ezekiel and Anna, you may come back in now." The two peeked from the doorway into the room. "Anna, you have a new baby brother! Would you and Zeke like to see him?" Ezekiel and Anna quickly spanned the room to join the others inside and Zeke voiced his sincere congratulations to Hannah and Anna for the tiny addition to their family. But Anna was speechless as she scooped up her little baby brother into her own arms, shed tears of joy for his safe delivery, smothered his face in kisses, and then took one of her mother's hands into her own in joy and thanksgiving that her mother had survived the ordeal of childbirth. Finally Hannah broke the silence by telling them the name of the child:

"My husband wants to call him Jesse!"

"That is a great name for a boy. But Anna tells me Ebed, Shallum, and Huldah are all at the palace right now."

"Yes, Ebed and Shallum are still at the palace, but Huldah went to get them to bring them back here."

"Good, but they need to hurry." Ezekiel was talking fast. "Quick. All of you. Come here."

As they gathered around Ezekiel, he spoke in hushed tones, "You're all in extreme danger. Since I'll become a priest at age 30, Yafa and I'll be classified as elite and be spared. So, you all need to know you are family now, and you've been living with us. But Saphah, …" He gave her with a solemn gaze. "you'll be recognized as foreign by your eyes, hair, and skin coloring. You won't pass as a Judahite. The cruel soldiers will try to kill you because we can't claim you as family."

Ezekiel's words were so blunt, they made Saphah step back. "Oh …!"

"You need to leave right now to escape to your own world." Ezekiel didn't pause. "We can't talk about it anymore now. I heard enemy troops coming closer, and they'll attempt to kill anyone mingled in with Jerusalem's soldiers. Everyone, say your goodbyes now, so perhaps Saphah can escape." But then he remembered. "She'll need water for her journey. Yafa, please get her a flask of water."

"Thank you," Saphah grabbed the flask and ran out the door. "Please pray for me, and I'll pray too!"

Oh dear! Saphah thought, *I can see the Babylonian soldiers approaching right now!* "My Lord and my God, please help me!" She prayed loudly as her heart beat wildly, *thump, thump, thump.* Saphah spun around in her tracks at the shriek of a woman's voice behind her. Aghast, she saw a Babylonian warrior pull the blade of a sword from the female's stomach. Instantly intestines and blood gushed from the victim's belly. Saphah thought she was going to vomit.

Blahhhh … Saphah expelled some of her previous meal. *Blahhhh* … She vomited again and wiped her mouth with her hand. Sick with anxiety, she crouched in the shadows and saw another soldier closer to her. He tore an infant from the clutch of a mother. The woman screamed as the soldier mercilessly slung the baby against the wall of a building and tossed the little one aside as if it were trash.

Oh my God, how evil! How cruel to kill a precious little baby like that! Saphah stifled her own cries. *Have they seen me? Have they heard me? Will they come for me next?* Frozen in fear, she couldn't move. But then, suddenly remembering her plight, she began to run as fast as she could.

"Kill them all," a rough voice yelled and then laughed as a man of war heard a little child's fearful cry for help.

Saphah dared to search for the child—only fifty feet behind her.

"Help me, help me!" the young child yelled over and over, "Hel …!" The child's words were snuffed out by the blade of a sword.

Saphah screamed, "I can't take anymore! Lord, please help me escape from this place!" Saphah prayed as she continued to run. Almost out of breath, she barely jumped over a big rock in the street. Then she heard a person who seemed to be in hot pursuit breathing heavily behind her. Her heart fell. *Has an enemy soldier almost caught up with me?* She turned just in time to see the pursuing soldier trip over the rock and fall flat to the ground.

"Praise God!" Saphah sighed in relief. "Praise God!"

Saphah spied a narrow side street and quickly took that route. *I'm getting close to the stairs to the Pool of Siloam. I think I know how to get there from here.* Dashing forward, she soon reached the steps. Making it to the bottom of the flight, she stopped to catch her breath. Then, pulling up her skirt tail between her legs and tying it on her sash in front, she took a deep breath and dove headfirst into the Pool of Siloam. Swimming toward the Hezekiah Tunnel, she soon came to the spot where she could stand on her feet. *Alright, I must wade the water from here forward into the tunnel,* she thought, remembering how she had waded it when she first came to Jerusalem.

Finally, reaching the wall separating the Siloam Spring from the cave, Saphah jumped as she heard the voice of someone already standing there. "Zephaniah," she gasped, recognizing her prophet friend in the light of his candle. "I'm so glad to see you!"

"As I am to see you," Prophet Zephaniah said. "God sent me here to tell you that you must return to your own world now."

"But what will you do, Zephaniah? Can you travel with me to the future?"

"No, I can't," the prophet replied. "But as God's will is performed in your life, it'll also be performed in mine, so you must leave now."

"Alright." Saphah gave him a big hug.

"God be with you." Prophet Zephaniah returned the hug.

"God be with you too." Saphah turned away and walked through the solid wall that separated the Hezekiah Tunnel from the cave.

It is so dark in here.

"Yes, it is," said a kind male voice. "Here, let me give you some light."

Saphah jumped at the sudden appearance of someone else in the cave. "You're a heavenly being, aren't you? I can tell by your glow." She continued to stare. "But who are you?"

"I'm here to light your pathway," the man said matter-of-factly. "So here, please take this candle."

Saphah reached over and took the lit candle in a holder from the celestial man. "Will you walk back with me all the way?"

Surely, I am with you always, to the very end of the age.[2] Then he was gone.

The watchwoman walked on, reflecting on what had just occurred. But then, holding the candle holder as she walked, Saphah began to reminisce on everything she'd learned during her journeys to Judah. Finally, she stopped short in her tracks and glanced upward in contemplation. *I think I need to pray for my nation,* she thought. *But who am I to pray for America?*

Saphah sat down on a ledge and considered Prophet Daniel's prayer from his book of the bible and what had happened: *When a remnant of people from Judah went into captivity in Babylon because they were judged for their sins, Daniel prayed a combination prayer asking forgiveness for both himself and his nation. I think I should pray for my nation too,* Saphah thought. *But I'm not a Daniel, I'm just a lowly servant of God from Missouri, one of the 50 states in America. Yet God has let me know that my nation, the United States of America, is under judgment.* Then she heard these words in her spirit:

Though the Lord is exalted, he looks kindly on the lowly; though lofty, he sees them from afar.[3]

Oh, my goodness! Saphah thought. *I think the Lord just let me know He 'looks kindly on the lowly' and 'sees them from afar,' so I think I do need to pray for my country, despite the fact I'm just an ordinary person.*

Thus, Saphah prayed God would hear her prayer just as He heard the prayers of people like David, Solomon, and Daniel. So, in her prayer for America, she requested God would have compassion on her nation, if in the future her people were taken into captivity under the conditions Solomon mentioned in his own prayer, as follows:

> *When a people sin against you—for there is no one who does not sin— and you become angry with them and give them over to their enemies, who take them captive to their own lands, far away or near, and if they have a change of heart in the land where they are held captive, and repent and plead with you in the land of their captors. …then from heaven …hear their prayer … forgive your people, …cause their captors to show them mercy …and bring them back to the land you gave to their ancestors.*[4]

Saphah also noted in prayer that while many of the citizens of the U. S. are Christians, yet all, including herself, have allowed the spiritual condition of the U.S. to deteriorate. Therefore, she confessed her guilt, like all the rest, of the sin of omission—apathy toward her duty to do something about the increase of evil in her land. So, first she prayed for God's forgiveness of her own sins and then for the forgiveness of the sins of the people of her nation.

Afterward, Saphah continued her walk in the cave until she rounded a bend and glimpsed the glow of the Aperture of Process beckoning her onward. At that moment, she heard a male voice.

"Hello, Saphah. I'm glad to see you, but I didn't expect you so soon."

"Hello, Nahal. I've arrived back early. The Babylonians broke through the wall in the second siege of Jerusalem and they're storming the city. Thus, Ezekiel and Zephaniah both told me I should go back to America."

"Oh, I see. So, was your walk in the cave uneventful?"

"Well, as I was walking here in the cave, I prayed for my nation."

"So, what did you pray?"

"I prayed that God would help America in the forthcoming days and that God would hear my prayer as he'd heard Daniel's prayer for his nation. I also reminded God about Solomon's prayer and asked him to respond as Solomon had requested if America is invaded by her enemies and people are taken captive into foreign lands, but then those people are sincerely repentant and ask God to forgive them."

"So, did God answer you?"

"He did, and it brought me to tears of thankfulness and joy. In my spirit he gave me four beautiful words:

"Stars and Stripes Forever."

"I knew immediately God was communicating with me by the phrase, 'Stars and Stripes Forever.' That is the name of the patriotic military march written and composed by John Philip Sousa and the Official National March of the United States of America. However, regarding the 'Stars and Stripes Forever' answer to my prayer, I knew it meant something special in regard to my nation."

"What do you think it means for your nation?"

"I think the Lord is referring to a future time when a remnant of American people may be sent into captivity in foreign lands. But at that time, if we the people of the U.S. turn to our God in humble repentance and ask forgiveness for what we've done, God will bring us out of captivity and return us home to the states. Then our flag will forever fly over America. It's a word of hope and promise for the United States: 'Stars and Stripes Forever.' Praise God!"

"Yes, praise God!"

"In the Book of Ezra, scripture relates how God's people of Judah were restored from Babylonian exile to the covenant land by God's doing:

> *In the first year of Cyrus king of Persia, in order to fulfill the word of the Lord spoken by Jeremiah, the Lord moved the heart of Cyrus king of Persia to make a proclamation throughout his realm and also to put it in writing: This is what Cyrus king of Persia says: 'The Lord, the God of heaven, has given me all the kingdoms of the earth and he has appointed me to build a temple for him at Jerusalem in Judah. Any of his people among you may go up to Jerusalem in Judah and build the temple of the Lord, the God of Israel, the God who is in Jerusalem, and may their God be with them. And in any locality where survivors may now be living, the people are to provide them with silver and gold, with goods and livestock, and with freewill offerings for the temple of God in Jerusalem.*[5]

But the Book of Isaiah also speaks about Jerusalem being reinhabited and provides additional insights. Here is the heading in my bible and the verses follow:

Jerusalem to Be Inhabited

> *'Remember these things, Jacob, for you, Israel, are my servant. I have made you, you are my servant; Israel I will not forget you. I have swept away your offenses like a cloud, your sins like the morning mist. Return to me for I have redeemed you.' Sing for joy you heavens, for the Lord has done this; shout aloud, you earth beneath. Burst into song, you mountains, you forests and all your trees, for the Lord has redeemed Jacob, he displays his glory in Israel.*

> *This is what the Lord says—your Redeemer, who formed you in the womb; I am the Lord, the Maker of all things, who stretches out the*

heavens, who spreads out the earth by myself, …who carries out the words of his servants and fulfills the predictions of his messengers, who says of Jerusalem, 'It shall be inhabited,' of the towns of Judah, 'They shall be rebuilt,' and of their ruins, 'I will restore them.' Who says to the watery deep, 'Be dry, and I will dry up your streams,' who says of Cyrus, 'He is my shepherd and will accomplish all I please; he will say of Jerusalem, 'Let it be rebuilt,' and of the temple, 'Let its foundations be laid.'

This is what the Lord says to his anointed, to Cyrus whose right hand I take hold of: …For the sake of Jacob my servant, of Israel my chosen, I summon you by name and bestow on you a title of honor, though you do not acknowledge me. I am the Lord, and there is no other, apart from me there is no God. I will strengthen you, though you have not acknowledged me, so that from the rising of the sun to the place of its setting people may know there is none besides me. I am the Lord, and there is no other. I form the light and create darkness, I bring prosperity and create disaster; I, the Lord, do all these things.

I will raise up Cyrus in my righteousness; I will make all his ways straight. He will rebuild my city and set my exiles free. [Then others] will come over to you and will be yours; they will bow down before you and plead with you, saying, 'Surely God is with you, and there is no other; there is no other God.'…[So} turn to me and be saved, all you ends of the earth; for I am God and there is no other. By myself I have sworn, my mouth has uttered in all integrity a word that will not be revoked: Before me every knee will bow; by me every tongue will swear. They will say of me, 'In the Lord alone are deliverance and strength. All who have raged against him will come to him and be put to shame. But all the descendants of Israel will find deliverance in the Lord and will make their boast in him.[6]

Thus, Isaiah gloriously sets out God's deliverance for his people. First, he says the suffering of the people has provided the way for their forgiveness and restoration. Then he points out that 'the Maker

of all things,' who carries out 'the words of his servants and fulfills
the predictions of his messengers,' will say of Jerusalem, 'Let it be
rebuilt,' and of the temple, 'Let it's foundations be laid.' But
then he relates that the Lord has bestowed on King Cyrus a title
of honor because the Lord has appointed him to carry out a divine
commission in his role as king. Therefore, the Lord summons Cyrus
by name and controls his actions. And God does all that so people
may know 'there is none beside me.' Only He is God."

"Yes," said Nahal. "But then, Isaiah lets us know God performs these
things 'in righteousness.' God is making all things right for the nation
through King Cyrus, enabling him to 'rebuild my city and set my
exiles free.' Then one day the nations will acknowledge Israel's God,
providing an invitation for them to 'turn to me and be saved.' Thus,
all the spiritual descendants of Israel (Jew and Gentile) who come
to believe, 'will find deliverance in the Lord, and make their boast in
him.'"

"There's also a heartfelt Psalm which speaks to restoration for Zion
and thus to the hope and promise of restoration for the U. S. too:

> *When the Lord turned again the captivity of Zion, we were like them
> that dreamed. Then was our mouth filled with laughter, and our tongue
> with singing: then said they among the heathen, The Lord hath done
> great things for them. The Lord hath done great things for us, whereof
> we are glad. Turn again our captivity, O Lord, as the streams in the
> south.*[7]

Here we see a restoration of Zion's fortunes: The land once again
overflows with God's blessings as the streams of the desert overflow
in the rainy season. And thus, we have these words from scripture to
pray in a future time for America: 'Turn again our captivity, O Lord,
as the streams in the south.' Amen."

"Amen," repeated Nahal. "Did the Lord say anything else after that?"

"Yes, He did. He said four bitter words to my ears to remind me once again of his judgment still impending on America:

"There will be war."

"So, Nahal, do you think there will be a time of revival and reform before that?"

"Perhaps. But only if the American people spiritually prepare as Prophet Zephaniah pointed out:

> *Gather together, gather yourselves together, you shameful nation, before the decree takes effect and that day passes like windblown chaff, before the Lord's fierce anger comes upon you, before the day of the Lord's wrath comes upon you. Seek the Lord, all you humble of the land, you who do what he commands. Seek righteousness, seek humility; perhaps you will be sheltered on the day of the Lord's anger.*"[8]

Note to the Reader

There is information of great importance you need to know about the story of Saphah, a fictional character in a work of Christian Fantasy, who gave warnings from God to the citizens of her nation. The words written in bold in the chapters are actual warnings given to me, the author of this book, in regard to my nation, America. They are words supplied to me by the Holy Spirit that God wants me to share with you, because He wants you to truly see them, hear them, and consider them in your heart.

You need to see, hear, and consider these words, because the Old Testament in Malachi 4 says the Lord is going to *send you Elijah the prophet before the coming of the great and dreadful day of the Lord: And he shall turn the heart of the fathers to the children, and the heart of the children to their fathers, lest I come and smite the earth with a curse.*[1] …[In addition], *remember ye the law of Moses my servant, which I commanded unto him in Horeb for all Israel* [all God's people in all eras], *with the statutes and judgements.*[2]

But what does scripture from Malachi 4 about parents and children really mean? The KJV Study Bible commentary notes the sense is not merely that when Elijah comes, it "will usher in a new harmony in family relationships. The mention of parents and children is a way of saying when the day of the Lord comes, He will turn everyone back to faithfulness to the covenant. This is a promise of great revival."[3] Hence, many people will turn to the Lord at that time, and there will be a faithful remnant ready for when the Lord returns for the second time, as Malachi noted:

> *Then they that feared the Lord spake often one to another: and the Lord hearkened and heard it, and a book of remembrance was written before him for them that feared the Lord, and that thought upon his name. And they shall be mine, saith the Lord of hosts, in that day when I make up my jewels; and I will spare them, as a man spareth his own son that serveth him.*[4]

The 'book of remembrance' here is possibly a scroll akin to the 'book of life,' as found in the book of Revelation.[5]

But how does Malachi's mention of Elijah and Moses fit in with the prophecies of the New Testament? Here is what Revelation 11 has to say about Elijah and Moses: *I will appoint my two witnesses, and they will prophesy for 1,260 days, clothed in sackcloth. They are the two olive trees and the two lampstands, and they stand before the Lord of the earth.*[6] Scripture says these two witnesses will have the ability to protect themselves from attack. Also, they can perform miracles, if necessary, such as preventing rain, causing plagues and turning water into blood. These abilities bring to mind Elijah and Moses, who exhibited such miracles in 1 Kings 17:1 and Exodus 7:19-20.

But who are these two figures of Elijah and Moses? The commentary of my NIV Bible says of the two witnesses: "Modeled after Moses and Elijah, they may symbolize testifying believers in the final period before Christ returns, or they may be two actual individuals who will be martyred for the proclamation of the truth."[7] The imagery of the two olive trees and the two lampstands "emphasizes that the power for [their] effective testimony is supplied by the Spirit of God."[8] So, the future forerunners of Messiah at His second coming may be persons clothed with Elijah's power who, with zealous upholders of the law clothed in the spirit of Moses, may be the forerunning witnesses alluded to in Malachi 3-4 and Revelation 11:3-12.

But what is the importance of all this information? First, all people need to remember that in the final period before Christ returns to judge the world, the Lord will appoint his testifying witnesses, whatever the number, and their power will be supplied by the Holy Spirit. Second, people need to keep in mind an even more important fact: The day is coming when the Lord shall "return and discern between the righteous and the wicked, between him that serveth God and him that serveth him not."[9]

For, behold, the day cometh, that shall burn as an oven; and all the proud, yea and all that do wickedly, shall be stubble: and the day that cometh shall burn them up, saith the LORD of hosts, that it shall leave them neither root nor branch. But unto you that fear my name shall the Sun of righteousness arise with healing in his wings; and ye shall go forth.[10]

So, which group will you be in when the Lord returns? Will you be in the group of the 'righteous that serveth God'? Or will you be in the group of the 'wicked that serveth him not'? God has given you warning that now is the time for you to make that choice 'before the coming of the great and dreadful day of the Lord.'

NOTES

CHAPTER 1: EZEKIEL & YAFA

[1]Matthew 28:20, emphasis added.

CHAPTER 2: JOURNEY INTO THE PAST

[1]See Genesis 18:1-19:23.

[2]See Judges 13:3-5.

[3]Mark: 10:27, emphasis added.

[4]John 1:5, emphasis added.

[5]Matthew 13:16, emphasis added.

[6]John 14:17, emphasis added.

[7]Ezekiel 3:17, emphasis added.

[8]Ezekiel 22:30, emphasis added.

CHAPTER 3: A CITY SET ON A HILL

[1]Ezekiel 12:2, emphasis added.

[2]Jeremiah 5:21; 23; 29, emphasis added.

[3]Matthew 13:14-15, which quotes Isaiah 6:8-10, emphasis added.

[4]John Winthrop, "A Model of Christian Charity," The Winthrop Society, 1630. Read online at: John Winthrop A Model of Christian Charity pdf.

[5]Matthew 5:14 (*The KJV Study Bible*), emphasis added.

[6]Winthrop, "A Model of Christian Charity."

[7]*Ibid.*

[8]Ephesians 5:15, emphasis added.

[9]Winthrop, "A Model of Christian Charity."

[10]1 Timothy 2:3-6, emphasis added.

[11]Psalm 139:2-3, emphasis added.

[12]"Softly and Tenderly, Jesus Is Calling," by Will L. Thompson, public domain.

[13]"When We All Get to Heaven," by Eliza E. Hewitt, public domain.

[14]"In the Sweet Bye and Bye," by Sanford F. Bennett, public domain.

[15]Just Over in the Glory Land," by Jas. W. Acuff, public domain.

CHAPTER 4: THE APERTURE OF PROCESS

[1]Esther 4:14, emphasis added.

[2]Esther 4:16, emphasis added.

[3]Matthew 28:18, 20 (KJV Study Bible), emphasis added.

[4]"There Shall Be Showers of Blessing," by Daniel W. Whittle, public domain.

CHAPTER 5: A PARALLEL TIME & PLACE

[1]Ezekiel 34:26, emphasis added.

[2]Isaiah 55:10-11, emphasis added.

[3]"There Shall Be Showers of Blessing," Whittle, public domain.

[4]*Ibid.*

[5]*Ibid.*

[6]*Ibid.*

[7]1 John 1:9, emphasis added.

[8]Isaiah 57:15, emphasis added.

[9]Leviticus 20:13, emphasis added.

[10]Romans 1:26, emphasis added.

[11]Romans 1:32, emphasis added.

[12]Genesis 1:27, emphasis added.

[13]Psalm 98:9, emphasis added.

[14]Ecclesiastes 3:15, emphasis added.

[15]Ecclesiastes 3:17, emphasis added.

[16]2 Peter 3:10, emphasis added.

[17]Psalm 139:13-16, emphasis added.

[18]Amos 3:7, emphasis added.

CHAPTER 6: WINNOW

[1]Jeremiah 15:1, emphasis added.

[2]Jeremiah 15:2, emphasis added.

[3]Jeremiah 15:4, emphasis added.

[4]2 Kings 21:3-6, 16, emphasis added.

[5]Jeremiah 15:6-7, emphasis added.

[6]See Revelation 6:1-8.

[7]Isaiah 53:6, emphasis added.

[8]1 Peter 2:24-25, emphasis added.

[9]Jeremiah 51:2, emphasis added.

[10]"At Calvary," by Wm. N. Newell, public domain.

[11]2 Kings 21:20, emphasis added.

[12]2 Kings 22:2, emphasis added.

[13]1 Kings 13:2, emphasis added.

[14]*Ibid.*

[15]Deuteronomy 30:15-18, emphasis added.

[16]Deuteronomy 30:11-14, emphasis added.

[17]Deuteronomy 28:1-2, emphasis added.

[18]2 Peter 3:4, 8-9, emphasis added.

[19]2 Peter 3:12-13, emphasis added.

[20]Isaiah 65:17, emphasis added.

[21]Revelation 21:1, 3-4, emphasis added.

[22]Psalm 121:1-4, 8, emphasis added.

[23]Psalm 73:24, 26, emphasis added.

CHAPTER 7: THE WALL

[1]Luke 10:18-19, emphasis added.

[2]"God Will Take Care of You," by Civilla D. Martin, public domain.

[3]Exodus 14:15 (NAS), emphasis added.

[4]See (*NIV Study Bible, Large Print*), "Hezekiah Tunnel and Water Projects," p. 609. See Wikipedia, "Siloam Inscription," p. 2.

CHAPTER 8: THE CITY OF GOD

[1]See 2 Kings 22:14.

[2]See 2 Kings 10:15-28.

[3]See 1 Chronicles 2:55.

[4]See Jeremiah 35:1-19.

[5]Psalm 19:1-2, emphasis added.

[6]See 1 Kings 13:1-2.

CHAPTER 9: SHALLUM & HULDAH

[1]See Genesis 2: 1-3.

[2]Philippians 4:13 (NAS), emphasis added.

CHAPTER 10: THE TWO PROPHETS

[1]Philippians 4:19, emphasis added.

CHAPTER 11: THE DAY OF THE LORD

[1]Psalm 16:2-5, 8, emphasis added.

[2]Isaiah 13:9-11, emphasis added.

[3]Joel 2:30-32, emphasis added.
[4]Mark 13:19-20, 24-26, emphasis added.
[5]See Deuteronomy 28:1-14.
[6]See Deuteronomy 28:15-68.
[7]See Mark 13:32-33.
[8]Deuteronomy 4:29-31, (*KJV Study Bible*), emphasis added.

CHAPTER 12: THE TWO MESSAGES

[1]Zephaniah 1:1, emphasis added.

CHAPTER 13: THE SHOPPING TRIP

[1]Matthew 6:9-13, (*KJV Study Bible*), emphasis added.
[2]Psalm 37:39-40, emphasis added.
[3]Psalm 46:1, emphasis added.
[4]2 Peter 1:21, emphasis added.
[5]1 Peter 1:25, emphasis added.
[6]Zephaniah 1:4-6, 8, emphasis added.

CHAPTER 14: THE ENCOUNTER

[1]Deuteronomy 23:17, emphasis added.
[2]Judges 2:17, emphasis added.
[3]Psalm 37: 39-40, emphasis added.
[4]Matthew 28:20, emphasis added.
[5]*Ibid.*

CHAPTER 15: THE WORD WAS GOD

[1]2 Chronicles 28:1, emphasis added.
[2]2 Chronicles 28:22, emphasis added.
[3]2 Chronicles 28:24-25, emphasis added.
[4]2 Chronicles 29:6-7, emphasis added.
[5]2 Chronicles 29:2-6, emphasis added.
[6]Jeremiah 11:10, 13, emphasis added.
[7]See Jeremiah 11:11.
[8]1 Timothy 2:5, emphasis added.
[9]John 14:6, emphasis added.
[10]Acts 4:10, emphasis added.
[11]Acts 4:12, emphasis added.
[12]Acts 10:43, emphasis added.
[13]Isaiah 16:5, emphasis added.

¹⁴Isaiah 7:14, emphasis added.
¹⁵Isaiah 9:2, 6-7, emphasis added.
¹⁶Matthew 1:1, emphasis added.
¹⁷Matthew 1:22-23, emphasis added.
¹⁸Luke 1:30-35, emphasis added.
¹⁹2 Samuel 7:16, emphasis added.
²⁰John 1:1, emphasis added.
²¹Genesis 1:1, emphasis added.
²²John 14:9-10, emphasis added.
²³John 14:12, emphasis added.
²⁴Luke 4:18-19, emphasis added.
²⁵Zephaniah 1:14, emphasis added.
²⁶Zephaniah 1:15, 17-18, emphasis added.
²⁷Zephaniah 2:1-3, emphasis added.

CHAPTER 16: LOOKOUT FOR ADVERSITY

[1]Read online at: https://www.newsmax/Newsfront/William-Cohen-defense-chief-terriorist-attack-powr-grid/2015/06/29/id/652742, pp. 1-2.

[2]Read online at: https://ge.com/news/reports/two-countries-waged-cyber-war-here's-expect, p. 2.

[3]Read online at: https://www.reuters.com/world/europe/russia-china-tell-nato-stop-expansion-moscow-backs-beijing-taiwan-2022-02-04/ p. 2.

[4]Read online at: https://www.foxnews.com/world/ukraine-conflict-heightens-the-risk-of-chinese-american-war-professor-says-3-5-22, p. 3.

[5]Read online at: https://www.newsmax.com/world/globaltalk/xijinping-china-military/2022/11/10/id/1095789, p.1.

[6]Read online at: https://www.newsmax.com/world/globaltalk/xijinping-china-military/2022/11/10/id/1095789, p. 2.

[7]Read online at: https://www.newsmax.com/newsfront/russia-china-naval/2022/12/28/id/1102188, p. 2.

[8]Read online at: https://www.newsmax.com/world/air-force-general-predicts-war-china-2025, p. 2.

[9]Read online at: https://www.newsmax.com/newsfront/mike-mc-caul-china/2023/01/29/id/1106350, p. 2.

[10]Read online at: https://www.foxnews.com/world/military-experts-provide-frank-assessment-us-shortcomings-potential-china-conflict, p. 3.

[11]Read online at: https://www.foxnews.com/world/china-confirms-balloon-theirs-spokeperson-claims-civilian-research-airship, p. 2.

[12]Read online at: https://www.foxnews.com/politics/spy/-balloon-likely-sent-extensive-intelligence-to-china-experts-say, p. 2.

[13]Read online at: https://www.foxnews.com/politics/spy/-balloon-likely-sent-extensive-intelligence-to-china-experts-say, p. 3.

[14]Read online at: https://frontierindia.com/briefs/chinese-spy-balloon-approaching-whiteman-air-force-base-with-b-2-stealth-aircraft/, p. 1.

[15]Read online at: https://www.newsmax.com/newsfront/china-spy-balloon/2023/02/03/id/1107243, p. 2.

[16]Read online at: https://www.newsmax.com/newsfront/china-spy-balloon/2023/02/03/id/1107243, p. 2.

[17]Read online at: https://www.newsmax.com/newsfront/south-korea-us/2023/02/19/id/1109228, p. 3.

[18]Read online at: https://www.foxnews.com/media/intel-community-blinking-red-over-isis-al-qaeda-rebuilding-make-waltz-simmering-powerkeg, p. 1.

[19]Read online at: https://www.newsmax.com/newsfront/iran-uranium-enrichment/2023/02/20/id/1109326, p. 1.

[20]Isaiah 5:20, emphasis added.

[21]2 Corinthians 4:4, emphasis added.

[22]Romans 1:18-20, emphasis added.

[23]Romans 1:21-23, emphasis added.

[24]Romans 1:24-27, emphasis added.

[25]Romans 1:28, emphasis added.

[26]1 Corinthians 10:13 (KJV Study Bible), emphasis added.

[27]Romans 1:29-31, emphasis added.

[29]Read online at: https://www.newsmax.com/newsmax-tv-cameron-woke-libraries/2022/12/08/id/1099726, p.2.

[30]Read online at: https://www.foxnews.com/politics/anti-religious-bigotry-nebraska-dems-bill-would-ban-kids-vacation-bible-school-church-youth-group, pp. 1-2.

[31]Read online at: https://www.foxnews.com/mediafbi-found-gateway-declare-christians-criminals-federal-whistleblower, p. 1.

[32]*Ibid*, pp. 1-2.

[33]*Ibid*, pp.2-4.

[34]Read online at: https://www.barrons.com/news/turkey-syria-quake--deaths-to-top-50,000-un-relief-chief-978ee2e4, p. 1.

[35]John 1:29, emphasis added.

[36]Romans 5:9-10, emphasis added.

[37]Romans 5:11 (KJV Study Bible), emphasis added.

CHAPTER 17: BEGINNING OF BIRTH PAINS

[1]Deuteronomy 27:9, emphasis added.

[2]Galatians 3:6-8, 26-29, emphasis added.

[3]William Hendrickson, More Than Conquerors, (Grand Rapids, Michigan; Baker Books, 1967), p. 152. See: Isaiah 54; Amos 9:11; Matthew 21:33; Romans 11:15-4; Galatians 3:9-16, 29; Ephesians 2:11; 1 Peter 2:9; Revelation 4:4; 21:12-14.

[4]Deuteronomy 28:1-14, emphasis added.

[5]Deuteronomy 28:15-62, emphasis added.

[6]Deuteronomy 28:49, emphasis added.

[7]Deuteronomy 28:59, emphasis added.

[8]Deuteronomy 28:64, emphasis added.

[9]Lamentations 3:33, emphasis added.

[10]Ezekiel 18:23, 30-32, emphasis added.

[11]See Psalm 106:6-13.

[12]See Psalm 106:14-33.

[13]Psalm 106:35-39, emphasis added.

[14]Psalm 106:40-46, emphasis added.

[15]2 Chronicles 33:9-10, emphasis added.

[16]2 Chronicles 33:20, emphasis added.

[17]2 Chronicles 33:22, emphasis added.

[18]Matthew 24:4-9, 12-14, emphasis added.

[19]Revelation 20:1-3, emphasis added.

[20]Matthew 28:18-20, emphasis added.

[21]See (NIV Study Bible, Large Print), Commentary on Revelation 20:2, (1) Amillennialism, p. 2174.

[22]Revelation 20:7-8, emphasis added.

[23]See Ezekiel 38-39 for the Old Testament background.

[24]Matthew 24:10, emphasis added.

[25]2 Thessalonians 2:3, emphasis added.

[26]2 Thessalonians 2:7, 9-12, emphasis added.

[27]Revelation 22:12, emphasis added.

CHAPTER 18: THE AUDIENCE

[1]Isaiah 42:18, 20-22, emphasis added.

[2]Isaiah 42:24-25, emphasis added.

[3]See NIV Commentary on Isaiah 42:25, p. 1094.

[4]Isaiah 42:25, emphasis added.

CHAPTER 19: FELLOWSHIP OF HIS SUFFERINGS

[1]1 John 3:8, emphasis added.

[2]1 John 3:4, emphasis added.

[3]John 8:44, emphasis added.

[4]1 John 4:3, emphasis added.

[5]1 John 5:19, emphasis added.

[6]Matthew 24:9-14, emphasis added.

[7]Revelation 3:10, emphasis added.

[8]See (NIV Study Bible, Large Print), Commentary on Revelation 3:10, p. 2154.

[9]Revelation 3:11-12, emphasis added.

[10]James 5:7, emphasis added.

[11]James 5:8-9, emphasis added.

[12]See (*NIV Study Bible, Large Print*), Commentary on James 5:8-9, p. 2096. See Hebrews 1:1-2.

[13]James 5:10-11, emphasis added.

[14]Revelation 13:1, emphasis added.

[15]Revelation 13:7-10, emphasis added.

[16]Daniel 12:1-4, emphasis added.

[17]Mark 13:19-20, 26-27, emphasis added.

[18]Ezekiel 34:13, emphasis added.

[19]Revelation 6:9-11, emphasis added.

[20]2 Timothy 3:1,12-13, emphasis added.

[21]1 Thessalonians 5:3 (*KJV Study Bible*), emphasis added.

[22]Matthew 5:10, emphasis added.

[23]Philippians 1:29-30 (*KJV Study Bible*), emphasis added.

[24]Philippians 3:10, emphasis added.

[25]Revelation 1:1-3, emphasis added.

[26]See (*NIV Study Bible*, Large Print), Commentary on Revelation 11:3, p. 2163.

[27]Revelation 11:7-10, emphasis added.

[28]See Revelation 6:10.

[29]See Revelation 8:3-5.

[30]See Revelation 5:10; 20:4; 22:5.

[31]See Revelation 20:10; 19:20; 18:2.

[32]Revelation 17:14, emphasis added.

[33]Revelation 7:14-17, emphasis added.

CHAPTER 20: LEARNING THE ROPES

[1]Matthew 19:14, emphasis added.

[2]Genesis 1:27, emphasis added.

[3]Isaiah 7:15, emphasis added.

[4]John 8:44, emphasis added.

[5]*Ibid.*

[6]John 8:47, emphasis added.

[7]Read online at: https://www.foxnews.com/opinion/students-deserve-know-shocking-truth-communism, p.3.

[8]*Ibid.*, p. 2.

[9]*Ibid.*, p. 3.

[10]*Ibid.*, p. 4.

[11]Read online at: https://www.foxnews.com/media/maryland-teacher-calls-urgent-war-capitalism-revolution-involve-viole, p. 2.

[12]Read online at: https://www.foxnews.com/us/minnesota-elementary-school-music-teacher-claims-goal-confuse-students-about-gendervideo, p. 2.

[13]Read online at: https://www.psychiatry.org/patients-families/gender/dysphoria/what-is-gender-dysphoria, p. 1.

[14]Read online at: https://healthline.com/health/news/surgery-gives-transgender-man-penis-from-own-body, pp. 6, 8.

[15]Genesis 1:27, emphasis added.

[16]Read online at: https://www.newsmax.com/newsfront/aaps-physician-statement/2023/02/27/id/1110391, pp. 2-3.

[17]Read online at: https://www.foxnews.com/us/school-choice-gives-parents-power-break-teachers-unions-chokeholds-students-coreydeangelis, p. 3.

[18]Read online at: https://www.foxnews.com/media/teacher-union-contracts-aimed-indoctrinate-students-leftist-ideas-promoted-race-based-hiring-report, pp. 1-3, 5-6.

[19]*Ibid.* p. 7.

CHAPTER 21: THE HULDAH GATE

[1]Psalm 30:5, emphasis added.

[2]Psalm 30:11-12, emphasis added.

[3]2 Samuel 12-23, emphasis added.

[4]Betsy DeVos, "Betsy DeVos Fights for Education Freedom," *Newsmax*, September 2022, p. 44.

[5]*Ibid.*, p. 44.

[6]*Ibid.*, p. 45.

[7]*Ibid.*, p. 45.

[8]Read online at: https://www.newsmax.com/newsfront/gov-desantis-school-choice-education/2023/03/27/id/1114016/, p. 2.

[9]Read online at: https://www.desmoinesregister.com/story/news/politics/2023/01/24/iowa-governor-kim-reynolds-signs-school-choice-scholarships-education-bill-into-law, p. 1.

[10]Read online at: https://www.foxnews.com/politics/north-carolina-go-gop-move-school-choice-with-new-supermajority-dems-stunning-party-switch, pp. 1-2.

[11]Nichole Stelle Garnett, "Time for Religious Charter Schools," *Newsmax*, March 2023, p. 22.

[12]*Ibid.*, p. 22.

[13]*Ibid.*, p. 22.

[14]*Ibid.*, p. 22.

[15]See https://en.wikipedia.org/wiki/Homeschooling, p. 1.

[16]Read online at: http://en.wikipedia.org/wiki/Classical-Education-Movement, p. 1.

[17]*Ibid.*, p. 1.

[18]*Ibid.*, p. 1.

[19]*Ibid.*, p. 5.

[20]Read online at: https://www.forbes.com/sites/brandon-busteed/2020/11/07/why-the-one-room-schoolhouse-is-a-vision-for-the-future-not-just-a-relic-of-the-past/?sh=57, p. 2.

[21]Read online at: https://www.foxnews.com/media/teachers-sound-alarm-growing-problems-schools-colleagjues-leaving-droves, p. 3.

[22]*Ibid.*, p. 2.

[23]*Ibid.*, p. 1.

[24]*Ibid.*, p. 2.

[25]*Ibid.*, p. 4.

[26]Proverbs 13:24, emphasis added.

[27]Proverbs 19:18, emphasis added.

[28]Proverbs 29:15, emphasis added.

[29]Proverbs 29:17, emphasis added.

[30]Proverbs 3:12, emphasis added.

[31]Hebrews 12:5-6, emphasis added.

[32]Hebrews 12:11, emphasis added.

[33]Read online at: https://www.forbes.com/sites/brandon-busteed/2020/11/07/why-the-one-room-schoolhouse-is-a-vision-for-the-future-not-just-a-relic-of-the-past/?sh=57, p. 3.

[34]*Ibid.*, p. 3-4.

[35]Read online at: https://www.npr.org/sections/ed/2014/07/02/326196530/the-return-of-the-one-room-schoolhouse, p. 2.

[36]*Ibid.*, p. 2.

[37]*Ibid.*, p. 3.

CHAPTER 22: THE BIRTHDAY CELEBRATION

[1]Psalm 107: 1, 9, 43, 31, emphasis added.

CHAPTER 23: THE JERUSALEM SCHOOL

[1] 2 Kings 9:1-3, 6-8, emphasis added.

[2] 2 Kings 21:25-26, emphasis added.

[3] 1 Kings 16:31-32, emphasis added.

[4] 2 Kings 10:15-16, emphasis added.

[5] See (NIV Study Bible, Large Print), Commentary on 10:15, p. 585.

[6] Isaiah 44:6, emphasis added.

[7] 2 Kings 10:25, 27, emphasis added.

[8] 1 Kings 19:15, emphasis added.

[9] 2 Kings 10:28, emphasis added.

[10] 2 Kings 10:31, emphasis added.

[11] 1 Chronicles 2:55, emphasis added.

[12] Judges 1:16, emphasis added.

[13] Isaiah 52:21, emphasis added.

CHAPTER 25: EVE

[1] 2 Samuel 12:23, emphasis added.

[2] Romans 8:28, emphasis added.

[3] 1 Kings 11:31, emphasis added.

[4] 1 Kings 11:35-36, emphasis added.

[5] 1 Kings 11:36, emphasis added.

[6] 1 Kings 11:37-38, emphasis added.

[7] 1 Kings 12:28, emphasis added.

[8] 1 Kings 12:29-30, emphasis added.

[9] 1 Kings, 12:31, emphasis added.

[10] 1 Kings, 13:1-2, emphasis added.

[11] See (*NIV Study Bible, Large Print*), p. 504.

CHAPTER 26: THE WEDDING CELEBRATION

[1] Psalm 128:1, emphasis added.

[2] Psalm 128:2, emphasis added.

[3] Psalm 128:3, emphasis added.

[4] Psalm 128:4, emphasis added.

[5] "The Wonder of Love," by Geraldine Koehn, public domain.

[6] Song of Solomon 4:9, emphasis added.

[7] Song of Solomon, 3:4, emphasis added.

[8]Song of Solomon, 8:6, emphasis added.
[9]Song of Solomon, 8:7, emphasis added.
[10]Song of Solomon, 2:16, emphasis added.
[11]*Ibid.*
[12]Genesis 2:24, emphasis added.
[13]Malachi 2:14, emphasis added.
[14]Ecclesiastes 4:11-12, emphasis added.
[15]Genesis 2:18, emphasis added.

[16]"Great Is Thy Faithfulness," by Thomas O. Chisholm, public domain.

CHAPTER 27: THE ALREADY & THE NOT YET

[1]Exodus 20:3, emphasis added.

[2]Read online at: https://thirdmill.org/answers/answer/asp/file143089, p. 1.

[3]1 Timothy 4:1, emphasis added.

[4]See (*NIV Study Bible, Large Print*), commentary on 4:1, p. 2041.

[5]Oscar Cullman, *Christ & Time: The Primitive Conception of Time and History*, trans. Floyd V Filson (Philadelphia: Westminster Press, 1950), p. 146.

[6]2 Samuel 7:11-12, 16, emphasis added.

[7]Joel 2:28-32, emphasis added.

[8]See Acts 2:17-21.

[9]Job 19: 26-27, emphasis added.

[10]1 John 3:2, emphasis added.

[11]Acts 24:14-15, emphasis added.

[12]Acts 26:22-23, emphasis added.

[13]Brandon D. Crowe, *The Hope of Israel: The Resurrection of Christ in the Acts of the Apostles*, (Grand Rapids: Baker Academics), 2020, pp. 85-86.

[14]John 11:25-26, emphasis added.

[15]John 5:28-29, emphasis added.

[16]Anthony Hoekema, *The Bible and the Future* (Grand Rapids, Eerdsman's 1979), pp. 21-22.

[17]Colossians 1:13, emphasis added.

[18]Romans 8:29, emphasis added.

[19]Matthew 6:10, emphasis added.
[20]Isaiah 43:15, emphasis added.
[21]Exodus 19:5-6, emphasis added.
[22]Isaiah 9:6-7, emphasis added.
[23]Jeremiah 31:33, emphasis added.
[24]Luke 1:31-33, emphasis added.
[25]Luke 2:10-11, emphasis added.
[26]Mark 1:25, emphasis added.
[27]Matthew 21:43, emphasis added.
[28]Revelation 1:6, emphasis added.
[29]Romans 5:17, emphasis added.
[30]Matthew 13:24-28, emphasis added.
[31]Matthew 13:29-30, emphasis added.
[32]Matthew 13:38-39 emphasis added.
[33]Jeremiah 1:1, emphasis added.
[34]See (*NIV Study Bible, Large Print*), Commentary on Jeremiah 1:2, p. 1223.

CHAPTER 28: AMERICA'S SPIRITUAL OUTLOOK

[1]Revelation 12:2, 5-6, emphasis added.
[2]Revelation 12:7-9, emphasis added.
[3]Revelation 12:12, emphasis added.
[4]Revelation 12:13-14, 17, emphasis added.
[5]Ephesians 6:10-12, emphasis added.
[6]Revelation 9:19, emphasis added.
[7]See (*NIV Study Bible, Large Print*), Commentary on Revelation 9:19, p. 2162.
[8]Revelation 9:20-21, emphasis added.
[9]1 Corinthians 10:7-8, emphasis added.
[10]Deuteronomy 32:17 (*The KJV Study Bible*), emphasis added.
[11]*Ibid.*, 32:16.
[12]Read online at: https://www.icr.org/article/worship-idols-demons, p. 1.
[13]1 Corinthians 10:14, emphasis added.
[14]Read online at: https://www.icr.org/article/worship-idols-demons, p. 1.

¹⁵Colossians 3:5, emphasis added.

¹⁶Read online at: https://www.newsweek.com/priest-two-women-arrested-alleged-group-sex-lousiana-church-altar-1537876, p. 1.

¹⁷Ibid.

¹⁸Read online at: https://www.wwltv.com/article/news/crime-pearl-river-priest-charged-with-vandelism-over-filmed-sex-with-dominatrices-on-altar/289-10497a2f-b3ea-4b, p. 2.

¹⁹*Ibid.*

²⁰Read online at: https://www.newsweek.com/priest-two-women-arrested-alleged-group-sex-lousiana-church-altar-1537876, p. 2.

²¹Read online at: https://www.gty.org/library/sermons/library/1261, p. 3.

²²Acts 19: 13, 15-17, emphasis added.

²³Acts 19:17-19, emphasis added.

²⁴See (*NIV Study Bible, Large Print*), Commentary on Acts 19:19, p. 1865.

²⁵Deuteronomy 18:10-11, emphasis added.

²⁶Read online at: www.hungrygen.com/moderndaywitchcraft, p. 2.

²⁷Read online at: https://www.caron-org/addiction-101/drug-use/statistics-and-demograpics, p. 1.

²⁸Read online at: https://www.dea.gov/resonding-america-over-dose-crisis, p. 2.

²⁹Ibid.

³⁰2 Thessalonians 3:11, emphasis added.

³¹2 Thessalonians 3:11-12, emphasis added.

³²1 Thessalonians 5:14, emphasis added.

³³Romans:2:5, emphasis added.

³⁴Read online at: https://www.newsmax.com/newsfront/united-states-china-malware--/2023/07/29/id/1128957/?ns_mail_uid=b3a1acd0-166a-ae63-60fee606432a&n, p. 2.

³⁵Ibid., pp. 2-3.

Chapter 29: A Priestly Outlook on Sin

¹Leviticus 10:11, emphasis added.

²Deuteronomy 16:18-20, emphasis added.

³Deuteronomy 16:21-22, emphasis added.

[4]Deuteronomy 17:2-4, 7, emphasis added.

[5]Deuteronomy 13:14, emphasis added.

[6]Deuteronomy 17:9-12, emphasis added.

[7]2Chronicles 28:2-5, emphasis added.

[8]See (*NIV Study Bible, Large Print*), Commentary on 2 Chronicles 28:5, p. 704.

[9]2 Kings 21:2-16, emphasis added.

[10]2 Kings 17:7, emphasis added.

[11]*The Baker Illustrated Bible Background Commentary*, edited by J. Scott Duvall & J. Daniel Hays, (Grand Rapids: Baker Publishing Group), 2020, p. 1317.

[12]Ezekiel 3:17-19, emphasis added. Also see: 2 Samuel 2:28; Leviticus 23:23-25; Joel 2:1; Matthew 24:31; 1 Thessalonians 4:16.

CHAPTER 30: LAST CHANCE TO REPENT

[1]Zephaniah 1:7, emphasis added.

[2]Zephaniah 3:20, (*The KJV Study Bible*) emphasis added.

[3]Zephaniah 3:1-5, emphasis added.

[4]Zephaniah 3:20, (*The KJV Study Bible*) emphasis added.

[5]Zephaniah 3:7, emphasis added.

[6]Zephaniah 3:20, (*The KJV Study Bible*) emphasis added.

[7]Zephaniah 1:4-6, 10-11, emphasis added.

[8]Zephaniah 3:20, (*The KJV Study Bible*)emphasis added.

[9]Zephaniah 1:12, emphasis added.

[10]Zephaniah 3:20, (*The KJV Study Bible*) emphasis added.

[11]Zephaniah 1:14-18, emphasis added.

[12]Zephaniah 3:20, (*The KJV Study Bible*) emphasis added.

[13]Zephaniah 2:1-3, emphasis added.

[14]Zephaniah 3:20, (*The KJV Study Bible*) emphasis added.

[15]Zephaniah 3:8, emphasis added.

[16]Zephaniah 3:20, (*The KJV Study Bible*) emphasis added.

[17]Zephaniah 1:2-3, emphasis added.

[18]Zephaniah 3:20, (*The KJV Study Bible*) emphasis added.

[19]Zephaniah 1:14, 18, emphasis added.

[20]Zephaniah 3:20, (*The KJV Study Bible*) emphasis added.

[21]Zephaniah 3:17-20, emphasis added.

[22]Zephaniah 3:20, (*The KJV Study Bible*) emphasis added.

[23]Zephaniah 3:12-13, 15, emphasis added.

[24]Zephaniah 3:20, (*The KJV Study Bible*) emphasis added.

[25]Genesis 6:5, emphasis added.

[26]2 Peter 1:19-21, emphasis added.

[27]Isaiah 46:10-11

CHAPTER 31: LADY ZEBIDAH

[1]Joel 2:12-14, emphasis added.

[2]Joel 2:30-32, emphasis added.

[3]Zephaniah 2:3, emphasis added.

[4]See 2 Kings 9:24, 27.

[5]See 2 Kings 9:34-37.

[6]2 Kings 10:15, emphasis added.

[7]2 Kings 10:16-17, emphasis added.

[8]See 2 Kings 10:18-28.

[9]2 Kings 10:29, emphasis added.

[10]2 Kings 10:31, emphasis added.

[11]Psalm 61:1-2 5-8, 63:11, emphasis added.

CHAPTER 32: SPYING OUT THE LAND

[1]Jeremiah 1:4-5, emphasis added.

[2]2 Kings 21:9, emphasis added.

[3]2 Kings 21:20, emphasis added.

[4]Psalm 23, emphasis added.

[5]James 2:25, emphasis added.

[6]1 Samuel 17:33, emphasis added.

[7]1 Samuel 17:40, emphasis added.

[8]1 Samuel 17:42-44, emphasis added.

[9]1 Samuel 17:45-46, emphasis added.

[11]1 Samuel 17:47, emphasis added.

[12]"Faith of our Fathers" by Frederick William Taber, public domain.

[13]2 Chronicles 28:3, emphasis added.

[14]2 Chronicles 33:6, emphasis added.

[15]2 Chronicles 33:22, emphasis added.

[16]Leviticus 18:21, emphasis added.

[17]Leviticus 18:3, emphasis added.

[18]Leviticus 18:6, emphasis added.

[19]Leviticus 18:22, emphasis added.

[20]Leviticus 18:23, emphasis added.

[21]Leviticus 18:24-26, emphasis added.

[22]Ecclesiastes 1:9, (*The KJV Study Bible*) emphasis added.

[23]Read online at: https://newlifedenton.org/2023/02/theval-ley=05-hinnom/11:~test=Later%2Cinaneffortasitcursedthesenses

Chapter 33: Ruin Upon Thine Habitation

[1]Jeremiah 9:6, (*The KJV Study Bible*) emphasis added.

[2]Jeremiah 9:7, emphasis added.

[3]Isaiah 48:10, emphasis added.

[4]Jeremiah 9:11-16, emphasis added.

[5]Joel 1:15, (*The KJV Study Bible*) emphasis added.

[6]See (*The KJV Study Bible*), commentary for Joel 1:15, p. 991.

[7]Psalm 103:19, emphasis added.

[8]2 Corinthians 4:4, emphasis added.

[9]Psalm 119:137, emphasis added.

[10]Psalm 7:11, emphasis added.

[11]Psalm 86:15, emphasis added.

[12]2 Peter 3:9, emphasis added.

[13]Isaiah 33:22, emphasis added.

[14]See Deuteronomy 28.

[15]Genesis 12:3, emphasis added.

[16]Romans 2:15, emphasis added.

[17]Acts 10:35, emphasis added.

[18]Jonah 1:1-3, emphasis added.

[19]Jonah 1:17-2:1, emphasis added.

[20]Jonah 2:10, 3:1-4, emphasis added.

[21]Jonah 3:5-10, emphasis added.

[22]See Luke 12:48.

[23]Jeremiah 1:10, emphasis added.

[24]Jeremiah 32:41, emphasis added.

[25]Micah 7:4, emphasis added.

[26]Jeremiah 26:18, emphasis added.

[27]Micah 2:12-13, emphasis added.

[28]See (*NIV Study Bible, Large Print*), Commentary on Micah 7:8-20, p. 1509.

[29]Micah 7:8-10, emphasis added.

[30]Micah 7:11-13, emphasis added.

[31]Micah 7:14-17, emphasis added.

[32]Micah 7:18-20, emphasis added.

[33]Genesis 17:5, emphasis added.

CHAPTER 34: TOPHETH

[1]Jeremiah 19:1, emphasis added.

[2]Psalm 23:4, emphasis added.

[3]2 Kings 23:10, emphasis added.

[4]Jeremiah 19:2, emphasis added.

CHAPTER 35: THE TWO JARS

[1]Jeremiah 18:5-12, emphasis added.

[2]Jeremiah 18:6, emphasis added.

[3]Jeremiah 18:12, emphasis added.

[4]Jeremiah 19: 3-4, emphasis added.

[5]Jeremiah 7:31-34, emphasis added.

[6]1 Kings 11:7, emphasis added.

[7]1 Kings 11:11, 13, emphasis added.

[8]Jeremiah 19:10, emphasis added.

[9]Jeremiah 19:11-13, emphasis added.

[10]Jeremiah 19:7-9, emphasis added.

[11]Zephaniah 2:1-3, emphasis added.

[12]Zephaniah 3:16-17, emphasis added.

CHAPTER 36: A NATION ON THE BRINK

[1]https://www.ajc.org/news/what-you-need-to-know-about-the-iran-backed-terror-group-hamas-and-its-attack-on-Israel, p. 1.

[2]*Ibid.*, pp. 5-7.

[3]https://www.fox.news.com/opinion/attacks-israel-only-beginning-democracies-risk, pp.2-3

[4]https://www.asc.org.news/5-facts-about-the-jewish-peoples-historic-connection-to-the-land-of-israel, p.1.

[5]*Ibid.*, p. 3.

[6]*Ibid.*, pp. 2, 1.

[7]*Ibid.*, pp.3, 1.

[8]*Ibid.*, p. 8.

[9]https://www.fox.news.com/opinion/attacks-israel-only-beginning-democracies-risk, p. 7.

[10]https://www.1000cranefoundation.org/hannah-milhouse-nixon, p. 2.

[11]*Ibid.*, p. 3.

[12]*Ibid.*

[13]Genesis 12:1-3, emphasis added.

[14]Zechariah 2:8, emphasis added.

[15]https://www.israelmyglory.org/article/q-what-does-the-apple-of-god's-eye-mean, pp.1-2.

[16]Jeremiah 31:35-36, emphasis added.

[17]https://www.fox.newsbusiness.com/politics/alan-dershowwitz-calls-obamas-deep-israel-ashamed, p. 1.

[18]https://www.fox.news.com/opinion/israel-war-hamas-surprise-attack-spotlights-biden-teams-failure-comes-next, pp. 1-2, 4.

[19]https://www.tabletmag.com/sections/israel-malley-lie-smith, p. 1.

[20]*Ibid.*

[21]https://www.fox.news.com/opinion/israel-war-hamas-surprise-attack-spotlights-biden-teams-failure-comes-next, p. 6.

[22]https://www.newsmax.com/world/globaltalk/gilad-erdan-united-states-terrorism/2023/11/05td/1141086/?ns-mail-utd=b3alacd0-166a-4053-ae63-60fe..., pp. 1-2

CHAPTER 37: LEARNING TRUTH

[1]https://www.fox.news.com/opinion/america-universities-become-hotbeds-terrorist-sympathizers, p. 2.

[2]Ibid, p. 2, 4.

[3]Ibid, p. 5.

[4]https://www.jpost.com/j-spot/article-771746, pp. 1-3.

[5]John 14:6, emphasis added.

[6]Acts 4:12, emphasis added.

[7]Psalm 119:142, emphasis added.

[8]John 1:1, emphasis added.

[9]John 14:19, emphasis added.

[10]Galatians 4:4, emphasis added.

[11]John 6:38, emphasis added.

[12]ohn 6:40, emphasis added.

[13]John 14:26, emphasis added.

CHAPTER 38: HAUNTED FOREVER

[1]https://www.fox.news.com/world/i-will-be-haunted-forever-israels-horrific-video-hamas-atrocities-leaves-viewers-shocked-sickened, p. 2.

[2]*Ibid.*, pp. 2-3.

[3]*Ibid.*, pp. 4-5.

[4]*Ibid.*, p. 6.

[5]*Ibid.*, p. 6.

[6]*Ibid.*, p. 6.

[7]*Ibid.*, p. 6.

[8]*Ibid.*, p. 7.

[9]*Ibid.*, pp. 8-9.

[10]*Ibid.*, pp. 10-11.

[11]*https:*//www.nationalww2museum.org/war/articles/ohr-druf-concentration-camp, pp. 1, 3-4.

[12]*Ibid.*, pp. 4-5.

[13]*Ibid.*, p. 5.

[14]https://www.fox.news.com/world/Israel-police-say-extreme-sexual-violence-rape-by-Hamas-terrorists-was-systemic, pp. 1-3.

[15]*Ibid*, pp. 6-7

[16]*Ibid*, p. 8.

[17]*Ibid*, p. 10.

[18]*Ibid*, p. 11.

CHAPTER 39: I DESIRE WORSHIP, NOT CONFLAGRATION

[1]*https:*//www.merriam-webster.com/dictionary/conflagration, p. 1.

[2]https://www.nationalreview.com/magazine/2023/12/its-looking-like-the-1930s/, p. 1.

[3]Genesis 6:5, 7-8, emphasis added.

[4]Genesis 13:13, 19:24-25, emphasis added.

[5]See (*NIV Study Bible, Large Print*), Introduction, p. 1493.

[6]Jonah 3:4-5, emphasis added.

[7]Jeremiah 44:4-6, emphasis added.

[8]Luke 21:6, emphasis added.

[9]See (*NIV Study Bible, Large Print*), Commentary on Luke 21:6, p. 1746.

[10]See (*NIV Study Bible, Large Print*), Commentary on Matthew 24:2, p. 1633.

[11]Luke 23:28-30, emphasis added.

[12]https://www.gotquestions.org/AD-70.html.

[13]Ezekiel 33:2-5, emphasis added.

[14]Ezekiel 33:6, emphasis added.

[15]Acts 17:26-27, emphasis added.

[16]See (*NIV Study Bible, Large Print*), Commentary on Acts 17:26, p. 1862.

[17]Psalm 144:15, 14, emphasis added.

[18]Proverbs 3:12, emphasis added.

[19]Revelation 3:19-20, emphasis added.

[20]Revelation 2:7, emphasis added.

CHAPTER 40: JOSIAH'S REFORMS

[1]2 Chronicles 34:6-7, emphasis added.

[2]2 Chronicles 34:14, emphasis added.

[3]2 Chronicles 34:18-19, emphasis added.

[4]2 Chronicles 34:21, emphasis added.

[5]*Ibid.*

[6]2 Chronicles 34:23-35, emphasis added.

[7]2 Chronicles 34:28, emphasis added.

[8]See (*NIV Study Bible, Large Print*), Commentary on 2 Kings 22:20, p. 612.

[9]2 Chronicles 34:30-32, emphasis added.

[10]2 Kings 23:4, 7, 11-13, emphasis added.

[11]2 Kings 23:10, emphasis added.

[12]2 Kings 23:15-16, emphasis added.

[13]1 Kings 13:1-2, emphasis added.

[14]See (*NIV Study Bible, Large Print*), Commentary on 1 Kings 13:2, p. 541.

[15]2 Chronicles 35:18, emphasis added.

[16]2 Kings 23:24-25, emphasis added.

[17]2 Chronicles 35:25, emphasis added.

[18]2 Chronicles 35:26, emphasis added.

[19]2 Kings 23:30-34, emphasis added.

[20]2 Kings 23:34, 36, 33, 35, 37.

[21]Daniel 1:1, emphasis added.

[22]2 Kings:24:1-3, 6, emphasis added.

[23]2 Kings 24:6, 8-10, emphasis added.

[24]Lamentations 4:9-10, emphasis added.

CHAPTER 41: APOSTATE JUDAH & AMERICA

[1]Ezekiel 19:1-4, emphasis added.

[2]Ezekiel 19:5-6, 8-9, emphasis added.

[3]1 Corinthians 10:11, emphasis added.

[4]See (*NIV Study Bible, Large Print*), Commentary on 1 Corinthians 10:11, p. 1936.

[5]Ezekiel 15:6-8, emphasis added.

[6]See (*NIV Study Bible, Large Print*), Commentary on Ezekiel 15:7, p. 1357.

[7]Ezekiel 16:1, emphasis added.

[8]2 Kings 22:2, emphasis added.

[9]Zephaniah 1:12, emphasis added.

[10]Read online at: https://www.foxnews.com/media/most-americans-think-religions-influence-declining-not-good-thing-poll-says, p.2.

[11]*Ibid.*, p.2.

[12]*Ibid.*, pp. 4-5.

[13]Read online at: https://www.worldchallenge.org/great-and-final-apostacy, p. 3.

[14]*Ibid.*

[15]*Ibid.*

[16]Read online at: https://www.newsmax.com/newsfront/franklin-graham-chastized-inclusive/2024/01/08/id/1148671/?ns_mail_uid=b3a1acd0-166a-4053-ae63-60fee606, p. 2.

[17]Read online at: https://www.worldchallenge.org/great-and-final-apostacy, p. 3.

[18]Isaiah 30:8-11, emphasis added.

[19]Isaiah 30:12-14, emphasis added.
[20]Isaiah 30:15-17, emphasis added.
[21]Isaiah 55:6-7, emphasis added.
[22]Romans 13:13-14, emphasis added.
[23]Ephesians 6:10-12, emphasis added.
[24]Jeremiah 6:22-26, emphasis added.
[25]Jeremiah 6:27-30, emphasis added.
[26]Ezekiel 34:26, emphasis added.
[27]Ezekiel 3:17, emphasis added.
[28]Ezekiel 3:18-19, emphasis added.
[29]Ezekiel 3:20-21, emphasis added.
[30]Acts 17:11, emphasis added.
[31]Philippians 2:7-8, emphasis added.
[32]"To God Be the Glory," by Fanny J. Crosby, public domain.

CHAPTER 42: THE MIRY CLAY

[1]https://www.fbi.gov/history/famous-cases/world-trade-center-bombing-1993, p. 1.

[2]https://www.newsmax.com/newsfront/fbi-southern-border-terrorism/2024/01/26/id/1151117/?ns--mail--uid=b3a1acd0-166a-4053-ae63-60fee606432a&, pp. 2-3.

[3]Psalm 40:1-3, (*The KJV Study Bible*), emphasis added.

[4]Isaiah 57:20-21, emphasis added.

[5]Isaiah 57:15, emphasis added.

[6]Isaiah 57:18, emphasis added.

CHAPTER 43: PREPARE THE WAY

[1]Isaiah 40:1-2, emphasis added.

[2]See (*NIV Study Bible, Large Print*), Commentary on Isaiah 40:1-66:24, p. 1172.

[3]Isaiah 40:3-5, emphasis added.

[4]1 Corinthians 15:2-3, emphasis added.

[5]John 1:23, emphasis added.

[6]https://www.woh.org/1998/05/10/john-the-baptist-the-fore-runner/, p. 5.

[7]Isaiah 62:10-12, emphasis added.

[8]Micah 2:12-13, emphasis added.

[9]Isaiah 62:1-4, emphasis added.

[10]Revelation 2:17, emphasis added.
[11]Isaiah 62:5, emphasis added.
[12]Revelation 19:7, emphasis added.
[13]Isaiah 62:6, emphasis added.
[14]Revelation 22:12-13, emphasis added.
[15]Revelation 22:14, emphasis added.
[16]Romans 1:28-29, emphasis added.
[17]Jeremiah 5:11-13, emphasis added.
[18]2 Peter 3:3-7, emphasis added.
[19]2 Peter 3:8-9, emphasis added.
[20]Matthew 25:1-7, emphasis added.
[21]Matthew 25:11, emphasis added.
[22]Matthew 25:12-13, emphasis added.
[23]Luke 18:8, emphasis added.
[24]Isaiah 50:4 (*New American Standard Bible*), emphasis added.
[25]Isaiah 50:5-9, emphasis added.
[26]Isaiah 51:7-8, emphasis added.

CHAPTER 44: DANIEL'S PRAYER
[1]Daniel 9:1-3, emphasis added.
[2]Deuteronomy 28:64-67, emphasis added.
[3]1 Kings 8:33-34, 46-51, emphasis added.
[4]Daniel 9:3, emphasis added.
[5]Daniel 9:4-7, 9-10, emphasis added.
[6]Daniel 9:11, 13-14, emphasis added.
[7]Daniel 9:15-19, emphasis added.
[8]Deuteronomy 30:1-6, emphasis added.
[9]Jeremiah 29:10-14, emphasis added.
[10]Matthew 26:26-30, emphasis added.
[11]Jeremiah 31:31-34, emphasis added.
[12]Galatians 3:10-11, emphasis added.
[13]James 1:22-25, emphasis added.
[14]Matthew 5:17-20, emphasis added.
[15]Psalm 51:1-4, emphasis added.
[16]Psalm 51:7-12, emphasis added.
[17]Psalm 51:13-17, emphasis added.

[18]Hebrews 10:12,14, emphasis added.

[19]2 Corinthians 7:10, emphasis added.

CHAPTER 45: GOD IS IN CONTROL

[1]Hebrews 13:8, emphasis added.

[2]Genesis 50:20-21, emphasis added

[3]Judges 16:28, 30, emphasis added.

[4]Joshua 6:16, 5, emphasis added.

[5]Judges 7:2, emphasis added.

[6]Daniel 12:1-3, emphasis added.

[7]Romans 8:28-32, emphasis added.

[8]Romans 8:33-39, emphasis added.

CHAPTER 46: PRAYER FOR A NATION

[1]Isaiah 41:13, emphasis added.

[2]Matthew 28:20, emphasis added.

[3]Psalm 138:6, emphasis added.

[4]1 Kings 8:46-47, 34, emphasis added.

[5]Ezra 1:1-4, emphasis added.

[6]Isaiah 44:21-24, 26-28, 45:1, 4-7, 13-14, 22-25.

[7]Psalm 126:1-4 (*The KJV Study Bible*), emphasis added.

[8]Zephaniah 2:1-3, emphasis added.

NOTE TO THE READER

[1]Malachi 4:5-6, (*The KJV Study Bible*), emphasis added.

[2]Malachi 4:4, (*The KJV Study Bible*), emphasis added.

[3]See (*The KJV Study Bible*), Commentary on Malachi 4:6, P. 1041.

[4]Malachi 3:16-17, (*The KJV Study Bible*), emphasis added.

[5]See (*The KJV Study Bible*), commentary on Malachi 3:16, p. 1041.

[6]Revelation 11:3-4, emphasis added.

[7]See (*NIV Study Bible, Large Print*), Commentary on Revelation 1:3, p. 2163.

[8]See (*NIV Study Bible, Large Print*), Commentary on Revelation 11:4, p. 2163.

[9]Malachi 3:18, (*The KJV Study Bible*), emphasis added.

[10]Malachi 4:1-2, (*The KJV Study Bible*), emphasis added.